THE NEXT STOP—MARS!

As our knowledge of our neighboring world continues to grow, our imaginative explorations of the fourth planet from the sun are still outdistancing our scientific studies. From what we know even now, however, Mars offers the greatest hope of a new, eventually self-sustaining home for humans within our solar system. So it is no wonder that Mars holds a special lure for many science fiction writers. Now, some of the top names in the field share their fascination with us, in such memorable tales as:

"The Love Affair"—He had remained in his private haven long after the rest of his people were gone, content with his existence until he saw *her*. She was human, she was irresistible, but would she prove his completion or his doom?

"Out of the Blue, Into the Red"—Could a father and son finally find a way to communicate when they were worlds apart?

"A Walk Across Mars"—No one could forget the heroic image of the two astronauts, best friends, defying the odds after a terrible accident and making it back to their base on Mars. Now, with one of the two long gone and the other facing his own imminent death, a ghostwriter is about to learn the *real* story behind that historic event. . . .

MARS PROBES

P9-EGL-610

More Stellar Anthologies Brought to You by DAW:

MOON SHOTS *Edited by Peter Crowther; with an Introduction by Ben Bova.* In honor of the *Apollo* Moon landings, some of today's finest science fiction writers—including Brian Aldiss, Gene Wolfe, Brian Stableford, Alan Dean Foster, and Robert Sheckley—have created original Moon tales to send your imagination soaring from the Earth to the Moon. From a computer-created doorway to the Moon . . . to a unique gathering on the Sea of Tranquillity . . . to a scheme to get rich selling Moon rocks . . . to an unexpected problem at a lunar-based fusion facility, here are stories to fill the space-yearnings of every would-be astronaut.

FAR FRONTIERS *Edited by Martin H. Greenberg and Larry Segriff.* Thirteen of today's top authors—including Robert J. Sawyer, Alan Dean Foster, Kristine Kathryn Rusch, Lawrence Watt-Evans, Julie E. Czerneda, and Andre Norton—blaze new pathways to worlds beyond imagining from: a civilization of humans living in a Dyson sphere to whom the idea of living on a planet is pure mythology . . . to an ancient man so obsessed with an alien legend that he will risk ship and crew in the Void in the hopes of proving it true . . . to the story of the last free segments of "humanity," forced to retreat to the very edge of the galaxy—in the hope of finding a way to save themselves when there is nowhere left to run.

STAR COLONIES *Edited by Martin H. Greenberg and John Helfers.* From the time the first Homo sapiens looked up at the night sky, the stars were there, sparkling, tempting us to reach out and seize them. Though humankind's push for the stars has at times slowed and stalled, there are still those who dare to dream, who work to build the bridge between the Earth and the universe. But while the scientists are still struggling to achieve this goal, science fiction writers have already found many ways to master space and time. Join Robert J. Sawyer, Jack Williamson, Alan Dean Foster, Allen Steele, Robert Charles Wilson, Pamela Sargent, Mike Resnick, Kristine Kathryn Rusch and their fellow explorers on these never before taken journeys to distant stars.

MARS
PROBES

edited by
Peter Crowther

DAW BOOKS, INC.
DONALD A. WOLLHEIM, FOUNDER
375 Hudson Street, New York, NY 10014
ELIZABETH R. WOLLHEIM
SHEILA E. GILBERT
PUBLISHERS
www.dawbooks.com

First Printing, June 2002
1 2 3 4 5 6 7 8 9

ACKNOWLEDGMENTS

Introduction: The Fascination of Mars © 2002 by Patrick Moore.

The Love Affair © 1982 by Ray Bradbury. Reprinted by permission of Don Congdon Associates, Inc.

Myths of the Martian Future © 2002 by Eric Brown.

A Martian Theodicy © 2002 by Paul Di Filippo.

The Real Story © 2002 by Alastair Reynolds.

Flower Children of Mars © 2002 by Mike Resnick and M. Shayne Bell.

Out of the Blue, Into the Red © 2002 by James Lovegrove.

Mom, the Martians, and Me © 2002 by Scott Edelman

The Old Cosmonaut and the Construction Worker Dream of Mars © 2002 by Ian McDonald.

A Walk Across Mars © 2002 by Allen Steele.

Martian Autumn © 2002 by Stephen Baxter.

Shields of Mars © 2002 by Gene Wolfe.

Under Mars © 2002 by Paul McAuley.

The War of the Worldviews © 2002 by James Morrow.

Near Earth Object © 2002 by Brian Aldiss.

The Me After the Rock © 2002 by Patrick O'Leary.

Lost Sorceress of the Silent Citadel © 2002 by Michael Moorcock.

CONTENTS

Contents

INTRODUCTION:
THE FASCINATION OF MARS

by Patrick Moore

WHEN I was a boy of seven—in 1930, I might add—two things happened to me. I had my first view of Mars through a telescope, and I read my first science fiction story.

Mars was a revelation. I was using a small telescope, but, even so, I could see the white polar ice cap, the dark markings, and the ocher deserts. Could there be anyone there, I wondered? After all, astronomers such as Percival Lowell had drawn what they believed to be Martian canals and in 1930 it was still generally believed that the dark areas were old seabeds filled with vegetation. This I knew, because my genuine interest in astronomy dated back over a year and it's fair to say that my reading ability made it possible for me to cope with adult books. Mars could be a living, vibrant world.

I had read *A Son of the Stars* by Fenton Ash, a boys' story which ran through a periodical called *Young England*. It had been published many years earlier, but somehow a bound copy had survived. It still does. I re-read that story the other day, and I was surprised to find how good it still is . . . though, of course, the theme seems somewhat hackneyed now. Two boys are taken to Mars in a spacecraft of the fleet commanded by King Amando, who has to face an onslaught on his home planet led by the wicked King Faronda.

Inevitably, the book has a happy ending, but so many stories about Mars do not. I suppose this goes back to *The War of the Worlds*, by H. G. Wells, which is widely read even now—and I remember the radio adaptation of it causing such panic just before the second world war. (I did meet Wells . . . I knew

Isaac Asimov well . . . and Arthur Clarke is a very old friend of mine—we first met as teenagers. Where *does* the time go!)

There are so many stories about the Red Planet, and they are generally of two kinds: those dealing with Wellsian monsters; and those which keep to known facts, as with Arthur Clarke's *The Sands of Mars.* Remember, too, the cloudlike Martians of Olaf Stapledon's *Last and First Men,* which I regard as the finest of all science fiction works and one of the most significant books I have ever read.

The important thing is that we can learn from all of these stories, no matter how old they are.

Science fiction has an uncanny habit of turning into science fact, and although we can rule out Olaf Stapledon's clouds, there is a great deal of resemblance between Jules Verne's Nautilus and a modern submarine—just as there is probably an equal affinity between Arthur Clarke's HAL and a computer of the not-too-distant future. Events are apt to overtake us, and I have the feeling that the twenty-first century will make the twentieth look very leisurely indeed.

We know so much more about Mars now than we did at the time I was taking my first look at it through my modest telescope. Lowell's brilliant-brained Martians have vanished into the realm of myth. There are no canals; the deserts are rusty, not sandy; and we could not breathe the atmosphere—it's too thin, and it is made of the wrong sort of gas. Yet terraforming Mars is often regarded as a real possibility, and I am bound to concede this, even though I admit to being something of a skeptic. We can most certainly live there, as men and women will do within the next few decades, but turning it into a second Earth is quite another matter. Moreover, we must appreciate that gravity there is only one third as strong as ours.

But colonies on Mars will come, and that poses the question as to whether a boy or girl born and raised in the Syrtis Major would ever be able to visit Earth. Here, perhaps, I may be forgiven for referring to a boys' novel I wrote in the early 1960s. It is called *The Voices of Mars,* and it describes a situation when the Martian colonies are flourishing but are under threat from accountants on Earth who are anxious to evacuate the whole planet in order to save money. This would mean certain death for the pioneers who have been on Mars for many years.

Two young colonists make the journey home to persuade the authorities to change their minds, and they are able to survive under the high terrestrial gravity for just long enough to make their case, after which they return through space to the safety of Mars. Juvenile fiction, yes . . . but could something of the sort ever happen? I would not rule it out.

Meanwhile, Mars continues to mystify and fascinate us.

Unmanned vehicles have been there, and we are searching for life—indeed, there may well be primitive organisms. But whatever the future holds, Mars is more like the Earth than any other world we know . . . and that is possibly why science fiction authors still like to write about it, just as science fiction readers still like to read about it.

Hence the book you now hold in your hands.

I am quite sure you will enjoy all the stories in *Mars Probes*, whether or not you feel they have any sound basis in fact, just as I enjoyed *A Son of the Stars* all that time ago. Less than seventy years separated Orville Wright's brief hop at Kitty Hawk from Neil Armstrong's "one small step" onto the bleak rocks of the Sea of Tranquillity, and, indeed the two men could have met . . . because their lives did overlap. I know Neil well and I met Orville Wright at the start of the war, when I was an underage Royal Air Force cadet learning how to fly.

So I have no doubt that the first man on Mars has already been born. And when he makes the journey, perhaps he'll take this book with him.

THE LOVE AFFAIR

by Ray Bradbury

ALL morning long the scent was in the clear air, of cut grain or green grass or flowers, Sio didn't know which, he couldn't tell. He would walk down the hill from his secret cave and turn about and raise his fine head and strain his eyes to see, and the breeze blew steadily, raising the tide of sweet odor about him. It was like a spring in autumn. He looked for the dark flowers that clustered under the hard rocks, probing up, but found none. He searched for a sign of grass, that swift tide that rolled over Mars for a brief week each spring, but the land was bone and the color of blood.

Sio returned to his cave, frowning. He watched the sky and saw the rockets of the Earthmen blaze down, far away, near the newly building towns. Sometimes, at night, he crept in a quiet, swimming silence down the canals by boat, lodged the boat in a hidden place, and then swam, with quiet hands and limbs, to the edge of the fresh towns, and there peered out at the hammering, nailing, painting men, at the men shouting late into the night at their labor of constructing a strange thing upon this planet. He would listen to their odd language and try to understand, and watch the rockets gather up great plumes of beautiful fire and go booming into the stars; an incredible people. And then, alive and undiseased, alone, Sio would return to his cave. Sometimes he walked many miles through the mountains to find others of his own hiding race, a few men, fewer women, to talk to, but now he had a habit of solitude, and lived alone, thinking on the destiny that had finally killed his people. He did not blame the Earthmen; it had been an accidental thing, the disease that had burned his father and mother in their sleep, and burned the fathers and mothers of great multitude of sons.

He sniffed the air again. That strange aroma. That sweet, drifting scent of compounded flowers and green moss.

"What is it?" He narrowed his golden eyes in four directions.

He was tall and a boy still, though eighteen summers had lengthened the muscles in his arms, and his legs were long from seasons of swimming in the canals and daring to run, take cover, run again, take swift cover, over the blazing dead sea bottoms or going on the long patrols with silver cages to bring back assassin-flowers and fire-lizards to feed them. It seemed that his life had been full of swimming and marching, the things young men do to take their energies and passions, until they are married and a woman soon does what mountains and rivers once did. He had carried the passion for distance and walking later into young manhood than most, and while many another man had been drifting off down the dying canals in a slim boat with a woman like a bas-relief across his body, Sio had continued leaping and sporting, much of the time by himself, often speaking alone to himself. The worry of his parents, he had been, and the despair of women who had watched his shadow lengthening handsomely from the hour of his fourteenth birthday, and nodded to each other, watching the calendar for another year and just *another* year to pass . . .

But since the invasion and the Disease, he had slowed to stillness. His universe was sunken away by death. The sawed and hammered and freshly painted towns were carriers of disease. The weight of so much dying rested heavily on his dreams. Often he woke weeping and put his hands out on the night air. But his parents were gone, and it was time, past time, for one special friend, one touching, one love.

The wind was circling and spreading the bright odor. Sio took a deeper breath and felt his flesh warm.

And then there was a sound. It was like a small orchestra playing. The music came up through the narrow stone valley to his cave.

A puff of smoke idled into the sky about a half mile away. Below, by the ancient canal, stood a small house that the men of Earth had built for an archaeological crew, a year ago. It had been abandoned, and Sio had crept down to peer into the empty rooms several times, not entering, for he was afraid of the black disease that might touch him.

The music was coming from that house.

"An entire orchestra in that small house?" he wondered, and ran silently down the valley in the early afternoon light.

The house looked empty, despite the music which poured out the open windows. Sio scrambled from rock to rock, taking half an hour to lie within thirty yards of the frightful, dinning house. He lay on his stomach, keeping close to the canal. If anything happened, he could leap into the water and let the current rush him swiftly back into the hills.

The music rose, crashed over the rocks, hummed in the hot air, quivered in his bones. Dust shook from the quaking roof of the house. Paint fell in a soft snowstorm from the peeling wood.

Sio leaped up and dropped back. He could see no orchestra within. Only flowery curtains. The front door stood wide.

The music stopped and started again. The same tune was repeated ten times. And the odor that had lured him down from his stone retreat was thick here, like a clear water moving about his perspiring face.

At last, in a burst of running, he reached the window, looked in.

Upon a low table, a brown machine glistened. In the machine, a silver needle pressed a spinning black disc. The orchestra thundered! Sio stared at the strange device.

The music paused. In that interval of hissing quiet, he heard footsteps. Running, he plunged into the canal.

Falling down under the cool water, he lay at the bottom, holding his breath, waiting. Had it been a trap? Had they lured him down to capture and kill him?

A minute ticked by, bubbles escaped his nostrils. He stirred and rose slowly toward the glassy wet world above.

He was swimming and looking up through the cool green current when he saw her.

Her face was like a white stone above him.

He did not move, nor stir for a moment; but he saw her. He held his breath. He let the current slide him slowly, slowly away, and she was very beautiful, she was from Earth, she had come in a rocket that scorched the land and baked the air, and she was as white as a stone.

The canal water carried him among the hills. He climbed out, dripping.

She was beautiful, he thought. He sat on the canal rim, gasping. His chest was constricted. The blood burned in his face. He looked at his hands. Was the black disease in him? Had looking at her contaminated him?

I should have gone up, he thought, *as she bent down, and clasped my hands to her neck. She killed us, she killed us.* He saw her white throat, her white shoulders. *What a peculiar color,* he thought. *But, no,* he thought, *she did not kill us. It was the disease. In so much whiteness, can darkness stay?*

"Did she see me?" He stood up, drying in the sun. He put his hand to his chest, his brown, slender hand. He felt his heart beating rapidly. "Oh," he said. "I saw *her*!"

He walked back to the cave, not slowly, not swiftly. The music still crashed from the house below, like a festival all to itself.

Without speaking, he began, certainly and accurately, to pack his belongings. He threw pieces of phosphorous chalk, food, and several books into a cloth, and tied them up firmly. He saw that his hands shook. He turned his fingers over, his eyes wide. He stood up hurriedly, the small packet under one arm, and walked out of the cave and started up the canyon, away from the music and the strong perfume.

He did not look back.

The sun was going down the sky now. He felt his shadow move away behind to stay where he should have stayed. It was not good, leaving the cave where he had often lived as a child. In that cave he had found for himself a dozen hobbies, developed a hundred tastes. He had hollowed a kiln in the rock and baked himself fresh cakes each day, of a marvelous texture and variety. He had raised grain for food in a little mountain field. He had made himself clear, sparkling wines. He had created musical instruments, flutes of silver and thorn-metal, and small harps. He had written songs. He had built small chairs and woven the fabric of his clothing. And he had painted pictures on the cave walls in crimson and cobalt phosphorous, pictures that glowed through the long nights, pictures of great intricacy and beauty. And he had often read a book of poems that he had written when he was fifteen and which, proudly but calmly, his parents had read aloud to a select few. It had been a good existence, the cave, his small arts.

As the sun was setting, he reached the top of the mountain pass. The music was gone. The scent was gone. He sighed and sat to rest a moment before going on over the mountains. He shut his eyes.

A white face came down through green water.

He put his fingers to his eyes, feeling.

White arms gestured through currents of rushing tide.

He started up, seized his packet of keepsakes, and was about to hurry off, when the wind shifted.

Faintly, faintly, there was the music. The insane, metallic blaring music, miles away.

Faintly, the last fragrance of perfume found its way among the rocks.

As the moons were rising, Sio turned and found his way back to the cave.

The cave was cold and alien. He built a fire and ate a small dinner of bread and wild berries from the moss-rocks. So soon, after he had left it, the cave had grown cold and hard. His own breathing sounded strangely off the walls.

He extinguished the fire and lay down to sleep. But now there was a dim shaft of light touching the cave wall. He knew that this light had traveled half a mile up from the windows of the house by the canal. He shut his eyes but the light was there. It was either the light or the music or the smell of flowers. He found himself looking or listening or breathing for any one of the incredible three.

At midnight he stood outside his cave.

Like a bright toy, the house lights were yellow in the valley. In one of the windows, it seemed he saw a figure dancing. "I must go down and kill her," he said. *That* is why I came back to the cave. To kill, to bury her."

When he was half asleep, he heard a lost voice say, "You are a great liar." He did not open his eyes.

She lived alone. On the second day, he saw her walking in the foothills. On the third day, she was swimming, swimming for hours, in the canal. On the fourth day and the fifth day, Sio came down nearer and nearer to the house, until, at sunset on the sixth day, with dark closing in, he stood outside the window of the house and watched the woman living there.

She sat at a table upon which stood twenty tiny brass tubes of red color. She slapped a white, cool-looking cream on her face, making a mask. She wiped it on tissues which she threw in a basket. She tested one tube of color, pressing it on her wide lips, clamping her lips together, wiping it, adding another color, wiping off, testing a third, a fifth, a ninth color, touching her cheeks with red, also, tweezing her brows with silver pincers. Rolling her hair up in incomprehensible devices, she buffed her fingernails while she sang a sweet strange alien song, a song in her own language, a song that must have been very beautiful. She hummed it, tapping her high heels on the hardwood floor. She sang it walking about the room, clothed only in her white body, or lying on the bed in her white flesh, her head down, the yellow hair flaming back to the floor, while she held a fire cylinder to her red, red lips, sucking, eyes closed, to let long slow chutes of smoke slip out her pinched nostrils and lazy mouth into great ghost forms on the air. Sio trembled. The ghosts. The strange ghosts from her mouth. So casually. So easily. Without looking at them, she created them.

Her feet, when she arose, exploded on the hardwood floor. Again she sang. She whirled about. She sang to the ceiling. She snapped her fingers. She put her hands out, like birds, flying, and danced alone, her heels cracking the floor, around, around.

The alien song. He wish he could understand. He wished, that he had the ability that some of his own people often had, to project the mind, to read, to know, to interpret, instantly; foreign tongues, foreign thoughts. He tried. But there was nothing. She went on singing the beautiful, unknown song, none of which he could understand:

"Ain't misbehavin', I'm savin' my love for you . . ."

He grew faint, watching her Earth body, her Earth beauty, so totally different, something from so many millions of miles away. His hands were moist, his eyelids jerked unpleasantly.

A bell rang.

There she was, picking up a strange black instrument, the function of which was not unlike a similar device of Sio's people.

"Hello, Janice? God, it's good to hear from you!"

Sio smiled. She was talking to a distant town. Her voice was thrilling to hear. But what were the words?

"God, Janice, what a hell-out-of-the-way place you sent me to. I know, honey, a vacation. But it's sixty miles from Nowhere. All I do is play cards and swim in the damned canal."

The black machine buzzed in reply.

"I can't stand it here, Janice. I know, I know. The churches. It's a damned shame they ever came up here. Everything was going so nice. What I want to know is when do we open up again?"

Lovely, thought Sio. *Gracious. Incredible.* He stood in the night beyond her open window, looking at her amazing face and body. And what were they talking about? Art, literature, music, yes, music, for she sang, she sang all of the time. An odd music, but one could not expect to understand the music of another world. Or the customs or the language or the literature. One must judge by instinct alone. The old ideas must be set aside. It was to be admitted that her beauty was not like Martian beauty, the soft slim brown beauty of the dying race. His mother had had golden eyes and slender hips. But here, this one, singing alone in the desert, she was of larger stuffs, large breasts, large hips, and the legs, yes, of white fire, and the peculiar custom of walking about without clothes, with only those strange knocking slippers on the feet. But all women of Earth did that, yes? He nodded, You must understand. The women of that far world, naked, yellow-haired, large-bodied, loud-heeled, he could see them. And the magic with the mouth and nostrils. The ghosts, the souls issuing from the lips in smoky patterns. Certainly a magical creature of fire and imagination. She shaped bodies in the air, with her brilliant mind. What else but a mind of clarity and clear genius could drink the gray cherry-red fire, and plume out architectural perfections of intricate and fine beauty from her nostrils. The genius! An artist! A creator! How was it done, how many years might one study to do this? How did one apply one's time? His head whirled with her presence. He felt he must cry out to her, 'Teach me!' But he was afraid. He felt like a child. He saw the forms, the lines, the smoke swirl into infinity. She was here, in the wilderness, to be alone, to create her fantasies in absolute security, unwatched. One did not bother creators, writers, painters. One stood back and kept one's thoughts silent.

What a people! he thought. *Are all of the women of that fiery green world like this? Are they fiery ghosts and music? Do they walk blazingly naked in their loud houses?*

"I must watch this," he said, half aloud. "I must study." He felt his hands curl. He wanted to touch. He wanted her to sing for him, to construct the artistic fragments in the air for him, to teach him, to tell him about that faraway world and its books and its fine music . . ."

"God, Janice, but how soon? What about the other girls? What about the other towns?"

The telephone burred like an insect.

"All of them closed down? On the whole damned planet? There must be *one* place! If you don't find a place for me soon, I'll . . . !"

Everything was strange about her. It was like seeing a woman for the first time. The way she held her head back, the way she moved her red-fingernailed hands, all new and different. She crossed her white legs, leaning forward, her elbow on a bare knee, summoning and exhaling spirits, talking, squinting at the window where he, yes, he stood in shadow, she looked right through him. Oh, if she knew, what would she do?

"Who, me, afraid of living out here alone?"

She laughed, Sio laughed in cadence, in the moonlit darkness. Oh, the beauty of her alien laughter, her head thrown back, the mystic clouds jetting and shaping from her nostrils.

He had to turn away from the window, gasping.

"Yeah! Sure!"

What fine rare words of living, music, poetry was she speaking now?

"Well, Janice, who's afraid of any Martian? How many are left, a dozen, two dozen. Line 'em up, bring 'em on, right? Right!"

Her laughter followed as he stumbled blindly around the corner of her house, his feet thrashing a litter of bottles. Eyes shut, he saw the print of her phosphorous skin, the phantoms leaping from her mouth in sorceries and evocations of cloud, rain, and wind. Oh, to translate! Oh, gods, to *know*. Listen!

What's that word, and that, and, yes then, that? Did she call out after him? No. Was that his name?

At the cave he ate but was not hungry.

He sat in the mouth of the cave for an hour, as the moons rose and hurtled across the cold sky, and he saw his breath on the air, like the spirits, the fiery silences that breathed about her face, and she was talking, talking, he heard or did not hear her voice moving up the hill, among the rocks, and he could smell her breath, that breath of smoking promise, of warm words heated in her mouth.

And at last he thought, *I will go down and speak to her very quietly, and speak to her every night until she understands what I say and I know her words and she then comes with me back into the hills where we will be content. I will tell her of my people and my being alone and how I have watched her and listened to her for so many nights . . .*

But . . . she is Death.

He shivered. The thought, the words would not go away.

How could he have forgotten?

He need only touch her hand, her cheek, and he would wither in a few hours, a week at the latest. He would change color and fall in folds of ink and turn to ash, black fragments of leaf that would break and fly away in the wind.

One touch and . . . Death.

But a further thought came. *She lives alone, away from the others of her race. She must like her own thoughts, to be so much apart. Are we not the same, then? And, because she is separate from the towns, perhaps the Death is not in her . . . ? Yes! Perhaps!*

How fine to be with her for a day, a week, a month, to swim with her in the canals, to walk in the hills and have her sing that strange song and he, in turn, would touch the old harp books and let them sing back to her! Wouldn't that be worth anything, everything? A man died when he was alone, did he not? So, consider the yellow lights in the house below. A month of real understanding and being and living with beauty and a maker of ghosts, the souls that came from the mouth, wouldn't it be a chance worth taking? And if death came . . . how fine and original it would be!

He stood up. He moved. He lit a candle in a niche of the

cave where the images of his parents trembled in the light. Outside, the dark flowers waited for the dawn when they would quiver and open and she would be here to see them and tend them and walk with him in the hills. The moons were gone now. He had to fix his special sight to see the way.

He listened. Below in the night, the music played. Below in the dark, her voice spoke wonders across time. Below in the shadow, her white flesh burned, and the ghosts danced about her head.

He moved swiftly now.

At precisely nine-forty-five that night, she heard the soft tapping at her front door.

MYTHS OF THE MARTIAN FUTURE

by Eric Brown

AT the end of the term, as was the custom among the Mountain Dwellers, the two eldest males of the most recent hatching left the living chambers and made the long climb toward the surface of the planet.

Tem scuttled ahead through unfamiliar chambers, eager to begin the great adventure. Olinka, a little older and wiser, conserved his energy: great hardship lay ahead if they were to succeed in the Outside World.

As he climbed, Olinka considered the stories of their people, the Myths of the Outside, which many of his contemporaries took to be factual accounts of the exploits of Initiates long gone. He had thought long and hard about this, and was not so sure. He was not even convinced as to the reason for the Rite of Initiation: but he kept his doubts to himself. Tem was naive and headstrong, and Olinka did not want to quash his touching enthusiasm.

One tenth of a term after setting out, they came to the outer exit, and even Olinka felt a bubbling sense of expectancy somewhere within his shell.

He watched Tem scurry up the incline and pause in the circular opening. After the lambent illumination of the living chambers, the light from Outside was blinding. Olinka retracted his four eyestalks and squinted at his friend. The sunlight struck Tem's etiolated shell and glanced off his six legs and madly waving pincers.

"The Outside World!" Tem signed. "It really is the Outside World! I never thought I'd ever see . . . ." The movement of his legs and pincers came to an awed halt.

Olinka hurried up the incline and joined his friend on the ledge.

The first thing he saw was the sun. It was huge and majestic and filled half the sky, a ruddy dome on the circumference of which exploded slow-motion jets and geysers of flame. Beneath the ancient star, the land stretched away for as far as the eye could see, close at hand a rumple of foothills flattening out to a vast, red desert.

Olinka opened his right pincer in wonder as he made out movement in the sky.

He signaled to Tem: "Look! Is that a . . . ? Can it be?"

"A Flyer, Olinka. Truly it is! A Flyer!"

Their eyestalks tracked the great silver bird as it flapped with lazy economy across the baleful eye of the sun.

"And there—and there!" Olinka signed.

Tem was signaling: "Are they Burrowers, Olinka? There, those snub-nosed creatures in the valley! And those circular beasts making their way toward the desert! They must be Rollers!"

The Outside World was positively teeming with all manner of life! Olinka discerned perhaps a dozen strange life-forms down below—creatures he had heard described in the telling of the Myths: the Flyers, Rollers, and Burrowers. Among them were things that he could not name, shaggy, lumbering beasts that kept to the shadows, and slick, slithering legless things that basked on rocks in the glare of the sun. Only one creature had he ever actually *seen* before, deep within the living chambers, and the sight of it now filled him with a reassuring sense of familiarity. High in the air, patrolling the foothills in search of life-forms which might wish to communicate, was the many tentacled form of a Speaker.

He turned his eyestalks toward the heavens and searched for other planets, but found none. Once, many thousands of terms ago, Initiates had reported witnessing the burning up of the solar system's third planet in the swelling wave-front of the expanding sun. And what of the people of that planet, Olinka had often wondered? Myth had it that, once, a proud race of bipeds had lived upon the third world: another myth, that they had at one time visited this planet in strange, silver flying machines . . . Olinka wondered where truth finished and myth began.

They paused on the threshold of the Outside World. Tem signaled: "You first, Olinka. You are my senior."

"I could not stand in the way of youthful enthusiasm," Olinka signed with a hint of condescension. "You first."

Nimble with importance, eyestalks quivering with excitement, Tem stepped from the shadow of the exit.

He semaphored the words of the Initiates upon Emerging: "We stand upon the cusp of adventure. We will be judged by our exploits. We ask nothing more than to return with tales to add to those of our illustrious forebears!"

Olinka kept his limbs, pincers, and eyestalks scrupulously immobile. The words of Emerging were nothing more than sentimental rubbish, but he was reluctant to tell Tem of his reasons for thinking so.

He followed his friend carefully down the hillside toward the desert, picking his way over and around the tumbled scree. The heat of the sun smote his shell like something physical, and Olinka wondered how he might survive ten terms of such inimical onslaught. Ten terms! If he were lucky, he might live for a hundred terms. And he was expected to survive out here for a tenth of a lifetime!

Five tenths of a term after leaving the mountain, Olinka and Tem arrived at the desert. Tem, eager as ever, scurried up the sliding face of a wind-sculptured dune. At the top he stood high and proud on his six bandy legs and waved his eyestalks impatiently for Olinka to join him.

Olinka navigated the curve of the dune and arrived beside his friend.

They had completed the first stage of their Initiation. Now they had an important choice to make, one which countless Initiates had made before them. The consensus of opinion was that to venture out into the merciless heat of the desert was risky indeed: few who made the journey returned to tell the tale. However, those few that did emerge triumphant from the ordeal by fire came back with stirring stories of valor and sacrifice, stories which immeasurably enriched the history of the Mountain Dwellers. The Initiates who took the safer option, the circumnavigation of the mountain via the foothills, brought back less colorful tales, and these Initiates, and their stories, were often forgotten in the long march of time.

Now Tem signaled: "Olinka?"

"Yes, Tem?"

"Do you know what I am thinking?"

"Hmmm . . . I can guess."

"And you?"

"I think you know what I suggest, Tem."

In high dudgeon, Tem signed: "What, Olinka? That we go around the mountain like timid hatchlings? Encounter what every thin-blooded Initiate has encountered before, and which every one of our people has forgotten?"

"Yes, rather that than face the uncertainties of the desert. The dangers—"

"But we can overcome the dangers, Olinka. We are young and strong!"

"Youth will not save us from the Eaters," Olinka pointed out. "Nor will our strength. The Eaters will take great delight in plucking our limbs one by one from our shells and sucking out our brains!"

Tem brought all four of his eyestalks to bear on Olinka. "What do you think is the reason for Initiation, then?" he signaled with acerbity. "Nothing is gained without risk. What is glory without the possibility of sacrifice!"

Angered, Olinka brought both his pincers up to eye level, for emphasis, and began: "Do you really want to know what I think initiation is for, Tem?" He almost stopped himself, there. But his friend's shortsightedness, his lack of insight, had angered him for many terms now. Tem had always gone with the flow, accepting whatever the Elders said, without thought or question. Now it was time to put him right.

Olinka continued: "Initiation is not what you think it is. It is not a means to provide our people with a history, with knowledge of the Outside World. Think about it. Consider the conditions in the living chambers. The fact is that our chambers and galleries are overcrowded. There is hardly enough food or water for everyone. It is a fact that males outnumber females almost six to one. Is it any wonder why only males are sent out on these great Initiations?"

Tem backed away, retracting his eyestalks in horror. "What are you saying?" he signed with his left rear leg, to denote shock and disbelief.

Olinka allowed a profound immobility to reign. Then he signaled: "I am saying that the Initiations are no more than a means by which our society regulates its numbers, a means of culling unwanted males, to ensure the survival of those who remain in the living chambers."

Tem shuffled sideways, putting distance between himself and the heretic notions of his fellow Initiate. "I cannot accept what you say! I will not accept . . ." His pincer was still. Then he waved: "But what about the Initiates who do return with magnificent tales of brave deeds?"

Olinka gestured placatingly. "I do not deny that these stories add to the richness of our culture—but how many males return, Tem? Six from every twenty? Which means that fourteen perish. Can you deny that our society is better off for the sacrifice of these Initiates?" He stopped suddenly and stared ahead.

At first, he thought that it was a trick of his eyestalks. He made out a slight irregularity on the northernmost fringe of the desert, a silver filament that seemed stationary. He looked away for a few seconds, and then glanced back. Certainly the filament had moved a fraction, was heading into the heart of the desert.

"What is it?" Tem asked.

"Look . . ."

The column was many thousands of body-lengths distant, and consisted of perhaps a hundred silver-gray individuals. They walked on four legs beneath cupola-shaped head-bodies, and from their craniums sprouted two eyestalks.

"I don't believe I'm seeing this!" Tem signed.

"Do you think . . . ? Olinka began. "Can they be?"

He turned his gaze skyward, looking for the tentacled shape of a Speaker. The bloated belly of the sun filled the sky, and against its light Olinka made out the relatively tiny shape of a floating Speaker. He signaled frantically, requesting that it descend and communicate with them.

Just when he thought that the creature had not seen his summons, or was ignoring him, the Speaker turned and swooped toward the dune.

It hung above their heads, its tentacles working in a passable imitation of their language.

"Two shell-heads, out in the open! How can I help you, Initiates?"

Olinka signaled: "The beings crossing the desert, there. Are they what I think they are, Speaker?"

The Speaker rotated to consider the column, but Olinka could not tell the difference between its tentacles and eyestalks. At last it signed: "If you think that they are Thinkers, Initiate, then they are what you think they are."

Olinka felt the blood surge around his head-shell. His six legs were suddenly weak.

Tem signaled frantically: "Thinkers! Are they *really* Thinkers?"

The Speaker signed: "They are Thinkers from the north, making their annual pilgrimage to the Southern Plain. There they will commune with the oracles, and contemplate the vast history of the planet for one long year before returning to their breeding grounds."

"Thinkers . . ." Olinka gestured in awe.

The history of the Mountain Dwellers was so vast that few stories reached them from the time when they had lived on the surface of the world. One story, however, had survived. It was a tale so fabulous that it had to be a myth.

It was said that long ago, a million generations in the past, the Thinkers and the race which eventually became the Mountain Dwellers were one and the same. A clan of Thinkers, so the story went, returning from their annual pilgrimage, had been caught in a sun storm, and in order to wait out the worst of the actinic sleet had sought refuge in the caves of the central mountains. Why they had remained in the mountain, and moved farther underground with every passing generation, was never adequately explained. According to the story, the Thinkers changed, became shorter, and grew more legs and eyestalks and pincers, and became in time the Mountain Dwellers. It was a strange and unlikely story, Olinka thought, but one which contained much poignancy.

To imagine that the Mountain Dwellers might be descended

from the mighty Thinkers, the ancient philosopher race which existed in some abstract realm of pure thought and reason!

Now Tem signaled impetuously. "Speaker! We require your assistance."

Olinka spun and stared at his friend with all four eyestalks. "We do?"

Tem ignored him. "Will you accompany us into the desert, Speaker, and translate whatever might pass between ourselves and the venerable Thinkers?"

The floating being signed: "They call me a Speaker because I speak, little one. I will follow you into the great desert."

"Wait!" Olinka gestured with two pincers in his most determined manner. "Who said anything about—?"

Tem turned and stared. "We must follow them! Don't you see that we cannot let this opportunity pass? Think of it, Olinka: we will determine once and for all the truth of our ancestry. We will be famous in every living chamber! Our names will never be forgotten, and our story will enrich the history of our people!"

Olinka turned to the patiently floating Speaker. "Please recount for the benefit of my headstrong friend the dangers awaiting us in the great desert."

The Speaker descended and hovered before Tem. "The dangers are indeed great for two puny little shell-heads such as yourselves."

"We can defend ourselves with these," Tem gestured, brandishing his pincers in demonstration.

The Speaker signed much humor. "Against a ravenous Eater, your claws will be useless! Also, the Thinkers move at prodigious speed and stop for no one. You will have difficulty catching them."

"That is a risk we will have to face," Tem signed, "along with the danger. Glory beckons! How can we turn our backs like two hatchlings on such an opportunity?"

Something in Olinka stirred. He thought of their reception, back in the living chambers, if indeed they did succeed in communicating with the Thinkers.

"Two terms," he gestured. "We will attempt to catch up with the column, but after two terms, if we have not overhauled them, then we turn back."

Tem hesitated, then waved a pincer in agreement. "Two
terms, then," he signed. He turned and scurried off down the
face of the dune.

Gesturing to himself, the Speaker hovering overhead,
Olinka gave chase.

For the duration of the next term, Olinka hurried alongside
Tem in a foam of excitement and apprehension. Ahead, the
shimmering column of Thinkers remained hopelessly distant.
He willed himself to greater speed, or the column to slow, so
they might achieve their aim and quiz the venerable beings,
and then return in safety to the foothills. With every passing
second he expected something vast and vicious to erupt from
the sand beside him and attack with savage tooth and claw. He
had heard many fearsome stories about the Eaters. As a hatch-
ling he had listened with terror as the Wise Elders described in
grotesque detail the dining habits of the desert dwellers.

The Thinkers seemed to get no nearer, and almost two
terms had elapsed when Tem paused in his headlong flight and
strained his eyestalks ahead. "They move with the speed of
Flyers!" he gestured, exasperated.

"It is time we turned and headed back," Olinka signed, in
sympathy, and not a little regret.

Tem ignored him. He gestured to the Speaker. "Will you fly
ahead, Speaker? Inform the column that we wish an audience."

The Speaker dipped before the Initiates. He gestured great
mirth. "The Thinkers pause in their pilgrimage for no one,
great or small, little ones."

Tem stamped in annoyance. "Tell them that we are descended from their kind, and wish to speak with them!"

Again the Speaker signed humor. "The Thinkers might take
offense that two shell-heads claim such a heritage," it gestured. "Be satisfied that your eyestalks have beheld such a procession, and that so far you have lived to tell the tale!"

"Come, Tem," Olinka gestured. "We will continue our Initiation in the foothills."

He turned, touching his friend's carapace with a consola-
tory claw, and they began the long trek back to the mountain.
He looked into his heart, and admitted to himself that he, too,

felt the burden of sadness at the fruitless outcome of the mission.

He was about to remind Tem that they had much time in which to accomplish notable deeds when, ahead, in the first gentle fold of the foothills, he saw a quick flash of light.

He turned his eyestalks in that direction, and beheld a large floating craft shaped like a water droplet, coruscating silver in the sunlight.

It was leaving the foothills and crossing the desert toward them.

Tem gave a gesture of fright and rapidly buried himself in the sand. Olinka twisted himself beneath the surface of the desert, then extended a periscopic eyestalk to track the craft's slow progress.

A rectangular section at the front of the droplet-shaped vehicle was made of some transparent material. Olinka made out two short, upright figures within the craft. One of the strange beings seemed to be directing the craft with a limb connected to a column, which it moved in the direction it wished the craft to follow.

Olinka wondered at the marvel of happening upon the column of Thinkers, and then this strange sight, so soon after leaving the mountain.

The craft approached the buried Mountain Dwellers and passed quickly overhead. Olinka bent his eye stalk to follow. Much to his excitement, the vehicle soon slowed and lowered itself to the ground. It sat immobile on the sand beneath the fierce sun, perhaps a hundred body-lengths away.

Then, startling him, a section of the droplet-shaped craft sprang open like the wing of an insect. Olinka watched with excitement. Beside him, he discerned Tem's timorous eyestalk, taking in the scene.

As he watched, two silver beings stepped from the craft and stood looking about them, and Olinka could not contain his excitement.

He shrugged all his eyestalks, and a pincer, free of the sand and communicated with Tem.

"Do you think it could be?" he asked. "Do you really think . . . ?"

Tem was slow in responding, as if dazed by the marvel unfolding before them.

"It can only be," he signaled. "It can only be the Silver Travelers!"

Olinka turned his eyestalks forward and watched as the Silver Travelers strode around their craft, sometimes pausing to examine the desert floor, sometimes gazing up at the swollen sun.

Olinka felt his lifeblood surge as he recalled the story of the Silver Travelers. It was an old tale, the details lost in the long history of their people. Many hundreds of thousands of terms ago, so the story went, two eager Initiates had ventured forth from the mountain and decided to cross the desert to the Southern Plain. It was a foolhardy choice to make, and one bound to end in disaster, as no Mountain Dweller had ever set eyestalks on the far distant flatland or the oracles said to reside there.

These two Initiates, however, were far from daunted. The story, no doubt much embroidered over time, went into great detail about the hardships they endured as they crossed the desert, the many perils they faced from predators and foe.

After seven terms beneath the merciless intensity of the sun, the two heroes weakened. They realized the absurdity of their attempt, and realized also the impossibility of turning back. They resigned themselves to death, and were about to bury themselves in the sand and await the end when, as if their plight was not dire enough, they were swooped upon by a pack of Eaters.

One of the Initiates was riven limb from pincer before the terrified eyestalks of his friend. The victim's shell was prized open by the Eaters' eager claws, his brain laid bare for the delectation of the ravenous beasts.

The surviving Initiate felt the claws of an Eater grab him. He was ready for death—but instead came salvation.

He was aware of commotion about him. He was dropped suddenly, and went rolling in ever decreasing circles around the desert floor, discovering as he did so that the Eaters were fleeing in fright. When he came to rest, he saw the reason for their sudden departure.

Two tall, upright silver figures stood over him. One knelt and reached out a limb, which terminated in five small digits.

Frightened, the Mountain Dweller summoned a Speaker, and communicated with the silver beings. The beings were first amazed by the fact of the Mountain Dweller's sentience, and then saddened by his companion's death.

The remaining Initiate asked if the silver beings might transport him back to the foothills in their craft, and they agreed. They ferried him safely to the entrance in the foothills, and thus ensured not only his survival, but one of the most famous rites of Initiation ever undertaken by a Mountain Dweller.

There was much speculation as to the provenance of the Silver Travelers. Some claimed that the beings were helpful ghosts, others that they were survivors who had fled the destruction of the system's third planet. . . .

Olinka had always considered the story more myth than fact, a far-fetched farrago of improbabilities concocted in the sun-crazed mind of an over-adventurous Initiate.

But here, before him, were two strange silver beings very much like those out of ancient myth.

"Should we approach them?" Olinka signaled to Tem, "attempt communication?" He scanned the sky for the Speaker.

"We might introduce ourselves!" Tem signed, excited.

The Silver Travelers were walking away from the craft, scanning the ground with strange instruments. From time to time they turned to each other, as if in communication— though the movement of their limbs was minimal. Olinka wondered how such obviously sentient creatures might effect communication with just four rudimentary limbs which seemed to lack anything but the most simple flexibility.

Olinka had sighted the Speaker high in the sky, and was about to ask its assistance, when disaster struck.

He felt the sand tremble around him, and thought at first that it was a quake similar to those which occasionally shook the mountain. Then the desert, in an approximate ring encompassing the two Silver Travelers, erupted and a dozen creatures, the like of which Olinka had never seen before, emerged and made for the two unwitting beings.

Olinka stared in horror, knowing full well that he was help-

less to intervene. The creatures were attenuated, insectlike
monsters twice as tall as the Silver Travelers, all jet-black
chitin and massive mandibles. Olinka expected them to devour
the silver beings straightaway, but the insects had other plans.

Four of their swarm took hold of the frantically struggling
beings, spread their iridescent wings and bore them off into the
air, followed by the remaining insects. They passed overhead
and made for the foothills, the Silver Travelers dangling.

Tem was flailing his limbs in an incomprehensible welter of
sadness and grief.

"We have to help them!" Olinka signed.

"Impossible! What are we beside those vile monsters?"

Olinka, without quite knowing what he intended, leaped
from his hiding place in the sand and hurried across the desert
toward the droplet-shaped craft. Tem scuttled in his wake, signaling a dozen frantic questions.

He reached the open hatch of the vehicle, hesitated only
briefly, and then jumped inside. Before he knew it, Tem was
beside him. "Have you taken leave of your senses, Olinka?
What are you doing?"

"I saw how the beings directed this craft," Olinka signed.
He reached out with his pincer and touched the column before
him. No sooner had his claw made contact than the hatch
swung shut and the craft bobbed sickeningly into the air.

With mounting fear Olinka watched through the viewscreen
as the desert receded beneath him. Tem huddled on the floor,
his limbs, pincers, and eyestalks waving in garbled distress.

Olinka fought the sensation of sickness that threatened to
overwhelm him. He pushed at the column, as he had seen the
Silver Traveler do, and the craft responded. It surged forward,
almost pitching Olinka to the floor. He eased the column to the
right, turning the craft in the direction of the foothills.

They were flying! They were the first Mountain Dwellers
ever to take control of a flying machine! Olinka marveled at
the miracle, hardly daring to believe what was happening.
What stories they would have to tell their people. Their exploits would be remembered for ever! Their names would
never be forgotten!

If, he reminded himself, they survived to tell the tale.

Ahead, through the viewscreen, he made out the distant

flight of insect-monsters, their dependent prey flashing in the sunlight. The insects swarmed across the desert toward the foothills. As Olinka gave chase, the beasts suddenly lost altitude and settled in an amphitheater enclosed by hills. As he watched, even more of the insect creatures emerged from holes in the ground.

Those carrying the Silver Travelers swooped in to land. Olinka knew that soon the opportunity to save the beings would be gone, once the insects took the captives to their underground lair.

He pushed the column forward and the craft dived.

"What are you doing!" Tem signaled in alarm.

Olinka was fueled by the desire to save the Silver Travelers, to do for them what their kind had done for the Initiate, long ago. Quite how he might effect such a rescue, he did not know. He was running on instinct, blind hope, and fear.

They fell toward the amphitheater.

The insects had landed and were scurrying across the sun-browned grass toward the nearest gaping hole in the ground.

The craft came into the amphitheater on a low trajectory, skimming the grass and heading toward the first of the insect-monsters.

"Hold tight!" Olinka warned Tem.

Through the viewscreen he beheld the looming shapes of a dozen insects, and then came the inevitable collision. The craft bowled through the creatures and flew on erratically. Olinka beheld halved insects littering the ground, and others, badly injured, attempting to crawl away. Ahead, he made out the insects bearing the Silver Travelers, and steered the craft full-tilt toward them. This time the impact, when it came, was jarring and final. There was a shell-shaking vibration, and then sudden immobility. He and Tem rattled around the interior of the craft, tumbling on top of each other in a tangle of legs and eyestalks.

Dazed, Olinka stood unsteadily and stared about him. Chitinous shrapnel and viscous ichor covered the viewscreen. Through a clear segment, he made out a scene of carnage, with fragments of insect shell scattered over a wide area.

As he stared, he heard the hatch open above him, and knew that the end had come. He hoped only that it would be swift, that the surviving insects would devour him quickly rather than desire to exact revenge.

He turned an eyestalk and looked up, and what he saw filled him with disbelief. A silver being was holding the hatch open and staring into the craft with two flat, round eyes. Its strange headpiece was enclosed within a bulbous, transparent shell, which was connected by two pipes to a bulky apparatus upon its back.

Olinka wished he could have made sense of the expression on the ugly headpiece as the Traveler took in the jumbled interior of its craft, and the two tiny Mountain Dwellers who had effected their salvation.

The face disappeared, and a second later the craft was righted, Olinka and Tem falling to the floor.

"What's happening!" Tem signaled. "Are we dead yet!"

Olinka had no time to reply. Through the viewscreen he made out the amphitheater. Panic seized him and his limbs signaled danger, as if the two Travelers might comprehend.

Across the amphitheater, the surviving insects were gathering their forces to attack. As Olinka watched in dread, they launched themselves toward the craft. He turned his eyestalks towards the hatch. He saw one Traveler kneeling beside the craft, perhaps attempting some form of repair. The second Traveler looked up, saw the approaching insects, and signaled to his friend.

They climbed quickly into the craft and slammed the hatch shut behind them, and not a moment too soon. The insects were swarming over the droplet-shaped vehicle, mandibles working to open its skin.

One of the Travelers reached out for the control column, easing it forward. Olinka was aware of a stalling vibration. The ship did not respond.

Outside, the craft was engulfed in a swarm of insects. Tem gestured in fear. Olinka felt the craft rock as the insects attempted to crack it open.

The first Traveler turned to the second. On its face, within the transparent shell, two thin strips of flesh surrounding a pink orifice made a minimal movement. Olinka found it amazing that such restricted gestures might convey any meaningful language.

The first being reached beyond the control column to a panel arrayed with tiny hieroglyphs. With its thin appendages, the Traveler tapped the console.

Instantly, the insects crowding the viewscreen disappeared, and light flashed outside the craft. Olinka felt suddenly nauseous. His limbs buckled and he slid toward Tem in the corner of the craft. He was aware of a constant vibration that threatened to shake his shell to fragments. He retracted his eyestalks and took refuge in darkness.

Then, just as suddenly as it had started, the nausea ceased. The vibration was no more. Cautiously, Olinka extended an eyestalk and peered around him.

All was immobile. The sun shone through the viewscreen. He looked out. All across the amphitheater lay the remains of shattered insects, wing cases and antennae, severed heads and legs. He looked away.

The Silver Travelers opened the hatch and climbed out. One reached back inside, picked up first Olinka, and then Tem, and lifted them out into the sunlight.

The Traveler placed Olinka and Tem side by side on the grass, then knelt to stare at the tiny Mountain Dwellers.

Olinka scanned the heavens for a Speaker. Within seconds his signals brought a response. A tentacled Speaker swooped to join them.

"The two shell-heads survive!" the Speaker gestured in patronizing disbelief. "You'll be heroes when your people hear of your exploits!"

"You followed us from the desert?" Olinka signed.

"Oh, it's more complicated than that, my friends!"

Tem signaled: "We wish to communicate with the Silver Travelers."

"And they," responded the Speaker, "wish to communicate with you!"

The first Traveler looked up at the floating Speaker. Again, the being moved the fleshy strips of its headpiece.

The Speaker rotated and addressed Olinka and Tem. "They wish to thank you," it signed. "Without your intervention, they would now be dead."

"Tell them," Olinka signaled, flashing pincers and limbs in joy, "that it was the least we could do. Many terms ago, so rumor has it, two of their kind also saved a Mountain Dweller from certain death."

The Speaker turned to address the Travelers. There followed a period of immobility. The Speaker did not use its tentacles to communicate, and Olinka was confused.

However, the Speaker must have conveyed Olinka's words, for they had an immediate effect The two Travelers turned to each other. Their headpieces shook from side to side and their fleshy strips moved animatedly.

The Speaker relayed what they had said. "They wish to tell you that it was *they* who saved your forebears in the desert."

"They?" Olinka responded. "But . . . how is that possible? It was many hundreds of terms ago! Surely no beings can live that long?"

Impatiently, Tem signaled to the Speaker. "Ask the Silver Travelers where they are from."

The Speaker conveyed the question, its tentacles immobile. The Travelers moved their heads and manipulated their inefficient signing strips.

At last the Speaker signaled: "They come, originally, from a place they call Earth—the third planet of this system."

"But their planet was destroyed, or so the story goes," Olinka signed. "Where do they dwell now?"

The Travelers were communicating again.

The Speaker reported: "Long ago they fled their planet when it was threatened by the expansion of the sun. Now, they travel through time," the Speaker went on. "They move through the long history of the solar system in their machine, alighting to study the many and various forms of life."

"Travel through *time* . . . ?" Olinka gestured, awed at the concept.

"How else do you think that they might have saved your distant forebear?" the Speaker asked.

Olinka's thoughts were in turmoil. He wished to ask the Travelers a thousand questions. He considered the many events since leaving the mountain. He recalled the column of Thinkers, and remembered the myth.

"If the Travelers do indeed travel through time," he signed to the Speaker, "then perhaps they might be able to answer my question?"

"And that is?"

Olinka turned his eyestalks and snapped his pincers. "Do they know if it is true," he began, "that once, many millions of terms ago, we Mountain Dwellers were one and the same as the Thinkers?"

As he waited for the Speaker to relay the question to the time-traveling bipeds, he thought ahead to their triumphal return to the living chambers, and the stories they would have to recount.

Perhaps, even, they might be able to report with certainty that their people were indeed descended from the venerable Thinkers!

The Travelers moved their fleshy strips. Olinka was aware of a dizziness within his shell as he awaited the reply.

"Over many millennia," the Speaker signed, "the Thinkers have made an annual pilgrimage to the Southern Plain. The time travelers have monitored their journeys."

"But are we descended from the Thinkers?" Tem was impatient to know.

"Sadly," the Speaker signed, "this is a groundless myth of your people. You are descended from lowly crustaceans which have always lived beneath the surface of the planet."

Olinka felt a crushing sense of disappointment. How might they return, now, with news that one of their long-held and most cherished stories was no more than a fanciful fairy tale?

He felt that all his exploits since leaving the mountain might have been for nothing.

The Travelers were communicating again. The Speaker turned. "They say that you should not be disappointed," it gestured. "For not only have they knowledge of your distant past—but also they know the course of your future."

"They do?" Tem signed.

"The only way they have of thanking you for saving their lives," the Speaker continued, "is to tell you to return to your living chambers and inform your people that, one day, your race will be great. You will leave your subterranean lair and live out in the open, under the sun. Then will begin the long period of your greatness. Over many terms, your kind will populate every corner of the planet, and become philosophers on a par with and even exceeding the venerable Thinkers."

Olinka's legs buckled and he collapsed to the ground. With his pincers he gestured: "They know this? They know this for sure?"

The Speaker replied: "They told me that the planet will never know of a race as intelligent and civilized as the people once known as the Mountain Dwellers."

For once, Olinka was speechless. He could not bring himself to move his limbs in any semblance of order.

"And now," the Speaker reported, "the Travelers must leave this time. They wish you well, and thank you once again."

The first biped reached out a long limb, extending its digits toward Olinka. Not knowing quite how to respond, but sensing that some gesture was required, he lifted his right pincer and gently touched the tip of the Traveler's digit, then repeated the gesture with the second creature.

The fleshy strips upon the Travelers' headpieces curled into a shape that might have been significant.

The Travelers stood, and lifted their limbs at Olinka and Tem, before climbing back into the time machine.

Olinka directed his eyestalks forward, overcome with sadness as the hatch closed. He expected to watch it fly away, but instead it vanished in a flash of light, once again on its mysterious errand through time.

Tem was beside himself with delight. He danced up the side of the amphitheater heading toward the entrance to the living chambers. His limbs flashed in glee, and Olinka made out brief phrases. "One day we will be great! Together, Olinka and I will lead our people from the living chambers! One day we will be *great!*"

Olinka, with the Speaker in attendance, followed Tem up the hillside.

Tem paused in his celebratory jig. "You will accompany us into the chambers, Speaker? You will corroborate the many wonderful stories Olinka and I have to tell our people?"

"I am a Speaker. That is my duty."

Olinka halted his friend with a gesture. "But we cannot return to the living chambers so soon," he signed. "The Elders will never believe us! We have been away hardly three terms!"

He was aware of the Speaker above them, signing his mirth.

"What?" Olinka asked.

The Speaker gestured. "You cannot guess?"

"Guess what?" Tem signed.

"How do you think you evaded the insect-monsters?" it asked. "Where do you think the insects vanished to, all of a sudden?"

Tem shrugged a pincer. Olinka recalled the nausea he had experienced in the craft, the eerie flashing light.

"Tell us, Speaker," he signed.

"To escape the remaining insects," it signed, "the Travelers moved the craft through *time*. The insects either died of their wounds in the interim, or fled."

Olinka marveled at the very idea. At last he found himself gesturing: "For how long did we travel through time?"

The Speaker responded: "A little over thirty terms."

Thirty terms! An Initiation was supposed to last only ten!

Olinka thought of his friends back in the chambers, the Wise Elders who had counseled them over the terms. They would have assumed the worst, by now. They would think that brave Initiates Olinka and Tem had left the mountain and met with a tragic end.

Their return would be a triumph indeed. Oh, the tales they would have to tell. . . .

Already Tem was skipping nimbly up the mountainside, followed by the floating Speaker.

Olinka, bursting with pride and joy, set off in pursuit.

A MARTIAN THEODICY

by Paul Di Filippo

> "Mars is a queer little world."
> —Stanley G. Weinbaum, "Martian Odyssey"

REMEMBER, men," Captain Harrison sternly advised, "we don't kill Dick Jarvis unless he forces our hand. Understood?"

In response to the captain's mortal admonition, Karl Putz, the engineer on mankind's second mission to Mars, spat derisively out the open air lock of their ship, the *Ares II*. His saliva landed on the dusty terra cotta soil of the Red Planet, instantly attracting a score of the walking native grass blades that roamed at random around their landing site.

"*Ja, ja,* agreed. But mine hand is damn near forced already, for truth."

Frenchy Leroy, crack biologist, absentmindedly fondled the butt of his own holstered radium pistol, as he watched the ambulatory grass blades surround and absorb the blob of his roughshod comrade's spit. Shivering, the dapper doctor said, "Zis world, she makes me itch. Too many strangenesses by far."

"Frenchy, you didn't signify your assent to my command."

Leroy ceased rubbing his gun butt and waved his hand dismissively. "*Oui, oui,* I will not slaughter zee traitor like zee *cochon* he is, until you permit it, *mon Capitaine.* Despite all zee grief he has caused us personally, despite zee five years of stagnation in the conquest of zee Solar System which can be laid directly at his renegade feet, he is still a human being deserving of civilized justice under zee League of Nations protocols."

"So we hope," said Captain Harrison grimly.

The three men stood at the head of the ship's extruded duralloy ramp in moody silence, breathing the thin but sufficient air of the alien world into their Himalayans-conditioned lungs, pondering the dangerous, uncertain, and even repugnant mission they were about to undertake. After a brief time spent in meditation and reminiscence, they were startled from their reverie by the arrival of the fourth crew member, who blithely allowed the screen door of the port to slam behind her.

"Hi, boys!" exclaimed Fancy Long gaily. The gorgeous blonde star of the *Yerba Mate* televid show filled out her regulation uniform in ways the solemn designers back at Space Command in Zurich could never have envisioned. Her lithe dancer's limbs carrying her even more frolicsomely in the reduced gravity, her trained singer's voice sounding elfishly attenuated in the lesser atmosphere of Earth's ruddy neighbor, Fancy Long was the brightest sight in millions of miles, and her advent cheered the men considerably.

Leroy took her hand and kissed it. "Ah, *Madamoiselle* Long, you discover us drearily engrossed in our responsibilities. Please forgive our manifold discourtesies."

Putz clicked his heels and saluted. "*Fraulein,* you are a testament to der bright Aryan spirit of adventure."

Captain Harrison blushed faintly at the way the ultra-vulcanized, vacuum-proof rubber fabric molded to the woman's form. "Ahem, Miss Long—Fancy—we were just discussing the outlines of our mission—"

Fancy batted her eyelashes and fluffed her Mars-bouncy hair. "Why so glum, then? We're finally going to rescue Dick from this awful fix he's gotten himself into, after five whole years! You should all be happy at the prospect of seeing your old shipmate again! Goodness knows, as his girlfriend, I'm terribly thrilled to think we'll be together again after so long!"

The men made no response to Fancy's bright chatter, and she became worried.

"What's wrong? Is there some new development you're not sharing with me? Have you had bad news from Dick over the radio? Or from Earth? Is the globe at war again? Have the Han Chinese broken out of the League blockade?"

Captain Harrison stroked his chiseled chin and spoke slowly, choosing his words carefully. "No, no, Miss Long, fortunately neither of your suppositions is correct. Earth contin-

ues to be blessed with peace—thanks to the cooperation of our
wise leaders—and the last communication we had from Dick
Jarvis left us assured that his, ah, situation remains stable. But
you see, there are certain, um, facts about Dick's continued
unplanned presence on Mars that neither you nor any other
civilians have ever been made aware of."

Fancy's pretty face expressed absolute confusion. "Why,
whatever do you mean, Captain?"

Harrison tried to approach the uncomfortable subject from
an angle. "Did you ever wonder, Miss Long, why you of all
people were selected for this rescue mission, rather than, say,
another scientist or even some practiced adventurer, such as
Lowell Thomas or Richard Halliburton?"

Plainly this thought had never occurred to Fancy. "No, I
can't say I ever wondered about it. Maybe I assumed that my
fame had something to do with my selection. You know, good
publicity for Space Command—"

Putz interrupted with Teutonic impatience. "You vere chosen, *madchen,* as a tool, a possible lever vee could use to pry
dot swine Jarvis out of his foul nest."

Fancy began to weep. "Oh, I don't understand! Why are
you all so mean all of a sudden? What did poor Dick ever do
to any of you, except get abducted by the rotten old Martians?"

Captain Harrison coughed, tugged at his collar braids, then
said, "Miss Long, your fiancé was not kidnapped by the Martians. He deserted. And he nearly doomed us before he left. Let
me fill you in on the secret aspects of our first mission to
Mars."

In short order, Captain Harrison recounted the bizarre adventures the crew of the original *Ares* had undergone, particularly Dick Jarvis.

During a recon mission in one of the two small fliers carried by the mother ship, Dick Jarvis had crashlanded in the
wastelands of Thyle, eight hundred miles from base camp, victim of his drive's defective atomic tubes. Uninjured, he had
gamely set out to walk home, burdened with massive amounts
of supplies made relatively light in the Red Planet's lesser
gravity.

Before too long, he encountered one of Mars's more intelligent life-forms, the ostrichlike sapient Jarvis came to call Tweel. Rescuing Tweel from a hypnotic carnivore, Jarvis had earned a friend for life. Together the two sentient beings began to traverse the hostile territory separating the human from the warmth and comfort of his own kind. The loquacious and helpful Tweel considerately kept his pace to the human's, restraining his one-hundred-and-fifty-foot jumps that ended beak-first in the rusty sands.

After encountering a strange, immortal silicon life-form that secreted bricks as part of its life-cycle, the two friends avoided yet another dream-beast—this time with Tweel rescuing Jarvis from a hallucination of Fancy Long herself—before finally coming upon a city of eight-limbed barrel-beings engaged in odd ritualistic construction duties. Tweel and Jarvis had wandered into the labyrinthine tunnels and chambers of the technologically sophisticated barrel creatures, ultimately becoming lost. Stealing a crystal talisman from the heretofore oblivious creatures, Jarvis incurred their wrath, just before man and Mars-bird broke through once more to the surface. Staging an Alamo-like last stand on the crimson sands, Tweel and Jarvis were on the point of being overwhelmed when a long-searching Putz dropped down with his own flier and rescued Jarvis. In the confusion, Tweel took off on his own, leaving Dick Jarvis inconsolable at the loss of his new alien friend.

"But this contradicts everything the public was told!" Fancy interrupted. "The whole world listened to your debriefing over all the televid networks with shock and sympathy! You reported that shortly after setting down on Mars, the first *Ares* was attacked without provocation by a horde of angry natives who damaged its propulsion tubes, We all know that Dick was captured when the vile creatures shot down his avenging scoutship. Then the rest of you brave adventurers, after laborious repairs, limped back home, to rouse Earth and mount a rescue mission."

"If only it were so," mused Captain Harrison, "the world would be a nobler place. But the authorities at Space Command and the League deemed the truth of our first expedition too volatile and shameful for general dissemination. We fabricated a cover story that we felt would encourage public support for a second mission. But allow me to continue with a summary of the actual events.

"That first night when Dick Jarvis lay safely in his bunk again, he apparently went mad. All that afternoon he had been fixated on that weird glowing egg-shaped crystal he had stolen from the barrel-beasts. He had told us previously how the crystal had cured an old wart on his left thumb when he touched it, and how the mystery stone had also eased the pain in his battered nose. We all speculated for a while about the curative properties of gamma rays. But when we asked to handle the miraculous object, he refused us! He clutched the alien bauble tightly and a horrible expression of greed, fear, and contempt flowed over his features as he defied us, with the crystal pressed to his brow like a radiant leech!"

Fancy shuddered at the image. "Poor Dick," she whispered. Harrison patted her shoulder in sympathy before resuming.

"'No, you can't have my treasure!' he hissed. 'You're all too ignorant of Mars. You don't deserve to handle it! None of you have been out there on foot like I was! I suffered for this! Immured behind your machines, you know nothing! It was different for Tweel and me. Tweel! Only Tweel knows! Tweel, where are you, Tweel? Save me!'"

Frenchy Leroy added to the captain's account. "In a blink, zat madman makes zee beeline for zee lock! Thank zee Lord, we have put zee latch upon zee screen door previously!"

"Vee had to wrestle him down," said Putz, "und jab him vit a sedative."

"Unfortunately," said Captain Harrison, "the sedative we used was not sufficient to counter his raging, jewel-influenced metabolism for long. Around midnight, while we all slept, Dick awoke. We had not bothered tying him very securely, and he escaped his bonds. He slipped out, hijacked our remaining scoutship, and took off. Awaking, we mourned and cursed this desertion. But it was only during a routine inspection the next day that we discovered your boyfriend's cruel parting gift."

A few tears trickled down Engineer Putz's cheeks. "Mine beautiful, beautiful tubes! Der *schweinhund* had scoured dem vit common kitchen grease from our galley! Bacon drippings and Crisco smeared all over dose delicate rockets! Somehow he knew dot der organics would foul dem beyond repair! Six months vee labored, first to discover a deposit of dohenium, den to excavate, smelt, refine and shape der material into new linings."

Captain Harrison nodded proudly at the heroic past exploits of his sturdy crew. "Even Doheny himself, that mad American who perfected the atomic blast, could not have done better."

Leroy spoke. "But zee new tubes were not perfect. We could not risk zee high-energy burns zat had brought us so swiftly to Mars. We had to crawl home on a slower ballistic. And once all zee Brie and Beaujolais ran out, it was hell!"

Captain Harrison added yet more infamy to Dick Jarvis' name, causing Fancy to weep quietly anew. "Of course we tried to raise Jarvis on the scoutship's radio and convince him to return and help us. The return of the scout would have made our repairs so much easier. But when he deigned to speak with us, all we could get from him were insane rants. Apparently, he had managed to hook up again with his beloved feather duster, Tweel. Together, they had taken over the city of the barrel-beasts, setting themselves up as despots with the aid of the healing crystal. But that wasn't the worst of it. Jarvis would rave for hours about the God of Mars. Somehow he had learned of the myth of this pagan deity through Tweel. Now he had some crazy plan for making contact with this superior being."

Putz patted his pistol. "I vill make contact vit dis God of Mars, all right. Right after vee settle Jarvis' hash."

Drying her eyes with a frilly hanky she removed from the hip pocket of her rubber coverall, Fancy put a bold and optimistic face on their mission. "I understand the situation more clearly now. I'll do everything in my power to convince Dick to abandon his megalomaniacal delusions and return with us to Earth for professional help from Zurich's best alienists." Fancy straightened her back and saluted winsomely. "You can count on me, Captain."

His stern mien brightening, Harrison returned the salute crisply, then said, "What are waiting for then, crew? Let's go corral our lost sheep!"

Several hours into their flight, as they soared across the barren, canal-slashed sands of the Red Planet, their underbelly film cameras recording every inch of the journey for rapt appreciation by the televid audience of Earth upon their return, the four people crammed into the small scoutship shared a certain apprehensive silence. Out the cockpit windshield clearly loomed the strange object that had cast the quartet into this blue funk. The anomalous fixed feature on the landscape had seemed to rise monolithically above the horizon as they rocketed around the curve of the globe. After several hours of supersonic flight, the enigmatic object had swelled to fill most of their forward-facing window.

"At first I thought it was some sort of natural bluff or mesa," said Captain Harrison, "although no such geographical feature appears on our maps. But now it's apparent that we're viewing some kind of construct. A monumental curving wall or tower larger than anything ever seen on Earth."

"Der lesser gravity permits extraordinary architectural feats," said Putz. "But how could Jarvis have accomplished so much in only five years?"

"Don't forget," Leroy said, "once he became zee Napoleon of zee barrel-beasts, he must have had all zair resources at his disposal."

"And most importantly," said Fancy, "despite his madness, he's still a human, the top-dog species in the solar system. And Dick was always a one-hundred-and-ten-percent he-man."

Putz snorted, Leroy rolled his eyes ceilingward, and Harrison coughed politely.

"What?" Fancy demanded. "What's the matter with you all? What are you trying to imply?"

"Miss Long," Harrison said gently, "I don't know how to break this to you, but your fiancé exhibited certain deviant tendencies to us on the first trip. Apparently, his libido, ah, flowed in wider channels than that of your normal man."

"Dot's putting it mildly," chimed in Putz. "Remember ven you accused him of being in love vit dot Tveel, und he said, 'So vot, I love you, too'!"

Fancy's face flushed nearly as red as the terrain below, and she uttered a stout defense of Dick Jarvis. "That's impossible! I'm sure you're all just misinterpreting some innocent banter. Dick has proved his passionate love for women physically to me many times!"

Leroy smoothed his own Lothario's mustache. "No doubt, *Ma'm'selle*. But trust a Frenchman in such matters: men who walk both sides of zee street of Eros are more common zen you might imagine."

Fancy snittily replied, "Well, I can't imagine what you need *me* for, then. Surely one of you nancy-boys could appeal to Dick's raging hormones as well as I could!"

Leroy was unruffled by Fancy's insult. "Perhaps, *cheri*. But why not have backup as well? Dick Jarvis has not seen a human woman in five years. Your presence might very well tip the scales in our favor."

No rebuttal to this cynical view occurred to Fancy, so she fell silent. Meanwhile, the men clustered about their instruments, intently examining the landscape ahead.

"Der optiscope under highest magnification has picked up der city of der barrel-beasts," Putz announced. "It is sitting right at der base of der construction."

"Any idea yet of exactly how big that wall is?"

"*Nein!* I have no sense of der proper scale yet, since I do not know der size of der city."

Harrison smacked a fist into his palm in frustration. "Damn! If only the eggheads back home had perfected that 'radar' gizmo they were yakking about before we left!"

"Vhen I rescued der traitor last time, der surface part of der city occupied only a few hectares dotted vit mounds made from dried mud. But mine guess is that it has expanded considerably since den."

Within half an hour their craft overflew the perimeter of the nonhuman city, and they could see that the newest buildings were sizable brick edifices. Now the still-distant yet dominating wall loomed over them balefully, its top unseen, more like one of Mars' two moons brought suddenly close than any artificial thing. In the labyrinthine streets below, the wiry-legged quadripedal barrel-beasts raced about on obscure errands, their upper four limbs engaged in carrying enigmatic objects or pushing their famous wheelbarrows so vividly described by Jarvis.

"Vhere should vee set down, Captain?"

"Try to find the original center of this cursed place. We'll have to assume Jarvis never bothered to move his HQ from its initial location."

Ten more minutes of flight carried them to the unchanged aboriginal portion of the city, a dusty clearing spotted with crumbling tumuli and the occasional scuttling barrel-creature. Careful not to injure any of the natives, Putz deftly set the scoutship down between two of the mounds, right next to the weather-corroded hull of the stolen scout from the first mission.

"I'm glad the *Ares II* is safely distant from here," said Harrison. "No sense in giving Jarvis a second chance at fouling our tubes! Well, men—Fancy—let's establish contact with these queer fellows!"

Once the ramp was extruded, the nervous humans descended at a deliberately dignified pace. A creature like a vertical oil drum with a ring of eyes all the way around its circumference awaited them at the foot of the ramp, its four unencumbered appendages wavering snakily, its four lower extremities firmly planted on the grounds.

Recalling how these aliens had once learned to parrot a single phrase Jarvis had once used, Harrison raised an open palm and said, "We are friends—ouch!"

The diaphragm at the top of the living drum vibrated in perfect replication of human speech.

"Please do not say 'ouch' unless you are actually feeling pain, Captain Harrison. That particular yokelish expression has become anathema among us, a reminder of our early nescience. Now come with me, please. The Highpriest Jarvis awaits you."

No attempt was made either to coerce them or to remove their weapons, so the humans warily accompanied their tubular guide, entering the hidden belowground city through the entrance in one of the mounds and embarking down a slanting, well lighted, temperate corridor.

Captain Harrison made proper introductions to the barrel-man, and then asked, "Do you have a name?"

"Stanley."

"Well, Stanley, perhaps you can tell us what this enormous construction outside is all about."

"I think the Highpriest himself would prefer to explain."

"Very well. We certainly have a lot of questions for Dick Jarvis."

"*Ja,* dot's for sure. Und he'd better have some damn good answers!"

Deeper and deeper under the surface they descended, twisting and spiraling past inexplicable mechanisms and scenes of antlike activity. Captain Harrison kept careful record of their trail, employing compass, pencil, and graph paper, so as to avoid getting lost as Jarvis had on his first visit. Leroy and Putz maintained a watchful defense of Fancy, who, to her credit under the trying circumstances, exhibited a calm and level head beneath her blonde curls.

Finally, they passed into a large domed room fit for a throne. But instead of any such formal seat, a welter of leathery pillows and exotic fabrics, seemingly more organically formed than artificial, filled the center of the hall.

Sprawled across the cushions in tangled intimacy like some evil Oriental potentate and concubine (as depicted on the nightly televid news) lay Dick Jarvis and his native birdfriend, Tweel.

Jarvis wore a kind of Robinson-Crusoe-on-Mars getup, native hides from some anonymous species roughly tailored into trews and vest. Beneath these new clothes, tattered remnants of his old undergarments remained. On his feet, clumsy sandals; on his head, a crude cap. A five-year-old beard draped his chest. Strapped to his brow with leather thongs like some barbaric fillet, the radioactive crystal talisman that the barrelbeasts worshiped glowed like a third eye.

Tweel, the sentient ostrich—thin legs with four-toed feet, rubbery neck, four-fingered hands, tiny head with eighteeninch, vaguely prehensile beak, plump body in which was secreted his powerful brain—that companion who had lured the human away from his very race, looked somewhat the worse for the passage of time as well. His mottled gray-blue feathers had lost their sheen, and a faintly dissolute droop to his neck conveyed some world-weary ennui, or exhaustion from attempting a task nearly too great for mortal strength.

Dick Jarvis registered the newcomers with only faint animation, as if drugged, his heavy-lidded eyes widening slightly

and a small smile twitching his chapped lips. He removed his
arm from where it had been slung around the feathered shoulders of his equally sluggish companion and forced himself
clumsily to his feet. He lumbered across the stretch of pillows
and extended his hand. Captain Harrison gingerly shook it,
then hastily let it go.

Jarvis spoke, and the visitors were washed by his oddly
spiced, not unpleasant breath. "Ah, my old friends! You'll
have to excuse Tweel and me, we were just indulging ourselves in a little recreational inebriation after a day's hard
labors." Jarvis removed a small canister from his pocket, un-
capped it, and poured some nearly weightless silicaceous BBs
into his palm. He snorted them, exhaled with a deep satisfaction, then seemed to gain new vigor.

Appalled, Harrison demanded, "What are those exotic
grains, Dick? Can you be certain they're safe?"

"Surely you recall my description of the spores discharged
by the brick-laying pyramid creature I encountered? Well, we
have enough of those beings here in the city now to fill all the
zoos of Earth, and they produce more spores than we need for
breeding purposes. I discovered their pharmaceutical properties strictly by accident one day, but you can bet that Tweel and
I have made good use of the surplus since!"

Leroy expressed the shock they all felt. "*Mon Dieu*, man!
You are snuffling up zee eggs of a non-carbon-based life-
form!"

At Jarvis' mention of his name, Tweel had levered himself
up on his stalky legs and sidled down to stand beside the
human renegade. After five years of tutoring, the Martian
bird's rubbery forebeak articulated human speech quite well,
in a reedy tenor.

"Cool your jets, Pierre. I bet you mugs all swill down the
hooch easy enough."

The quartet from the *Ares II* gaped in astonishment at being
thus reprimanded in slang by a sentient struthiod, and received
a further shock when Jarvis seconded the bird.

"If you've come all this way just to lay a Carrie Nation
spiel on me, you might as well go home now. Tweel and I
don't need your hypocritical do-gooding. We're on a mission
from God."

Harrison tried to smooth the waters. "We're not interested in criticizing your mode of living, Dick. I imagine that isolation and deprivation have bred some sloppy habits that we can help you kick. But we do need to know why you abandoned us so precipitously five years ago—nearly condemning us by your mean-spirited sabotage to join your exile—and what you've been up to since."

"Fair enough. I can sum up all my activities since we parted in a single phrase: the Tower of Babel."

The stunned silence that greeted this insane declaration was shattered by the harsh voice of the ship's engineer.

"Vot nonsense is dis!" bellowed the short-tempered Putz.

Possessed of an unflappable calm, Jarvis replied easily, "No nonsense of any kind, Karl. I am in contact with the God of Mars, who dwells on the satellite Deimos. Tweel and I are engaged in a project to bring us closer to Him, so that we may more fully receive his divine instructions."

"I haff had enough—" said Putz, making a move for his sidearm. But Harrison restrained him and said, "Let us hear Dick out, Karl."

Jarvis had not blinked at the threat, and now continued his strange story with easy equanimity, lightly touching the crystal indenting his brow as he spoke.

"When I first came into possession of this gem, I began to receive the most bizarre mental impressions, as if some superior being were trying to contact me via telepathy. At first, I thought I was going mad! Evidently you all did, too, forcing you to dope me and loosely secure me to my bunk. But during that fateful night, as the information began to sort itself out and my overworked brain began to make some partial accommodations, I realized the veracity of my experience, and what I must do.

"In a nutshell, here is what I learned.

"Millions of years ago, extrasolar visitors of surpassing intelligence and moral probity—call them gods, for by our standards they were—established outposts on both Luna and Deimos. They seeded the two prehistoric planets around which the satellites orbited—in both cases, home at this time only to brutish beasts—with thousands of these artificial gemstones, endowing the baubles with curative powers to insure that any intelligent individual yet to develop would cherish them upon discovery. The crystals also had another function, that of communicator with the undying guardian entity left behind on the moon of each world. When utilized by an individual of the appropriate mental development and receptivity, the crystal would unload its story into him.

"And he would be assigned a task.

"The construction of a tower at least one mile high.

"The accomplishment of this feat—a marvel of engineering and social skills—would signal the fitness of his race for the ultimate transcendence. The God left behind would initiate the uplifting of the native race to a level close to His Own, and that race would afterward join the intergalactic community.

"Mankind had its chance. The Biblical legend of the Tower of Babel is pure fact. But the Biblical Tower was not shattered by an imaginary Jehovah, angry at man's hubris. Rather, after work on the project was abandoned by an impious citizenry, the God of Luna turned his back on mankind. That is the true meaning of the Old Testament allegory. Nowadays, all of Earth's gems are lost. But Mars still has a chance for its own epiphany, and I intend to be the instrument of that salvation."

Jarvis finished his peroration with a valedictory air, and awaited a response.

His four auditors stood openmouthed in disbelief. At last Fancy Long spoke, causing Jarvis to take real cognizance of her for the first time.

"Oh, Dick, you sound nuttier than Father Coughlin and Aimee Semple McPherson combined! Surely you can't believe all that bushwa!"

"Fancy—is that really you? I thought you were just an afterimage from a dream-beast session. What are you doing here?"

"I'm a real flesh-and-blood girl, Dick! Your girl, if you want her! And I'm here to try to talk some sense into you."

Tweel edged closer to Jarvis, plucking at the human's rude shirt with his odd hand. "Don't listen to her, Dick. Don't listen to any of them. They want you to fail, just like your predecessor on Earth failed. They're from the Devil."

Jarvis passed a hand across his face, seemingly confused.

"I—I don't know what to say right now. I need some air." But
then, without exterior cause, the exile straightened decisively,
as if receiving an inner prompting. "Let me show you the
tower. Surely you'll sense the reality of the situation then.
Stanley!"

The attentive cylindrical Jeeves responded, "Yes, Highpriest?"

"Arrange transport for us immediately!"

Somehow Stanley communicated invisibly with his fellows, perhaps via radio waves, and in a short time six more
barrel-beasts arrived, each pushing a kind of rickshaw.

"Please, be seated," Jarvis graciously commanded. And
after everyone had complied, the train set off.

The rickshaws popped out onto the surface miles away, at a
busy construction site. The sun was well past its meridian, and
already the bone-penetrating chill of the Martian night could
be warily anticipated. This far from the shelter of the scout-
craft, the humans would be reliant on the good will of Dick
Jarvis, Tweel, and their uncanny subjects in order to survive
the night.

Clustering uneasily around Jarvis and Tweel, the Earth
people found their attention inevitably drawn to the incredible
wall only a few hundred yards away. This close, its known cur-
vature was masked. Looking heavenward, the humans could
gain no sight of its top. The structure was compounded of
nothing more substantial than small bricks in an infinity of
courses.

Dick Jarvis regarded his accomplishment proudly, like
some Pharaoh ogling his pyramid. "Ten miles in diameter at
the base here, tapering as she ascends. And after a mere five
years, she's already half a mile high. The outer wall has two
integral helical ramps, the clockwise one for upward traffic,
the other for down. You should see the intersections, it's like a
barrel-beast ballet. If there are any collisions, we just push the
victims over the edge. Ground crews clean up that debris.
Sometimes they get hit by the falling trash, and have to get
swept away themselves! Let me show you one of the brick
lines."

Jarvis conducted them across the bustling grounds, across

which innumerable barrel-beasts pushed wheelbarrows both
empty and full. They came upon a long row of lumpy rugose
creatures anchored in the sand, paralleled by a slowly but effi-
ciently moving procession of cylindrical workers and their
wheeled hods. Now Tweel took over the lecture.

"When Dick and I discovered the first of these creatures,
we noted that it produced one brick internally for its monumental carapace approximately every ten minutes. We were
able to stimulate this rate of brick-creation considerably. Now
each creature makes one brick every ninety seconds. By precisely staggering their start-up times, we contrive an assembly
line such that a barreloid can fill its empty wheelbarrow with
one hundred bricks simply by walking down the line at a mod-
erate pace. Observe."

The process was just as described: the first featureless gray
creature moored in the soil reached down its gullet with its
lone arm, extracted a brick and laid it in the empty barrow
poised to intercept it. The brick-carrier moved on a few paces
to the next living kiln and garnered a second brick. And so on
for a hundred instances. Once its barrow was loaded to capacity, the barrel-beast raced away to the foot of the ascending
ramp. Meanwhile, staggered ninety seconds after one barrel-
beast came another.

Dick Jarvis beamed. "All the components of the system
work around the clock. And when they wear out, we just bring
young, fresh units onto the line. Our breeding programs are
tremendously efficient. You know how the brickmakers reproduce—those loco-coco BBs! But perhaps you forgot what I
learned years ago about the barreloids. Stanley, come here!"

The loyal factotum approached, and Jarvis searched its
body for a moment before finding what he wanted. "Look
here! A bud! These things reproduce like Brussels sprouts!"
Jarvis pinched the immature offspring nodule on Stanley's
hide, twisted, and off it came. He popped it into his mouth,
chewed and swallowed. "And they taste pretty much like
Brussels sprouts too. That's how I've survived so well!"

Captain Harrison stammered out a horrified response
shared by one and all. "Guh-guh-good Lord, Dick! But this is
monstrous! You've perverted the sacred principles of Henry
Ford into a kind of nightmarish slave society even Edgar Rice

Burroughs himself couldn't envision! And all in the service of a mystical delusion!"

Tweel stepped forward, his close-set avian eyes hard as the tower's bricks. "You must not criticize the Highpriest."

The muzzle of Putz's gun centered on Jarvis' stomach. "Vee vill continue dis fascinating discussion back on der ship. Get your hands in der air, Dick, and do as I—"

Putz ceased speaking, and looked down at himself in horror.

Tweel's light feathery body seemed glued to Putz's torso, while from the engineer's back protruded the gore-smeared beak and head of the javelin-deadly ostrich.

Pierced front to back through heart, lung, and other essential organs, Putz dropped his gun, burbled, and collapsed to the unforgiving sands in a welter of blood. Tweel adroitly withdrew his deadly head and neck before becoming pinned down, and hopped backward from the corpse. The bird opened the leather pouch he wore about his long neck, withdrew a square of cloth, and began to clean himself fastidiously of the evidence of the hideous murder.

Before any of Putz's comrades could come to succor him in his dying moments, they found themselves pinioned by several of the barrel-beasts summoned by Stanley. Fancy, Leroy, and Captain Harrison struggled in vain against the tendrils enwrapping them.

Dick Jarvis exhibited no emotion other than a faint distaste. "Too bad for Karl, but he brought it on himself. Tweel is my brother. We guard each other's back. And nothing must be allowed to interfere with our holy tower."

Tweel had finished his finicky ablutions. "Quite correct, Dick."

"What are you going to do with us now, you madman?" demanded a shaken but defiant Captain Harrison.

"You and Leroy will be locked up. But you won't mind, since your jailer will be pleasant company. As for Fancy, I think Tweel and I will entertain her ourselves."

At this unwelcome announcement, the lady under discussion fainted dead away, prevented from falling only by the embrace of her barreloid captor. Without further ado, all three

captives were lifted off their feet and carried away at high
speed, while Jarvis and Tweel followed in their rickshaws.

Down, down, down they went, to a dim dungeon level of
the city. The barrel-beasts unceremoniously thrust Captain
Harrison and Frenchy Leroy into a small cell, which, oddly
enough, boasted neither door nor bars. Seated in his carriage
in the corridor, Jarvis spoke.

"I'm certain you recall my description of the carnivorous
dream-creature from which I first rescued Tweel. A nest of
ropy limbs and a slavering maw, able to project hallucinations
that lure its victims to their doom. Well, you two men start
with the advantage of knowing that what you face is a deadly
illusion. But even so, we will see how long you are able to resist the beckoning allure of the telepathic monster!"

Jarvis reached out to press a button inset beside the doorway, and the rear wall of the cubicle began to slide upward, re-
vealing the hideous pedal extremities of the captive
dream-devil. Harrison and Leroy backed up into the farthest
corners of the cell as the first burgeoning fingers of the seductive mesmeric impulses reached them, conjuring up private visions of longing.

Laughing insanely, Jarvis signaled departure for the rest of
his entourage.

Fancy Long awoke in a warm, pleasantly scented bed,
keeping her eyes closed for a moment just to savor the com-
forting sensations. What a nightmare she had had! No doubt
she would open her eyes to see the familiar outlines of the
cabin of the *Ares II*. No, make that her Hollywood hacienda.
She was home in the Los Angeles hills, and tomorrow she
would go shopping at all her favorite stores—

"Fancy, my dear, you cannot know how many times I have
dreamed of this moment."

Fancy shrieked, and her eyelids flew upward like snapped
roller-shades.

Naked except for a pair of ragged Earth briefs, Dick Jarvis
had considerably shaved off his long beard and scrubbed himself clean of Martian grit. For one brief moment, Fancy could
almost believe that her old suitor stood before her, and that
they occupied a suite in the Waldorf. But then her eyes fas-

tened on the cursed jewel bound to his brow, and she knew
herself in the direst of straits.

Jarvis cooed to her in what he must have assumed was a reassuring tone, but which had the opposite effect. "Oh, my tame
dream-beast could always provide a simulacrum of you obedi-
ent to my every command, for my erotic enjoyment. But having the real, tangible woman here—that is a paradise beyond
compare. And to be able to share with my brother—!"

Horrified, Fancy turned her head to find Tweel's head resting on a pillow only inches from hers.

"I am most anxious to observe the mechanics of human
mating. Perhaps I might even be able to assist at some point,
although from what I am given to understand by Dick, my private anatomy is most unsuitable."

Fancy willed herself to lose consciousness, but apparently
she had used up her fainting resources during Putz's murder.
The most she could do was close her eyes, grit her teeth, and
pretend that she lay upon the casting couch of the least loath-
some televid producer.

The next interval was always to remain a merciful blur in
Fancy's memory, a period of a thousand mingled sensual impressions, some of them not unpleasant, some of them approaching pain, with the former perhaps more disturbing than
the latter. The roving hands, the twining legs, the feather-
seated probing appendage, the rubbery prehensile beak— No,
best to draw a curtain over it all.

When Fancy's personality finally reassembled itself into a
coherent whole, the naked woman found both her sated as-
sailants fast asleep beside her. Taking stock of the chamber,
Fancy noted a small shrine of terrestrial possessions maintained by Jarvis: a framed 3-D portrait of Fancy herself, an
empty can of coffee, a radio set—and a standard-issue Space
Command .45 pistol.

Praying fervently, Fancy slid slowly out from between man
and bird without waking them. She moved on tiptoe to the
shrine, took the pistol in hand—

"What are you doing, Miss Long?"

Standing up, Tweel confronted her impassively from the
rumpled bedclothes.

No thoughts passed through Fancy's mind before she fired, blowing off Tweel's tiny head.

Naturally the shot awoke Dick Jarvis, who sized up the situation instantly. The man uttered a wild ululation of grief and flung himself upon the writhing Tweel, whose midriff-concealed brain strove to deal with the pain of decapitation and loss of sensory organs. Jarvis grabbed a bit of cloth to fashion a tourniquet for Tweel's bleeding stump, and at that exact moment Fancy dived in to rip the jewel from his forehead.

The evil crystal came away with a harsh tearing sound, and Jarvis bellowed, then collapsed. Still nude, Fancy dashed from the room.

Encountering a lone barrel-beast in the corridors, Fancy flashed the gemstone at it and commanded, "Take me to the other humans!"

Wrapping her voluptuous form in its neutral, dry embrace, the alien promptly complied.

Harrison and Leroy had cast themselves upon the floor of their cell in an effort to crawl to freedom. Their bloodied fingertips testified to their determined striving to counter the compulsion to submit to the slavering dream-beast. But otherwise they proved unharmed as Fancy lowered the shielding wall, freeing them from the ill effects of the telepathic carnivore.

Gaining his feet, Captain Harrison sized up Fancy's condition, and swiftly realized she had made the ultimate sacrifice for their rescue. He saluted her bravely, then took command.

"Back to the scout! Once we're board the *Ares,* we'll even the score!"

The leaderless, disorganized barreloids could offer no interference to the human attack. It took hours and hours of steady play of the inexhaustible Doheny jets at several points along the base of the tower to weaken it sufficiently to trigger its collapse. But when half a mile of masonry finally came down, the results repaid their efforts with a cataclysm equal to several N-bombs, effectively vaporizing the city of the barrel-beasts, including the unfortunately abandoned corpse of Putz, and—presumably—Dick Jarvis and his avian catamite, Tweel.

In orbit around the ruddy world, preparing for the long trip home, the survivors of the second Terran mission to Mars exhibited a sober demeanor consonant with their horrible experiences. Finally, Fancy broke the introspective funk.

"You don't suppose there was any sense in Dick's madness, do you? Could there be representatives of an intergalactic civilization on Luna and Deimos, virtual gods?"

Captain Harrison stroked his chiseled chin thoughtfully before replying. "If we ever find them, a few N-bombs should settle their hash. What nerve, interfering with human destiny!"

Fancy made no reply, but merely considered the small crystal souvenir stashed among her personal luggage. Not that she would ever use it, after seeing what the gem had done to poor Dick. But diamonds *were* a girl's best friend.

THE REAL STORY

by Alastair Reynolds

I CUPPED a bowl of coffee in my hands, wondering what I was doing back home. A single word had brought me from Earth; one I'd always expected to hear but after seventeen years had almost forgotten.

That word was *shit*: more or less my state of mind.

Grossart had promised to meet me in a coffeehouse called *Sloths*, halfway up Strata City. I'd had to fight my way to a two-seater table by the window, wondering why that table—with easily the best view—just happened to be empty. I soon found out: *Sloths* was directly under the jumping-off point for the divers, and one of them would often slam past the window. It was like being in a skyscraper after a stock market crash.

"Another drink, Madame?" A furry robot waiter had crossed the intestinal tangle of ceiling pipes to arrive above my table.

I stood up decisively. "No thanks. I'm leaving. And if a man asks for me—for Carrie Clay—you can tell him to take a piss in a sandstorm."

"Well, now, that wouldn't actually be very nice, would it?"

The man had appeared at the table like a ghost. I looked at him as he lowered himself into the other chair and then sighed, shaking my head.

"Christ. You could have at least made an effort to look like Grossart, even if being on time was beyond you."

"Sorry about that. You know what it is with us Martians and punctuality. Or I'm assuming you used to."

My hackles rose. "What's that supposed to mean?"

"Well, you've been on Earth for a while, haven't you?" He

snapped his fingers at the waiter, which had begun to work its way back across the ceiling. "We're like the Japanese, really—we never truly trust anyone who goes away and comes back. Two coffees, please."

I flinched as a diver zipped by. "Make that one . . ." I started saying, but the waiter had already left.

"See, you're committed now."

I gave the balding, late middle-aged man another appraisal. "You're not Jim Grossart. You're not even close. I've seen more convincing . . ."

"Elvis impersonators?"

"What?"

"That's what they said about Elvis when he came out of hiding. That he didn't look the way they'd been expecting."

"I haven't got a clue who or what you're talking about."

"Of course you haven't," he said, hurriedly apologetic. "Nor should you. It's my fault—I keep forgetting that not everyone remembers things from as far back as I do." He gestured toward my vacant chair. "Now, why don't you sit down so that we can talk properly?"

"Thanks, but no thanks."

"And I suppose me saying *shit* at this point wouldn't help matters?"

"Sorry," I said, shaking my head. "You're going to have to do much better than that."

It *was* the word, of course—but him knowing it was hardly startling. I wouldn't have come to Mars if someone hadn't contacted my agency with it. The problem was that man didn't seem to be the one I'd been looking for.

It all went back a long time.

I'd made my name covering big stories around Earth—I was the only journalist in Vatican City during the Papal Reboot—but before that I'd been a moderately respected reporter on Mars. I'd covered many stories, but the one of which I was proudest had concerned the first landing; an event which had become murkier and more myth-ridden with every passing decade. It was generally assumed that Jim Grossart and the others had died during the turmoil, but I'd shown that this wasn't necessarily the case. No body had ever been found, after all. The turmoil could just as easily have been an oppor-

tunity to vanish out of the public eye, before the pressure of
fame became too much. And it was worth remembering that
the medical breakthrough which triggered the turmoil in the
first place could have allowed anyone from that era to remain
alive until now, even though the *Hydra*'s landing had been a
century ago.

I'd known even then that it was a long shot, but—by deliberately omitting a single fact that I'd uncovered during my investigations—I'd left a way to be contacted.

"All right," he said. "Let me fill you in on some background. The first word spoken on Mars was *shit*—we agree on
that—but not everyone knows I said it because I lost my foot-
ing on the last-but-one rung of the ladder."

I allowed my eyebrows to register the tiniest amount of surprise; no more than that. He continued: "They edited it out of
the transmission without anyone noticing. There was already a
twenty-minute delay on messages back to Earth, so no one noticed the extra few seconds due to the censorship software. Remember how Neil Armstrong fluffed his lines on the Moon?
No one was going to let that happen again."

The waiter arrived with our coffees, hanging from the ceiling by its four rear limbs while the long front pair placed
steaming bowls on the table. The waiter's cheap brown fur
didn't quite disguise its underlying robotic skeleton.

"Actually, I think it was Louis who fluffed his lines," I said.
"Louis?"

"Armstrong." I took a sip of my coffee, the deep butter-
scotch of a true Martian sky. "The first man on the moon. But
I'll let that pass."

He waved a hand, dismissing his error. "Whatever. The
point is—or was—that everything said on Mars was relayed to
Earth via the *Hydra*. But she didn't just boost the messages;
she also kept a copy, burned onto a memory chip. And nothing
on the chip was censored."

I took another cautious sip from the bowl. I'd forgotten how
we Martians liked our drinks: beer in Viking-impressing steins
and coffee in the sort of bowl Genghis Khan might have
sipped koumiss from after a good day's butchering.

"Tell me how I found the chip, and I might stay to finish
this."

"That I can't know for sure."

"Ah." I smiled. "The catch."

"No, it's just that I don't know who Eddie might have sold the chip to. But Eddie was definitely the man I sold it to. He was a Rastafarian, dealing in trinkets from early Martian history. But the last time I saw Eddie was a fair few decades ago."

This was, all of a sudden, beginning to look like less of a wasted trip. "Eddie's just about still in business," I said, remembering the smell of ganja wafting through his mobile scavenger caravan out on the gentle slopes of the Ares Vallis. "He never sold the chip, except to me, when I was making my investigations for the *Hydra* piece."

He pushed himself back in his seat. "So. Are you prepared to accept that I'm who I say I am?"

"I'm not sure. Yet."

"But you're less skeptical than a few minutes ago?"

"Possibly," I said, all that I was going to concede there and then.

"Listen, the way I look isn't my fault. The Grossart you knew from your investigations was a kid; a thirty-year-old man."

"But you must have obtained longevity treatment at some point, or we wouldn't be having this conversation."

"Correct, but it wasn't the instant the treatment arrived on Mars. Remember that if the treatment had been easily obtainable, there wouldn't have *been* any turmoil. And I was too busy vanishing to worry about it immediately." He rubbed a hand along his crown; weathered red skin fringed by a bristly white tonsure. "My physiological age is about seventy, even though I was born one hundred and thirty-two years ago."

I looked at him more closely now; thinking back to the images of Jim Grossart with which I'd become familiar all those years ago. His face had been so devoid of character—so much a blank canvas—that it had always seemed pointless trying to guess how he would look when he was older. And yet none of my expectations were actually contradicted by the man sitting opposite me.

"If you are Jim Grossart . . ." My voice was low now.

"There's no 'if' about it, Carrie."

"Then why the hell have you waited seventeen years to speak to me?"

He smiled. "Finished with that coffee?"

We left *Sloths* and took an elevator up sixteen city levels to the place where the divers were jumping off. They started the drop from a walkway which jutted out from the city's side for thirty meters, tipped by a ring-shaped platform. Brightly clothed divers waited around the ring—it only had railings on the outside—and now and then one of them would step into the middle and drop. Sometimes they went down in pairs or threes; sometimes joined together. Breathing equipment and a squirrel-suit was all they ever wore; no one ever carried a parachute or a rocket harness.

It looked a lot like suicide. Sometimes, that was just what it was.

"That's got to be fun," Grossart said, the two of us still snug within the pressurized viewing gallery.

"Yes. If you're clinically insane."

I immediately wanted to bite back what I'd just said, but Grossart seemed unoffended.

"Oh, cliff diving can't be that difficult—not if you've got a reasonably intuitive grasp of the Navier-Stokes equations and a few basic aerodynamic principles. You can even rent two-person squirrel-suits over there."

"Don't even think about it."

"Heights not your thing?" he said, turning—to my immense relief—away from the window. "Not very Martian of you."

He was right, though I didn't like admitting it. Gravity on Mars was only slightly less than two fifths of Earth's—not enough to make much difference if you were planning on falling more than a few meters—but it *was* enough to ensure that Martians grew up experiencing few of the bruising collisions between bone and ground which people on Earth took for granted. Martians viewed heights the way the rest of humanity viewed electricity: merely *understood* to be dangerous, rather than something felt in the pit of the stomach.

And I'd been away too damned long.

"C'mon," I said. "Let's check out the tourist tat. My great-

great-grandmother'll never forgive me if I don't send her back something seriously tacky."

Grossart and I went into one of the shops which lined the canyon-side wall of the viewing gallery, pushing past postcard stands flanking the door. The shops were busy, but no one gave us a second glance.

"Christ, look at this," Grossart said, hefting a paperweight. It was a snow-filled dome with a model of the *Hydra* parked on a red plastic base. There was even a replica of Grossart; a tiny space-suited figure not much smaller than the lander itself.

"Tasteful," I said. "Or at least, it is compared to this." I held up a keyring holder, shaped like a sloth if you were feeling generous.

"No, that's definitely at the quality end of the merchandise. Look." Grossart picked up an amber stone and read from the label. "Sloth healing crystal. This gem modifies and focuses the body's natural chromodynamic fields, ensuring mental and physical harmony."

"You can't prove it doesn't, can you?"

"No, but I think Brad Treichler might have a few interesting things to say to the proprietor."

I perked at the mention of the *Hydra*'s geologist. "I'd like to meet Treichler as well. And Manuel D'Oliveira, while we're at it. Is it possible?"

"Of course."

"I mean here, today."

"I know what you mean, and—yes—it's possible. They're all here, after all."

"And you don't mind speaking about them?"

"Not at all." He put down the stone. "Those guys kept me alive, Carrie. I'll never forget the debt I owe them."

"I think we all owe them one, in that case." As I spoke I rummaged through a rack of what purported to be recordings of sloth compositions, some of which were combined with whale sounds or Eskimo throat music. "Having said that, seeing this must be depressing beyond words."

"Why, because I was the first man on Mars?" He shook his head. "I know how you think I should feel. Like Elvis in the Graceland's souvenir shop, inspecting an exquisite plastic dashboard figurine of himself. White jumpsuits and hamburgers era, of course."

I looked at him blankly.

"But I'm not horrified, Carrie. As a matter of fact, it actually amuses me."

I examined a garment. *My best friend went to Strata City, Mars, and all I got was this lousy T-shirt,* it said on the front.

"I find that pretty hard to believe, Jim."

"Then you don't really understand me. What did you think I wanted? Reverence? No. I came to Mars to begin the process of human colonization. That's why others followed me, because I made that first, difficult step. Oh, and it was difficult, believe me—but I made it all the same."

I nodded. Though seventeen years had passed since I'd written the piece on the landing, I remembered it all: how Jim Grossart had left Earth in a privately-funded expedition done the cheap way—done, in fact, more cheaply than anyone else ever thought possible—with only a vague idea of how to get back from Mars afterward. His sponsors were going to send out supplies, and then more settlers, until there was a self-sustaining colony. Eventually they'd send a bigger ship to take back anyone who wanted to return, but the expectation was that few people would plan on leaving for good. And that, more or less, was how it had happened—but Grossart's crossing had been every bit as difficult as it had been expected to be, and there had been enough crises along the way to push him to the edge of sanity, and—perhaps—slightly beyond.

It all depended, I supposed, on what you meant by sanity.

Grossart continued: "You know what would worry me more? A planet that took its past too seriously. Because that would mean there was something human we hadn't brought with us."

"What, the ineffable tendency to produce and consume bad-taste tourist crap?"

"Something like that, yes." And then he held up a crude plastic mask to his face, and suddenly I was looking at the face of the man I had hoped to meet in *Sloths;* the young Jim Grossart.

"I don't think you need to worry," I said.

Grossart returned the mask to a tray with a hundred others,

just as the manager of the shop started eyeing us unwelcomingly. "No, I don't think I do. Now . . ." He beamed and rubbed his hands together. "You know what I'm going to suggest, don't you?"

He was looking out of the shop, back toward the jump-off point.

I suppose the technical term was blackmail. I wanted a story (or at least some idea of why Grossart had contacted me after all these years), and he wanted to take the big dive. More than that, he wanted to do the dive with someone else.

"Look," I said. "If it's such a big deal, can't you just do it and I'll see you at the bottom? Or back here?"

"And what if I decided to vanish again? You'd kick yourself, wouldn't you, for letting me out of your sight?"

"Very possibly, but at least I'd have the satisfaction of knowing I hadn't been talked into doing something monumentally stupid."

We were already in the line for the squirrel-suits. "Yes," he said. "But you'd also have to live with the knowledge that—when you come to write this up, as I know you will—you won't be able to include the sequence in which you took the big dive with Captain Jim Grossart."

I looked at him coldly. "Bastard."

But he was right: personal fear was one thing; compromising a story another.

"Now there's no need for that."

"Just tell me you know what you're doing, all right?"

"Well, of course I do. Sort of."

We got our squirrel-suits. The first thing you did was get the breathing and comms gear attached. Each suit had only a few minutes of air, but that was all you needed. The suits themselves were lurid skintight affairs, padded and marked with glowing logos and slogans. They were so named because they had folds of elastic material sewn between the arms and legs, like the skin of a flying squirrel—enough to double your surface area during a fall. Mine was only moderately stiff across the chest and belly, but Grossart's had a six-inch-thick extra layer of frontal armor. We settled on our helmets, locked our visors down and established that we could communicate.

"I'm really not pushing you into this," Grossart said.

"No; merely playing on the fact that I'm a mercenary bitch who'll do just about anything for a story. Let's just get this over with, shall we?"

We filtered through the air lock which led to the jump-off stage. Strata City reached away on either side for several hundred meters; buildings crammed as close as the wall's topology would allow. Pressurized walkways snaked between the larger structures, while elevator tubes and staircases connected the city's levels. Not far above, perched on the canyon's lip, a series of large hotel complexes thrust their neon signs against the early dusk sky: *Hilton, Holiday Inn, Best Martian.*

Then—realizing as I did so that it was probably going to be a bad idea—I looked down. The city continued below us for several kilometers before thinning out into an expanse of sheer, smooth canyon wall which dropped away even more sickeningly. The Valles Marineris was the deepest canyon on Mars, and now that its deepest parts were in shadow, all I could see at the bottom was a concentrated sprinkling of very tiny, distant-looking lights.

"I hope to God you know what you're doing, Jim."

At the end of the platform an attendant coupled us together, me riding Grossart. With my legs bound together and my arms anchored uncomfortably against my sides, I was little more than a large dead weight on his back.

Another attendant unplugged our air lines from the platform's outlets, so that we were breathing from the suits. Then we shuffled forward and waited our turn.

I wondered what I was doing. I'd met a man in a bar who had given me some plausible answers about the first landing, but I didn't have a shred of evidence that I was really dealing with Jim Grossart. Perhaps when they peeled me off the bottom of the canyon, they'd find that the man was just a local nutcase who'd done his homework.

"Miss?" he said, when we had shuffled closer to the edge.

"What is it?"

"Something you should probably know at this point. I'm not Jim Grossart."

"No?"

"No. I'm Commander Manuel D'Oliveira. And is there anyone else who you'd rather have for the big dive?"

I thought about what lay ahead—my stomach butterflies doing an aerobatics display by now—and decided he was probably right. D'Oliveira was the *Hydra*'s pilot; the one who had brought the tiny lander down even though half her aerobrake shielding had been ripped off by a mid-flight explosion. It had not been a textbook landing, but given that the alternative consisted of becoming an interesting new smear on the Argyre Planitia, D'Oliveira had not done too badly.

"You'll do nicely, Commander."

"Manuel, please." He spoke almost flawless American English, but with the tiniest trace of a Latin accent. "Tell me—how did you get on with Jim?"

"Oh, fine. I liked him. Apart from the fact that he kept going on about some dead person called Elvis, of course."

"Yes. You have to humor him in that respect. But he's not too bad, all things considered. We could have had a worse captain, I think. He glued us together. Now, then. It seems to be our turn. Are you ready for this, Miss . . . ?"

"Carrie Clay." It was strange introducing myself again, but it seemed rude not to. "Yes, I'm ready."

We shuffled forward and jumped; falling through the middle of the ring-shaped platform. I looked up—though I was attached to D'Oliveira, I could still move my head—and saw the ring-shaped platform dwindling into the vertical distance. After only a couple of heartbeats we flashed past the level of *Sloths*, and then we were falling still faster. The feeling of weightlessness was not totally new to me, of course, but the sensation of mounting speed and proximity to the rushing wall of the city more than compensated.

"There's a trick to this, of course," D'Oliveira said. He had positioned us into a belly-down configuration, with his arms and legs spread out. "A lot of people haven't got the nerve to keep this close to the side of the city."

"No shit."

"But it's a big mistake not to," D'Oliveira said. "If you know the city well, you can keep in nice and close like this. The fatal error is moving too far out."

"Really."

"Oh, yes; major mistake." He paused. "Hmm. Notice anything? We're not accelerating. You've got your weight back."

"Silly me. Didn't . . . notice."

"Terminal velocity after forty-five seconds. Already dropped four kilometers—but you wouldn't guess it, would you?"

Now we were dropping down a narrow, vertical canyon with buildings on either side of us and rock on the third face. D'Oliveira started giving me a lecture on terminal velocities which might well have been fascinating at any other time; how the refineries had ramped up the air pressure on Mars to around five percent of Earth normal, which—while neither thick nor warm enough to breathe—was enough to stop a human in a squirrel-suit from dropping like a stone, even if terminal velocity was still a hair-raising one sixth of a kilometer per second.

It was about as welcome as a lecture on human neck anatomy to someone on the guillotine.

I looked down again and saw that we were beginning to reach the city's lower-level outskirts. But the canyon wall itself seemed as high as ever; the lights at the bottom just as far away.

"You know how this city came about, don't you?" D'Oliveira said.

"No . . . but I'm . . . damn sure you're . . . going to . . . tell me."

"It all began with geologists, not long after the turmoil." He flipped us around and altered our angle of attack, so that we were slightly head down. "They were looking for traces of ancient fossil life, buried in rock layers. Eight vertical kilometers wasn't good enough for them, so they dug out the canyon's base for two or three more, then covered a whole vertical strip in scaffolding. They built labs and living modules on the scaffolding, to save going back up to the top all the time." A chunk of building zipped past close enough to touch—it looked that close, anyway—and then we were falling past rough rock face with only the very occasional structure perched on a ledge. "But then somewhere else on Mars they uncovered the first sloth relics. The geologists didn't want to miss the action, so they cleared out like shit on wheels, leaving all their things behind." D'Oliveira steered us around a fingerlike rock protrusion which would have speared us otherwise. "By the time they got back, the scaffolding had been taken over by squatters. Kids, mostly—climbers and BASE jumpers looking for new thrills. Then someone opened a bar, and before you knew it the place had gone *mainstream*." He spoke the last word with exquisite distaste. "But I guess it's not so bad for the tourists."

"Jim didn't mind, did he?"

"No, but he's not me. I don't mind the fact that we came here either, and I don't mind the fact that people came after us. But did it have to be so many?"

"You can't ration a planet."

"I don't want to. But it used to be hard to get here. Months of travel in cramped surroundings. How long did it take you, Miss Clay?"

"Five days on the *Hiawatha*." It was easier to talk now; what had been terror not many seconds ago transmuting into something almost pleasant. "And I wouldn't exactly call her cramped. You could argue about the decor in the promenade lounge, but beyond that . . ."

"I know. I've seen those tourist liners parking around Mars, lighting up the night sky."

"But if you hadn't come to Mars, we might not have discovered the sloth relics, Manuel. And it was those relics which showed us how to get from Earth to Mars in five days. You can't have it both ways."

"I know. No one's more fascinated by the sloths than me. It's just—did we have to learn so much, so soon?"

"Well, you'd better get used to it. They're talking about building a starship, you know—a lot sooner than any of us think."

The rock face had become much smoother now—it was difficult to judge speed, in fact—and the lights at the bottom of the canyon no longer seemed infinitely distant.

"I know. I've heard about that. Sometimes I almost think I'd like to . . ."

"What, Manuel?"

"Hang on. Time to start slowing down, I think."

There were only two orthodox ways of slowing down from

a big dive, the less skilled of which involved slamming into the ground. The other, trickier way, was to use the fact that the lower part of the canyon wall began to deviate slightly from true vertical. The idea was to drop until you began to scrape against the wall at a tiny grazing angle and then use friction to kill your speed. Lower down, the wall curved out to merge with the canyon floor, so if you did it properly you could come to a perfect sliding halt with no major injuries. It sounded easy, but—as D'Oliveira told me—it wasn't. The main problem was that people were usually too scared to stay close to the rushing side of the wall when it was sheer. You couldn't blame them for that, since it was pretty nerve-racking and you did have to know exactly where it was safe to fall. But if they stayed too far out, they were prolonging the point at which they came into contact with the canyon wall, and by then it wouldn't be a gentle kiss but a high-speed collision at an appreciable angle.

Still, as D'Oliveira assured me, they probably had the best view, while it lasted.

He brought us in for a delicate meeting against the wall, head down, and then used the six-inch armor on his front as a friction break, as if we were tobogganing down a near-vertical slope. The lower part of the wall had already been smooth, but thousands of previous cliff-divers had polished it to glassy perfection.

When it was over—when we had come to an undignified but injury-free halt—attendants escorted us out of the danger zone. The first thing they did was release the fasteners so that we could stand independently. My legs felt like jelly.

"Well?" D'Oliveira said.

"All right; I'll admit it. That was reasonably entertaining. I might even consider doing . . ."

"Great. There's an elevator which'll take us straight back . . ."

"Or, on second thought, you could show me to the nearest stiff drink."

I needn't have worried; D'Oliveira was happy to postpone his next cliff dive, and I was assured that there was a well-stocked bar at the base of the canyon. For a moment, however, we lingered, looking back up that impossible wall of rock, to where the lights of Strata City glimmered far above us. The city had seemed enormous when I'd been inside it; not much smaller when we'd been falling past it—but now it looked tiny; a thin skein of human presence against the monumental vastness of the canyon side.

D'Oliveira put a hand on my forearm. "Something up?"

"Just thinking, that's all."

"Bad habit." He patted me on the back. "We'll get you that drink now."

An hour or so later, D'Oliveira and I were sharing a compartment in a train heading away from Strata City.

"We could go somewhere else," I'd said. "It's still early, after all, and my body clock still thinks it's midafternoon."

"Bored with Strata City already?"

"Not exactly, no—but somewhere else would make a good contrast." I was seeing off a vodka, and I could feel my cheeks flushing. "I'm going to write this meeting up, you understand."

"Why not." He shrugged. "Jim's told you what he thinks about Mars, so I might as well have my say."

"Some of it you've already told me."

He nodded. "But I could talk all night if you let me. Listen—how about taking a train to Golombek?"

"It's not that far," I said, after a moment's thought. "But you know what's there, don't you."

"It's not a problem for me, Miss Clay. And it isn't the reason I suggested Golombek anyway. They've recently opened a sloth grotto up for public viewing. Haven't had a chance to see it, to be honest, but I'd very much like to."

I shrugged. "Well, what are expense accounts for, if not to burn."

So we'd taken an elevator back up to the top of the canyon and picked up the first train heading out to Golombek. The express shot across gently undulating Martian desert, spanning canyons on elegant white bridges grown from structural bone. It was dark, most of the landscape black except for the distant lights of settlements or the vast, squatting shapes of refineries.

"I think I understand now," I said. "Why you contacted me."

The man sitting opposite me shrugged. "It wasn't really me. Jim was the one."

"Well, maybe. But the point remains. It was time to be heard, wasn't it? Time to set the record straight. That was the problem with vanishing—it let people put things into your mouths that you wouldn't necessarily have agreed with."

He nodded. "We've been used by every faction you can think of, whether it's to justify evacuating Mars completely or covering it with mile-deep oceans. And it's all bullshit; all lies."

"But it's not as if you even agree with each other."

"No, but . . ." He paused. "We might not agree, but at least this is the truth; what we really think; not something invented to suit someone else's agenda. At least it's the real story."

"And if the real story isn't exactly neat and tidy?"

"It's still true."

He looked, of course, very much like Jim Grossart. I won't say they were precisely the same, since D'Oliveira seemed to inhabit the same face differently; pulling the facial muscles into a configuration all of his own. He deported himself differently, as well, sitting with slightly more military bearing.

Even by the time I'd done my article—more than eighty years after the landing—no one really understood quite what had happened to Captain Jim Grossart. All anyone agreed on was the basics: that Grossart had been normal when he left Earth as the only inhabitant of a one-man Mars expedition.

Maybe it was the accident that had done it; the explosion in deep space which had damaged *Hydra*'s aerobraking shields. The explosion also caused a communication blackout which lasted several weeks, and it was only when the antenna began working again that anyone could be sure that Grossart had survived at all. Over the next few days, as he began sending messages back home, the truth slowly dawned. Jim Grossart had cracked; fracturing into three personalities. Grossart himself was only one third of the whole, with two new and entirely fictitious selves sharing his head. Each took on some of the skills which had previously been part of Grossart's overall expertise; D'Oliveira inheriting Grossart's piloting abilities and Treichler the specialist in Martian physics and geology. And—worried about inflicting more harm than necessary on a man who was almost over the edge—the mission controllers back on Earth played along with him. They must have hoped he'd reintegrate as soon as the crisis was over; perhaps when the *Hydra* had safely landed.

But it never happened.

"Do you ever think back to what it was like before?" I said, aware that I was on dangerous ground.

"Before what, exactly?"

"The crossing."

He shook his head. "I'm not really one to dwell on the past, I'm of afraid."

Golombek was a glittery, gaudy sprawl of domes, towers, and connecting tubes; a pile of Christmas tree decorations strewn with tinsel. The train dived into a tunnel, then emerged into a dizzying underground mall. We got off, spending a lazy hour wandering the shopping galleries before stopping for a drink in a theme bar called *Sojourners*. The floor was covered in fake dust, and the hideously overpriced drinks arrived on little flat-topped six-wheeled rovers which kept breaking down. I ended up paying, just as I'd paid for the train tickets, but I didn't mind. D'Oliveira, or Grossart, or whoever it was best to think of him as, obviously didn't have much money to throw around. He must have been nearly invisible as far as the Martian economy was concerned.

"It was true what you said earlier on, wasn't it?" I said, while we rode a tram toward the sloth grotto. "About no one being more fascinated by the aliens than you were."

"Yes. Even if the others sometimes call me a mystical fool. To Jim they're just dead aliens; a useful source of new technologies but nothing more than that. Me, I think there's something deeper; that we were *meant* to find them; meant to come this far and then continue the search, even if that means some of us leaving Mars altogether . . ." He smiled. "Maybe I've just listened to too much of their music while doing the big dive."

"And what does Brad Treichler think about them?"

He was silent for a few moments. "Brad doesn't feel the same way I do."

"To what extent?"

"To the extent of wondering whether the relics are a poisoned chalice, the extent of wondering whether we should have come to Mars at all."

"That's an extreme viewpoint for someone who risked his life coming here."

"I know. And not one I share, I hasten to add."

I made an effort to lighten the mood. "I'm glad. If you hadn't come to Mars, there'd have been no big dive, and I'd have had to find another way of having the living shit scared out of me."

"Yes, it does tend to do that first time, doesn't it?"

"And the second?"

"It's generally worse. The third time, though . . ."

"I don't think there'll be a third time, Manuel."

"Not even for a vodka?"

"Not even."

By then we had arrived at the grotto; a real one that had been laboriously dismantled and relocated from elsewhere on Mars. Apparently the original site was right under one of the aqueducts and would have been flooded in a few years, as soon as they tapped the polar ice.

Inside, it all felt strangely over-familiar. I kept having to remind myself that these were *real* sloth rooms; *real* sloth artifacts and *real* wall frescoes; that the sloths had actually inhabited this grotto. Part of my brain, nonetheless, still insisted that the place was just a better-than-average museum mock-up or an up-market but still slightly kitsch theme-style restaurant—*Sloths* with better décor.

But they'd really been here. Unlike any mock-up I'd been in, for instance, there was really no floor. Floor was a concept the sloths had never got their furry heads around; the walls merging like an inverted cave roof. Supposedly they'd evolved on a densely forested planet where gruesome predators used to live on the ground. The sloths must have come down at some point—they hadn't evolved an advanced civilization by wiping their bottoms on leaves all day—but that dislike of the ground must have remained with them. Just as we humans still liked to shut out the dark, the sloths liked to get off the ground and just hang around.

It was all very interesting; I would have been happy to

spend hours there, but not all in one go. After two hours of showing scholarly fascination in every exhibit, I'd had enough six-limbed furry aliens to last me a fortnight.

We met up in the souvenir shop attached to the grotto. I bought a T-shirt with a tasteful sloth motif on it; very discreet with the words *Sloth Grotto, Golombek, Mars* in writing that had been made to look slightly like sloth script if you were not an expert in xeno-linguistics.

"Well," I said, beginning to feel just the tiniest bit tired. "That was fun. What next?"

"The lander's not far from here," he said. "We could check it out, if you like."

I should have talked him out of it.

It was all very well D'Oliveira and the others talking as if they were distinct individuals, but the tiny, single-seat lander would be in screaming contradiction to that. Something was surely bound to happen . . . but I'd hardly be able to write up my story without dealing with the lander issue.

More than that, D'Oliveira seemed willing to go along with it.

It was another tram ride to the outskirts of Golombek. The city was the first port of call for people coming down from space, so it was teeming at all hours with red-eyed newcomers. Most of the shops, bars, and restaurants stayed open around the clock, and that also went for the major tourist attractions. Of these, the *Hydra* was easily the oldest. There'd been a time—long before I was born—when you actually had to take a tour from Golombek to the landing site, but that wasn't the case now. The mountain had come to Mohammed; the city's outskirts surrounding the ship in a pincer movement.

D'Oliveira and I spent a while looking down from the pressurized viewing gallery. On either side the city reached away from us in a horseshoe shape, enclosing a square half-kilometer of Martian surface. The lander was in the middle; a tiny, lopsided silver cone looking slightly less impressive than the one in the paperweight Jim had shown me. I looked at the other visitors, and observed the way they couldn't quite hide their disappointment. I couldn't blame them: I remembered the way I'd first felt on seeing *Hydra*.

Is that all there is?

But I was older now, and I didn't feel the same way. Yes, it was tiny; yes, it looked barely capable of surviving the next dust storm—but that was the point. If the lander had been more impressive, Jim Grossart's achievement wouldn't have been half the thing it was.

"Fancy taking a closer look?" I said eventually.

"For old time's sake . . . why not."

I should have realized then, of course: there was something different about his voice.

We made our way from the gallery to the surface level. People were waiting to board robot buses which followed a pre-programmed track around the landing site, exactly the way I'd done as a child.

"We don't need to do it like that," he said. "You can rent a space suit and walk out there if you like."

"All the way to the lander?"

"No—they don't allow that. But you can still get a lot closer than with the buses."

I looked out into the arena and saw that there were three people wandering around in sand-colored suits. One was taking photos of the other two standing in front of the lander, obviously trying to frame the picture so that the backdrop didn't include any parts of the city. My companion was right; the people in suits were nearer to the ship than the buses allowed, but they were still forty or fifty meters from the lander, and they didn't seem inclined to get any closer.

Most of the tourists couldn't be bothered with the hassle of renting the suits, so it didn't take long to get outfitted.

"I think they come in two sizes," I said, when we were waiting in the air lock. "Too small and too large."

He looked at me without a trace of humor. "They'll suffice."

The penny dropped. "Of course, Brad."

We stepped outside. It was dark overhead, but the landing site was daytime-bright; almost shadowless. The lander stood two hundred meters from us, surrounded by a collection of equipment modules, surface rovers, scientific instruments and survival packages. It looked like a weatherworn Celtic obelisk encircled by a collection of marginally less sacred stones.

"Well, Brad," I said. "I've heard a lot about you."

"I know what you heard."

"You do?"

We started walking across the rust-colored ground.

"I know what Grossart and D'Oliveira say about me, don't you worry."

"What, that you're not as convinced as they are that coming to Mars was such a good idea? It's hardly intended as criticism. Everyone's entitled to an opinion."

Even three at the same time, I thought.

"They're right, of course—I don't think we should have come here—but if that was all they said . . ." He paused, allowing a glass-bodied bus to cross in front of us, surfing through the loosely-packed dust on its wide balloon wheels. The tourists were crammed inside, but some of them looked more interested in their snacks than in the *Hydra*.

"What else do they say, Brad?"

"You know, of course, so why pretend otherwise?"

"I'm really not sure—"

"The explosion, damn you. The one that happened in midcrossing. The one that nearly prevented us landing at all. They say I did it; tried to sabotage the mission."

"Actually, they hardly mentioned it at all, if ever."

"Oh, you're good, I'll grant you that."

"I know, but that's not the point. You couldn't have sabotaged the mission anyway . . ." But I stopped, because there was only one place that particular argument was headed. *Because you didn't exist then; just as you don't exist now. Because back then Jim Grossart was all there was. . . .*

I said lamely: "Even if you'd had second thoughts, you wouldn't have done something like that."

"No." His voice was softer now—almost trusting. "But perhaps I should have."

"I don't agree. Mars wasn't some pristine wilderness before we came, Brad. It was nothing; just a miserably cold and sterile blank canvas. We haven't ruined it; haven't spoiled anything."

He stopped and looked around, taking in the tiered galleries of the city, leaning over us like a frozen wave. "You call this an improvement?"

"On nothing at all, yes."

"I call it an abomination."

"Christ, we've only been here a century. This is just our first draft at living on Mars. So what if it isn't the best we could ever do? There'll be time for us to do better."

He didn't answer for a few seconds. "You sound like you agree with Jim Grossart."

"No; I could live without some of the things Jim seems to cherish, believe me. Maybe when it all comes home, I'm closer to Manuel D'Oliveira."

We carried on walking again, approaching the lander's encirclement.

"That mystical fool?"

"He may be a mystical fool, but he can sure as hell do the big dive." I paused, wondering why I was defending one aspect of a man's personality against another. But D'Oliveira felt as real to me then as anyone I'd ever met; as equally worthy of my loyalty. "And he's right, too—not coming to Mars would have been the greatest mistake humanity could have made. I'm not just talking about the relics either. They'll open a few doors for us, but even if we'd come here and found nothing but dust, it would still have been right. It's the space Mars gives us that makes the difference; the room to make mistakes."

"No," he said. "We already made the greatest mistake. And I could have stopped it."

We were close to the lander now—no more than forty-odd meters from it, I'd have guessed, but I noticed that the other people were no nearer. Walking side by side, we took a few more footsteps toward the center, but then our suits began to warn us against getting closer; lights flashing around the faceplate and a softly-insistent voice in the headphones. I felt my suit stiffen slightly as well—it was suddenly harder to take the next step.

"Then speak out about it," I said forcefully. "Come out of hiding. Tell everyone what you think. I guarantee they'll listen. No one else has your perspective."

"That's the problem. Too much perspective."

We were close enough to the lander now that he must have been finding it hard to sustain the illusion that three men had come down in it. I'd feared this moment and at the same time felt a spine-tingling sense of anticipation about what would happen.

"I'll make sure they listen, Brad. That was why Jim contacted me, wasn't it? To have his story heard; his views on Mars known? And didn't he mean for all of you to have your say?"

"No." He began fiddling with the latch of his helmet. "Because it wasn't Jim who contacted you, it was me. Jim Grossart isn't real, don't you understand? There was only ever me." He nodded at the lander, even while he struggled with his helmet. "You don't think I'm stupid, do you?"

I tried to pull his hands away from the neck-ring. "What are you doing?" I shouted.

"What I always planned to do. What it took me seventeen years to summon up the courage to do."

"I don't understand."

"Words won't make a difference now. Mars needs something stronger. It needs a martyr."

"No!"

I fought with him, but he was stronger than me. There was no unnecessary violence in the way he pushed me away—it was done as gently as circumstances allowed—but I ended up on my back in the dust, looking up as he removed his helmet and took a last long inhalation of thin, cold Martian air.

He took a few steps toward the lander, his skin turning blue, his eyes frosting over, and then stumbled, one arm extended, fingers grasping toward the *Hydra*. Then his suit must have locked rigid, immobilizing him.

He looked like a statue that had been there for years.

It shouldn't have been possible, I kept telling myself. There are supposed to be safeguards that stop you doing that kind of thing in anything less than a breathable atmosphere; rigidly-adhered-to rules ensuring that equipment for hire is checked and rechecked for compliance; double and triply redundant protective systems.

But I guess the suits we'd rented just didn't quite live up to those high ideals.

He died, but that means even less now than it did once upon a time. They got him inside reasonably quickly, and though the exposure to the Martian atmosphere had done a lot of harm, and although there was extensive neural damage, all of these things could be repaired given time and—more importantly—money.

"Who's the old man, anyway?" the medics asked me, after I had arranged for my firm to pay for his medical care, no matter how long it took. That had taken some arguing, incidentally, especially after I told them there wasn't going to be a story for a while.

"I don't know," I said. "He never did tell me his name, but he was interesting enough company."

The tech had smiled. "We ran a gene profile, but the old coot didn't show up in the records. Doesn't mean much, of course."

"No. A lot of people with criminal pasts vanished during the turmoil."

"Yeah," the medic said, already losing interest.

They kept talking about him as an old man, and it wasn't until I saw his comatose body that I understood why. He did look much older than he had ever seemed in any of his three guises; as if even his semblance of middle age had been an illusion.

His coma was deep, and the restorative brain surgery was performed slowly and painstakingly. I followed the progress closely at first—checking up on him every week, then every month. But nothing ever happened; he never showed any signs of emerging and all the usual techniques for kickstarting a mind back to consciousness were unsuccessful. The medics kept suggesting they call it a day, but so long as funds were arriving from my firm, they didn't mind wasting their time.

I checked on progress every six months, then perhaps once a year.

And life, of course, went on. I couldn't see any dignified way of finishing the story—not while the principal player was in a coma—so it just stalled while I covered other pieces. Some of them were moderately big, and after a while there came a point when I consigned the whole Jim Grossart story to the bottom drawer: a wild-goose chase that hadn't ended up anywhere. I even stopped being sure that I'd ever met him at all. After that, it was a simple matter of forgetting all about him.

I don't think I've given him a moment's thought in the last two or three years.

Until today.

I still visit *Sloths* now and then. It happens to be a reasonably trendy media hangout now; a place to pick up the ground tremors of rumor ahead of the pack.

And there he was, in approximately the same window seat where Jim Grossart had sat ten years ago, looking out at the divers. I read his expression in the window; one of calm, critical detachment, like a judge at a major sporting event.

His face was that of a young man I recognized, but had only ever seen in photographs.

I looked at him for long moments. Perhaps it was just a genetic fluke that had thrown up this man who looked like the young Jim Grossart, but I doubted it. It was the way he sat; the stiff, slightly formal bearing. Except that hadn't been Jim, had it?

Manuel D'Oliveira.

I stared for a moment too long, and somehow my eye caught his, and we found ourselves staring at each other across the room. He didn't turn around from the window but after a few seconds he smiled and nodded.

The bar was packed that night, and a crowd of drinkers surged in front of me, interrupting my line of sight.

When they'd passed, the table was vacant.

I checked with the hospital the day after—it had been at least two years since I'd been in touch—and I was informed that the old man had at last emerged into consciousness. There'd been nothing unusual about him, they said; nothing odd about his psychology.

"What happened then?" I said.

"The funds allowed for some fairly simple rejuvenative procedures," the medic said, as if restoring youth was about as technically complex—and as interesting—as splinting a fracture.

He hadn't left any means for me to contact him, though.

It might not have been him, I know. It might never have

been Jim Grossart I met, and the young man in *Sloths* could
have been anyone with the same set of blandly handsome facial genes.

But there was one other thing.

The old man had emerged from his coma eighteen months
before the meeting in the bar, and his rejuvenation had taken
place not long after. Which might have meant nothing, except
there was something different about the night I saw him;
something which was entirely consistent with him having been
Manuel D'Oliveira. It was the night the starship left Mars
orbit; the one they've been building up there for the last five
years; the one that's going out into the galaxy to search for the
sloth.

The ship they've named the *Captain James Grossart*.

I like to think he was on his way up to her. I checked the
ship's manifest, of course, and there was no one called
Grossart, or D'Oliveira, or even Treichler—but that doesn't
mean it wasn't him. He'd be traveling under a new name now;
one I couldn't even guess. No one would know who he was;
just a young man who had volunteered to join the starship's
crew; a young man whose interest in the aliens might at times
verge on the mystical.

And—on his way up—he hadn't been able resist one last
look at the divers.

Maybe I'm wrong; maybe it was only ever my subcon-
scious playing tricks with a stranger's face; supplying the clo-
sure my journalistic instincts demanded, but, the way I see it,
it almost doesn't matter. Because all I was ever looking for
was a way to finish their story.

Now it can be told.

FLOWER CHILDREN OF MARS

by Mike Resnick and M. Shayne Bell

*B*ETWEEN *his first and second trips to Mars, or Garsoom as the natives call it (at least, I think it's Garsoom; handwriting is not our family's long and strong suit), my uncle, James Carruthers, made another journey there, one which has gone unrecorded in any of the books of his adventures that I have brought to the public.*

He seems to have been caught in a time warp of some sort—although there are some, including the Swordmaster himself, who would say that it was a culture warp. Anyway, I have instructed the executors of my estate not to release these notes of his until 200 years after my death.

(signature illegible)
January 23, 1950

Dear Hadj Tajus:

I was just cleaning out my desk, and I came upon the old diary that described that strange visitor we had. I was going to throw it out, but then I thought, what the hell, maybe you or Nigel might get a kick out of reading about it once more. So here it is.

Yours,
Ollie Willowby

I cannot describe the agony of those years after I had been drawn back to Earth. I thought of my fourteen years on Mars and wondered if they had all been a dream, but I knew they had not: I had traveled to Mars, by whatever means I did not understand, and I had lived and fought there and I had won the love of a woman I had to reach again. Every night of those Earth-bound years, I would stand and stare at that red gem in the night sky, Mars, and I would hold my arms up to it and ache to be drawn across the dark, cold void separating me from it.

Until one night a great nausea overcame me, then a paralysis of all my muscles, and after I had fallen to the ground, I heard a rustling behind me as if some great and evil being were creeping up on me. In my struggle to move to defend myself, I looked to Mars and felt myself drawn there, suddenly—except that this passage was warm, not cold. I woke naked and sweating on the shore of a vast, shallow sea that lapped placidly against the warm sand I lay on. I knew at once that I was on Mars, but it was not the Mars I had known.

If Mars were thus changed, I wondered, for the seabed had before been dry, what had become of my wife, the incomparable Jedib Pharis, and the others I had come to love and admire here? When the nausea had passed and I could stand again, I set out to find the answer.

To my great surprise, the beach gave way to a plain of tall grass and that, as the land began to rise, to a forest of mighty trees. I entered a fragrant parkland that showed every sign of diligent cultivation. No tree seemed misplaced, and each was shapely and majestic. The path I soon encountered and followed opened to views of the sea or of the far-off mountains, each framed by the trees as if in a painting. It was at one of these overlooks that I found an ancient, rusted sword hidden between the stones of a ruined wall; I was glad for the defense it would provide, however brittle. It was at another overlook that I heard music start up, not far off, and I hurried toward it.

I shall always remember the scene I shortly encountered. It was as unlike anything Mars had previously shown me as night is to day. The forest opened onto a broad, grassy meadow, and among the flowers there lay fifty of the fierce four-armed chartreuse Throops that had before held nomadic sway over the vast plains of the once dry sea. With them lay an equal number of the puce men and women of Mars, all of them picnicking together on breads and luscious fruits.

These people were all clothed in flowing white robes, while on the Mars I knew men and women of both races had gone through their days practically naked. One of the Throops strummed an enormous instrument with his four hands, and he sang a not unharmonious melody. I rushed up to the nearest Martians and introduced myself.

"I am James Carruthers," I said, "a duke among the Throops, a prince of Nitrogen, husband to Jedib Pharis, and Swordmaster of all Garsoom. I am lost. Can you help me find my way?"

There was a low murmur among the recumbent crowd, and many regarded my naked form wide-eyed. Some stood and bowed mockingly to me. "Oh, duke!" they said. "Oh, prince!" They drew me toward the singer, who regarded me languidly.

I knew that I somehow had to make these people believe I was who I claimed to be, and that I had to find my way home.

We moved here to Get Away From It All—from the wars, from the moralists, from the bureaucrats who taxed us to within an inch of our lives and then ran what was left. We thought we'd made it free and clear.

Then *he* showed up.

I think it was Nigel who first spotted him.

"You'll never believe what's approaching us," he whispered.

I stopped fondling Lucretia and Gwen long enough to peer off into the distance.

"What is it?" I asked. Ordinarily I've got vision like a hawk, but I'd had a little too much to drink, and I couldn't get my eyes to focus.

"A naked man," said Nigel. "With a sword."

Lucretia sat up and stared at him. "With two swords!" she giggled.

"Poor chap seems rather pale," remarked Nigel.

"Who cares?" said Lucretia, staring at what I shall call his second sword. "You're all brothers under the skin."

"Except for those of us who are sisters," said Hadj Tajus, blushing a deep chartreuse.

"Is he still coming?" I asked.

"Yes."

I got to my feet. "Well, I suppose we ought to greet him and welcome him to our little community."

"He seems well-prepared for it," said Nigel. "Why else would he leave his clothes behind?"

The naked man finally reached us.

"Welcome," I said. "My name is Ollie."

He mumbled something about princes and Nitrogen and emperors, and that his name was James something-or-other.

"Well, James," I said, "you're just in time for the festivities."

"Festivities?" he repeated.

"The wining and wenching," I said.

He stared disapprovingly at me. "Garsoomians don't do such things."

Everyone laughed at that.

"What's so funny?" he demanded.

"How long have you lived on Garsoom?" I asked.

"A long time," he said, frowning. "But I've been away."

"I can tell," I said. "Welcome to Happy Valley."

"I have never heard of a Happy Valley on Garsoom," he said. "Indeed, you seem unlike any Garsoomians I have ever encountered."

"The realtors just opened it up five years ago," I explained. "Most of us come from Earth, but we've got a few Throops and puce Martians here, too."

"Where is Happy Valley in relation to my beloved Nitrogen?" asked John.

"Oh, we're about two thousand miles away. Maybe a little more."

"But philosophically, we're at the other end of the universe," added Nigel. "We believe in peace, sexual experimentation, and artificial stimulants."

The stranger looked around. "I see no flags," he said. "What are your battle colors?"

"Black lace," said Gwen, which brought forth another burst of laughter.

"Now, what was all this about you being a duke?" asked Wilber.

"He's a duke?" asked a couple of the Throops, who hadn't been paying much attention up to now.

"Oh, duke!" said Lucretia, letting her robe drop to the ground. "You can impale me upon your sword any time you want!"

I thought he was going to have a stroke.

"What is the matter with you people?" he shouted. "Where is the manly comradeship, the lust for battle, the brave martial hymns?"

"Maybe you want *East* Garsoom," suggested Nigel. "I understand they have boxing matches on the third Friday of every month."

"Mock me not, you vile scum!" said James, drawing his sword. "I am the greatest swordsman of two worlds!"

"And I'm the greatest lover of two worlds," shot back Nigel. "Which of us do you think has more fun?"

"One more such remark and I'll run you through," said James, and I suddenly perceived that he wasn't kidding.

I have never killed out of sheer annoyance. I have killed to defend myself; I have killed to defend those I love; and I have killed to defend the two nations to which I swear allegiance: The Republic of the United States of America and the Kingdom of Nitrogen. But that day, I came close to killing for petty reasons. Any decent man or woman who heard and saw Nigel and those others at that moment would have forgiven me, but I could not have forgiven myself. A duke and prince— a fighting man of honor—must always demonstrate better self-control.

So it was that through their snickering and crude jokes I struggled for a moment to regain my composure. Then I spoke slowly and forcefully to the people mocking me. "I am who I claim to be," I said. "And I must return to Nitrogen as quickly as possible. I have a wife there and a child I have never seen. Please direct me to the person who can help me to Nitrogen."

Some of them grew quiet then, and I thought for a brief moment that my words had moved them.

Lucretia, the woman who had invited me to "impale" her, bent down to gather up her robe. "How long have you been away from your Jedib Pharis?" she asked.

"Fourteen years," I said.

"And you left her a single mother in one of those Martian hellholes all that time?" she said, the contempt in her voice too clear.

"Leaving was against my will," I explained.

Lucretia said nothing while she pulled on her robe and tied it around her. "The poor girl's had nothing from you in all that time, and you expect her to believe your story now and take you back?"

It was my turn to be quiet. I had always imagined a happy homecoming—Jedib Pharis rushing into my arms, my son— for such I imagined our child to be—anxious to meet his father.

"No," said Lucretia, "unless this Jedib Pharis is a dim-witted sap with no other options, she's moved on by now, and your return home will only be cause for a lawsuit to recover unpaid child support. I hope Nitrogen has decent laws against deadbeat dads!"

I had expected to be believed. I am an honest man, and honest men expect to be taken at their word. But I had to admit that, if these people could travel to Mars so easily— with the help of realtors, no less—Jedib Pharis and the authorities of Nitrogen would certainly question my fourteen-year absence.

The music started up and the picnic commenced again around me, though I scarcely noticed. How had I missed all this? How and when had Earth and Mars established contact? When had travel between the worlds become, apparently, commonplace? I listened to the people from Earth. Some spoke with British accents, but some were clearly American. Their presence on Mars did not make sense. Interplanetary travel had not been in the American and British papers, of that I was certain. I would have gone to Mars as part of the first exploratory expedition from Earth if there had ever been one— nothing could have kept me from it—but I had never heard of such an expedition! I could not understand how this had come to pass. I felt more alone and disoriented than I have ever felt before or since. The happy homecoming of my dreams vanished and was replaced, instead, with disquiet. I began to doubt my own sanity.

It was presently evening, and a chill fell across the vale. I sat shivering in the grass and knew that, whatever had happened, I would soon need shelter. Martian nights were still cold.

Ollie approached me while his friends gathered up their picnic. "James," he said, "we don't know quite what to make of you, but you're in a funk, I can see that. Why don't you come back to Arcadia with us? Maybe things will be clearer for you in the morning."

It could only be so. I have often found that a night's sleep restores the world's balance, at least in my own head. So it was that I followed Ollie and the others up to a ridgeline. We stopped in the dusk to look out across Happy Valley. The lights of Arcadia twinkled below us.

We hit the outskirts of Arcadia. Nigel raised his hand, and we all stopped.

"What is the problem?" asked James.

"No problem," I explained. "We do this every night."

"You camp outside the city?"

"No, we stop for just a few minutes."

"What for?"

"To determine," I said, as all the women began tossing their house keys into a pile, "who goes home with whom."

"But surely each man goes home with his own wife," said James, obviously shocked.

"What century were you born in?" giggled Gwen.

"The nineteenth," he answered.

"Somehow I'm not surprised," said Oglethorpe, walking over and picking up a key. He held it up in the air.

"That's mine!" squealed Veronica happily.

"This is outrageous!" shouted James. "I demand that you stop, in the name of the Swordmaster!"

"You want us to spend all night out here?" said Wilber. "Do you know what the wind chill on Garsoom is at three in the morning?"

"I suppose the only way to combat it is animal warmth," said Lucretia. "Still, it would be rude to ignore a suggestion from our visitor." She sidled over to him. "I'll warm you top to bottom, James baby."

He backed away as if she was a starving sewer rat about to nibble on his toes, or even more delicate parts. His mouth moved, but no words came forth.

"I think James is having some difficulty adjusting," said Nigel. He thrust a gourd forward. "Here you go, James. It'll help you put things in perspective."

James took a sip, instantly spat it on the ground, and coughed violently. "What is it?" he managed to gasp.

"A little something from the brewery at Zobingo," answered Nigel, taking a long swallow. "It opens the pores, lowers the voice, and sets the adrenaline racing."

"I feel ill," said James. "And dizzy."

"Yeah, good Zobingan pure will do that to you," replied Wilber.

"Maybe we should take him into town and bed him down, and then come back for the keys," suggested Hadj Tajus.

No one had any objections, so Nigel and I supported James as we ambled down the hill and into Arcadia. Suddenly I felt his muscles tense.

"What manner of place is this?" he demanded.

"It's Arcadia," I replied.

"But where are the stately palaces, the oversized barracks, the weapon shops? Where are the slaves going about their masters' business? Why are there no swordsmen stationed at every approach to the city?"

"We prefer the contemporary look," said Nigel. "Long, low, and functional."

"Besides, I've got a game knee," added Wilber. "What would I do with a castle that had staircases leading everywhere?"

"We believe in minimalist landscaping," I pointed out. "After all, we came here to enjoy ourselves, not to spend all our time working in the yards and repainting all the closets."

"But if you are attacked . . ." began James, blinking furiously as he tried to comprehend what he saw.

"Who would want to attack us?" asked Nigel. "What have we got that anyone would want?"

James thought for a moment. "Your women," he said at last.

"We're happy to share them," said Oglethorpe.

"Make love, not war," echoed Veronica.

James looked around again. "Where are the blazing torches that light the night thoroughfares?"

"There was this guy called Edison," said Oglethorpe. "I guess you don't read the papers much, huh?"

"This is madness!" cried James.

"No," we assured him. "This is Garsoom."

I lay awake that night—alone and shivering under blankets that had labels marked Sears, Roebuck and Co.—and attempted to determine the facts of my situation. First, I did not believe myself to be mad. I considered my actions and studies of the previous fourteen years and found nothing to indicate insanity. Second, I had returned to Mars. I did not doubt that. I had known I was on Mars when I was first brought here, and I knew it now with the same certainty. Third, Mars—my beloved Garsoom—had changed utterly. If the oceans, grasses, and trees weren't enough to convince me, if hedonistic Throops and voluptuous Anglo-Saxons could be considered insufficient evidence, the taste of liquor from Zobingo could not. Zobingo had been one of Nitrogen's principal enemies, a city I had often compared to ancient Greece's renowned Sparta, spartan and severe in every respect. But Nigel had set the bottle of Zobingan brew down beside me in case I might want its contents in the night, and I had read its label before he and Ollie had turned out the lights. It was marked with the instantly recognizable seal of the Zobingan royal house. Such a thing would never have been allowed inside the city walls of the Zobingo I had known, let alone sanctioned by its royal family. Unless everything here was a vast forgery, Mars had indeed changed utterly. That Zobingo had sunk to the production and export of intoxicating drink announced just how complete and swift had been those changes.

But how all of this had happened, I did not know. There was a mystery here, and I was determined to solve it.

I sat up and wrapped myself in blankets. At the back of my mind was the nagging insistence that I was missing some important fact, some detail that might account for all of the changes around me. I thought for some time, trying to deduce or recall what it might be, but I could not.

I realized that finding further answers in the middle of the night might prove equally problematic, but resolved to do what I could. I turned on the electric lights, and commenced a more detailed examination of the room Ollie had lent me (for they had taken me to his house). That soon led to an examination of the main rooms. I hoped to find newspapers, printed histories—brochures, even, from the supposed Terran-Garsoomian real estate agency.

What I found was a telephone.

The disparaging remarks of Oglethorpe to the contrary, I considered myself an avid student of all the practical sciences. I had made detailed studies of the great inventors and inventions of my day, intending to introduce their time- and life-saving works to Garsoom upon my return. I had witnessed my countryman Alexander Bell's telephone demonstrations at the Centennial celebrations in Philadelphia, and had followed his court battles to defend his patent with interest (and the growth of local and long-distance telephone exchanges with even greater interest). I had intended to be one of the first subscribers when memberships in a telephone exchange were offered to residents of the Missouri Valley, my temporary (I had hoped) home on Earth.

I picked up the receiver. A female voice spoke to me at once.

"What number, please?"

I thought quickly. "I don't know a number to request," I said. "But is it possible to place a call to Nitrogen?"

"That will be long distance. Do you accept the charges, or will you be reversing them?"

I did not want to encumber my host with costs I could not immediately repay, and I felt certain that the royal house of Nitrogen would gladly pay for any communication from me. "Reverse them," I instructed. "I need to speak to my wife, Jedib Pharis."

"Checking," the voice said, and there was a pause. "There are 158 Jedib Pharises listed in Nitrogen. Do you have a street address?"

"She is the princess of that city. "

Or was when I left, *I thought.* Who could tell now?

"Oh. You want the Incomparable Jedib Pharis. She's listed under 'I.'"

"Yes," I said, thinking that we were finally getting some-where, and actually trembling at the thought of hearing my wife's voice again.

"At this hour?"

"She will want to speak with me."

"Your name, please?"

I told her.

"One moment."

I heard a series of clicks, then ringing. On the sixth ring, the call was answered. "Royal Palace," announced a male voice.

"I have a collect call for the Incomparable Jedib Pharis from a Mr. James Carruthers. Do you accept the charges?"

"That's the tenth such call tonight. Of course we don't ac-cept them."

"Let me say something," I said. "This is James Carruthers. To whom am I speaking? Do you recognize my voice?"

"Sir!" the operator said. "You cannot speak until the charges are cleared."

"I'm hanging up now," the voice in Nitrogen said.

And I spoke one more word. It is a word authorized to be spoken by only a select few of the royal house of Nitrogen. When it is uttered, doors open, discussions end, actions com-mence. I will not repeat it here, because it is still not common knowledge.

"By all the gods!" exclaimed the voice in distant Nitrogen. "We accept the charges! Hold the line!"

I heard the sound of running feet, then silence in Nitrogen.

"James?" said a voice behind me. "Do you think this is ad-visable?"

It was Ollie. He and Lucretia stood shivering behind me, wrapped as I was in blankets.

"Advisable or not," I said, "I have called my wife to the telephone."

And then I remembered what I should have remembered earlier. It was the sight, I think, of Ollie and Lucretia shiver-ing that made me remember. My first passage to Mars had been unbearably cold. I had felt the chill of it for days after-ward. The passage to this Mars, as I now considered it, had been warm. I was on Mars, but perhaps Mars of a different age, or Mars in a universe organized on different principles. There was apparently a woman named Jedib Pharis in a palace in Helium, but I now doubted it was the woman I knew and loved. I concluded instantly that I must return to Earth to begin my journey again, a journey that would take me, finally, to the Mars of the time and place I sought. That it still existed I could not doubt. That I could reach it again, I had never doubted.

"Sir, " a voice spoke suddenly in the receiver. "The incomparable princess has not yet returned from dancing in the clubs. Can you leave a number where you might be reached?"

I was certain then. The Jedib Pharis I knew would never comport herself thus. I replaced the receiver without saying another word. "I must return to Earth," I announced to my host and his paramour.

"Leave?" I said. "But you just got here!"

"I cannot abide the pit of immorality into which you have all fallen," said James.

"Stay a while," I urged. "It'll grow on you."

"Like a fungus," laughed Hadj Tajus.

"You!" snarled James to Hadj Tajus. "You of all people should be ashamed of yourself. If my old fighting companion Lars Barkas could but see you . . ."

"Barkus? The one with four arms, not the one who is willing?" she replied. "He's pretty laid back these days. Perhaps you'd care to talk to him? Of course, he doesn't make a lot of sense when he's been snorting coke, but . . ."

James just glared at her for a moment, then turned back to me. "I must get back to Earth. I can bear this no longer."

"I don't know how to lay this on you, James," I said, "but the next spaceliner isn't due for another nine days."

"I don't use spaceliners."

"Cargo ships don't land anywhere near here."

"I don't use *them* either."

"What else is there?" asked Nigel, a puzzled expression on his handsome face.

"I reach my hands out, and close my eyes, and I am instantly transported."

"Yeah?" said Oglethorpe. "Does the space pilots' union know about this?"

"I've got a better question," said Lucretia. "If you close your eyes, how do you know you're not reaching for Arcturus, or even the Andromeda galaxy?"

"I just reach," said James, suddenly looking a little unsure of himself.

"Let's put it to the test," continued Lucretia. "Point out Earth to me."

He looked up and frowned. "There are so many stars . . ."

"Earth is a planet, not a star," offered Nigel helpfully.

"I never concerned myself about it before," said James. "I just reached my hands out and suddenly I was there."

"Well, if you want my opinion, you were damned lucky not to wind up on a frigid methane world," said Lucretia. "Or maybe a world awash in chlorine oceans."

"I always wind up on Earth or Mars," he said adamantly. "That's just the way it is."

"Don't you get cold traveling through interstellar space?" asked Nigel. "It's not as if you're dressed for it, you know."

"I leave my body here."

"What do you do when you get there?" asked Gwen, puzzled.

"I find myself in my original body."

"You mean this body you're wearing is just a spare?" persisted Gwen.

"I don't know," he admitted. "I'm a fighting man, not a scientist. I've never given the matter much thought."

"Well, I think it's worth some thought," said Gwen. "I mean, if I had a spare body, I could have twice the fun."

"Do all your weapons go with you?" asked Nigel.

"Sometimes."

"If they don't this time, can I have the sword?" said Nigel. "It would look great over my fireplace."

"You are all mad!" cried James, running off to a small hill.

No one followed him. I mean, after all, here was this unhappy nut case running around with a lethal weapon in his hand, so we decided not to get too close to him.

Anyway, he stood there, motionless, for a moment. Then he

gave us one last contemptuous look, raised his hands to the
heavens, and vanished.

We never saw him again. His sword still hangs above
Nigel's fireplace.

*I found myself back on Earth. I looked ruefully at the Red
Planet, realizing that my incomparable princess was lost to me
forever.*

*Then, suddenly, I felt a surge of inner strength, and I was
spurred on by my indomitable will. There are, after all, always
more princesses. Tomorrow I begin my journey to Palos of the
Dog Star Pack in search of a suitable replacement.*

One night later a well-built almost-naked blond man approached our happy little group.

"Hello," he said. "My name is Cramer Wilson, but you may
call me simply Cramer of Venus. I'm looking for my
princess . . ."

OUT OF THE BLUE, INTO THE RED

by James Lovegrove

THE CEDARS
Upper Wolcott
near Middleton
East Sussex

Dear Richard,
I suppose, if you're reading this, the first thing I should say is congratulations. I'll confess to you now, I had my doubts about whether you would make it, and happily, I was wrong. And if you're not reading this—well, then, I derive no satisfaction at all in knowing that I was right.

It required some subterfuge, I can tell you, to get this letter to you (assuming all has gone as arranged). The plan is as follows: Caroline will be taking it over to America with her when she goes to watch the launch, and she's going to pass it on to your mission controller who'll get it to the relevant technician who'll tuck it somewhere safely away in your—I think it's called—"environment suit locker," which you won't have access to till after you touch down. Quite a chain of potential foul-ups there, starting with your sister who, let's be honest, doesn't always keep as firm a grip on things as she should. (Or am I judging her too harshly? *You* would probably say that I am.)

Anyway, the mission controller seemed quite taken with the notion of this letter being there for you to discover after you land. He got all sentimental over it and said it would be good for your morale and *he* wished he had had a father like me. He also advised me that the letter shouldn't weigh more than an ounce, otherwise it might throw out the "onboard weight-distribution ratios" or some such thing, so I'm using airmail paper, as you see, and I'll try to keep this as short as I can. I never appreciated just how exact a business spaceflight is!

I suspect your mission controller thinks this'll be a nice surprise for you.

It'll be a surprise anyway.

Now that I've got this far in, I still don't actually know where to begin. I suppose it won't hurt to say that your mother and I are very proud of you, Richard. I know you know Mum is, not least because of the way she embarrassed you when you were over here last month. She all but dragged you round the village to show you off to the neighbors, didn't she? And then that party she insisted we have! All those friends of ours swarming around you . . . I felt sorry for you, but you handled it all very well, I thought. Very graciously. But that's your mother for you: so up-front, so demonstrative about everything. Over the years I've rather let her take over that aspect of life from me. She has such a capacity for it—the emotions, all that stuff—that it's become simplest for me just to confer the responsibility to her and let her act on my behalf in that arena.

But be under no illusion, Richard. Though I've not said as much, I *am* proud of you, too. Even prouder than your mother is, possibly.

And that's because of, not in spite of, our frequent differences of opinion. When you first announced your intention to become an astronaut, remember the argument we had? Well, strictly speaking, the first time you announced you were going to become an astronaut you were five years old, and we didn't have an argument. All I said was, I think, something like, "Oh, that's interesting," because every small boy wants to be an astronaut at some time or other, doesn't he? But I'm referring to the time when you were twenty-three—or was it twenty-four?—and we were having that discussion over supper about what you were going to do with your life, because let's face it, Richard, at that point you were a bit of a wastrel. You had a splendid engineering degree and you were just arsing around, doing odd jobs, living in London and, I don't know, getting "potted" all day and listening to music, or whatever it is young people get up to when they should be earning a living and getting a career off the ground. You said you needed time to "sort your head out." You wanted to travel, see a bit of the world, and then—and these were your exact words—"maybe I'll go and be an astronaut or something."

You can understand why I hit the roof, can't you? I mean, that's hardly what you might call a clear and unambiguous statement of intent. That's not the same as "Well, Dad, I'm planning on making an application to NASA to see if I'm accepted for training for the Mars settlement programme." (That should be "program," shouldn't it?) You can see my point, can't you? Whatever your real feelings, you could hardly have come across as more vague.

I'm not writing this to justify myself, however. I've looked back over the previous two paragraphs and I realize that that's how it reads, and that's not my intention at all. Besides, it's a little late for self-justification. Here you are. You're on Mars. You've proved your old man wrong.

Maybe that argument we had— Well, it was a row, really, wasn't it? Maybe that row we had was the catalyst you needed. Maybe it was what finally fired you up and got you going. I have to hope that it was, because I know that things were never quite the same between us afterward. It was as though we'd broken some delicate linking structure that neither of us realized was quite as fragile as it was. I remember you looking at me across the dining table, the very same table I'm sitting at now, and I remember the expression on your face. It was beyond anger. It was pure contempt. And I couldn't understand what it was I'd said that had earned that contempt. All I'd been talking about was the need for responsibility, the need not to waste your life. I'd always had such hopes for you, Richard. Caroline was, and is, never going to set the world alight. She's a lovely girl, as we all know, but it was clear from pretty early on that her best bet would be to find a decent fellow, marry him, and have kids. She's managed that—although Andrew isn't *precisely* the kind of husband I had in mind for her. He's well-meaning enough, but he's not got much up top and he's feckless, and if it wasn't for the money he inherited . . . But that's not relevant. You were the one who was going to go far, Richard. I always believed that, and then when I watched you frittering (as I thought) your life away, it just really irked me. You had all these prospects, all these opportunities . . .

And now you *have* gone far, haven't you? Forty-nine million miles. And you're not coming back. You've abandoned this planet to start a new life—and a new world—somewhere else. You've become an émigré, an exile, a pioneer. You and I will never see each other again.

And I cannot shake the feeling that I am the one who drove you away.

Now we're getting to the nub of it, aren't we?

I talked to your mother about this a couple of nights ago. I said to her that I thought I was the one responsible for your going. I'd had a whiskey or three, so my guard was down. And do you know what? Your mother looked surprised at what I'd said, but also (I could see it in her eyes) she wasn't surprised at all. As if she'd been expecting this. She's not as bubble-headed as she sometimes makes herself out to be, your mother. Her reply was straightforward and succinct, at any rate, as if it was something she had prepared in advance long ago. "If you feel that, Charles," she said, "why don't you say something about it to him? We have Richard's number in Florida. Why don't you phone him before it's too late?"

I don't know why I haven't done so. Yes, I do. Cowardice, plain and simple. I don't want to call you and ask you if I'm the reason you're going to Mars and for you to say, "Yes, Dad, actually you are." I don't think I could bear to hear that.

Shall I tell you something? Back when your mother and I were courting—yes, "courting," that's what it was, a desperately old-fashioned term I realize, but I don't apologize for using it—back when she and I were *courting*, I remember one night I took her out for a drive, to the South Downs, up to Ditchling Beacon. It was summer, a beautiful clear night, more stars up there in the sky than you ever see these days, in this light-polluted age. We sat in the car, that old topless MG of mine, and I remember between hand-holdings and kisses—and I know, I know, it's embarrassing to hear about your parents when they were young doing young-people things—I pointed out some of the constellations to your mother, and what impressed her the most was when I pointed out Mars. It impressed her, or so she said, because Mars is a planet, not a star.

"I didn't know we could see *planets* as well," she said. She's since told me that she *did* know this, but she wanted me to feel like I was teaching her something. Such are women's wiles. But she's told me, too, that she was genuinely impressed by my ability to pick out and name one single star from all the hundreds up there in the heavens. It's easy, of course. Mars is quite readily identifiable by its brightness and its pink tinge. Even so, the fact that I could pinpoint it played a significant part in my wooing of your mother. ("Wooing"—there's another word you don't hear used nowadays.) Certainly it was that night that I decided I was going to ask her to marry me. And since then, for that very reason, often when I've been out at night I've looked up and looked for Mars and been moved to offer it a small prayer of gratitude.

Anyway, I think I'm close to reaching the weight allowance for this letter, meager as it is. So I'll try to wrap things up as best I can.

You've spent five years of your life training and preparing for this mission, Richard. Even though you've been on another continent, I have a good idea how hard-working and dedicated you've been. Reports of your progress have been filtering back to me via Caroline: the rigors, the regimen, the single-mindedness, the eschewing of all pleasures and distractions. And when you came back to England last month to say goodbye, I could see how you'd changed. There was a determination in your eyes that I'd never seen there before, a zest, a zeal. We hardly spoke to each other, did we, but all the same I knew that you had found your purpose, and I was glad.

I still have my fears that something will go wrong. A couple of the unmanned probes crashed, didn't they, and then there was that terrible accident on the third *De Gama* mission. I have this horrible feeling that your spacecraft isn't going to make it, and all fifty of you aboard are going to perish. Rationally I know it's unlikely, but still I have that fear. That's father's fear. That's why I'm not coming over for the launch. I'm not even going to watch it on TV. And whether you die or not, I know I'm never going to see you again, so either way I've lost you.

I have to hope that you've made it to Mars alive and you're reading this. This is my humble little arrival gift to you.

Welcome to your new home, Richard.
Yours,
Dad

                              ***

ares/geo uplink message
ident: personal/richarddaniels   encryption code: 17/d
date of transmission: L+97   time of transmission: 2413
local

Dear Dad,
You think *your letter* had a complicated routepath? This is
going to be beamed across the void to Canaveral, whereupon
it will be decrypted and transferred to Caroline's e-mail address and printed out by her and sent on via conventional post
until it at last finds its way into your Luddite hands. The "potential foul-ups" are myriad, although knowing the cackhand-
edness of the Upper Wolcott postie, I think this has a better
chance of crossing 49,000,000 miles of space safely than it
does of making it, without mishap, from the depot at Middleton to your front doormat.

Sorry it's taken so long to respond, but all of us have,
frankly, been worked off our arses here, and this is virtually
the first opportunity I've had since landing to sit down and
compose a reply. It's getting on for midnight and I'm completely exhausted, but I know I can't postpone this any longer
than I already have.

Well, finding that envelope in my environment suit locker
was a surprise, no doubt about it. If you could have seen my
face! I'd gone to check the equipment, make sure nothing had
been damaged in transit, and I was running diagnostics on the
suits and I got to mine and there was your letter, lodged between thumb and forefinger of the left glove. Like the suit was
delivering it to me. Whichever techie put it there, he or she has
got a sense of humor.

I recognize your handwriting straight away. And I love the
way you addressed it: Richard Daniels, De Gama Base, Amazonis Planitia, Mars.

As for the contents . . .

Well, Dad, I think you've been making a mountain out of a molehill. (And I know all about mountains now. We've got a good view of Olympus Mons from where we are here. It's so vast it makes Kilimanjaro look like a pimple on a pygmy's backside.) You and I have been at loggerheads since I was a teenager, and even before then. We were always disagreeing about something or other, don't you recall? I didn't want to go to boarding school. You wanted me to go. I didn't want to try for Imperial College. You made me try. Remember when I was eight, and you asked me if I wanted to learn the piano? I said no, and that made you utterly determined that I would. You booked the lessons and you made me go to them and made me practice and practice till I actually got quite proficient. There was always a friction between us, a mismatching of cogs. Yet somehow, for some reason, our relationship worked. Probably because we're both so strong-willed. I'd refuse to do something, and that would make you adamant that I was going to do it. Maybe something similar applied the other way round, too, I don't know. Was there ever an occasion when I objected to you doing something and that made you do it? Perhaps. I can't think of an instance right off the top of my head, but I'm sure it must have happened. Anyway, the thing is, that's just how we are. Some fathers and sons get along and cooperate, and some don't but get things done regardless.

So here I am. As you know by now, liftoff and landing both went flawlessly. I can't convey how exhilarating—and terrifying—they both were. Liftoff, I thought I was going to be shaken to pieces. Landing, I thought we were plunging to our doom, but in fact we were descending to the surface like a falling feather, and I barely felt it when we actually touched down. My hat goes off to the guys and girls responsible. They were cool and calm and confident as anything throughout.

Since then it's been a hundred days nearly—a hundred days on Mars!—of unloading and unpacking and constructing and connecting and setting up and adjusting and putting in place and founding and establishing, and each evening I've staggered back to my bunk after supper and fallen asleep before I've barely laid my head down. We're all getting used to one another now, and though there have been a couple of arguments, it's never been anything serious—just tempers fraying at the end of another long hard day.

It's extraordinary here, Dad. The images from the De Gama missions don't even begin to prepare you for the experience. The vistas, the texture of the light, the constant freezing cold, the low gravity, the *emptiness* of the place . . . At first I thought I was never going to adjust. Now I can't imagine anything else. It gets to you, this world. It creeps up on you and infiltrates your heart. It touches you like nowhere on Earth could touch you—none of the places I've seen, at any rate.

I get pangs of homesickness, of course. Now and then, all of a sudden it'll hit me: I'm never going back to Earth. I'm never going to see any of my friends and family again. But the pangs aren't nearly as bad as they were in the first few weeks after we arrived. Fewer and farther between now, and fainter.

But look . . . You mustn't go beating yourself up, Dad, about anything. Yes, I know that row we had, the one you mentioned, was a bad one. The worst. But it was, when all's said and done, only one of many. We'd built up a sort of tolerance to disagreement, hadn't we, so that when we rowed on that occasion, though it was volcanic, it was the equivalent to us of what would have been to anyone else a mildly severe spat. We didn't quite mend fences afterward, which maybe we should have done, and then I buggered off backpacking around the world and wound up at Canaveral and that was that. My course was set.

You're right to take responsibility for me being here, Dad, but responsibility in the sense of credit. Without you, I'd never have done this. I'd never have had the drive or the ability to make the necessary sacrifices.

We just have to face the simple fact that one planet wasn't big enough for the both of us. Two planets, on the other hand—well, maybe that'll do.

Like you, I'm a bit limited as to how much I can write here. They're pretty miserly about uplink time and transmission size for personal communications. But I don't think this is going to be the last time I'll be getting in touch—particularly if you drag yourself into the twenty-first century and get yourself a damn computer!

You're naturally hard on everyone, Dad, but you're hardest

of all on yourself. I accept that. It's not necessarily a bad quality. But I think you might just have to learn to ease up somewhat.

I'll tell you one thing, though. That story in your letter, the one about you pointing Mars out to Mum? Well, there's a biochemist here, a Swiss girl. She and I have been getting along pretty well, if you know what I mean. There was never much time for fraternizing and socializing while we were training, and it was sort of frowned on anyway, in case you got too friendly with someone who didn't then make the cut to the final fifty, but now that we're here, people have begun pairing off. It's not only sanctioned, it's actively encouraged.

Anyway, she and I went out the other night for a starlit stroll. (You can't exactly "stroll" in environment suits, you can only really do a kind of modified plodding, but a "stroll" was the import of it, if not the precise action.) And remembering what you said, I thought I'd try and impress her by picking out Earth in the sky.

It's easy, of course. Earth is quite readily identifiable by its brightness and its blue tinge.

All the same, it's a handy little trick. And I think it worked.

Love,

Richard

MOM, THE MARTIANS, AND ME

by Scott Edelman

AFTER Dad ran off with that art assistant from Chico State, Mom became convinced that he'd been kidnapped by aliens. And not just the kind from Mexico, either.

Hers were from Mars. At least, that's what she told me. I did my best to show her otherwise.

I hate people who lie, even to themselves. Being a journalist does that to you. Putting out a small-town weekly paper isn't exactly investigative reporting, since the catalogs and sales circulars we have to do on the side to stay afloat mean we end up making more allowances for advertisers than *The New York Times* has to, but still . . . I take pride in my profession. I do.

So when Mom first started talking about Martians right after Dad disappeared, I found it hard to listen, and harder to answer. I love her, you see, which made what I had to do that much harder. It would have been far easier for me if she'd been a stranger. With family, pain inflicted is pain received. So I tried to be gentle about it, to give her the chance to figure things out for herself. It's what I would have wanted, had I been in her position. Rather than offer her words in response to her strange statements, I led her down to Dad's office. I wanted to show her the state in which I had found it after he vanished so she could see the story that it told:

Half-empty liquor bottles and full ashtrays, evidencing an evening not dedicated entirely to business. Torn clothing, both Dad's and Lorraine's, ripped off each other as their passions rose and overwhelmed them, covered with sweat and lipstick, scattered about the room. A chair on its side, overturned as they'd rolled about on the floor, devouring each other's bodies. Spilled ink bottles. An impression of Dad's shoulder here, Lorraine's buttocks there, as they'd imprinted their rutting on the linoleum. The weekend travel section of *The Examiner,* decorated with magic marker circles, bold question marks, and bolder exclamation points. The safe, its door open wide, empty of contents.

I know what image these things made me see. I could imagine them standing there naked as he spun the dial, she behind him, her breath hot in his ear, her long hair pasted by sweat to his back, one firm breast flattened against his inky shoulder.

I'd walked Mom slowly through this scene that still smelled of their sex, saying here, "See, Mom, you're an adult, you can handle this, I know you can," saying there, "Look at that, you know what this means." I waited for a glimmer of recognition to come to her eyes. She'd always been a realist, before, but I guess it was too much to expect that her rational side would win in a situation like this.

She nodded her head, whispering incoherently the whole time I talked, forcing what I hoped would be an honest dialogue to be a stilted monologue instead. She never gave me the chance to comfort her, because she never admitted for an instant that she'd been wronged. At least, not by him. It was the Martians that were at fault. She was mumbling words I'd already grown tired of hearing, phrases like *Candor Chasma* and *Chryse Planitia,* sounds that when I'd first heard them had me thinking she was speaking in tongues. She then walked away looking slightly dazed, but still undeniably believing. I was left to straighten up the office myself, while she wandered off to nurture her fantasies that Dad was being held against his will for experimentation in a dark cave on a rust-colored planet.

"Experimentation's the only part you've got right," I told her then, and often in similar words since, as I thought of Dad and Lorraine rolling under the sheets in positions Mom would never attempt. I hate having to tell you that those were my words, my thoughts, because I'd regretted what I'd said instantly. But I'm supposed to be truthful here, right? No matter how I tried to stay calm, she'd inevitably do something that would get to me. This more often than not resulted in mean-

spirited needling like that cheap experimentation shot, which I
would regret for a short while, wishing I could pull my words
back to my tongue—but only until her behavior would humil-
iate or disgust me again.

She was happier the way she was, the way she chose to be.
People pretty much believe what they need to in order to survive. I guess I should have let her be, then maybe this all
would have worked out differently. I knew that regardless of
my jabs meant to force her to confront reality, she never took
a single step closer to acknowledging the truth than the first
day she discovered him gone and started moaning about Martians. Still, that didn't forgive the way I'd act toward her or
make our relationship any healthier.

The sad thing is, I'm all she's got.

Sadder still, with Dad gone, she's all I've got.

With Dad gone, the bedroom that they had shared for years
was transformed into a makeshift astronomical museum. Star
maps covered every available inch of wall space, even hiding
the bay window that had once cast light over their twin beds.
A floor-to-ceiling mosaic of the surface of Mars as seen from
space filled one wall of the room, looming like a giant un-
blinking eye. Mom had planted a silver pushpin where she was
sure he was being kept.

Odd books were everywhere. She'd always been an avid
reader, but only of nonfiction. She could not stand made-up
lives. Science fiction distressed her most of all. It had nothing
to do with real life, she said. Now, she might as well have been
living in a science fiction novel, for the library she'd built to
wall off the world was so fantastic as to make any fiction,
however wild, seem mundane by comparison. Until Mom
went strange and I lost her, I had not realized that there were
so many first-person accounts by people who claimed to have
been scooped up by spacecraft and later returned. On the
bulging shelves next to these grew scrapbooks of clippings
from supermarket gossip rags, stories telling of women who
had been impregnated by Martians, teenagers who had been
stolen as youths and returned middle-aged, and old men whose
end-stage colon cancer had been cured by the touch of alien
fingers.

Children's small windup toys decorated her end table,

rocket ships and alien robots that were sometimes left scattered on the floor where I would trip over them. The area around her bed became littered with badly printed newsletters which purported to tell the truth about a government conspiracy to hide from the public the secrets of crashed alien crafts and their inhabitants. All of these objects combined to tell a sad story. Unfortunately, she could not see that story, any more than she could see the tale Dad's office told.

I did not like knowing so much about what went on in there, but I was trapped having to pass her bedroom to reach mine.

After a long day downstairs at our office, I would walk up to our living quarters and be unavoidably assaulted by her open bedroom doorway. I could no more avert my eyes from the sight of her lost in there in a world of her own than you could ignore a smoking car crash. Mom would be lying atop the bedspread, her head propped up by pillows, not having bothered to get out of her clothes or under the covers, staring at the phosphorescent stars and planets which she had climbed a ladder to arrange on the ceiling.

"There," she once said, extending a trembling finger ceilingward toward the glowing circle that represented the fourth planet from the sun. "He's out there."

"Try to forget him, Mom," I'd said, hoping to calm her, but unwilling to respond directly to her ludicrous statement. How could I? What would have been the point of trying to argue her out of it? It was too late at night for that. From my vantage point of the doorway, I watched the stars glow, thinking myself as shielded from her delusion as I would have been from an earthquake. I was a fool. After her breathing slowed, I would shut her door and go to my own room, where as she dreamed of stars I would ponder how to rescue her from her chosen fate. A son's supposed to do that, isn't he?

Of what did her dreams consist, really? I was never on the receiving end of anything more than hints. Did she plan on tracking him to some hot Martian wasteland, where she could rescue him so that afterward they could continue living what she had believed to have been a utopian existence? Or had some of her realer, unconfessed feelings bled through to her fantasies? Did she perhaps figure to coldcock a Martian guard for his disintegrator pistol only to turn it on Dad, obliterating the old man with a death ray? Somehow I thought that second possibility would have been much healthier. It would have meant that she'd begun confronting the truth of her marriage. But I couldn't learn which of the two was more likely. Our relationship was not such that I ever would.

I keep telling people that Mom didn't start acting funny until after Dad disappeared, but they don't believe me. Even the customers we had from long before, the ones who knew us when it was just Mom and Dad and me killing ourselves night and day putting out shopping center circulars, began to doubt that they'd ever known her sane. It's as if people tend to think of you as being forever frozen as you are, no matter how they watched you grow and change . . . or in Mom's case, warp. Well, once she wasn't warped, and once her part in our business was not an embarrassment. They couldn't remember it, and to tell you the truth, at times, neither could I. She once performed just like the rest of us—sold ads, wrote filler copy, worked late correcting the final proofs, drove the delivery truck, whatever it took. She was a good woman. And she even looked like a normal human being, too. Have you seen her recently? She's let herself go. Hard to believe. Once her appearance was so important to her. Used to take care of herself, her things.

But that was before.

Before Lorraine.

Before it all changed.

She started stealing hours away from the business to devote to her private obsessions, which I'll admit began to get to me. I was killing myself as it was and could have used her help. But I would have been luckier if she'd given up *all* her hours, because it turned out that when I wasn't looking she started sneaking in filler copy on UFOs and inserting hidden messages between sentences of news stories. Readers noticed and complained. What's worse was when I caught her fiddling with the ads themselves, and I was forced to spend time before each issue was put to bed blearily proofing every page yet again so I could delete some of her more bizarre articles and replace them with text of my own.

I think I'd have been able to keep a cool head about her behavior if it hadn't started affecting the stability of the business.

After all, everyone has at least one eccentric in his family; Mom just turned out to be mine. I could have lived with a milder form of it, I guess. But you see, when Dad left, our business was thriving. Profits were as high as they'd ever been. Higher. I'd always assumed that eventually Mom and Dad would retire and leave the business to me. Now it started to look as if there wasn't going to be a business to inherit. Publishing is all I know, you know that. Sometimes, in my more paranoid moments, I'd start to think that Mom was trying to destroy it deliberately, to get back at Dad through me.

But I'm getting ahead of myself.

It was on the day that our town celebrated its one hundred and fiftieth anniversary that whatever traces of amusement which might have been left in me were chased away and replaced by fear and despair.

I hadn't noticed Mom around much during that previous week. The few times I asked her how she was occupying her time, she was chipper, but evasive. I was pleased with her demeanor, so I didn't press her. I know now that I should have. But the less time she spent around the home or office, the less time I needed to spend cleaning up after her, so I let it slide. Besides, I was her son. I did not see myself becoming her father. I know that's what's predicted as coming for all of us if we and our parents live long enough, but I didn't want to think of it then.

As you know by now, that was a bad mistake.

If I thought at all about her comings and goings during that time, I think a part of me had a fantasy it meant that she'd found herself a boyfriend, that that was why she hadn't been speaking of Mars as much in my presence. It would be good, I thought, for Mom to start a new relationship—that the effort might help snap her out of her delusion. Turns out I was the one being deluded.

What I remember most about the day of the parade is the laughter. As I stood in front of our office home waving to the girl scouts and firemen who passed by, I could hear that laughter approach in waves. At first I thought the crowd was reacting to the clowns and jugglers that the sheriff's office always provided, and I was anxious for them to turn the corner. After these rough months, I needed something to cheer me up.

But when Mom came barreling down Main Street with a fishbowl over her head, wearing a gold lamé jumpsuit, and driving our delivery truck which had a papier-mâché flying saucer constructed around it, I realized to my horror why they were really laughing. You see, as much as I'd tried to keep her new behavior quiet, the whole town had been gossiping about her for months. They'd never laughed in my presence, but now, it was as if they were being given permission to take their mocking public.

It was only then that I realized that Mom hadn't been forgetting about her delusions during her absences. She'd just been diving into them more deeply, hiding from me while building me a nightmare:

The damned thing was over twenty feet in diameter. It was painted purple and silver, and had been wired so that the portholes flashed whenever Mom hit the brakes. Over the saucer stretched a sequined banner that read, "The Martians Are Coming!"

Those standing closest to me pointed to the float and then at me. Some of the ones laughing the loudest even came closer to slap me on the back. I shrugged off their hands and forced my way toward Mom through the crowd. One of the cops grabbed my arm as I charged through the barriers, but I broke free and ran out in the middle of the street. I dodged through a maze of marching band members to reach Mom. I climbed into the saucer and pushed her away from the wheel.

At the next corner I steered us away from the path of the parade, heading down a side street. Some of the crowd followed after us on foot, trying to keep up. I floored the accelerator and could hear the saucer creak around us. Mom shouted at me to stop, but I sped along as quickly as I could until the trailing mockers vanished behind us. Were you one of them?

I drove to the town dump, keeping Mom at bay as she tried to peel my fingers from the wheel. When I crashed through the gate, some of the skin shredded off the saucer. I didn't kill the engine until I was safely in the heart of the dump. Pocketing the key, I slid out of the driver's seat. The place looked very familiar to me. When I was younger, I used to hang out there all the time, rummaging through junk with friends, looking for hidden treasures. The sight just reminded me that I wasn't young anymore. My chest hurt, and I felt my knees give out. I sat on the edge of an abandoned refrigerator. Some fool had forgotten to detach the door, and I thought, *Jesus, Mom! Martians? It's more likely that Dad's in* there!

Sitting on the refrigerator, breathing heavily, I was so angry that I could not speak. I could only tremble. Before I could calm myself enough to reason with her, Mom filled in the silence.

"Don't you dare do anything like that ever again!" she shouted as she dropped from the saucer, her gold lamé jumpsuit shining in the moonlight. "What are all of those people going to think of us now? You've humiliated me in front of my friends!"

When I laughed, she leapt across the dirt, knocked me from the fridge, and started beating me. As far as I can remember, that was the only time she ever hit me, so I was too much in shock to defend myself. I just lay there and took it. The next thing I know she had the keys in her hand and was heading off in the saucer.

By the time I'd limped the ten miles home, she'd already had the ugly thing planted in our backyard and was repairing what damage I'd done. I don't think I've ever seen anything quite as horrifying as the sight of her standing there in the moonlight, applying damp strips of old newspaper to that monstrosity. It frightened me. I couldn't even bear to enter our property. Sitting on the curb and watching her, I contemplated what I could do with the lighter fluid we had left over from our summer barbecues.

But you know me. Unfortunately, I didn't have the guts to end things that way.

She worked until dawn, and did not turn to look at me even once the entire time. When the saucer was restored to some semblance of its original grotesqueness, she stepped back and admired her work in the early morning sun. She nodded. Then she looked up, heavenward, and I knew she saw stars through the sun's rays, saw my father's footprints on Martian soil.

"This will never take you anywhere," I called to her. I was afraid that if I came too close I'd get caught in her delusion. My voice echoed though the stillness. I did not want to be brutal with her, but I saw no other path than the truth. "Besides, I don't believe you really want him back. You know where he is, and it isn't Mars. You don't really want to go after him. Mom, listen to me. This saucer won't take you to Mars."

"It won't have to take me anywhere," she said, her face brightening. She had not yet looked down from the sky, and I wondered how her neck could endure the strain. "You're mistaken. This isn't transportation. It's a *beacon.* Someday your father will escape. Martians unconscious around him, he will commandeer a ship. He'll need to be able to find Earth. He'll need help finding me. *This* will lead him here."

"Mom . . . listen to me, Mom. Her name was Lorraine."

She wouldn't take the bait, wouldn't respond with more denials, and, oh, how I wanted her to. I was worn down, losing the patience to be tender toward her. I wanted the license to blast her again with the facts, and blast her hard. Instead, she shook her head sadly and walked into the house.

The next day, before I could even say good morning to her, Mom announced that she wasn't going to have time to help me at the paper anymore, because she was going to start publishing her own UFO magazine, which she'd decided would be called *The Martian Messenger.*

"For whom?" I asked her. "There surely aren't that many people whose husbands have run off with younger women."

"You'll just have to start getting by on your own," was all she said to that. I tried it for a couple of days, too, but I soon realized that there was simply too much work. I'd need to hire an assistant to replace her.

That's how I first met Julie. Found her through an ad I ran in one of our own flyers, in fact.

The day I met her brought the one moment in all of this when I thought Mom's facade was going to crack, that she was finally going to be forced to drop this whole silly obsession; that was when she stalked in to glare at me during my interview with Julie. Though Mom would not speak of it, behind her eyes I saw memories of a certain previous interview, the one during which Dad, though he might not have realized it at that instant, had begun his exit.

I was studying page layouts while interviewing at the same time, and when Mom came in I thought she was going to forbid me to hire her. I could tell that she was looking at Julie, but that she was seeing Lorraine. But instead, she simply nodded and said, "If you don't watch out, the Martians are going to take you next."

And then she returned to her room, where she'd begun taking to bed even earlier in the day, mesmerized by the stars.

When I saw how nervous Mom had become, I hired Julie on the spot. She was a student at our local community college's art and design department, and I quickly saw that she was better at the job than Mom ever was. Julie moved through our office like she'd been born to it. Me, I was good, but I was only good because I worked hard at it—I'm one of those 99% perspiration types. Julie was a natural.

We quickly became a team. A good team.

But I saw it couldn't go on. With Mom the way she'd become, nothing good ever could.

After that parade incident, we lost a number of our best customers, and every few days that passed we lost others. After a lifetime of service, you'd think I'd have some credibility, even if Mom had lost hers. But it wasn't just that they no longer trusted us—they didn't want to be associated with us at all. I assured them that Mom no longer got to the files to insert her crazy messages anymore, I told them about how Julie had improved our organization, but the damage had already been done. Advertisers thought it hurt their image to be seen in the paper, or to have us be involved with their circulars. Money was not coming in as fast as it once had.

Mom made sure it went out a lot faster, though. Her loony projects were draining whatever income we were lucky enough to get from the few advertisers who still looked kindly on us. Our basement was filling with unsold copies of all her newsletters and magazines. Even though she was only able to unload a handful of copies of each issue, and those mostly by mailing them gratis to all of the magazines *she* subscribed to, she'd still print thousands of copies of each issue, as if expecting the world to suddenly wake up and agree with her.

I began to go down to the basement with a beer each night. I would sit on the steps and stare at the sickening towers of boxes. It seemed as if those boxes contained my entire future, stolen from me and packed up to rot. As I watched the stacks grow, I wondered whether there was any future left.

Sometimes, if I happened to bring an extra beer or two down there with me, my thoughts would turn to Julie. I counted up what I could have bought for her had all that money not been tied up in useless stacks of wasted paper. Where we could have gone together if it had ended up in my pocket instead.

I had no hope at all if things continued the way Mom insisted.

One night, six-pack tucked under an arm, I went down to the basement for my ritual of despair and discovered that the boxes were gone. All of them. The beers slipped away and clunked down the remaining stairs. One can burst open when it hit bottom, fizzing and spinning in the empty room. For a brief moment, I hoped that some force unknown to me had propelled Mom to her senses. But I wasn't allowed to hang onto that moment long.

A banging at the front door called me upstairs. Jack Blanchard, owner of the Multi Mall up in the southeast corner, was there with a cigar clenched tightly between his tobacco-stained teeth. Once, we had played high school football together, and now he made ten times my salary and had an amount of control over my life too great for me to voluntarily consider. Funny how things work out that way.

He did not look happy. When I let him in, and he told me what Mom had been doing all day, my mood quickly matched his. She had been driving through the town for hours, dropping multiple copies of her wacky newsletter in everybody's mailboxes, a violation of both postal laws and good taste. But that wasn't enough. She wallpapered the billboards entering and leaving town. She stuck them under the windshield wiper blades of each car out at the mall. Jack's mall. And now he'd had enough. He'd been thinking for awhile of hiring some staff artists of his own to produce his monthly flyers, and he had come by to tell me that he didn't want anything more to do with our company. He wanted me to hear it straight from his mouth and not through the town gossip. He felt he owed me that much.

Thank God I was able to talk him out of it.

How? In the long run, having played ball together didn't count for as much as we'd thought it would when we were teenagers. A cut in his rates for the next six months accounted for far more leverage than either of us would care to admit, but since I'm talking to you, I figure I can be open about it.

I have to be open about it.

I didn't mention the visit to Mom after she finally came home. I figured it wouldn't have done any good. It was far too late to scare her out of her lunacy. She was too far gone.

I told Julie about it first thing the next morning, though. I needed her to help me decide what to do next. But she didn't seem as concerned as I'd hoped she would.

"A job's a job," she said. "I'll be able to find another one. So will you."

That was not what I wanted to hear.

I was losing her, and I'd never even had a fair chance.

Do I have to go on?

Yes, it was a stroke of good luck for Mom to disappear like that. What do you expect me to say? I wouldn't lie to you. The company finances have bounced back into shape again, and Julie has become even more valuable to me and to the business than ever. But you must have noticed Mom isn't the only thing that's gone—Mom's saucer vanished as well. All that's left is a spot of dead grass on the lawn.

I am positive, officer, that regardless of your suspicions, you'll surely realize that there can be but one solution. What else could it be? As I told you before, people generally believe what they need to believe in order to survive. We all know what Mom believed. Well, this is what I believe.

Julie and I have talked about it at great length, and we both agree—Mom was right all along.

I owe her an apology.

Mom must have been kidnapped by Martians, too.

THE OLD COSMONAUT AND THE CONSTRUCTION WORKER DREAM OF MARS

by Ian McDonald

FROM the summer room he watched the car wind along the road by the bay, and he thought, *They will be bringing the dog.* His pleasure at seeing them all again did a sharp downturn at that. He did not like the dog. He did not like dogs in general; fawning, attention-seeking things, with a surfeit of bodily fluids, and this dog in particular owned a superabundance of those things. It was a tatty white-and-black urchin with a need for human attention so consuming that once, coming down in the night for a drink of water, he caught it foursquare in the middle of the kitchen table, enthusiastically pissing on the tablecloth. It had been lonely. He had scrubbed, steeped, disinfected twice, and said nothing as Paavo and Raisa and Yuri sat around it pouring their coffee and breaking their rolls.

You can no more kick a man's dog than his child. Even for pissing on the table. And Yuri adored the beast.

As he always did when they came on their twice yearly visits, he lit all the house lights so that there should be a welcome as they came across the causeway over the frozen inlet. Last of all were the porch lights, as he stood by the open door in the knifing cold of December and the car turned in the gravel drive, sending its headlight beams washing over him. He could hear the dog barking in the back. It had probably been barking like that all the way from Haapsalu.

Yuri came running in first; then his son and Raisa, beating their hands and stamping their feet. Breath-steamy kisses with the dog leaping up at him, leaping and leaping and leaping until he stove in its ribs with a timely-lifted knee.

"The roads bad?"

Paavo lumbered in with the bags.

"Bad enough. Down to thirty this side of Tallinn. Repair budget's probably putting some councillor's kid through university."

"Ah, no budget for anything, these days." He looked out at the setting indigo before closing the porch door on the winter. The silhouettes of the trees across the bay were still discernible, shadows against the infra-blue; low over them, Jupiter rising, and the early stars. Another thing we couldn't afford.

"You can cut the rest, but you have to have infrastructure," Paavo was saying as he moved the bags into the hall.

"Spoken like a good new Russian," the old man said, but Yuri was running ahead of any of them, even the dog.

"Where are they, can I see them?" he called out, questing in at the open door though he knew what room they were in, where they would always remain, that they were always his to look at and marvel over. Grandfather Antti paused in the study doorway, reluctant to break the shell of unalloyed wonder. Yuri stood in the center of the threadbare Kazakh rug, head thrown back, looking up at the models hanging from the ceiling. Revolving slowly, unconsciously; the photographs and certificates and engineering diagrams and artist's impressions spinning around him. Relativity.

The dog scuffled at his heels, horrified that it was missing something. Antti shoved it away with his foot. *Dare break the moment and, Yuri notwithstanding, I will poison you.* Twice a year, summer and winter, was a meager ration of wonder stuff, and its half-life was so short. Years and peers and sophistication would kill that thing you feel, orbiting beneath the models of the ships that should have taken us to Mars.

Yuri stopped.

"That one. That wasn't here before."

"It's new, that's why."

"I can see that. Show me."

Antti pulled over the peeling swivel chair to stand on and unhook the curved delta of aerobody from its fishing line rig.

"What's that bit?"

"That's the fuel processing module. The idea was that it

would go down first, maybe even six months before, and manufacture the fuel for the return trip."

"An empty tank mission."

"Empty tanks." The boy had the language. "That's right."

Yuri turned the aerodynamic plastic wedge over in his hands, stopped at a hieroglyph in curvilinear blue.

"This isn't Russian," he pronounced. "I know this sign. That says NASA. But I don't know this bit." A line of red, alien letters above the noble blue insignia.

"It says 'Astrodyne Systems MOREL 2'."

"An American ship."

"I have friends in America. I send them mine, they send me theirs. We're all the same, really."

"They didn't get there either."

"No, they left it too late. Do you know what they ask for most? The Americans?" He nodded Yuri to the disk of embroidered fabric, insignificant among the prints and plans of the boosters and orbiters. Vorontsev, Nitin, Rozdevshensky, Selkokari: *Novy Mir.* And the date, so many decades ago he could not believe the hubris of those who had planned to send men to another world. Another Russia, then. "I'll never let them have it. A photograph, that's what they'll get. At least we made it to the pad."

The hatch-dog spinning. The gloved hand reaching in: the thick, black glove. The glove, the hand that should not have been there. The gold-plated audio jacks pulling free from the helmet sockets, dangling on their glossy black wire coils. Commander Rozdevshensky hitting his chest release and surging up from his restraint straps—slowly, so slowly—as the white digits on the countdown timer remained forever frozen between the flip and flop. Better to die that way. Better by far than to be talked to death by pragmatists and right Christians.

And it still hurt, by God, still brought that involuntary twitch to the corners of the mouth. Thirty-five years since the light of a Kazakhstan morning flooded through the hatch into the capsule, the hatch that should have opened on another light altogether. Scrap now. Plumbing in the Presidential palaces of new Republics. Pig sheds. He had heard that one of the preignition pumps had turned up as a vodka still. New Russia. Dismembered. But in this shrine to a lost space age deep in

Baltic winter, ATOM 12 still stood as he remembered her that morning as they drove across the steppe, high and lovely and unbelievably white. Its model in the corner by the curtained window towered over Yuri. *Towers over us all,* his grandfather thought. *We are never out of its shadow, the rocket that would have taken Antti Selkokari, Cosmonaut, to Mars.*

***

The holy woman has been in the tomb five days now and the crowds are gathering again. Most are there to witness a miracle, a triumph of faith and will. They are easy to spot: many wear the sadhu's unbraided hair and go flagrantly naked, skin daubed with holy ash. Spirit clad. Some practice asceticism; burning cones of incense on their skin, driving hooks through folds of flesh, tongue, eyelids. One man walks around for the admiration of the crowd, his right arm held aloft by a devotee declaring that the sadhu had held his arm fifteen years thus in asceticism. Fifteen years! The arm is withered as a stick in a drought. It will never bend again. The joints are fused, locked. The holy man s eyes glare spiritual challenge at the crowds thronging the station approach. See what I do: who in this corrupt century dares attempt such practice to sever soul from flesh?

This corrupt century has surer and swifter ways to samadhi, Ashwin thinks, smiling to himself, as he joins the queue for holy breakfast. He has done this every morning since the sacred woman's coffin was sealed, lowered into the dusty grave, and buried. Behind him, a band tootles. Off-shift jitneys and money-kids on biomotor scooters dart around the musicians. The sky is already that flat, dusty steel blue of the most ferociously hot days; the sun a savage copper atom. Ashwin thanks whatever gods mind buried women for the air-conditioning of the cyber-*mahals* of Chandigarh. The line shuffles forward, toward the shade of the tent where Ashwin can make out the bobbing, nodding head of the benefactor; a *datarajah:* grown sleek on the global market's hunger for cheap IT labor. His expiation: a pile of chapattis and a pot of *daal.*

Ashwin reaches the folding deal table where the alms are bestowed. The old man bows to him in blessing, an assistant hands him a chapati. Ashwin cannot but notice the barrier gloves. He looks a moment at the bowed head of the rich man, the saffron mark on the forehead, the simple white robes. *Are you the one whose machines split my mind from my body and send it across the solar system?* A nudge moves him on.

"How long?" Ashwin asks the man at the end of the row of tables, whose job seems to be to keep the beneficiaries moving. He nods to the richly patterned cloth draped over the pile.

"Looking like today," the minder says.

By the time Ashwin reaches the station, he has finished the holy breakfast. With each step up, the sound from within increases until it seems as solid as the four-hundred-year-old Raj-brick walls. Hand-scrawled signs apologize again for the delay in final construction of the nano-carbon diamond train shed. Labor shortages. More money to be made, *out there.* The spars of the half-completed dome reach over the crumbling station like a hunting hawk's claws, stooping. Beneath them, legions of shift workers clash on the platforms, merge, flow through each, separate, neither the victor. Clocking on, clocking off. Families camped on the platforms make meals, wipe children, tend elders. Water sellers clack bronze water cups, newsplug hawkers hold up five fingers full of the days' headlines; wallahs lift baskets of guavas and mangoes; battered tin trays of samosas and nimki; paper-wrapped pokes of *channa.* Buy eat buy eat. Ashwin half-hears an announcement, half-glimpses a platform change on a hovering roll-screen, then is almost carried off his feet as a thousand people move as one. *Out there*, a sleek little electric commuter train slides stealthily into its platform. He makes it as the doors close, dodges the Sikh packer who would seize him by collar and seat of pants and wedge him between that oily man with the big mustache and that girl in the suddenly self-consciously short skirt. Ashwin swings into the gap between carriages: hands reach down, pull him up the ladder as the fast little train begins to accelerate.

The inside monthly ticket has gone up again.

Roof-riders shuffle aside for Ashwin as the train pulls out of the cracked dome of Kharar station. He grips tight as the carriage lurches over points. If you slide down between the carriages, there is no hope. But it is cheap, and the air is fresher than the hot spew pushed around by the carriage ventilators. From his high seat, it seems to Ashwin that even in one night the slum *chawls* have divided and grown denser again, like bacteria doubling, in a sample dish. They seem to shoulder closer to the line. *Chawl* life as a series of snapshots. *Flash*: a dirty little urchin girl, wide-eyed at the wonderful train, one hand in her mouth, the other held up in salutation. Hello hello hello . . . *Flash*: three men in dhotis drag the corpse of a pickup on frayed nylon ropes, like an ox hauled to the slaughter. *Flash*: two barefoot women push a water-barrow, leaning hard into the shafts to shift the heavy leaking plastic barrel. *Flash*: a leathery old man angles a solar umbrella into the best light to power his sewing machine. *Flash*: A skeletal yellow cow stares dully at the level crossing, unfazed by the train hurtling past its nose. Don't test your sacred status this morning. Panjab Rapid Transit respects you not.

Ashwin thinks of his own tenaciously held few rooms, the roof garden where his mother tends a small urban farm, the balcony; his father's pride, the mark of a man, a place where he may entertain his friends, read the paper of a morning, watch the satellite sports of an evening. But a proper house; no slum, no cardboard shanty, no. So proud they are. He thinks of the world he will build that day, the homes and towns they will design beneath the glass sky. Cities. Hundreds of cities; cities built for people, with districts where everyone knows your name and open spaces where you can meet and talk and markets where you can buy goods from two worlds and then a cup of coffee in a bar where you may watch sports. Cities big enough to be thrilling, small enough to be intimate. And *chawls*? Ashwin looks at the sprawling degradation with a new eye. Yes, chawls! *Of course chawls*! Where there are people, there will always be the cities we build for ourselves, out of our deepest needs, not given by those who tell us how we should live. Human cities. He imagines the people of Old Kharar and Basi and Kurali flocking from their hovels, along the sewage-seeping lanes to the roads, to the rail, south, ever south, to the girdle of space elevators ringing the world's waist. He sees them flowing up those spun-diamond towers, sailing across space in colossal arks, whole families together. He imagines them coming down the hundred thousand pier-

towers, spreading out under his glass roof across the virgin
grasslands, taking the things they find and building from them
their homes.

A sudden slam of sound and air and movement jars him out
of his dreams. Ashwin slides on his tender perch, grabs, finds
human bodies. Hands seize him, steady him. The 07:00 Jul-
lundur express hurtles past on the main line, a blurred streak
of steel and windows and speed. Ashwin laughs. And trains.
Of course trains. The only practical transport. No plane can
operate in the cold, primeval atmosphere beyond the roof, and
none but a fool or a sparrow would fly inside a glass house.
Trains, then. Already, he has heard, engineers are designing
fusion-powered juggernauts the size of city blocks riding
tracks wide as a house. Grand journeys they shall go on; not
gritty little commuter runs, but voyages across whole conti-
nents. Those who ride up on the roofs of these titans will see
entire landscapes unfolding before their eyes, new vistas, ge-
ographies; new worlds that have never felt the foot of man.

When the fast train slams past, Ashwin always looks forward for the first glints from the towers of Chandigarh through
the smog haze. Ghost cities in the mist. The Cybermahals of
the Indian Tiger. Curving scimitars of construction crystal,
minarets of spun titanium and glass, curtain walls of solar
tiling, battlements half a kilometer above the *chawl* sprawl of
the Panjab. Ashwin seeks particularly the golden glint of the
huge solar disk that fronts the Ambedkar tower, the vanity of
corporada architecture but also the device that will spin his
mind, his perceptions, his abilities, across the solar system to
that new world. Ashwin thinks again of the holy woman by the
station, buried in dirt. Can you promise them anything like
this? Or is it all internal, all for the next world? There is the
next world, hanging up there. All you have to do is look. A
promise, a lure. A world of your own. Your Mars. For how
many years had the disciple lifted his own arm, uncomplain-
ingly, unnoticed, to bear aloft his master's?

Then cutting walls seal off the vision as the overburdened
little commuter train dives into the approach tunnel to Chandigarh station.

***

The others were asleep now, and the house was quiet and dark. A time for men. A time for father and son. They sat by the fire in the drawing room. Burning wood gave the only light. Paavo had brought a bottle of good vodka: Polish, none of that Russian dung. The dog lay at his feet, but it did not lie easily. Every creak, every click of the geriatric heating, every pop of the fire roused it: enemy/interest/attention. *Lie at peace like a proper dog,* Antti thought. *Proper dogs trust their masters.*

The long, bad winter drive had drained Paavo; it did not take much vodka, Polish or not, to bring him to the point where he could speak the truth. He lifted his glass, turned it to catch the light from the fire, send its rays into his eyes, his soul of souls.

"I thought twice about bringing Yuri with us this time."

A brief knurl of cold in Antti's chest. Cold of winter, cold of space. Cold of an old man alone in a wooden house by the sea.

"Why would you do that?"

Paavo shifted uncomfortably in his chair. The bloody dog started.

"He has exams."

"I thought he was doing well at school."

"He is. He is. Just . . ."

"Not at the right subjects."

"His science grades have been dropping."

Antti eyed the bottle, thought the Polish vodka made what he had to say next slip out so much more easily.

"So, why should he not come to see me for New Year? I'm a scientist. Scientist first class. I've got the medal, from Comrade Kosygin himself. I could help him with his grades." He waved down any interruption Paavo might make. "I know, I know. It's the wrong kind of science. Space travel. Stars, galaxies, planets. Missions to Mars. Old science. Wrong science. Not the kind you can make money from. Not technology. Not computers." The dog was edgy now, sensing an arousal beyond its primeval levels of reaction and response. Its velvet mongrel ears lifted. "All that time and research and effort and money to send men to Mars, and how many people get to go? Four men. All that money and time and effort. And the stars? Impossible! The universe is too big for us. Let's explore inner space instead. Cyberspace. Everyone can go there. All you need is a computer. And look at the wonders you find there! All those wonderful things you can buy, if you have the money. All those beautiful women who want you to look at them having sex with donkeys or drinking each other's piss. If you have the money. All the famous people; you can find out about their lives and their clothes and what they eat and how they make love, but you can never ever be like them. Reach the stars? Impossible."

He snatched up the bottle. Surprised, the dog gave a little grizzle. *And you,* the old man thought at it.

"Are you finished?" Paavo asked.

"No, not nearly; I've hardly even begun."

"Well, when you're done, give me a shot of that and I'll show you something."

Antti handed the bottle through the firelight. Paavo poured, and the two men drank in silence, one too proud to admit his hurt, the other to apologize. *When you were Yuri's age, on such a night as this we went out through those French windows into the gardens and named the winter constellations together,* Antti thought. *I saw you look up. I saw their light in your eyes. I have always respected your work, even if I haven't always comprehended it, and if I am scornful, if I am critical and bitter, it is because, like my ATOM project, there, too, a great promise has been betrayed. Buy things. Look at things. The constellations in this cyberspace have no shine, no wonder. They are shaped like Coke logos and Nike swooshes. There is no sparkle in them to catch in your eye. They don't call you outward from home.*

Now Paavo was taking a flat case from his bag beside his chair. He set it on his lap, unfolded it. Blue screen light illuminated his face.

"This is the thing you wanted to show me?" Antti asked. "Another laptop."

"No," Paavo said carefully. "Not another laptop. You were saying about the universe being too big for us? No, it's not. I've got it right in here." He tapped the translucent blue polycarbonate casing. "I've got them all in here. Infinite universes, in one small box."

"You got it to work, then."

The son nodded.

"If Einstein couldn't get his head around quantum theory, I don't imagine that I ever will," Antti said, realizing as the words left him how mealy they sounded. "This quantum computing: calculations being made simultaneously in thousands of parallel universes, each as real as this room, as us, that dog. . . ."

Other rooms, like reflections of reflections. Mirror in mirror. Other worlds. One where the crew of *Novy Mir* were not pulled from the capsule at T-minus-seven because the booster, the ATOM mission, the entire Mars project had been so rotten with corruption and creaming-off that safety standards had been squandered.

The moment you went for throttle-up, the fuel lines would have ruptured, Launch Controller Barsamian had said as the army transporter sped away from the launch site, the summer dust pluming up behind it. *The call came through from Kirilenko. The whole thing is rotten. Rotten to the heart. It always was. A quick, cheap fix.*

He had glanced back through the window at the great white tower on the scorched steppe and thought, *Was there a chance it could have flown, or had it been quick and cheap and botched from the start? All a feint in the game with the Americans?*

In another world, the word did not come from Kirilenko in time. They went for throttle-up. It blew.

In another universe, they went for throttle-up. It flew. It flew right off this world, on to another. They came burning down in an arc of fire clear across Amazonis Planitia and the calderas of Elysium. Ten kilometers above Isidia Planitia the descent stage fired. They came down in fire and steam in the crater shadow of Nili Patera. The hammer and sickle of the Union of Soviet Socialist Republics was stabbed into the regolith and unfurled in the winds of Syrtis Major.

Somewhere in that thin plastic case, that possibility existed.

"Can I see it?"

Paavo gave a shrug of assent. Antti lifted the plastic shell as if what it held were terribly terribly fragile. It was lighter than he had imagined.

"All these . . ."

Paavo smiled. Antti turned the screen toward him, angled it to make sense and shape out of the plasma film screen. A brief frown of disappointment: the display was a standard operating system interface. But its pristine touch pads, white as milk teeth, called his fingers to type. *Test us if we speak the truth.*

"I feel I should ask it something."

"It's not an oracle. It's just a computer."

"All the same . . ."

"It's still garbage in, garbage out in every universe." The coals collapsed, sending up a spear of flame, and the dog started, and they were two men together with the mad cold outside the window. "If it were an oracle, if it could send one question out into all universes and all times, what would you ask?"

Paavo saw his father smile, then think, then the light from the surge of fire fade from his face. Slowly, deliberately, with winter-stiff fingers, not wanting to get one holy word wrong, Antti began to type.

***

The locker rooms are all numbered and work in strict rotation. Fifteen hundred workers off-shifting as the next battalion shift on would clash like Vedic armies in the corridors and changing rooms, so they are channeled into separate sectors. Ashwin always imagines he can feel the drub of feet through the carbon steel skeleton of the tower. Likewise, though he never met his shift predecessor, Ashwin knows the heat and particular perfume of his body (irrefutably a *his*) from the imprint on the live-leather transfer seat.

Men here, women there. Shirt on this peg. Shoes on that shelf. Pants here. Always folded, neatly folded. A gentlemen looks after his clothes. A nod, a word to the number up and the number down and the number across as he changes into the simple white coverall. Sometimes, in the transfer, the body forgets itself; a soiling, a leaking, at least, a drooling. As ever, the papery thing catches at the crotch. Ready. Fifteen hundred locker doors clatter shut, ranked and filed. People moving, always moving, along streets, down platform, onto trains, into rooms, down plastic clad corridors, moving together, a herd of bodies under the utilitarian strip light.

He nods to his fellow on-shifters. He does not confuse them with workmates any more. Once you get in that chair, they can send you anywhere. The thin Sikh man next him could work an entire quartersphere away. His own closest workmate is a black man from Senegal. Ashwin carries, he bolts.

But the room catches him, every time. He flies heavy-lift rosettes through the staggering canyon lands of Valles Marineris, but a thousand black-chairs, row upon row, all facing in the same direction, is awe-full.

As ever, the air hums to barely audible mantras to relax the on-workers and set the brain-wave patterns ready for the transfer. The scent is mood blue. Ashwin has come to hate that stink up his nose. He finds his seat, twenty along by thirty-five deep. Still warm. He knows its every creak as he lowers himself onto the skin. A nod to the Sikh, mumbling a prayer to himself. Ashwin lies back, stretches. The sensory array arms unfold over his face like a mantis over her husband.

A start, something, down at the foot of the room. A noise raised over the mantra-wash; wailing, animal noise. Ashwin props himself up, the machine arms with their eyecups and earplugs and skull taps scurry away. Thrashing: something is spasming its couch. Attendants come running through the rows of transfer couches, screening the sight with their bodies, but the fear has rippled out to every corner of the huge room.

The technology is safe, they said. *Tested, tried, true, safe. You need have no fear. We are paying for your soul, but nothing will go wrong.*

But things go wrong. Things have always gone wrong. The ones who settled under the skull-tap probes and went into seizures. The ones who built up an allergic response to the nanoprocessors. The ones who, like this one, come out in pieces, broken in the head. The ones, they rumor, who never come out at all. Who go *somewhere else.*

Ashwin watches the electric gurney weave its load back between the couches. Nothing to see here, nothing's happened, everything will be fine, go about your work, you have great work to do today, great work. And Ashwin feels part of him saying, yes, yes to the blandishments of the company medics

and he knows that part is the pretransfer drugs suffusing up
through the skin of the seat, through his own skin, into his
blood. Let go. All is illusion: mind, body . . . illusion. Free
your mind. Let us park your body. Go. Commute.

Soft bioplastic fingers unfold over Ashwin. Eyecups press
over his sockets: A moment's panic as the plugs seek out the
contours of his inner ears and fill them. The breathing tubes
worm down his nostrils, into his lungs. The drip-feed needles
and blood scrubbers are busy at his wrists. Last of all, the taps
caress his skull as the nanoprocessors swarm through the cra-
nium into his selfhood and wrench it away from him.

But another Ashwin, one the drugs and tiny skull machines
can not touch, shouts through the drugs and the seethe of
nanomachines, the sweat-reek of the workroom, the *corporada*
mantra-blur. What kind of world? What kind of Mars, you
asked yourself, up on the roof, riding with the poor men like
the poor man you are? That kind of Mars, where poor men are
taken away quietly on a cart, where there is no fuss, no mess,
nothing to spoil the *corporada* image. You think your people
will ever ride on the roof of those great fusion-power
expresses? There will never be enough cars on the space-
elevator, there will never be enough berths in the transplane-
tary ships, enough lovely, habitable cities for all the poor of
Chandigarh and the Punjab and all of Bharat, let alone the children they squeeze into being every second of every day. Rich
men build a rich world. You go to construct a golf course in the
sky. A country club for the *datarajahs*.

Then that Ashwin is snuffed out, and there is the black of
light-speed for a time the mind cannot clock. And after that instant: light, mass, sensation, existence. A world. His world.
Ashwin Mehta has arrived on Mars.

***

The old man came down the stairs sniffing. No salty tang of
mongrel urine in the porch. He threw back the heavy night curtains. The outer windows were leafy with frost. No taint in the
hall. In the study the splendid erection of ATOM 12 was un-
defiled; a natural challenge to a dog. Why did he always forget to close the door when that thing came to call? Nothing and

no one to close them on, most of the time. The living room smelled of vodka and gentle sweat, but no taint of piss. The fire had burned down to gray charcoals. New morning now. Antti wrenched open the curtains, admitting watery, destroying light into every part of the room. He waved clear a circle in the frosted mist inside the window. Real mist beyond, moving slowly across the frozen bay. The sun was high and wan, seeming to dash and veer through the upper streamers of the fog. If it were a morning hoar, it would boil off, but the speed with which the trees on Kuresaari Island were fading hinted at an inversion layer forming out at the limit of the pack ice. They could lie out there for days. Weeks, in a stable winter anticyclone. Breath steaming, Antti watched the ice crystals reform and close as cold coils of fog hastened across the ice to swaddle the wooden house.

In the unsympathetic morning light, the oracle-machine was just a wafer of translucent aquamarine plastic. No more wisdom than a credit card. Wincing at the foolishness of old men and firelight and vodka, Antti slipped open the lid. Still there from the night before. He had forgotten to shut the program down. So clever, and yet too stupid to think of doing it itself.

WHAT WILL HAPPEN TO MY DREAM OF MARS?

Dining room unsullied. Dining table polished and perfect. Table linen pure and unpolluted. Kitchen. And there it was, one paw in a shallow lagoon of cold, orange piss, proudly wagging its tail.

"Hiii! Hutt! Hutt! Hutt! Out with you, pissing beast! Go on, out, out, away with you."

The thing had a terrible temper, but the wrath of old men is swift and fearless. The vile thing was bundled out the back door before it could open its jaw. It stood there, grubby white on the white, stunned by the suddenness of the cold. Antti bent to the undersink cupboard to fetch cleaner and cloths and disinfectant before young feet in search of cereals came skidding through the amber slick. It was crying now, a kind of sobbing keen that made Antti despise it all the more. *Learn Darwin,* he thought as he went down on his knees to the crusted piss.

Only when he heard Yuri's voice from outside did Antti realize he had not heard the dog's yip for some minutes now. He

ran to the door to scold Yuri about silly boys who went rushing out into the cold not properly dressed. He listened. Yuri's
voice was getting farther away. He was out on the ice.

"Bloody cur!" Antti cursed. He dashed down the back path
as fast as his years and the winter would let him.

"Yuri!"

The boy was farther even than he had feared, calling into
the white fog that came weaving thicker every moment
through the trees across the inlet.

"Yuri!"

Come back, oh, come back now, don't let this be the moment when you decide that everything old men say is stupid
and you can safely disregard them.

"Yuri!"

The boy stopped, on the edge of melting into the white and
white.

"Come back, come on back. It's not safe; you can't see a
foot in front of you in this fog, and the ice can still be rotten."

"But my dog . . ."

"Come back to the house." He saw the boy look back to the
dimensionless white of the closing fog and knew what he must
offer to buy his safety. "I'll go look for him. You go on back.
It'll be all right."

Hunting through the drawer of the study desk, Antti looked
at his private space fleet and shivered. *Venture into the unknown. The alien on your doorstep.* He found his mission
training compass. *It saw me through Kamchatka, it won't let
me down within sight of my own back door.* Outside, the cold
was paralyzing. Antti took a bearing on the house and went
down to the edge of the ice. Pebbles grated beneath his booted
feet. And he was *there.* The door opening, everyone waiting
for that first crack of light, that pale slit widening into a
wedge, a rectangle of illumination, beyond which lay a new
world. Cranking down the ladder, everyone getting into proper
order in the lock as narrow as a birth canal; bulking in their ex-
cursion suits, rehearsing their lines. Rozdevshensky first, then
him, last Nitin. The top of Rozdevshensky's helmet vanishing
over the platform. Rozdevshensky down, a breath—more a
sigh—on the helmet intercoms. Then him, lumbering out
backward, clumsy as a spring-woken bear. Looking at the

strangely lit metal, until the crunch of stones under his booted feet. *You're down. Now, you can turn and look. How it would have been. Should have been.*

Antti Selkokari stepped out onto the frozen world.

Within twenty paces, the house was a ghost. Another ten, and it was gone. Antti was embedded in white from the surface of his skin to infinity. He looked around, suddenly cold and fearful in the knowledge that he had let his need to be admired by his grandson push him into folly. Pale fronds of trees swam momentarily through the nothing. He checked the compass. It pointed true. It pointed home. He struck out into the mist.

"Hiii! Hey! Here, boy!" he called. "Come on, where are you, you stupid mutt?"

No sign, no sound. He half-hoped that it was drowned already. It would wash up with the thaw, recognizable only by its blue plastic webbing collar. Thing-that-was-a-dog. Let it go. *Your kitchen is warm, there is coffee, and you are no Mars explorer. Anything lost in this is dead.*

But Yuri, he told himself. *How can I tell him this and retain any honor?*

Another reading on the compass, another tentative shuffle forward into the featureless white. Every footfall a test. *Will it bear me. Is it rotten to its blue heart?*

On Mars, there are craters silted so full of dust they cannot be seen on the surface. They wait, drowning traps of red, like buried ant-lions.

Lost in remembrance, Antti realized with a shock of cold that he had been walking without thought. He flipped open the compass. The needle was spinning, swinging wildly from point to point, hunting for home and unable to find it.

Antti Selkokari tapped the compass.

Still the needle swung.

He closed the compass, opened it again, hit it with the heel of his hand, held it upside down, shook it, shook it like he would a dog that had pissed on his dining table, pressed it up to his ear as if it might tell him the reason for its betrayal. Still, it lied. It would not tell the way home. Antti was lost. The ice held no footprints, no track back.

"Hello!" Antti shouted. "Hello! Can you hear me!"

The ice fog took his words, smeared them, returned them as

whispering echoes. Echoes. Nothing in this dimensionlessness should echo.

"Hello!"

Hello hello hello hellooo hellllooooo said the echoes, in voices not his, that did not die away, but whispered on, into a mumble of conversations half heard, from another room, another universe.

Hello?

Against sense, Antti spun toward the voice so clear behind him.

Is anyone there? Who is that?

The voice was at once out there in the white and inside his head, speaking in his own Estonian and another language he did not recognize.

"Who is this?" Antti asked, and heard his own voice speak in two places, two languages, two worlds. He frowned, a thickening of the fog, a curdling of the white, a solidity, a shape. A shadow, moving toward him across the ice plain. The white swirled, and a man walked out of it.

***

White on gold. A line, a crack. Peer into it: a sliver of eye, a line of cheek, the corner of a lip. A face under the gold. Pull out: the crack is a hairbreadth in a curve of gold: another step's remove, and the golden arc is the laminated visor of a pressure-suit helmet. Reflected in the visor, a landscape curved like an image in a state fair hall of mirrors. Where visor seals to helmet, the golden landscape curves away to nothing. There are hills mirrored here on either side; they slide off into nothingness, the mere suggestion of altitude. Optical lies: in truth, they are vast rim-walls, kilometers high. This same distortion gives undue prominence to the objects at the center of the field of vision. Immediate foreground: an insectlike vehicle, spiky with antennae, huge balloon wheels at the end of each of the six sprung legs. Behind it, a squat brick structure, incongruously like a Hopi pueblo, down to the satellite dish on the flat roof. Its location only adds to the likeness: a wide, dry plain of wind-eroded stones. Beyond, and dwarfing the little adobe home, a hovering saucer, keeping its station a handful of meters above the ground with twitches of its nacelle-mounted fans. The distortion of the reflection thrusts the logo on the aircraft's nose into focus: ROTECH. It has colleagues, they hold tight formation across the valley floor as far as the visor reflections allow seeing. And beyond the flotilla of airships, and dwarfing them as they dwarf the house, the house the vehicle, the vehicle the man, the man the scratch etched by some accident in his helmet visor, the pillar. It is surely stupendous. It is buttressed like the roots of a rain-forest tree: tiny flakes of dirt cling to them. There are other pueblos, hanging from the lower slopes, insignificant as grains of salt. An airship drifts across the sheer face of the tower. It is tiny and bright as a five *pice* coin. Follow the huge structure up until it curves away off the edge of the visor. Look beyond: like the airships, this pillar is one of a mass. The floor of this vast canyon is forested with thousands of pillars, three kilometers high.

Pull out again, in a long, astronomical-scale zoom. The pressure-suited figure is just one of many, human and machine. The machines outnumber the humans in number and variety. The valley floor is a hive of machine species. There are high-stepping nanofacturing robots, pausing to stab proboscises into the surface and release swarms of nanoassemblers. There are surveying machines, exchanging heliographs of laser light. There are great orange worm machines, burrowing deep in the regolith, chewing dead red rock into pumice. There are planters and fermentories—great, slow, sessile things—gulping in carbon dioxide atmosphere by the ton and reacting it with water and wan sunlight into organic matter. Living stuff. The stuff of worlds. There are the fleets of heavy-lift LTAs—the man in the suit is marshaling them on some precision maneuver—and smaller, nimbler skycraft, zipping between the big slow dirigibles on their priority missions. There are track layers and road builders and brick makers and patient little spider machines that mortar them into the neat adobes for the humans. There are machines that build machines and machines that service machines and machines that program machines and machines that repair machines and everywhere is the green circle logo and sigil of ROTECH. Remote Orbital Terraform and Environmental Control Headquarters. Swarming machine life calls green out of the red;

tentative, fragile plantations of gene-tweak grasses and mosses. Beneath human perceptions, the cleverest, the most important machines, the nanoassemblers, fuse red sand into silicon pillar. On the scale of planets, other hives of machines extend primeval run-water channels into canals to carry water from the thawing north pole to the terraformed lands of Grand Valley. A flash of light: eighty kilometers up in low, fast orbit, a vana, a spinning mirror of silver polymer, frail as a hope, rolls its focus on to its true target; the northern polar cap. The scale of the work in this four-thousand kilometer rift valley only becomes apparent at this kind of altitude. To the northwest the forest of towers rise above our ascending point of view. Their tops open out into branches, those branches into twigs, bare, waiting. To the east the towers are still growing, one kilometer, two kilometers. Farther east still, trillions of assemblers swarming in the subsoil are pushing the great root-buttresses out of chaotic mesa-lands of Eos and Capri. The wave of construction passes down the chasm like a slow, silicon spring. Another glitter of light, not from an orbital mirror this time, but sun catching the edge of the world roof, five kilometers above the wind-shaved hills of Coprates. Above it now, climbing fast. The world roof flows from the east like a river of glass that falls into red emptiness.

How to terraform Mars. Easy. Stick a roof over Valles Marineris. Real greenhouse effect. By the time it is complete, it will be visible from Earth, a bright white mote in the eye of the ancient red war god.

Higher now, past the littler, lower moon. Keeping precise pace with it on the other side of the planet is the SkyWheel, the spinning ground-to-orbit space-cable. All the humans, all the machines that build the bases and plants and the machines, were spun down this cable. But the real work of terraforming, the RO in the ROTECH, is done from orbit. Up beyond the vanas and the supercores, weaving a magnetic cocoon around this tectonically dead, defenseless world, are the orbital habitats and factories and mass drivers of the planetary engineers and terraformers. By the time humans can walk unclad under the Grand Valley roof, they will form a ring around the planet, a band of satellites. The night will glitter with them.

All in a construction worker's visor; reflected.

Ashwin Mehta edges the heavy-lift flotilla in over the construction site. His belly sensors and satellite uplinks to ROTECH's moon ring redoubt could guide him in with laser precision but human atavism endures. The gloved hands wave him down, and he follows. Spinners skitter clear. The winds that howl the full length of the rift valley have buried the load with sand: Ashwin's trim-fans sweep it clear as he maneuvers with millimeter precision. He feels the lift cables go out of him: it is a physical, pleasurable sensation but not one for which his flesh body has an analogue.

Despite Bharat trumpeting the largest IT skill pool on the planet, Ashwin knows that he and every other body on its live-skin couch only got there because of strong body mapping. It still took him many shifts to feel his way into a new, weightless body to which modules could be added or swapped. His hands and arms are obviously the wiry little manipulators—though no human arm ever experienced the sensation of detaching itself and swinging, hand-over-hand to a new attachment point elsewhere on the body. His legs he regards as the fan-pods, his lungs the lift bags and the curved silver shell his body, the center of his being. The slave units, hooked up according to work schedule, were more difficult, but he has learned a way; he expands his sense of self to incorporate them. *I am vast, I contain multitudes.* It still takes some minutes after the computers flick him home at light-speed to snap out of three-hundred-sixty-degree vision. The rabbit-eye sight of his hundreds of optical sensors has taught Ashwin truths about how body shapes consciousness. The universe of meat is divided rigidly into front and back, visible and invisible. Objects are sought out, selected, made part of the view. Morphology begets psychology. Ashwin, like a divinity, sees everywhere at once. There is no forward or backward, up or down, just movement toward a destination or away from it.

It is this aspect of his job that he finds hardest to tell others. His parents nod and say how good it is that he has employment and good steady money but they do not comprehend what he is doing up there, let alone how he feels doing it. They are one generation away from believing that gods live in the sky. He does not want to tell them that, in a sense, they do. The girls are a little more sophisticated; they know about other planets and terraforming. *Mars! How exciting! How romantic! Is it re-ally really dangerous? Do you face sandstorms and explosions and volcanoes?* Telling them that Mars is a quiet, placid sort of place, where what action there ever was happened billions of years ago, is not what they want to hear but they have passed on anyway, for these women also know what kind of work the *corporadas* hire for, and how little it pays.

He feels lock. The cable grippers bind molecule to molecule with the lift points. *Ready,* Ashwin says. Coprates control whispers clearance in his inner ear: the site foreman waves her hand. Take her up. Fans swivel to full lift. Winches wind in the strain. Flicker-lasers torch up: these loads require every gram of lift. Ashwin feels motor/muscles tense, strut-bones strain. He mentally grits his teeth. *You are a weight lifter, going for the clean lift.*

The rosette of twelve linked LTAs pulls the five-hundred-meter diameter glass hexagon clear from the sand. Ashwin lifts straight for a hundred meters, then tilts the whole array from side to side to clear it of lingering dust and dead glass-weavers. Gently, gently. The glass is engineered to tolerances far beyond terrestrial norms, and the gravity slight, but one crack, three kilometers up . . . Tiny crystal shells cascade from the edges of the roof pane like iridescent snow. The great glass light heliographs in the sun. The forewoman raises an arm in salute as Ashwin gains cruising altitude. It is a sight he never tires of, this resurrection of glass from the earth. Two kilometers up, bearing 5.3 pi rad, Pier 112, 328. Pane 662, 259.

Telephone number engineering.

Beneath him graders are leveling billion-year-old outwash hills for new glass fields. Ahead, the buried panes are stains in the sand, a mesh of linked hexagons. Tiny machines, working, working. Ashwin reflects a moment on the incomplete dome of Kharar railway station, then a proximity alert gently chides him: Heavy Lift Array 2238 is on approach to pick up. Day and night the LTAs carry and set, busy and sterile as drone bees.

In the air lane now. The lifters move in strictly regulated traffic zones over cleared terrain. There has not been an accidental drop since Ashwin started on the job, but a five-hundred hexagon of fifty-centimeter glass falling from three kays is the stuff of health and safety legend. HLA 1956 comes up from the glass fields of Cander and slips in ahead of Ashwin: a colleague, though Ashwin has never seen his flesh face, nor knows where his meat is based. He sends a greeting message over the com channels; truckers flashing their headlights. Closing on the target now. The front edge of the construction is visible as a line of white light. Ashwin has never seen the sea, but he always thinks of the edge of the world roof as a line of surf breaking on a beach, frozen, turned to slow-flowing glass, inching forward day by day, hour by hour. One kilometer out, construction control taps into Ashwin's neural matrix and dispatches him and his load into an approach pattern to Pier 112, 328. As he moves in high over the open fingers of the Main Left Branch, he sees another heavy-lift cluster retract cables and slide away from the pier top. Spider-welders skitter across the glass on delicate sucker feet to bolt the plate to the struts. That is what Ashwin's friend from Senegal does: Ashwin can see his spider-welder hugging the pure white spar like a tick as he swivels the rig on its belly fans. They earn more than lifter pilots. They have more responsibility.

Lasers flicker from all around Ashwin's multiple body—another sensation for which his meat has no likeness—guiding him in onto the baffle plates. The alignment must be millimeter perfect. Ashwin tunes the ducted fans to compensate for an unseasonable breeze he can feel picking up across his sensory skin, descends steadily through the mesh of laser light. Thirty meters. Twenty.

Looking good, Ash, says the bolter from Senegal on the innercom.

Ten meters

Looking good. A simple expression of solidarity, but it opens Ashwin's extended senses like a key. From skin to horizon in every direction he can look, his world rushes in on him. He sees it all fresh, entire, as one thing. The stupendous canyon, one end to the other, wall to wall. The thin pink sky, the wisps of high cirrus. The surface three kilometers beneath him; the constructions of man, the patterns they make on the soil as they fuse sand to glass. The machines: those above, those below, those between, that crawl upon the pillars and roof of the world. The SkyWheel on its ponderous orbits,

ROTECH's habitats wheeling overhead in a carousel of satellites. The men and minds that looked on this world, and set their will upon it. He sees it all, and it looks good to him. Very good indeed. He is so proud of all that he is part of, this Bharati boy one foot out of the *chawl*, who is become Creator of Worlds.

Five meters.

And in that instant, everything goes white. . . .

***

Is this what it is to be dead? he thinks and thinking so, knows himself to be alive. An image: the holy woman, buried alive for righteousness' sake. Real? Imaginary? Is the darkness of the grave really a white so intense it cannot be regarded by the eye? Is there any difference between outside and inside in this featureless white? A freezing thought. This is the pure white light of cyberspace. There has been an error in the mindlink, a fault in the tap-head technology. The kind of thing that sends some people thrashing and fitting on their couches. You, it has sent into nowhere. No thing. A mind without a body.

He cannot tell if he has flesh perception or machine sense: everything in every direction looks the same and therefore robs him of dimension. An uncle driven blind by cataracts once told him the horror of blindness. It is not not seeing. It is everything white.

A mind, with no senses, no connection to the outside world. He could be lying on his couch at the Ambedkar *corporada,* in a hospital, at home. A mind with only its own thoughts for company. A thought to make the heart kick coldly in the chest. At least, he can still feel. And if he can feel . . .

"Hello?" Ashwin ventures. He can hear himself. His own voice, inside, and outside. "Hello? Can anyone hear me?"

Does he hear an echo, or is it the resonance of his own skull? If he does, is it in another voice, another accent?

"Hello?"

Hello.

And the white: is it moving, are there shapes within it, like figures in a fog? Ashwin is sure now; the fog boils like milk and he can sense up and down, forward, back. Dimensions. Gravity. Slowly he becomes aware that he has a body, his own body, his home flesh. There is a surface under his feet, and there is a human shape walking toward him through the white fog. A white man in a white fog, an old man, dressed for cold, with a compass in his hand. He steps into clear focus and frowns at Ashwin.

"Who the hell are you?" he says.

***

A milky blue box on a living-room table. A photonic array tumbling over Terra Tyrrhena. Calculations made in billions of parallel universes. Each computer contains the other, and millions more besides.

The machines that are building Mars have more than just the viewpoint of gods. They have something of the power. Quantum computing, quantum engineering. If calculations can be made in multiple universes, one of which supplies the perfect solution, how much simpler to cut out the application of that answer and cut straight to the result? It's mere extension of theory into practice to take those solutions out of the abstract into the real world. Model a thousand, a million, a billion quantum Mars; a slew of possibilities from Barsoom at one end of the probability spread to tripod fighting machines and delicate crystal cities at the other. Humped along the bell-shaped curve in the middle, the likelier, possible Marses. Simple school algebra will give you the best likely solution. Output, and let that be your reality. Terraforming by quantum leap. Nudges along the path to inhabitability. More than terraforming. Whole-universe-forming. The quantum machines, the AIs that have, in the private mindspaces where humans cannot go, given themselves the names and natures of angels, have always understood that reality is a construct of language. They know what the shamans knew; that words, whether in primal chant or machine code, have power over the physical universe.

And somewhere in that polyverse, lies that answer that makes the theory real, and, by the gods whose power they have usurped, the machines are going to have a go at it. But what kind of Mars? Whose dreams will frame it? An old cosmonaut, left on the pad like a jilted bride, who casually asked a foolish prophetic question of a plastic box. A young construction worker, who is shown the glory every day and every night has it taken away from him, whose mind is sent spinning across space by quantum computers. These, certainly, and others besides, millions of others, brought to this place that is white with the light of millions of universes, to speak their dreams and tell their stories.

***

"Well, I could as well argue you're my illusion," Antti Selkokari said to the young Indian man standing before him barefoot in an incongruous paper coverall. "After all, I can understand you and you can understand me, And where does that happen except in dreams? And you're hardly dressed for the cold. You'd be dead after ten minutes in that, where I come from."

"And what about you?" Ashwin Mehta argued. "An old man with a compass? Very allegorical."

"All right, then," Antti said. "We'll agree that each is a figment of the other's imagination. So, then, who imagined all these?"

Figures were advancing through the white fog on all sides. Men, women, children, all ages and races and stations, walking patiently, silently. Between them, Antti and Ashwin saw other figures emerging from indeterminacy. Beyond them, yet others. The two lost men stood at the center of a great congregation of people.

"Who are you?" Antti demanded, more bold than Ashwin in the face of a faceless mass. "Where is this place? What do you want?"

A woman stepped forward. She was small, dressed in a simple shift frock, barefoot, her hair badly cut, urchin crop. She had soft black eyes and when she spoke, both men heard her in their own tongues, with an American accent. She said, "In answer to your questions: first; my folk don't really do names—we're AIs—but if you want to call me something, call me Catherine. It's as good as any. Second: that entirely depends on you, all, but at the moment it might help to think of yourselves as individuals accidentally caught up in an experimental superimposed quantum state. Or a convocation, if that helps. Third: your stories. Your visions. Your hopes. Your Marses."

Silence across the white plain. The shabby little woman turned to the great mass of people.

"Hey! It's your world. You all have a say in it. Say nothing, and that bit goes unsaid. Your works build it, your stories tell it. Listen: quantum reality is information, pure and simple. Language defines what's real: it's the same for AIs as it is for humans. Deep down, everything is a story. We're all tales. Tell me. Tell me your stories. We've got a world to build, and build it right."

Against reason, Antti found words bubbling up in his throat. They were not demands for explanations that made sense, to be shown the way home. They were heart words, old memories and passions surging up like water from a deep aquifer struck by a well. It was a story of Mars, and the story of his own life.

He told of the night with the crisp of autumn first on the air when his father lit a bonfire on the beach and his children, following the sparks up into the night sky, had seen one that did not fly and fade. "That is no spark," he remembered his father saying. "That is another world. Its name is Mars." Another world! As complete and self-contained and full as this. A childhood of frequent illnesses was self-educated with old *People's Encyclopedias*. Short on the rest of the world, but long on the wonders of astronomy. Sitting up late, late to listen to the beep on the radio that was Sputnik calling Earth. Again, that hot summer day when his father came running from the house to call him in from football to see the pictures of the capitalists walking on the Moon.

"That was when I decided I wanted to be a cosmonaut," Antti said. "The Americans had put their flag on the Moon, but Mars, Red Mars; that was always ours."

As he spoke, he became aware of the young man Ashwin's voice, telling his own story: a strange and mighty one, of a world very alien to his own, and all the other voices on this featureless white plain, telling their tales and dreams of that little red light in the night.

Antti told then of the Air Force, when it had been a thing of pride and honor, and the passion and energy of young men who drive themselves toward a single ambition. The trials, the tests, the skills, the physical rigors and disciplines, the sacramental hours alone in the training jet, up on the lonely edge of the world, only the stars above him. The tensor mathematics would have finished him had he not found the humility to go home to his father, a schoolteacher, and ask his help.

"And cosmonaut training!"

It was only after that Kazakhstan morning, when ATOM 12 died, that Antti Selkokari realized his entire life and energy had been focused on that red dot in the sky, like a laser sight. As he told of the hours in the centrifuge, the constant medical testing—his childhood sickness a permanent dread—the team-building exercises, the Kamchatka survival course, the hours in the underwater tank, the hours and hours in the mock-ups and simulators, doing it over and over and over and over until they could do it blindfolded; the hours and hours and hours at the desks in front of the blackboards, working it out again and again and again. The crew interviews; how he thought his heart would stop when the letter came with the crest of the space agency, yet his fingers had no hesitation ripping it open. He still could not remember what it said beyond the key words. Glad. Successful. Mars. *Novy Mir.* Report.

He told about Milena. How overjoyed she had been, how proud! A cosmonaut's wife! They celebrated with Cuban cigars and good vodka. A party member's daughter could get the good stuff. She came at him fast and hot that night: there was a child to be conceived. A keep-safe, in case. Space was big. Radiation hard. Mars far and cold. Unflinching how it had all fallen apart, afterward. The failure had not been his, but it is a sin women do not forgive.

That morning, always coming back to that morning. The cold; clear Kazakhstan light; the jokes in the back of the truck that died one by one as they drew nearer to the great white rocket. The frosting he had noticed on the rippled white skin as they rode up the elevator, helmets under their arms. The cameraman crouching beside the gantry, their nonchalant waves. *Hi, we're going to Mars!* Vorontsev, Nitin, Rozdev-shensky, Selkokari. The startled birds flapping across the steppe. The hatch dogging, screwing the umbilical into the LSU. The startled grunt on the intercom as Mission Commander Rozdevshensky was told something they could not hear and he could not quite believe. The dogs turning. The ray of golden morning light. Barsamian's hand reaching in: *come now, quick now, get unfastened there and come with me.* The ride down in the elevator. The ride no one had ever thought to take. The van bouncing over the rutted dirt road to the control bunker, and the word from Kirilenko that the thing was poisoned, had always been poisoned, was nothing but a tool in Politburo maneuvers.

From his trip to Mars, Antti Selkokari brought back a Kazakh rug and a fabric badge with the names of the crew of *Novy Mir.* He brought them home to the wooden house by the Baltic that had been his father's and, since his death, was now his, his alone. A party official invited himself for tea to tell Cosmonaut Selkokari Mars was dead, no one was going now or ever, never to mention Mars; forget Mars, but even then their authority was on the wane and Antti had nodded and signed the forms and consents and that night gone out on the pale sand beach to look up at that red dot in the sky. First loves are enduring loves.

As he spoke, Antti became aware that the other voices telling their tales of their Marses were fading; the figures, though still pressed close as far as he could see into the white, were becoming less distinct. They became whispers, shadows, until all that remained with any clarity was the Indian youth, confessing his hopes and dreams for the world he was building, a world for all the dispossessed; with trains! Trains! Antti smiled. The construction worker smiled back and, like the cat in that English children's story he never liked, faded too, the white of the smile lingering. Back to his future, his universe, his incomplete solution to Mars. Now Antti was alone with the ragged little woman, the saint, the angel, the artificial intelligence.

"Will this do?" he asked. "It's all I have."

"This will do very well," she said, turned, and was gone, too.

Antti was alone in the featureless white, and, as if held in abeyance, the cold rushed in.

Time, he knew, had restarted somewhere. And space. Space! The compass. He flipped it open. The needle quested, then settled firmly on north. Antti tapped it. No lie. As if in confirmation, he heard a dog barking, muffled, but closing with every yap. It came bowling out of the white, breath steaming, curling up in itself, wagging its tail furiously in its delight to have found him. It made to jump up, Antti stepped back.

"Enough of that!" It cringed. "Here! Hutttt! Heel!"

Too much to expect of such a creature, but it did draw close, looking up at him, and together they followed the way the compass said to home, man and mongrel.

***

Before the train has even come to a halt the roof-riders are swinging down over the doors and windows, hitting the platform at a run, some slipping and falling, some hitting into people waiting for the train out. Racing to beat the crowd. Racing to get home. Work. Home. Sleep. Work.

Every other evening, Ashwin would have been among the first of the first. Tonight, he waits for the roof to empty around him. He looks up at the fragmented station dome. The memories of the time that was not a time in that other place that was not a place are less clear now. In time they will fade. All such encounters with the numinous, the miraculous must. It is written.

Quantum interference, they said in the medical center. *A random superposition of states. Less than a second, no permanent damage done.* But in that second, he had flat-lined. Brain-dead. Mind . . . elsewhere. Elsewhen. The *corporada* doctors ran their diagnostics and did their tests and pronounced him fit to work and travel. It would have cost too much money to have pronounced him anything else.

New passengers are scrambling up as Ashwin climbs down from the train. He passes through the ceaseless, changeless bustle of the station in a state of beatification.

I've seen you all, over there, in the new world. I told them

*about you, what you needed, what you dreamed. It may be
your future, it may be someone else's future, but I spoke for
you. And somebody listened.*

In the square a great crowd has gathered, all attention
turned to the street where the holy woman has buried herself
alive. The kids have got off their scooters and are peering,
questing over the heads, *What's happening, what's going on?*
The band is playing like a pack of maniacs and over the general hubbub Ashwin can hear the *sadhus* proclaiming loudly
that a miracle has taken place, a miracle, a sign for corrupt,
materialist days. This woman! This holy woman! For five days
she has mortified the flesh in the earth, she has practiced the
fiercest of asceticisms, she has come forth and she has
achieved *samadhi.*

From the top of the station steps, Ashwin catches sight of
her. She is smaller than he had imagined and, despite five days
fasting in the earth, plumper. her hair is wound in a long greasy
pigtail, and a circle of *sadhus* surrounds her, proclaiming her
virtues to the crowd, who thrust out their hands to be touched,
to take some of her spirituality. But something stops her.
Something turns her head. She looks up. She seeks out Ashwin
on the far side of the crowd. Their eyes lock.

I saw you, there, Ashwin thinks. *And you saw me. We know
each other. We know what we have done.*

Self-mortification as a quantum state? What are the physics
of the soul?

He nods. The holy woman smiles, then goes back to her
adoration. Ashwin skirts the crowd, then the smell stops him.
It has been a long, strange day of hard work. he could eat the
beard of the *sadhu.* He might trouble the *datarajah* for another
of his chapatis, he thinks.

***

The thing ate like a pig. Worse, for a pig, despite its lack of
grace, has some utility. He had put his life on the line out there
on the ice (*and beyond*, something whispers) and it hadn't
even the grace to look up from its food bowl.

Displacement, Antti thought. *It's the boy you are really an-
noyed with. He went straight to the dog, not to you. What did*

*you expect? But you cannot be angry with our grandson. So
curse his dog, and watch it scatter its food that looks and
smells like shit over the kitchen floor.*

Paavo had that look he got when he wanted to lecture his
father again for his stupidity. Antti knew that he would say it
was a bad example to Yuri, going out on the ice alone, not
leaving a note, a message—why, he even has a GPS tracker in
the car—trusting your life to some ancient compass. All for
Yuri's benefit, but it would be son to father. Strange, the nu-
ances of parents. Everything mediated through the children.

Nursing his mug of coffee—shot through with the last of
the night's good Polish vodka—Antti excused himself from
the kitchen table.

"If that thing has to pee, take it out on a bit of string," he
admonished Yuri.

He hesitated at the door to his study. All that Mars, shut inside. Hallucination? People did go crazy in whiteout. Winter-
mad. And he knew he had been closer to hypothermia out there
than he liked to think. But it had seemed so real, so true. He
had told those people things he had not even told his own son,
certainly not the woman who had been his wife. Things he had
only alluded to with his truest family; the brethren of rocke-
teers and Areologists and Mars dreamers.

He opened the door, peeked in. There, in the corner, a
glimpse of another world: a ragbag place that held the dreams
of everyone who had ever looked up into the autumn sky and
wondered at that little red fast traveler. Ten thousand cities
under a glass roof. SkyWheels and moon rings and terraforming machines and reality shaping angels and airship legions
and trains the size of ocean liners. And more, so much more;
more wonders. As many wonders and incongruities as only a
real world can hold. And people. Of course, people. People
make it a world. Their stories, their words, their never-ceasing
definition of its reality. Without them, it is just a planet. Dead.

He looked again and it was just badges and models and toy
spaceships hanging from the ceiling on fishing line. He closed
the door. He would take his coffee in the living room. He could
poke some life into the embers of the other night; there was
wood, he might coax up a blaze. He settled in his chair,
watched curls of red creep across the charcoals, almost alive.

The quantum computer still stood open on the table. Antti turned it to him. His wish, his prophecy, burned on the screen. WHAT WILL HAPPEN TO MY DREAM OF MARS? He closed the blue plastic lid and settled down to have his coffee.

A WALK ACROSS MARS

by Allen Steele

IT'S an image which has remained with us for over twenty-five years, one which appears in every history textbook, has been printed on posters and digitalized on countless web sites. It's familiar even to those who hadn't been born yet and thus don't remember when it was on the front page of every newspaper in the world. It's more famous than the picture of Neil Armstrong descending the ladder of *Ares 2* or the one of Alexei Leonov standing on the Martian surface between the raised flags of the United States and the Union of Soviet Socialist Republics. It looks like this . . .

Two men in Mars suits caked with red dust, struggling across the stony tundra of Utopia Planitia. The figure on the right is barely able to walk: his right leg is limp and twisted, his boot dragging against the ground. His left arm is clumsily draped across the shoulders of the figure on the left, who somehow manages to stand erect; his right arm is wrapped around his comrade's waist, his left hand raised toward the camera. The astronaut on the right is looking down, but the man on the left stares straight at us; his helmet's sun visor is raised, and we can see his face: haggard, exhausted, grimly determined to stay alive.

You've seen this photo countless times. I shouldn't have to remind you what it's about. Lieutenant Commander Jeffrey Carroll and Major David Park, two American members of the International Mars Expedition, returning to Utopia Base after being lost on Mars for eighteen hours. During what should have been a routine sortie, their rover rolled down a dry river channel nearly twenty miles from camp. The rover lost pressure and its high-gain antenna was snapped off, and Park's leg was broken, yet both men managed to survive the crash. With long-distance radio contact with *Ares 1* lost and only four tanks of air between the two of them, they set out across the unmapped wilderness, Carroll half-carrying Park as they fought their way through the cold Martian night until, midway through the following morning, they came within sight of Utopia Base.

The picture was taken by Sergei Roskov, the first man to reach Carroll and Park, and it came to symbolize the International Mars Expedition. There may never be another Mars mission; nearly three decades later, public opinion is still divided over how worthwhile it may have been to spend nearly $100 billion on a project which resulted in few tangible benefits. Yet only the most cynical can deny that Carroll and Park's ordeal was the great story of 1976 . . . and twenty-five years later, everyone still wants to know how these two men remained alive against all odds.

I know. And God help me, I wish I didn't.

***

I'm a word doctor.

When someone asks me what I do for a living, I tell them I'm a writer, and when they ask me what I write, I say that I'm a biographer, yet both descriptions are inadequate and somewhat elusive. Oh I've written a couple of novels, but I've seldom met anyone who has ever read them; my third book was a biography of John F. Kennedy, but since few people today remember the Massachusetts senator who lost to Nixon in the 1960 presidential election, there's not much point in mentioning it. Yet the JFK book received a few favorable reviews—*Publishers Weekly* called it "one of the best political biographies of the past few years"—and a couple of editors took notice.

Not long after the Kennedy book was published, someone I knew at Random House phoned to ask whether I was interested in doing a little rewrite work on an autobiography of . . . well, since my contract forbids me from identifying her, let's put it this way: she's a legendary film actress, she's not very bright, and she once slept with Jack. Random House paid her a large advance for her memoirs, but she seemed to be having trouble with it—two years later, all she had produced were ten pages—and her editor felt that the time had come for someone else to come in and give her a little advice and assistance.

Advice and assistance. The next time you see a best-seller allegedly written by an actor, a sports figure, a rock star, or a major politician—that is, a celebrity who shouldn't have enough time, talent, or intelligence to write a book—flip to the acknowledgments page. Somewhere in there, usually near the bottom, will be something like this: ". . . and many thanks to so-and-so, for all his advice and assistance in writing these memoirs."

Chances are, this is the person who really wrote the book. The celeb may have gone so far as to actually write the first draft, but more often than not a ghostwriter cobbled together the book from a handful of notes and several hours of tape-recorded interviews. The real author receives a flat fee for his or her work, but it's the celeb who does the book tours and makes late-night guest appearances with David, Conan, and Jay. It's not a book so much as it is another consumer item featuring their likeness, no different than a cereal box or a wall calendar.

The actress' memoirs sold a couple of million copies, and word got around that I was a reliable wordsmith. Over the course of the next several years, I rendered advice and assistance to a rapper who could barely spell his real name, an actor whom I interviewed in his trailer between takes of his next Oscar-nominated film, a Colorado congressman with presidential aspirations (my least successful project; his autobiography was published the week after he finished last in the New Hampshire primary), and a radio talk-show host who spent most of his time lying about the size of his . . . um, microphone. I receive my usual mid-five figure fee for these book products, which resemble literature in much the same way that cheese product tastes like cheese, and when I feel creative I bang out mystery stories. Yes, I'm a hack, but I'm a damn good hack. It pays the rent, and it beats working for living.

In the autumn of 2000, I got a call from a certain editor with whom I had worked before, wondering if I was presently available. I wanted to work on a novel, my first in quite some time, but Christmas was just a few months away and I needed the money. So I asked who the author was, and my friend in New York told me it was Jeffrey Carroll.

I'm not a space buff, but I was aware that he was one of the men in that famous photo. The editor informed me that, twelve months earlier, Jeff Carroll had quietly signed a contract for his memoirs. The deal had been in the seven-figure range, yet his publisher considered it a good investment. After all, Jeff Carroll was not only the pilot who had managed to guide *Ares 2* to a safe landing despite unexpected difficulties, but he was also the man who had carried Dave Park back to Utopia Base. Even more than Alexei Leonov or Neil Armstrong, the coleaders of the International Mars Expedition, he was considered the hero of the *Ares* mission. Leonov had produced his memoir, *Journey to A Red Planet,* almost twenty years ago—a bestseller then, now out of print and largely forgotten—and Armstrong had remained reticent about his role in history, preferring an anonymous life in Ohio. A heart attack had killed Park six years ago, so no one would ever get his side of the story. This left Carroll as the *Ares* alumnus most likely to produce a *New York Times* best-seller.

Yet nearly a year had gone by, and Carroll hadn't delivered so much as an outline. When the editor phoned Carroll's literary agent to inquire about the delay, he was told that Jeff Carroll had recently been diagnosed with liver cancer. Although chemotherapy had knocked it into remission, no one was sure how much longer he would live. Carroll still wanted to publish his memoirs—in fact, now faced with his own mortality, the former astronaut was determined to tell his story—yet it was no longer possible for him to write the book himself.

Was I interested in taking the job? Of course I was, and not just because the money was good. For some time now, I had wanted to write about someone whose fame had come from something less ephemeral than pop culture. Jeffrey Carroll wasn't the product of starmaking machinery; he had once walked on Mars, and this was a more significant achievement than making movies or cutting rap albums.

So I told the editor to fax me a contract, and that's how I became Jeff Carroll's confessor.

***

Jeffrey Carroll lived in western Massachusetts, his home an eighteenth century cedar-shingle farmhouse on a hilltop outside Northampton. A country road no one can find without specific directions, a mailbox with only a number on it, and a view of the Holyoke mountain range: if you wanted to get away from everyone, you couldn't do much better.

His live-in nurse answered the door: a broad-shouldered woman in her mid-fifties, no-nonsense yet polite and soft-spoken in a Yankee sort of way. Since Jeff Carroll's former wife Patty had passed away several years ago—indeed, they had divorced only a couple of months after he returned from Mars—and they didn't have any children, she was the only person who saw Carroll on a daily basis. After taking my coat and offering me a cup of coffee, Dorothy led me through the living room. I caught a brief glimpse of various mementos—a group photo of the *Ares* crew, a wood model of the *Ares 2* lander, his Congressional Medal of Honor framed above the fieldstone hearth—before we reached the glass door leading to a screened-in back porch.

She opened it quietly, peered outside. "You awake?" she asked softly. A pause. "The writer's here." Another pause, then she stepped aside. "He's expecting you. Go on. I'll bring you your coffee."

In all the pictures I'd seen of Jeffrey Carroll during my preliminary research, he had been a robust, dark-haired man with stylish '70s sideburns, his demeanor usually taciturn although the camera had occasionally caught a wry grin. That wasn't the person who waited for me on his back porch; pale and shrunken, nearly bald save for a few wisps of white hair, seated in a steel-frame wheelchair with a blanket around his waist even though it was a warm Indian summer afternoon. He was sixty-nine years old. He could have easily passed for ninety.

The years hadn't been kind to him, and he knew it. Carroll peered at me through heavy-lidded eyes. "Who were you expecting?" he rasped. "Neil Armstrong?"

"No, sir," I said. "Never met him."

It was the best I could manage, but he seemed to think it was funny. He grinned and favored me with a dry laugh. "You and me both, and I went to Mars with him. Either he's the smartest guy I've ever known or . . ."

He stopped, shook his head. "Never mind. Rule one . . . let the living speak for themselves. And if we slander the dead, they're just going to have to sue." The grin faded, and he gave me a sharp look. "Think you can live with that?"

There was a wicker chair across from him. I settled into it, placing my notebook and cassette recorder on the low table between us. "No problem at all, Colonel. Besides, the dead can't sue for libel . . ."

"Nice thing to know. Rule two . . . I'm Jeff. Haven't been a colonel in twenty years . . . twenty-two years . . . whatever." His gaze drifted toward the mowed hayfield beyond his porch. The fall foliage was at its peak; reddish-gold maple leaves lay across the yellow meadow, the wooded hillside draped with harlequin colors. He savored this beauty through the eyes of a man who knew he wouldn't see another autumn.

"This is supposed to be when we get to know each other," he said. "Small talk about things that don't matter . . . how your flight was, how my day has been, how cold it was here this morning, how it's still warm where you live." He sighed. "But you know, there comes a time when . . . well, you just don't have any time left to waste. No offense, but let's just get on with it, okay?"

He was dying, and he was telling me this was to be his final testament. Without bothering to ask his permission to do so, I reached forward to switch on my recorder. He must have heard the sound, for he glanced in my direction. "You ready?" he asked, and I nodded. "Okay, let's get started."

I opened my notebook, flipped to the first page of the questions I wanted to ask. "So, Colonel . . . Jeff, I mean . . . when were you born?"

He ignored me. Still gazing at the autumn hills, he began to speak. "On Wednesday, July 28, 1976, I tried to kill Dave

Park . . ." And then he looked back at me. "Or would you rather that I start at the beginning?"

***

The relationship between Jeff Carroll and Dave Park went back almost fifteen years, when they were recruited from their respective services—the Navy for Carroll, the Air Force for Park—for the U.S. Space Force astronaut training program. At first they were little more than fighter jocks vying for the same job, yet as they made their way through the program, the two men developed a deep friendship. Although there was often cutthroat rivalry among the other candidates, Carroll and Park preferred to work together rather than try to trip up the other guy. They helped each other cram for exams, supported one another during survival training in Arizona, and worked together to figure out how to beat the cockpit simulators. The washout rate was high; although sixty rookies tried out for the USSF during the summer of 1962, only twenty remained eight weeks later. It came as no surprise to anyone that both Carroll and Park received their astronaut wings and were formally invited to join the USSF.

In retrospect, it was easy to see why the pair got along so well, for they had much in common. Both were originally from the South—Jeff Carroll born and raised in Virginia, Dave Park a Florida native—and both had joined the armed services with the ambition of becoming fliers, although only Carroll had seen active duty as a carrier pilot aboard the U.S.S. *Nimitz* while Park was stationed in West Germany. Both had married their teenage sweethearts; Patty Carroll met her future husband when he had played center on the high school football team, and Louise Park found Dave when they had worked together on the yearbook staff. Both were clean-cut, conservative young men who voted Republican, regularly attended church, and had no trouble with being straight arrows at a time when many guys their age were letting their hair grow over their collars and smoking reefers.

"Maybe that's hard to swallow, but we liked it that way." Thirty years later, there was a wistful smile on Jeff Carroll's face. "I mean, here was all this stuff breaking out all over . . .

antiwar protests, sit-ins at lunch counters . . . and we just didn't want to have anything to do with it. Dave and I had our own agenda."

"You wanted to go into space."

"Right on." He laughed, a little self-conscious about using an expression he probably disdained when it was popular. "So far as we were concerned, there was only one thing worth doing, and that was beating the Russians to the Moon." He gave me a sidewise wink. "And, of course, we wanted to be there when it happened."

Yet history didn't work in their favor. While Jeff became a pilot for the Atlas-class shuttles which regularly lifted off from Merritt Island, ferrying into orbit the components of Space Station One, Dave opted instead to train as navigator for the lunar reconnaissance mission scheduled to be a precursor to *Eagle One*. Each man thought his career choices would put him on the shortlist for the first lunar expedition; indeed, Dave was aboard the *Columbus* when it flew around the Moon on Christmas Eve, 1968. Yet Jeff continued to be a shuttle jockey long after *Eagle One* touched down in the Sea of Tranquillity; he and his best friend sat in the TV room of Jeff's house in Cocoa Beach, drinking beer and trying not to feel sorry for themselves the night they watched John Harper Wilson set foot on the Moon.

"Why did you get passed up?"

"Politics." Jeff shrugged. "Officially, I was told I was too valuable as an *Atlas* pilot, and Dave was told that he got the cut because he'd been to the Moon once already. But the fact of the matter was that the Space Force was already on the way out, and I guess we were seen as being part of the old guard."

Dorothy returned to make sure he was comfortable. She asked if I wanted another cup of coffee; I told her I did, and took the opportunity to flip the cassette. Jeff waited until I was ready, then continued.

"The night Johnny Wilson walked on the Moon, Dave and I got drunk. I mean, really loaded. Whiskey, beer . . . we were gonzo. My place was on the beach, so we left the girls behind and went for a long walk on the sand. Just hanging onto each other, not knowing whether we wanted to laugh or cry, doing a little of both. And somewhere along the way, I fell down on my knees and . . . I dunno, maybe it was just the booze, but I made a solemn vow.

" 'Screw the Moon,' I said, 'we're going to Mars. You and me, man, we're going to Mars.' And Dave said, 'I'm with you. Hell or high water, we're going to Mars.' "

It may have been a drunken vow, yet they both remembered it. Robert F. Kennedy was the new President, and he favored the creation of a new civilian space agency which would pursue nonmilitary objectives. On September 6, 1969, Congress passed the Space Act which established the National Aeronautics and Space Administration. NASA needed a major objective to justify its existence, and the Russians had become interested in establishing detente with the Americans, so ten months later the US and the USSR signed the International Space Treaty which, among other things, called for a joint American-Russian expedition to Mars.

With the USSF being phased out, many Space Force astronauts tendered their resignations. Carroll and Park stayed on, however, and when NASA and Glavkosmos began putting together the twelve-man team for the International Mars Expedition, they found themselves near the top of the list. On September 2, 1971, the prime crew for Project Ares was publicly announced during a Washington press conference. Colonel Neil Armstrong and Colonel Alexei Leonov were presented as the mission's coleaders, and standing next to them were Lieutenant Commander Jeffrey Carroll, the pilot of *Ares 2,* and Major Dave Park, the navigator of *Ares 1.*

"That was the proudest moment of my life, being introduced as the man who'd land a ship on Mars," Jeff says. "There was a reception for us that evening at the White House, and after it was over, Dave and I went back to the Hilton. We got out of our monkey suits and had a nightcap in the bar. A quiet little celebration, just the two of us. We were on our way to Mars. Nothing could stop us now."

Yet there was no warmth in his eyes, no trace of nostalgia in his voice. "I didn't know it then, but that was the last night we'd meet as friends."

***

Shortly after Christmas, 1971, the six American members of the *Ares* flight crew relocated to Houston, where they would undergo mission training at the Von Braun Manned Space Center for the next four years. No one liked moving to Texas. Their families had established roots in Florida; the nearest beach was hundreds of miles away, and instead of Route A1A and Disneyworld all Houston had to offer were miles of strip malls and the NFL's worst football team. Not only that, but every two or three months the astronauts had to fly to the USSR, where they would spend several weeks training with their Russian teammates at the Star City complex.

"It may have been tough for us, but it was even worse for our families." Jeff shakes his head. "Patty never saw me except on the rare weekend or holiday . . . sometimes not even then. Dave was in Houston a little more frequently than I was, but I don't think he saw much of Louise either. By then they had a little boy, Scott, but . . . well, I don't think Dave got much chance to see his boy grown up.

"After the first few months, I started to notice a change in Patty. She became distant. We'd always been close, never keeping anything from each other. Even when we argued . . . and, y'know, old married couples often quarrel, because that's the way they hash out their problems . . . we always ended up the same way. Usually in bed." A reticent smile, quickly gone. "But now there wasn't even that. We'd have a disagreement over something, and she'd simply surrender. 'Whatever you want, Jeff,' even when I knew she didn't like it. But we didn't . . . I mean, she wouldn't . . . ."

"A problem with sex?"

His face darkened and he glanced away. This wasn't something he was comfortable talking about. "When we . . . when we did it, it wasn't because she wanted to. Before we moved to Houston, there had never been . . . y'know, that sort of problem. Now I was spending twelve, sometimes sixteen hours a day at the space center, and then I'd be gone for a few weeks, either off to Russia or up to the Wheel, and then I'd come home and . . . well, she simply didn't want to be with me."

All of a sudden, he became impatient. Tossing aside his blanket, Jeff raised himself from his wheelchair, let his felt slippers touch the floor for the first time. "It's too cold out here," he muttered, reaching for the gnarled walking stick resting against the wall. "Dorothy! Coming in!"

The porch door opened, banged shut. His nurse gently helped Jeff hobble across the porch, scolding him for walking without permission. I looked away as she guided him into the house; for the first time, I noticed the aluminum bedpan tucked beneath his wheelchair. Dorothy returned a minute later; she gave me an apologetic smile as she picked up the bedpan. "Give us a moment," she said quietly, then she whisked through the porch door into the living room.

I made a few notes, put in a fresh tape. Early afternoon; the day was warm, but a northern breeze had come in, rustling the fallen leaves beneath the porch. Looking out over the mountains, I noticed a daytime moon hovering in the bright blue sky. Jeff Carroll never went there, but Dave Park was one of the first men to see its far side. I found myself wondering what it must be like to see another world, not as a distant and abstract object but as a real thing. . . .

But when you're so far from Earth, what is it that you leave behind?

"You can come in now." Framed within the porch door, Dorothy waited for me. "He's a little tired, but he wants to go on." And, softly: "Please . . . be gentle. This is taking a lot out of him."

I picked up my recorder and notebook. The interview would continue, but I doubted it would be gentle. There were too many secrets, and my subject was unburdening himself of them, one at a time.

***

Ares 2, the larger of the two ships which went to Mars, was a monster. With a wingspan of 450 feet and weighing more than 1,800 tons, it was the largest vehicle ever assembled in space. Twenty-one *Atlas* flights were needed to carry its components up from the Cape, and sixteen more to bring up the pieces of *Ares 1,* the passenger vessel which would remain in orbit above Mars and eventually bring the crew back to Earth.

During the winters of '74 and '75, Jeff Carroll was a regular visitor to Space Station One. His training in Houston and

Russia now largely complete, one of his major tasks was overseeing construction of *Ares 2*. It wasn't easy. Several racks of electrical cable were laid in backward, two of the enormous fuel spheres belonging to the booster stage had hairline fractures which weren't discovered until after the spheres were test-pressurized, and one of the astronauts building the vehicle was killed while the return rocket was being mated to the wing fuselage. Jeff found himself sleeping more often in a narrow berth aboard the Wheel than in his own bed back home, and sometimes it would be weeks before he'd see his front lawn again.

"And all this time, Dave was in Houston." As he spoke, Jeff gazed at the polished wooden model of *Ares 2* upon the coffee table. "Most of his training was now being done in the simulator at Von Braun, so he wasn't going to Russia quite so often, and once *Ares 1* was finished, he came up to the Wheel only a couple of times. I'd see him now and then, usually during mission briefings, and we'd say hello, sometimes grab lunch. I'd ask how Louise was doing, and he'd ask how Patty was doing, but . . . well, since we weren't seeing much of either of them, it was just polite conversation."

He was looking at the framed photo of his late wife, placed on the rough oak mantle above the fireplace. Dorothy quietly entered the living room, the floor creaking beneath her rubber-soled shoes. "Then one night in late May, just after the Memorial Day weekend, I returned early from a trip to the Wheel. Wasn't supposed to be back for another day or so, but at the last minute I managed to snag a ride back to the Cape aboard a cargo shuttle, then grabbed a commercial flight out of Orlando to Houston. Patty's birthday was coming up, and I wanted some time to go shopping for her."

He picked up a glass of water, took a sip. "It was raining that night, really coming down hard. Didn't get home till around midnight. I was about to pull into the driveway when I saw there was already a car parked in front of the garage. I recognized it at once . . . it was Dave's Camero."

He glanced at me. "Guess you can already see where this is leading, right?" I said nothing, and he went on. "Anyway, I drove down the street, then circled back and parked across from the house under a tree. Turned off the engine and waited.

About a half hour went by, then the front door opened. Someone came out . . . he was wearing a raincoat with the hood
pulled up over his head . . . and he stopped on the porch. I saw
Patty for a moment . . . she was standing just inside the door,
wearing her robe . . . and then the guy in the raincoat turned
around and kissed her.

A pause. "He kissed her. That's what I saw. Then he dashed
out to his car and got in. The car started up, backed out of the
driveway, and went down the street. Patty shut the door, and a
couple of minutes later I saw the upstairs lights go out."

Jeff looked away. "I sat out there for a good, long time . . .
another hour at least . . . not knowing what to do, not even
what to think. Or maybe I was thinking lots of things. After a
while I started up the car, pulled into my driveway, got out,
and walked into my house just like I always did. Had a glass
of milk in the kitchen, then went upstairs. Patty was asleep, so
I put on my pajamas and crawled into bed, trying not to wake
her. The next morning I told her I had come home late, but I
didn't tell her what I'd seen."

"You didn't . . .?"

He shook his head. "No . . . not then, or later. And I didn't
take it up with Dave either. Not that I wasn't tempted. When I
saw him the next day, I was ready to punch him through the
wall. Instead I left the room, went to the bathroom, and threw
some cold water on my face. After that, I tried to have as little
to do with him as possible . . . but I never touched him, never
made any threats, never said a word about what I had seen."

His eyes met mine. "And you know why? Because I wanted
to go to Mars."

Regardless of how angry or hurt he was, Jeff Carroll knew
that, if he confronted Dave Park or separated from his wife, it
would mean the end of his involvement with *Ares*. Just like the
Space Force, NASA management was preoccupied with pro-
jecting a squeaky-clean public image; astronauts had been
grounded for as little reason as being spotted drinking in a bar.
Dave was all too aware that, if anyone discovered that one
American member of the *Ares* team was having an affair with
the wife of another member, they both would be dismissed
from the mission and replaced by members of the backup

crew. Therefore, Jeff couldn't tell anyone what he had seen that night—not Patty, and not even Dave.

"I just . . ." He sighed, shook his head. "I just let it go. Chalked it up as a one-night stand, maybe a bad mistake. Whatever the reason, I fell out of love with Patty that night, and Dave was no longer my friend. I tried to pretend like nothing happened. I never saw Dave's car at my house again, but Patty didn't seem to mind when I started sleeping in the guest room. I tried to make love to her a couple of times, but . . . well, it wasn't the same. She just went through the motions, and after the second time, I gave up."

"And what about Dave?"

"Dave was . . ." Jeff considers the question, looked away. "Dave was my navigator. I needed him to get to Mars. And that's all there was to it."

***

On November 2, 1975, *Ares 1* and *Ares 2* simultaneously fired their main engines, and the two giant spacecraft began the long voyage to Mars.

Spending eight months in close quarters with a man who'd been sleeping with your wife might seem intolerable, yet *Ares 1*'s crew sphere had three decks, and when that wasn't room enough, there were many occasions to taxi over to *Ares 2*. Although it soon became obvious to everyone aboard that Carroll and Park weren't getting along, neither was there any outright animosity. Dave stayed away from Jeff, and Jeff . . .

"I blocked it out." Nestling a mug of hot chocolate against his stomach, Carroll leaned back in his chair. With late afternoon setting in, Dorothy brought some split wood and stoked a fire in the hearth, then retreated to an armchair on the other side of the living room. "Just put it out of my mind as best I could. I played chess with the Russians, wrote in my journal, rehearsed landing procedures with Neil. That sort of thing. When Dave and I had to interact with each other, we did so as professionally as possible." He shrugs. "And that's how we went to Mars. Not as enemies, but not as friends either."

The months went past, each day grinding against the next, as Mars gradually swelled in size, growing from a red-tinted star to a distinct sphere. During this time, the crew regularly received messages from home. Because of the ever-increasing time delay, these communiques were usually transmitted as text messages, printed out on the com station's CRT screen. Although the Russians and most of the Americans received frequent letters from friends and family back home, Jeff seldom heard from Patty, and even then it was only the most terse greetings. On the other hand, Jeff observed that Dave received frequent letters from Louise. The fact that Louise Park was blissfully unaware that her husband recently had an affair with his best friend's wife rubbed salt in the wound, yet Jeff chose to bite his lip and look the other way. He turned his attention upon Mars, focused upon completing the mission.

It was good that he did so, for landing on Mars was more difficult than anyone expected. When the expedition reached its destination and *Ares 1* commenced its orbital survey, it was then that they found that the landing site was much rougher than expected. Instead of a vast plain of rolling dunes, Utopia Planitia was strewn with boulders, some large enough to damage the landing skids. Leonov was in favor of finding an alternate landing site, but Armstrong held out for Utopia Planitia; the terrain wasn't much better anywhere else they looked, and at least it was flat enough for the high-speed horizontal landing *Ares 2* was designed to make. Never once did anyone aboard seriously consider turning back, although many at NASA were in favor of aborting the mission.

On July 20, the ten members of the landing party boarded *Ares 2,* leaving two men aboard *Ares 1.* With Jeff Carroll in the left seat and Neil Armstrong in the right, the pilot fired the booster rockets for the final time, then jettisoned the stage and commenced the long, swift glide toward Mars.

Back on Earth, hundreds of millions of people were glued to their TVs, watching as Walter Cronkite and CBS science correspondent Arthur C. Clarke delivered a play-by-play commentary on the craft's perilous descent. In Houston, NASA flight controllers listened anxiously to the distant voices within their headsets, all too aware that, if something were to go catastrophically wrong, it would be fifteen minutes before they knew about it.

Yet within *Ares 2,* there was an almost eerie sense of calm. "No one really said anything on the way down," Jeff said, remembering the descent. "I just sat there, right hand on the stick, listening to Neil as he called out the numbers. I kept waiting for something to blow up, but it never did. In fact, it was easier than flying the simulator."

"Weren't you nervous?"

He smiled, shaking his head. "Not really. I knew that if we crashed, we'd be dead before we knew it. So long as we didn't crash, everything would be fine." He chuckled. "Besides, I was too busy handling that beast to have time to be scared."

False modesty or not, it was an extraordinary feat of flying. During the last few hundred feet of descent, Carroll spotted a stretch of ground which seemed a little less rocky; at the last possible moment, he turned the massive ship in that direction. Had he done otherwise, *Ares 2* would have touched down in the middle of a boulder field, possibly snapping one of the skids and causing the ship to crash. As it turned out, he brought *Ares 2* to a safe landing, albeit one which rattled their teeth.

"Once Neil informed Mission Control that we were on the ground and I raised the return rocket to take-off position, I just lay back and stared up through the canopy. Below me, I could hear the rest of the guys yelling at each other, yelling at me . . . they were going nuts." Carroll shrugged, picked up his water glass. "The only thing on my mind was how weird it was to see a pink sky."

***

The expedition had been on Mars for little more than a week when Jeff Carroll tried to kill Dave Park.

By then they had unloaded their equipment from the lander and had set up camp: three hemispherical inflated tents and a small, semi-rigid greenhouse, powered by a solar-cell array with a small nuclear generator as backup. The tents were cold at first, so much that the crew was reluctant to remove their suits after they cycled through the air lock, but after a couple of days the interior temperature rose to seventy-two degrees and they were able to walk around in shirtsleeves. Five men bunked in each of two tents—Carroll made sure that he didn't have to share quarters with Park—and the third tent served as laboratory, mess hall, and rec room. A narrow well was plunged through the floor of Tent Three, where it tapped into the permafrost layer deep beneath the Martian regolith. Six days after landing, they had enough water to drink, with even a little left over for the occasional sponge bath.

Once the explorers made themselves at home, the rover was lowered from the lander's cargo bay and assembled on the surface. Designed and built by General Motors, it had oversized wire-mesh tires, four-wheel drive, and was powered by photovoltaic cells. Its maximum distance was fifty miles, which meant that it could travel twenty-five miles in any direction before it had to turn around and come back. The ride was bumpy and its pressurized two-seat cab wasn't much larger than a Volkswagen Beetle, but everyone wanted to take it for a cruise. The first soil tests hadn't revealed the presence of microbiological life, and the water melted from the permafrost was sterile, but everyone was convinced that, if they drove just ten or fifteen miles thataway, they'd find an oasis hiding beyond the horizon.

"One night over dinner, Alexei drew up a list of survey teams," Jeff said. "He and Neil were on the first one, of course, and then everyone else got their turn. I intended to team up with Yuri Antonov, but before I could say so, Dave said he wanted to go out with me."

"I thought you two weren't getting along."

"We weren't. That's why it surprised me." Jeff shook his head. "I think Alexei was surprised, too, because he gave Dave and me an uncertain look. Like, 'you sure you want to do this?' But Dave seemed insistent, and I couldn't think of a good reason to object, so Alexei wrote down our names. We were the third team."

On the morning of July 28, Carroll and Park climbed aboard the rover and set out to the northeast. Their primary objective was a dry channel about twenty miles from Utopia Base; there they were to obtain core samples from beneath the soil of the ancient riverbed. Carroll took the wheel, and Park was in the passenger seat. Although the rover was pressurized, Jeff kept his helmet on, only opening its visor. Dave removed his helmet, though, and placed it in his lap.

"We went for a couple of hours or so without saying much of anything," Jeff recalled. "I think we could have gone all day without speaking. Or at least I could have. But we were about eighteen miles from the base when Dave reached over and switched off the radio. Then he looked at me and said, 'Y'-know, I think we need to talk.'

"'About what?' I said. 'I don't think we've got anything to talk about.' And that was the truth, so far as I was concerned. I had done my best to forget it, and the last thing I wanted was to discuss something that had happened thirteen months ago and fifty million miles away.

"But Dave wasn't going to let it drop. 'You know what I mean,' he said. 'That night you came home early, saw my car in your driveway.'

"'I think you ought to shut up,' I said. 'I really don't want to discuss it.' He didn't say anything for a while. We were very close to the channel, and I was skirting along the edge, trying to find a good place where we could go down and collect our samples. That's when he opened his mouth again. 'Has it ever occurred to you,' he said, 'that you didn't see what you thought you saw?'"

"Well, that got me mad. 'Oh, c'mon, you think I'm stupid? What are you going to tell me, you had dropped by to borrow a cup of sugar?'

"I didn't meant to yell, but I was angry. I mean, really furious. 'No, that's not what I'm saying,' he says. "'I'm just trying to tell you that you're not the only one who got hurt that night.'

Jeff hesitated, staring into the fireplace. I've seen people clam up when they get close to something they've kept secret for many years. Sometimes they fall back, tell you to stop the tape and forget everything you've just heard. But after a moment he drew a deep breath, forcing himself to go on.

"'That was my car you saw, all right,' he said, 'but I wasn't the one driving it. Fact was, I was flying back from Russia that night. If you'd asked me, I would have told you . . . even showed you the ticket stub to prove it.'"

"By now I was so furious I wasn't even looking where I was driving. 'If that wasn't you,' I said, 'then who was the guy I saw kiss Patty good night at my front door?' "

" 'That wasn't me,' he said. 'That was Louise.' "

***

A long silence. Jeff let out his breath and picked up his drink. The glass was empty, yet when he turned to call for Dorothy, she reappeared from the kitchen, bringing him another glass of water. As she bent down to give it to him, she whispered something in his ear. He shook his head and she nodded reluctantly, then turned to leave the room again.

"Patty and Louise . . . I never suspected." The glass trembled in his hand as he took a sip. "Neither did Dave, for that matter. He didn't figure it out for a couple of months after I spotted his wife leaving my house, and then only after Louise came right out and told him."

"Why did she . . . ?"

"Want to hear something funny?" He grinned. "He thought I was having an affair with her . . . but he didn't say or do anything about it for the same reason I didn't! He didn't want to get booted off the mission!"

The grin vanished. "So here we were, two stupid bastards, each thinking the other guy's fooling around with his wife when the fact of the matter was that they were fooling around with each other. Two All-American boys off playing astronaut, never suspecting that their All-American girls could . . ."

He shrugged. "Anyway, when he learned the truth, he decided not to tell me. He knew how much it would hurt, and that was the last thing he wanted to do. So he kept mum and hoped things would work out on their own. And when he couldn't stay quiet any longer . . . well, I was hurt all right. In fact, I went berserk."

"You said you tried to kill him."

He looked back at me. "When he told me it was Louise I'd seen leaving my house, I simply couldn't believe it. It was like . . . I don't know, like a red curtain came down in front of my eyes. I forgot where I was, what I was doing, just threw myself at him."

Jeff close his eyes. "I had my hands around Dave's throat, and he was trying to fight me off when everything turned upside down. All of a sudden, we were rolling end over end down the side of the channel."

The rover crashed at the bottom of the dry channel. Although Dave was knocked out, Jeff remained conscious. The fact that he hadn't removed his helmet was what saved them both, because the rover began to leak air as soon as it came to rest. Jeff found Dave's helmet, put it over his head, and managed to repressurize his suit before he suffered a fatal embolism. He then managed to prize open the door and drag Dave from the wreckage. Dave was alive, but his right leg was broken just below the knee.

Even worse, the rover's high-gain antenna had been demolished, as was the satellite dish which would have enabled them to contact *Ares 1*. However, there were two replacement oxygen tanks in the rover; neither had been ruptured, and since their suit tanks were fully charged, they had enough air for another twenty hours. So the two men had two choices: either remain where they were and pray for rescue, or walk back to Utopia Base.

They decided to walk.

***

"We worked out a lot of things that night, Dave and I. Perhaps we should have been saving our air, but when you're facing death, it's easier to talk than not to."

The fire was dying out. Jeff reached over to pick up a cane resting against the hearth, then carefully eased himself out of his chair. I almost got up to help him, then remembered this was someone who once carried another man on his shoulder across nineteen miles of the most lonesome desert known to humankind. I stayed in my seat and watched as he hobbled to the fireplace.

"I won't go into what we talked about," he said as he opened the screen and prodded the cinders with an iron poker. "Perhaps some things should be left private. Suffice it to say, by the time we made it back to camp, we were friends again.

Sergei saw us coming, and just before he reached us, he raised his camera and took that shot everyone's seen."

"I've always wondered about that. You've got your hand raised toward the camera. What were you trying to do?"

"A lot of people have asked me that. Everyone thinks I was pleading for help." He shut the screen, put the poker back in its rack. "Truth is, I was trying to stop Sergei from taking that shot. I thought we looked like idiots, and I didn't want anyone to see us crawling back into camp with dirt all over our suits."

He moved slowly across the living room. "Dave and I spent the rest of our time on Mars as friends, and we stayed friends long after we returned to Earth. Patty and I divorced not long afterward . . . fact is, we separated even before I came back, but kept it a secret until we were no longer in the public eye. Dave had been trying to patch things up with Louise . . . that's what all those messages were about . . . but she was already in a relationship with another woman . . . not Patty, thank God . . . and she had moved out by the time we got home. She made one brief appearance with him, when we received our Congressional Medals of Honor, but that was the last time I saw her. Patty was there also, under the same pretense, but . . . well, she had her own life, and it didn't include me."

He stopped in front of an antique rolltop desk and opened a drawer. "Anyway, that's pretty much it. That's all I have to tell you. You got it, right?"

"Well, yes, but . . . " I glance at my recorder. It held a two-hour cassette, the second one I'd used during our interview, and there were at least twenty minutes of tape left. "There's more, isn't there? I mean, that's just part of the story."

"Uh-huh. The hard part . . . the part I couldn't bring myself to write." As he turned away from the desk, he was holding three spiral-bound notebooks. "I hope you don't have trouble with my handwriting, and I apologize for my grammar . . . anyway, it's all there."

I stared at the manuscript as he placed it in my hands. He lurched back to his chair, collapsing into it with visible relief. "Sorry, but I had to do it this way," he said. "My words weren't . . . well, maybe you can do better."

I opened the top notebook, and skimmed a couple of pages. His handscript was neat, his prose effortless to read. Perhaps it could use a little line-editing, but on the whole it didn't appear to need much revision. "So what do you want me to . . . I mean, what you've just told me?"

Jeff said nothing for a few moments. His gaze returned to the fireplace; he appeared very tired, and somehow no longer interested. "Do with it as you will. It's your book now."

I took Jeffrey Carroll's manuscript home and worked on it for next eight weeks. It was the easiest rewrite job I'd ever done: a little chapter restructuring here, some scene embellishment there. His spelling and punctuation were awful, but nothing a good copyeditor couldn't have handled. Easiest money I ever made . . .

Except when it came to writing the chapter where he spoke the truth about what happened on Mars. Even after I transcribed our interview and wrote it as straight first-person text, I went through several drafts, trying to find just the right tone. Yet never could I imagine the way he must have felt, all those lonely hours hiking through the Martian night, coming to grips with the fact that Dave Park, a friend whom he thought had betrayed him, had instead tried to protect him.

So much pain. So much courage.

I was almost through with the book and my editor was breathing down my neck when, two weeks before Christmas, Dorothy called to tell me that Jeff had passed away. He had gone upstairs to take a midafternoon nap, and when she went up to wake him for dinner, she discovered he had died in his sleep.

I attended the funeral. Colonel Jeffrey Carroll was buried with full military honors at Arlington National Cemetery; the President delivered a brief eulogy, then a Marine Corps honor guard fired a twenty-one gun salute as Navy jets roared across the slate sky in the missing-man formation. I stood in the back of a crowd of nearly five hundred people, none of whom I knew except for Dorothy. I saw her, but she didn't see me, and I didn't try to approach her. When it was over, I caught the next flight home.

I finished the book and sent it to the publisher. My editor loved it, and even paid me a, bonus. *A Walk Across Mars* was published the following summer and became a major best-seller. If you haven't read it you should, because it's good and it's true, and most of the words were his own. Except for the parts I decided to leave out.

So far as I'm concerned, that's no one's business. We need heroes. And sometimes, a lie is better than the truth.

MARTIAN AUTUMN

by Stephen Baxter

I *WILL tell the story much as I set it out in my journal at the time. Old-fashioned, I know. But I can't think of any better way to tell how it happened to me.*
If there is anybody to read it.

***

Bob ran one last check of his skinsuit. He did this without thinking, an ingrained habit for a fourteen-year-old born on Mars. Then, following Lyall, he let the lock run through its cycle, and he stepped out of the tractor and onto Martian dirt.

This was Isidis Planitia, a great basin that straddled Mars' northern plains and ancient southern highlands. It was late afternoon, a still day at the start of the long, languid Martian autumn. Everything was a cruddy red-brown: the dirty sky, the lines of shallow dunes lapping against the walls of an enclosing crater.

A cloud of camera fireflies hovered around his head. The moment was newsworthy, Mars' youngest resident visiting the oldest. Bob ignored the flies. They had followed him around all his life.

Meg Lyall was standing with her arms spread wide, as if crucified. She turned around and around, with the creaky, uncertain motions of great age, enjoying Mars.

Bob stood there, hideously embarrassed.

She said, "You want to know the best thing about modern Mars? Skinsuits." She flexed her hand, watching the fabric crumple and stretch, waves of color crossing its surface.

"Back in '29 we had to lock ourselves up in great clunky lob-
ster suits, all hard shells and padding, so heavy you could
barely take a step. Now it's like we're not wearing anything
at all."

"Not really."

She looked up at him, her rheumy eyes Earth-blue. "No.
You're right. It's not *really* like walking over a grassy field,
out in the open air, is it? Which is what you think you'll be
doing in six months' time." She looked up at Earth's bright
glint. "Sixty years after the Reboot, Earth is a world of
fortresses. Even the grass is under guard. But maybe they'll let
you walk on it even so. After all, you're famous!"

Resentment sparked easily, as it always did. "You won't put
me off going."

"Oh, no." She seemed shocked at the suggestion. "That
isn't it at all. You have to go. It's very important. There may
be nothing more important. You'll see. Walk with me."

He couldn't refuse. But he wouldn't let her hold his hand.

***

April 2008

*Tricester is in Oxfordshire, England. It is a strange place, I
suppose: both old and new, an ancient leafy village in the
shadow of a huge particle accelerator facility called Corwell,
a giant circular ridge of green landscaping. It is a place
crowded with history.*

*My name is Marshall Reid, by the way. In April 2008 I am
a science teacher at the village school.*

Here's how it begins for me.

*On a bright spring afternoon I lead a field trip of eleven
schoolchildren to the Corwell plant. As we troop past the
anonymous buildings, there is an emergency, some failure of
containment, and a blue flash overwhelms us all. I am dazzled
but unhurt. Some of the children are still, silent, as if distracted, others very frightened. They all seem unharmed.*

*There are predictable fears of a radiation leak. The guides
quickly herd us into a holding area.*

*Miranda Stewart is called in, and introduced to us. She is
Emergency Planning Officer for the region, the local author-*

ity official in nominal charge of such operations, supposedly coordinating the various emergency services. She is 50-ish, a Geordie, a former soldier. I like her immediately; she is a reassuring presence.

But Stewart is overwhelmed by the techs and suits and experts from the environment ministry. Scientists in protection gear crawl scarily over the site with Geiger counters.

We teachers and pupils are held in the middle of all this, sitting in our neat rows, surrounded by officials and police and medics, our mobile phones besieged by anxious parents. We are all bewildered and scared.

Reluctantly Stewart concedes that the village should be cordoned off, proper tests run on the inhabitants and the local crops, and so on. But no alarm will be raised; there will be a cover story about a chemical leak.

The police set up blocks around the plant and village. There is press attention, and Green protesters quickly appear at the barriers. Emma, my wife, encounters this perimeter, returning from work in London.

Emma, at thirty-one a little younger than me, is a PR consultant. She misses life in the capital. Emma is seven months pregnant. To her, the Corwell incident is the final straw; this is not a safe place to raise a kid. Later that day we argue again about moving back to London. But I am devoted to my job, and loyal to the kids. The argument is inconclusive, as usual.

Meanwhile, at the plant (so I learn later), the technicians are finding no signs of radiation damage. But one technician, checking surrounding foliage, finds a nest of mice—a nest without babies.

I have the feeling this is only the start of something larger. Hence my decision to keep this journal.

***

When Bob looked back, he saw that the tractor had already sunk behind Mars' close horizon. He had no idea where they were going. He wasn't enjoying the oily feel of his suit's smart material as it slithered over his skin, seeking to equalize temperature and pressure over his body. It was like being held in a huge moist hand.

He'd only stepped on the raw surface of Mars a dozen times in his life. It was a frozen desert—what was there to see? He had spent all his life rattling around in the cramped corridors of Mangala or Ares or Hellas, surrounded by walls painted the glowing colors of Earth, purple and blue and green.

Earth! He could see it now, a blue-white evening star just rising, the only color in this whole rust-ridden landscape— Earth, where he had dreamed of escaping even before he had realized that he was a freak.

He was the youngest child on Mars: the last to be born, as colonists abandoned by Earth dutifully shut down their lives. A little later he had been orphaned, making him even more of a freak.

He owed Mars nothing. He didn't fit. Everybody stared at him pityingly. Well, another week and he was out of here: the only evacuee Earth would allow.

But first he had to get through this gruesome ritual of a visit with Meg Lyall.

On she talked.

"I guess you're used to the fireflies. Surely they are going to watch you all the way home. Just like when I rode the *Ares* out here, back in 2029 . . ." More old-woman reminiscing, he thought gloomily. "There we were, in our big ugly hab module, and we were surrounded by drifting cams the whole way out. At first I figured people were watching to see us screw, or take a dump, or fight. But it turned out the highest ratings were for ordinary times, when we were just working calmly, making our meals, sleeping. Like watching fish in a tank. But you've never seen a fish. Maybe even then people were too isolated. Now it's a lot worse, of course. But we're social animals; we need people around us. What do you think?"

"I think you ought to tell me where we're going."

She stopped and turned, breathing hard, to face him. "Why, we're already there. Don't you know your history?"

She led him over a shallow rise. And there, under a low translucent dome only thinly coated with Martian dust, sat the *Beagle 2*.

***

May 2008

After a couple of weeks the cordon has been lifted. But technicians still patrol the area with their anonymous instruments, and the children and I are subject to ongoing medical checks.

I have tried to protect the children. But there is media attention: unwelcome headlines, cartoons of huge-brained kids glowing in the dark. I am angry, of course. My pupils have already been betrayed by the authorities who should protect them, and now they are depicted as freaks.

The school's pet rabbits have produced no young.

Paul Merrick has shown up, rucksack on his back, looking for a place to stay.

Merrick, 40-ish, is a Jeff Goldblum-look-alike American environmental scientist. He has become something of a maverick, with controversial theories about holistic aspects of the environment. At college he taught Emma.

And they had a relationship.

Now Emma has called him in; she knew Merrick would be intrigued by the accident and she wants to know his views.

I am not pleased to see this ghost from Emma's past.

Merrick and Emma do some unauthorized exploration of Corwell. I suspect Emma, now on maternity leave, wants something to take her mind off the approaching upheaval in her own life: a last youthful adventure.

They find birds' nests without eggs.

They are discovered by Emergency Planning Officer Stewart. She tries to throw them out, and blusters about this being a routine cleanup operation. But Merrick asks probing questions about the instances of sterility, which are already the talk of the village. Stewart points out that the sheep and cattle in neighboring farms are giving birth as usual. Merrick says this may be because of different gestation periods; if some kind of sterilization effect has occurred, short-gestation creatures would be the first to be affected. Stewart—not a scientist and, I suspect, not kept fully in the know by the ministry types—is disturbed, but is sure there is a "rational" explanation.

When she tells me this part of the story, Emma rubs her bump thoughtfully.

Merrick, Emma, and I talk it over in the pub. To my discomfiture, Emma tells Merrick too much personal stuff: that her conception was an accident while we were on holiday, for example. Merrick, though restrained, is obviously jealous.

Merrick says predictable things. That it is as if we are running a huge, uncontrolled experiment on nature. That England is a small and crowded place, where nature has been saturated by everything we could throw at her—electromagnetic radiation, pesticides, genetic modification, acid rain, and now even exotic radiation from the nuclear accident. That we have stressed natural systems beyond their limits. That something strange is happening here as a result—but who knows what?

Meaningless talk. I resolve to focus on the immediate issues before me, on the people I care for, Emma and the field-trip kids.

***

The *Beagle* wasn't much to look at. It was just a pie-dish pod that had bounced down from the sky under a system of parachutes and gasbags. Disk-shaped solar cell panels had unfolded over the dirt, and a wand of sensors had stuck up like a periscope. And that was it. When people had come looking for it five decades after its landing, *Beagle* had been all but buried by windblown toxic dust.

And yet, by baking its tiny soil samples and sniffing the thin air, *Beagle 2* had discovered life on Mars.

"It was the atmospheric sensor that did it," Lyall said. "The probe could directly examine only one little patch of landscape, but a Martian cow could fart anywhere on Mars and *Beagle* could sense the methane. It took another thirty years before anybody had a sample they could hold in their hand, but *Beagle* proved it was here to be found."

Even before Lyall and her crew had left Earth, the findings of unmanned probes had already shattered many ancient dreams of Mars. There were no canal builders, no lusty princesses, no wistful golden-eyed poets, no leathery lung-plants. For a time, Mars had been thought to be dead altogether.

But then a meteorite, a fossil-laden scrap of Mars brought to Earth by cosmic chance, had changed all that.

Young Mars and Earth, billions of years ago, had been like sisters: both warm, both glistening with shallow oceans and ponds. And both had harbored life—sister life, as it turned out, spawned on one world or the other and blown across space on the meteorite wind.

Lyall turned around, letting her gloved fingertips trace out the line of the crater walls. "I don't think you can imagine how strange this scenery is to me, still. To see a crater like this with water features in it: gully networks and dried riverbeds and the rippling beaches of ancient lakes . . . A crater punched in rock that formed at the bottom of a sea, a crater that later got flooded, over, and over. When I was your age, I'd have given anything to be transported here, to stand where you are standing—to know what I know now." Bob thought she behaved as if she had just stepped down out of that creaky old spaceship of hers.

Mars had been too small. It could not hold onto the gases its volcanoes vented, and without tectonic recycling the atmosphere became locked in carbonate rocks. The air thinned, the oceans and land froze, and the harsh sunlight destroyed the water.

And yet life persisted.

"Slime," Bob said. "Life on Mars is pond scum, kilometers down."

Lyall glared, as if he'd insulted her personally. "Not pond scum. Biofilms. Martian life is not primitive. It is the result of four billion years of evolution—a different evolution. The anaerobic life-forms organize themselves, working together, one living off the output of another. Life on Mars is all about cooperation. Some say that the whole Martian biota, stuck down in those deep thermal vents, is nothing but one vast community."

"Sure. But so what? You can't eat it. It doesn't do anything."

Lyall struggled to remain serious, then a grin cracked her leathery face. "Okay. I felt the same as you, even though I was

forty years old before I got here. Once we got through the first
phase surface op, I made it my mission to find something
more."

"More?"

"More than a damn microbe. Something with a backbone
and a brain. Something like me."

***

June 2008

*Frogs in the school pond have produced spawn, but no tad-
poles.*

*As rumors spread of the sterilities, the children remain the
focus of unwelcome attention. Some of them are showing signs
of stress—strange paintings and stories, odd games in the
playground—they are becoming withdrawn, turning to each
other for comfort.*

*They are just victims of the same hypertechnological acci-
dent which apparently triggered the sterility problems. But it
is as if the children are being transformed into witches, in
some monstrous mass mind. Absurd, paradoxical, frightening.*

*Meanwhile the ministry scientists are considering pulling
out. Their tests have proved inconclusive.*

*Merrick argues against this. He says that something subtle
and strange is unfolding here, which we must study. He walks
Stewart, Emma, and me through a tree-of-life evolution wall
chart; the sterility effects are working their way "down" the
tree, from younger and more complex forms of life, like mam-
mals, to the older. He predicts that reptiles will be the next animal group to show symptoms.*

*Stewart sticks to her chain of command, determined to keep
control and minimize disorder and panic.*

*But now a personal crisis looms for us. Emma has gone into
labor. A doctor and midwife attend.*

*Merrick, typically, uses the event to gather more data. He
asks distracting questions about instances of human conception in the village since the accident. The midwife repeats a
few rumors.*

*And meanwhile there are more stories of empty nests, va-
cant ponds, all over this scrap of ancient English countryside.*

***

She had sent Bob the letter: a genuine letter, written by hand on flimsy sheets of plastic-sealed paper. Bob didn't understand the half of it. But he knew it was about the Reboot, the origin of Earth's disaster.

"I never knew him," she said. "Reid, I mean. He was just some English guy. Dead now, I guess. I don't even know why he sent me the letter. We were first on Mars; we got mails from all over. Maybe he saw a bond between us. He was there at the beginning of a new world, as was I."

"Doctor Lyall—"

She laid her hand on his shoulder—softly, but her fingers were strong, like claws. "Indulge me a little more. It's important. Believe me."

She took a few steps away from the memorialized *Beagle,* and scuffed at ruddy Martian dirt with her toe. "I learned my fossil hunting before I left Earth. I worked out in the desert heartlands of Kenya. That's in Africa. You've heard of Africa? You know, people have lived in that area for two million years or more. But even there you don't find bones just sticking out of the ground. You have to be systematic. You have to know where to look and how to look.

"The landscape of Mars is billions of years older than Africa. Everything is worn to dust. Fossil-hunting here is unimaginably harder." She pointed to the distant crater walls. "But not impossible. I looked in craters like this, at exposed layers of sedimentary rock."

Bob felt a remote curiosity stir. "And you found something?"

Lyall smiled. " It took years." From a pocket in her suit she dug out a scrap of rock, embedded in a disk of clear plastic. She handed it to Bob.

He turned it over and over. It was like a paperweight. Except for the fact that it contained two bands of shading, divided by a neat, sharp line, it looked like every other rock on Mars.

He was obscurely disappointed. "I can't see anything."

"The evidence is microscopic. This is only a show sample anyhow. But *they were here,* Bob: multicellular life, complex life, a whole community. There seems to have been an evolutionary explosion like Earth's Precambrian, buried in Mars' deep past—*much* earlier than anything comparable on Earth. They lived in the oceans. There were squat bottom feeders, and sleek-shelled swimmers that seem to have been functionally equivalent to fish—"

"Why doesn't everybody know about this?"

"Because we are still trying to figure out how they all died."

He shrugged. "What is there to figure? Mars dried out and froze."

"But the extinction was sudden," she said. She pointed to the line between the different-colored layers in the rock. "You find rocks like this on Earth. The lines mark places in the geological record where there have been great extinction events. Below, life. Above, no life—or at any rate, a different life, a sparser life."

"Like the dinosaurs."

She nodded approvingly. "Yes. These are Mars' dinosaurs, Bob. But it wasn't a comet that killed them. It wasn't the freeze—not directly; it happened much too rapidly for that."

Then Bob saw it; it was as if the ruddy landscape swiveled around the bit of rock. "It was a Reboot."

"Yes," she said.

"Just like Earth."

"Just like Earth."

***

July 2008

Now, Merrick has found, even insects are failing to reproduce, and on the farms crops are failing.

This unfolding environmental disaster is, of course, impossible to conceal. The cordon is back. Government officials, scientists and the press are crawling over the area. There is a news blackout on the school and heavy security—"for the children's protection" I am glad Miranda Stewart is still involved, trying to maintain decent conditions for the children, responding to my requests for normality.

But the children have been isolated. Once more they are subject to scrutiny and endless tests from doctors, social work-

ers, educationists, psychologists, other scientists. These "experts" find nothing, of course. I see it as all part of the absurd witch-hunt.

The children's parents are agitated, frightened, angry. "We don't want our child to be special. Why us?" Some are threatening to sue me or the government. But the children have not actually been injured. There is nothing I can say to reassure them.

Joel is one of the field-trip kids. Through him I learn that his family of farmers have been badly affected. They blame the government, the kids. Even Joel himself, says the poor child. I wonder what is happening in his home, away from official eyes.

I am staying with the kids as much as I can. But my situation is difficult. I am delighted with our baby boy, and I think we are both secretly relieved that he is "normal." But Emma is scared and thinks we should be planning to get as far from here as possible.

My conflict of loyalties deepens.

***

"When the desiccation came, evolution slowed to a crawl. Life was forced to be thrifty, to evolve toward simplicity, robustness, and cooperation. Any fancy multicellular design became a liability. Great communities emerged with a new kind of distributed complexity, with simple, interchangeable components."

"Instead of people, slime."

"You got it. *But it had to happen fast.* On an evolutionary timescale anyhow . . . Look, I can't tell this story right. There is nothing conscious about the direction of evolution, nothing purposeful. But there was something in the genes, something that found itself activated when the conditions were right, when the stress got too great. Something that shut down what could no longer survive the desiccation."

"Something?"

"We think we understand the mechanism," Lyall said darkly. "Bob, your DNA isn't a seamless piece of genetic machinery. Your genes contain endogenous retroviruses—ERVs."

"Retroviruses—like HIV?"

"That's right. ERVs were once independent life-forms like HIV—viruses that invaded the cells of our ancestors millions of years ago. But ERVs liked it so much they decided to stay. They have become integrated into the human genome, reproduced and passed down through the generations. This has been going on for at least thirty million years: maybe one per cent of your genome is represented by ERVs and fragments. And every mammal species we've examined contains ERVs, too.

"Cohabitation makes the viruses settle down: it's a poor parasite that destroys its host. But sometimes the tamed viruses turn feral. Retroviruses seem to be responsible for autoimmune diseases: when they kick in, it's like your body is mounting an immune attack against your own cells. And that's not all they can do. In certain circumstances, it seems, they can stop the replication of DNA molecules altogether . . ." Lyall shrugged. "Look, kid, I'm a propulsion engineer—not even a rock hound, and still less a microbiologist. But what I do understand—"

"The Martian Reboot was caused by ERVs."

She nodded grimly. "Or something like them. The evidence is iffy—it's been a *long* time—but that's how it looks."

Bob struggled to understand what she was telling him. "Was it an ERV on Earth, too?"

"Yes." She watched him, letting him figure it out for himself.

"Oh," he said. "The same ERV."

"The same ERV."

***

August 2008

Now the plants are dying in earnest—wheat, grasses, weeds. In the very center, close to Corwell itself, only single-celled organisms are reproducing, the very root of the evolutionary tree. Merrick has followed this grim progression with my classroom tree-of-life diagram, step by step.

There is growing hostility to the children.

It is a hot August, and tempers are inflamed.

It comes to a head.

Some of the locals mount a drunken attack. The soldiers on guard are hesitant, their sympathies split, their orders unclear. Stewart, Merrick, Emma, and myself rush to defend the children. Joel's father, drunk and in despair, improvises a petrol bomb and throws it. His own child is his target.

I have never held a lower opinion of the human species. With a possibly terminal catastrophe gathering around us, all we can do is seek someone to blame, and to harass the innocent and helpless. Perhaps we do not deserve to survive.

The children are saved from the fire.

Emma is killed.

I don't know how else to tell such a thing.

***

She stood there, the lower half of her suit stained bright red by the dust, gazing up at Earth. "*Earth doesn't have to die,*" she said. "That's the point. Earth isn't freezing and drying like ancient Mars. I think that damn ERV got triggered by accident. It was the pressures of that one shithole place in England, the mix of ground toxins and atmospheric pollution and whatever the hell else was going on there. Our fault, sure—but an accident all the same. *It isn't Earth's time.*"

Bob, still resentful, was growing frightened of this eighty year old, and the huge biological disaster that lay behind her, a billion-year shadow. "Why doesn't Earth do something about it?"

She sighed. "Because there is no 'Earth.' There are only factions and nations and corporations. For a time, even as the disaster unfolded, we were hopeful. We even mounted missions to Mars, for God's sake. I guess we always thought we'd defeat the plague. But we didn't. Hope died. Now there are enclaves, fortresses. And you can't do science from inside a fortress.

"Listen to me. You are Mars' last child. On Earth you will be a sentimental token, a five-minute wonder. You will have a platform. You have to use it." She closed her hand around his, around the rock. "Make them listen. Drag them out of their fortresses, their cowering madness. Read the letter. Make them put together the lessons of this ancient rock, and what's going on all around them. We learned more from the first scraping of Martian bugs than in fifty years of one-planet biology, and I believe it can be so again. In a way it's beautiful—the ancient life of one abandoned world coming to the aid of its suffering sister . . . Make them see that." She searched his face anxiously. "Do you understand?"

Bob opened his palm. In the slowly fading light he stared at the innocent bit of rock, longing to see the creatures who had once swum vanished Martian seas.

***

September 2008

Merrick, my dead wife's lover, has stayed with us. Emma's death has drawn us together.

Merrick's counsel is oddly reassuring, in an abstract way. He says that essentially a "reboot" mechanism is operating. Just as a crashed computer can be restored from reboot files, so the biosphere, stressed beyond endurance, is "dumping" higher biological forms, abandoning all but the most basic forms of life, perhaps in the hope of re-evolving to suit the new conditions. Merrick speculates that this mechanism may have operated before, after the great extinction events of the past.

This all seems a little spooky to me; it smacks of Mother Gaia taking revenge. But I know little about the science and I keep my counsel.

The virus is spread by air, water, contact. Merrick hacks into Internet sites to find evidence that the virus is already working its effects elsewhere, far from Tricester.

Merrick predicts we have maybe a century left. A hundred years, as humans and other higher forms are discarded like autumn leaves.

I cradle my baby, and wonder how many more like him will be born.

(For Colin Pillinger and the *Beagle* 2 team.)

SHIELDS OF MARS

by Gene Wolfe

ONCE they had dueled beneath the russet Martian sky for the hand of a princess—had dueled with swords that, not long before, had been the plastic handles of a rake and a spade.

Jeff Shonto had driven the final nail into the first Realwood plank when he realized that Zaa was standing six-legged, ankle-deep in red dust, watching him. He turned a little in case Zaa wanted to say something; Zaa did not, but he four-legged, rearing his thorax so that his arms hung like arms (perhaps in order to look more human) before he became a glaucous statue once again, a statue with formidable muscles in unexpected locations.

Zaa's face was skull-like, as were the faces of all the people from his star, with double canines jutting from its massive jaw and eyes at its temples. It was a good face, Jeff thought, a kind and an honest face.

He picked up the second Realwood plank, laid it against the window so it rested on the first, and plucked a nail from his mouth.

Zaa's gray Department shirt ("Zaa Leem, Director of Maintenance") had been dirty. No doubt Zaa had put it on clean that morning, but there was a black smear under the left pocket now. What if they wanted to talk to Zaa, too?

Jeff's power-hammer said *bang,* and the nail sank to the head. Faint echoes from inside the store that had been his father's might almost have been the sound of funeral drums. Shrugging, he took another nail from his mouth.

A good and a kind face, and he and Zaa had been friends

since Mom and Dad were young, and what did a little grease matter? Didn't they want Zaa to work? When you worked, you got dirty.

Another nail, in the diagonal corner. *Bang.* Mind pictures, daydream pictures showed him the masked dancers who ought to have been there when they buried Dad in the desert. And were not.

Again he turned to look at Zaa, expecting Zaa to say something, to make some comment. Zaa did not. Beyond Zaa were thirty bungalows, twenty-nine white and one a flaking blue that had once been bright. Twenty-eight bungalows that were boarded up, two that were still in use.

Beyond the last, the one that had been Diane's family's, empty miles of barren desert, Then the aching void of the immense chasm that had been renamed the Grand Canal. Beyond it, a range of rust-red cliff that was in reality the far side of the Grand Canal, a glowing escarpment lit at its summit by declining Sol.

Jeff shrugged and turned back to his plank. A third nail. *Bang.* The dancers were sharp-edged this time, the drums louder. "You're closing your store."

He fished more nails from his pocket. "Not to you. If you want something I'll sell it to you."

"Thanks." Zaa picked up a plank and stood ready to pass it to Jeff.

Bang. Echoes of thousands of years just beginning.

"I've got one in the shop that feeds the nails. Want me to get it?"

Jeff shook his head. "For a little job like this, what I've got is fine."

Bang.

"Back at the plant in a couple hours?"

"At twenty-four ten they're supposed to call me." Jeff had said this before, and he knew Zaa knew it as well as he did. "You don't have to be there . . ."

"But maybe they'll close it."

And I won't have to be the one who tells you.

Jeff turned away, staring at the plank. He wanted to drive more nails into it, but there was one at each corner already. He could not remember driving that many.

"Here." Zaa was putting up another plank. "I would have done this whole job for you. You know?"

"It was my store." Jeff squared the new plank on the second and reached to his mouth for a nail, but there were no nails there. He positioned his little ladder, leaning it on the newly nailed one, got up on the lowest step, and fished a fresh nail from his pocket.

Bang.

"Those paintings of mine? Give them back and I'll give you what you paid."

"No." Jeff did not look around.

"You'll never sell them now."

"They're mine," Jeff said. "I paid you for them, and I'm keeping them."

"There won't ever be any more tourists, Jeff."

"Things will get better."

"Where would they stay?"

"Camp in the desert. Rough it." *Bang.*

There was a silence, during which Jeff drove more nails.

"If they close the plant, I guess they'll send a crawler to take us to some other town."

Jeff shrugged. "Or an orthopter, like Channel Two has. You saw *Scenic Mars*. They might even do that."

Impelled by an instinct he could not have described but could not counter, he stepped down—short, dark, and stocky—to face Zaa. "Listen here. In the first place, they can't close the plant. What'd they breathe?"

Even four-legging, Zaa was taller by more than a full head; he shrugged, massive shoulders lifting and falling. "The others could take up the slack, maybe."

"Maybe they could. What if something went wrong at one of them?"

"There'd be plenty of time to fix it. Air doesn't go that fast."

"You come here."

He took Zaa by the arm, and Zaa paced beside him, intermediate armlike legs helping support his thorax and abdomen.

"I want to show you the plant."

"I've seen it."

"Come on. I want to see it myself." Together, the last two inhabitants of the settlement called Grand Canal went around the wind-worn store and climbed a low hill. The chain-link fence enclosing the plant was tall and still strong, but the main gate stood open, and there was no one in the guard shack. A half mile more of dusty road, then the towers and the glassy prisms, and the great pale domes, overshadowed by the awe-inspiring cooling stack of the nuclear reactor. On the left, the spherical hydrogen tanks and thousands upon thousands of canisters of hydrogen awaiting the crawler. Beyond those, nearly lost in the twilight, Number One Crusher. It would have been a very big plant anywhere on Earth; here, beneath the vastness of the russet sky, standing alone in the endless red-and-black desert, it was tiny and vulnerable, something any wandering meteor might crush like a toy.

"Take a good look," Jeff said, wishing Zaa could see it through his eyes.

"I just did. We might as well go now. They'll be wanting to call you pretty soon."

"In a minute. What do you suppose all that stuff's worth? All the equipment?"

Zaa picked his teeth with a sharp claw. "I don't know. I guess I never thought about it. A couple hundred million?"

"More than a billion. Listen up." Jeff felt his own conviction growing as he spoke. "I can lock the door on my store and board up the windows and walk away. I can do that because I'm still here. Suppose you and I just locked the gate and got on that crawler and went off. How long before somebody was out here with ten more crawlers, loading up stainless pipe, and motors, and all that stuff? You could make a better stab at this than I could, but I say give me three big crawlers and three men who knew what they were doing and I'd have ten million on those crawlers in a week."

Zaa shook his head. "Twelve hours. Eight, if they never took a break and really knew their business."

"Fine. So is the Department going to lock the door and walk away? Either they gut it themselves—not ten million, over a billion—or they'll keep somebody here to keep an eye on things. They'll have to."

"I guess."

"Suppose they've decided to stop production altogether. How long to shut down the pile and mothball everything? With two men?"

"To do it right?" Zaa fingered the point of one canine. "A year."

Jeff nodded. "A year. And they'd have to do it right, because someday they might have to start up again. We're pretty well terraformed these days. This out here isn't much worse than the Gobi Desert on Earth. A hundred years ago you couldn't breathe right where we're standing."

He studied Zaa's face, trying to see if his words were sinking in, if they were making an impression. Zaa said, "Sure."

"And everybody knows that. Okay, suppose one of the other plants went down. Totally. Suppose they lost the pile or something. Meltdown."

"I got it."

"Like you say, the air goes slow now. We've added to the planetary mass—covered the whole thing with an ocean of air and water vapor three miles thick, so there's more gravity." Jeff paused for emphasis. "But it goes, and as it goes, we lose gravity. The more air we lose, the faster we lose more."

"I know that."

"Sure. I know you do. I'm just reminding you. All right, they lose one whole plant, like I said."

"You never lose the pile if you do it right."

"Sure. But not everybody's as smart as you are, okay? They get some clown in there and he screws up. Let's take the Schiaparelli plant, just to talk about. How much fossil water have they got?"

Zaa shrugged.

"I don't know either, and neither do they. They could give you some number, but it's just a guess. Suppose they run out of water."

Zaa nodded and turned away, four-legging toward the main gate.

Jeff hurried after him. "How long before people panic? A week? A month?"

"You never finished boarding up."

"I'll get it later. I have to be there when they call."

"Sure," Zaa said.

Together, as they had been together since Jeff was born, they strode through the plant gate upon two legs and four, leaving it open behind them. "They're going to have to give us power wagons," Jeff said. "Suppose we're at home and we have to get here fast."

"Bikes." Zaa looked at him, then looked away. "In here you're the boss. All right, you had your say. I listened to everything."

It was Jeff's turn to nod. He said, "Uh-huh."

"So do I get to talk now?"

Jeff nodded again. "Shoot."

"You said it was going to get better, people were going to come out here from Elysium again. But you were boarding up your store. So you know, only you're scared I'll leave."

Jeff did not speak.

"We're not like you." To illustrate what he meant, Zaa began six-legging. "I been raised with you—with you Sol people is what I mean. I feel like I'm one of you, and maybe once a week I'll see myself in a mirror or someplace and I think, my gosh, I'm an alien."

"You're a Martian," Jeff told him firmly. "I am, too. You call us Sols or Earthmen or something, and most of my folks were Navajo. But I'm Martian, just like you."

"Thanks. Only we get attached to places, you know? We're like cats. I hatched in this town. I grew up here. As long as I can stay, I'm not going."

"There's food in the store. Canned and dried stuff, a lot of it. I'll leave you the key. You can look after it for me."

Zaa took a deep breath, filling a chest thicker even than Jeff's with thin Martian air that they had made. "You said we'd added to the mass with our air. Made more gravity. Only we didn't. The nitrogen's from the rock we dig and crush. You know that. The oxygen's from splitting water. Fossil water from underground. Sure, we bring stuff from Earth, but it doesn't amount to shit. We've still got the same gravity we always did."

"I guess I wasn't thinking," Jeff conceded.

"You were thinking. You were scraping up any kind of an argument you could to make yourself think they weren't going to shut us down. To make me think that, too."

Jeff looked at his watch.

"It's a long time yet."

"Sure."

He pressed the combination on the keypad—nine, nine, two, five, seven, seven. You could not leave the door of the Administration Building open; an alarm would sound.

"What's that?" Zaa caught his arm.

It was a voice from deep inside the building. Zaa leaped away with Jeff after him, long bounds carrying them the length of the corridor and up the stair.

"Mister Shonto? Administrator Shonto?"

"Here I am!" Panting, Jeff spoke as loudly as he could. "I'm coming!"

Undersecretary R. Lowell Bensen, almost in person, was seated in the holoconference theater; in that dim light, he looked fully as real as Zaa.

"Ah, there you are." He smiled; and Jeff, who was superstitious about smiles, winced inwardly.

"Leem, too. Good. Good! I realized you two might be busy elsewhere, but good God, twenty-four fifteen. A time convenient for us, a convenient time to get you two out of bed. Believe me, the Department treats me like that, too. Fourteen hours on a good day, twice around the clock on the bad ones. How are things in Grand Canal?"

"Quiet," Jeff said. "The plant's running at fifteen percent, per instructions. We've got a weak hydraulic pump on Number One Crusher, so we're running Number Two." All this would have been on the printout Bensen had undoubtedly read before making his call, but it would be impolite to mention it. "Zaa Leem here is making oversized rings and a new piston for that pump while we wait for a new one." Not in the least intending to do it, Jeff gulped. "We're afraid we may not get a new pump, sir, and we want to be capable of one hundred percent whenever you need us."

Bensen nodded, and Jeff turned to Zaa. "How are those new parts coming, Leem?"

"Just have to be installed, sir."

"You two are the entire staff of the Grand Canal Plant now? You don't even have a secretary? That came up during our meeting."

Jeff said, "That's right, sir."

"But there's a town there, isn't there? Grand Canal City or some such? A place where you can hire more staff when you need them?"

Here it came. Jeff's mouth felt so dry that he could scarcely speak. "There is a town, Mr. Bensen. You're right about that, sir. But I couldn't hire more personnel there. Nobody's left besides—besides ourselves, sir. Leem and me."

Bensen looked troubled. "A ghost town, is it?"

Zaa spoke up, surprising Jeff. "It was a tourist town, Mr. Bensen. That's why my family moved here. People wanted to see aliens back then, and talk to some, and they'd buy our art to do it. Now—well, sir, when my folks came to the Sol system, it took them two sidereal years just to get here. You know how it is these days, sir. Where'd you take your last vacation?"

"Isis, a lovely world. I see what you mean."

"The Department pays me pretty well, sir, and I save my money, most of it. My boss here wants me to go off to our home planet, where there are a lot more people like me. He says I ought to buy a ticket, whenever I've got the money, just to have a look at it."

Bensen frowned. "We'd hate to lose you, Leem."

"You're not going to, Mr. Bensen. I've got the money now, and more besides. But I don't speak the language or know the customs, and if I did, I wouldn't like them. Do you like aliens, sir?"

"I don't dislike them."

"That's exactly how I feel, sir. Nobody comes to Grand Canal anymore, sir. Why should they? It's just more Mars, and they live here already. Me and Mr. Shonto, we work here, and we think our work's important. So we stay. Only there's nobody else."

For a moment no one spoke.

"This came up in our meeting, too." Bensen cleared his throat, and suddenly Jeff understood that Bensen felt almost as embarrassed and self-conscious as he had. "Betty Collins told us Grand Canal had become a ghost town, but I wanted to make sure."

"It is," Jeff muttered. "If you're going to shut down our plant, sir, I can draw up a plan—"

Bensen was shaking his head. "How many security bots have you got, Shonto?"

"None, sir."

"None?"

"No, sir. We had human guards, sir. The Plant Police. They were only police in Grand Canal, actually. They were laid off one by one. I reported it—or my predecessor and I did, sir, I ought to say."

Bensen sighed. "I didn't see your reports. I wish I had. You're in some danger, I'm afraid, you and Leem."

"Really, sir?"

"Yes. Terrorists have been threatening to wreck the plants. Give in to their demands, or everyone suffocates. You know the kind of thing. Did you see it on vid?"

Jeff shook his head. "I don't watch much, sir. Maybe not as much as I should."

Bensen sighed again. "One of the news shows got hold of it and ran it. Just one show. After that, we persuaded them to keep a lid on it. That kind of publicity just plays into the terrorists' hands."

For a moment he was silent again, seeming to collect his thoughts; Zaa squirmed uncomfortably.

"Out there where you are, you're safer than any of the others. Still, you ought to have security. You get supplies each thirty-day?"

Jeff shook his head again. "Every other thirty-day, sir."

"I see. I'm going to change that. A supply crawler will come around every thirty-day from now on. I'll see to it that the next one carries that new pump."

"Thank you, sir."

"But you'll be getting a special resupply as quickly as I can arrange it. Security bots. Twenty, if I can scrape that many together. Whatever I can send."

Jeff began to thank him again, but Benson cut him off. "It may take a while. Weeks. Until you get them, you'll have to be on guard every moment. You're running at fifteen percent, you said. Could you up that to twenty-five?"

"Yes, sir. To one hundred within a few days."

"Good. Good! Make it twenty-five now, and let us know if you run into any problems."

Abruptly, Benson was gone. Jeff looked at Zaa, and Zaa looked at Jeff. Both grinned.

At last Jeff managed to say, "They're not shutting us down. Not yet anyhow."

Zaa rose, two-legging and seeming as tall as the main cooling stack. "These terrorist have them pissing in their pants, Jeff. Pissing in their pants! We're their ace in the hole. There's nobody out here but us."

"It'll blow over." Jeff found he was still grinning. "It's bound to, in a year or two. Meanwhile we better get Number One back on line."

They did, and when they had finished, Zaa snatched up a push broom, holding it with his right hand and his right intermediate foot as if it were a two-handed sword. "Defend yourself, Earther!"

Jeff backed away hurriedly until Zaa tossed him a mop, shouting, "They can mark your lonely grave with this!"

"Die, alien scum!" Jeff made a long thrust that Zaa parried just in time. "I rid the spaceways of their filth today!" Insulting the opponent had always been one of the best parts of their battles.

This one was furious. Jeff was smaller and not quite so strong. Zaa was slower; and though his visual field was larger, he lacked the binocular vision that let Jeff judge distances.

Even so, he prevailed in the end, driving Jeff through an open door and into the outdoor storage park, where after more furious fighting he slipped on the coarse red gravel and fell laughing and panting with the handle of Zaa's push broom at his throat.

"Man, that was fun!" He dropped his mop and held up his hands to indicate surrender. "How long since we did this?"

Zaa considered as he helped him up. "Ten years, maybe."

"Way too long!"

"Sure." Sharp claws scratched Zaa's scaly chin. "Hey, I've got an idea. We always wanted real swords, remember?"

As a boy, Jeff would have traded everything he owned for a real sword; the spot had been touched, and he found that there was still—still—a little, wailing ghost of his old desire.

"We could make swords," Zaa said. "Real swords. I could and you could help." Abruptly, he seemed to overflow with enthusiasm. "This rock's got a lot of iron in it. We could smelt it, make a crucible somehow. Make steel. I'd hammer it out—"

He dissolved in laughter beneath Jeff's stare. "Just kidding. But, hey, I got some high-carbon steel strip that would do for blades. I could grind one in an hour or so, and I could make hilts out of brass bar stock, spruce them up with file work, and fasten them on with epoxy."

Though mightily tempted, Jeff muttered, "It's Department property, Zaa."

Zaa laid a large, clawed hand upon his shoulder. "Boss boy, you fail to understand. We're arming ourselves. What if the terrorists get here before the security bots do?"

The idea swept over Jeff like the west wind in the Mare Erythraeum, carrying him along like so much dust. "How come I'm the administrator and you're the maintenance guy?"

"Simple. You're not smart enough for maintenance. Tomorrow?"

"Sure. And we'll have to practice with them a little before we get them sharp, right? It won't be enough to have them, we have to know how to use them, and that would be too dangerous if they had sharp edges and points."

"It's going to be dangerous anyhow," Zaa told him thoughtfully, "but we can wear safety helmets with face shields, and I'll make us some real shields, too."

The shields required more work than the swords, because Zaa covered their welded aluminum frames with densely woven plastic-coated wire, and wove a flattering portrait of Diane Seyn (whom he had won in battle long ago) into his, and an imagined picture of such a woman as he thought Jeff might like into Jeff's.

Although the shields had taken a full day each, both swords and shields were ready in under a week, and the fight that followed—the most epic of all their epic battles—ranged from the boarded up bungalows of Grand Canal to the lip of the Grand Canal itself, a setting so dramatic that each was nearly persuaded to kill the other, driving him over the edge to fall— a living meteor—to his death tens of thousands of feet below. The pure poetry of the thing seemed almost worth a life, as long as it was not one's own.

Neither did, of course. But an orthopter taped them as it shot footage for a special called *Haunted Mars*. And among the tens of billions on Earth who watched a few seconds of their duel were women who took note of their shields and understood.

UNDER MARS

by Paul McAuley

FOUR in the afternoon, and at last it's the end of Bill "Buzz" Brown's shift on the Marsport shuttle ride. The other steward, Cristal, hands out lollipops to half a dozen fretting kiddies while Buzz does his bit about how it might be a bumpy ride because there's a dust storm in the upper atmosphere, "So make sure those seat belts are done up tight, folks," and then zones out in his bucket seat, his long fingers surreptitiously kneading a scrap of paper, Homer's mysterious message, while the shuttle bucks and slews, red light flaring through the viewscreen portholes and most of the guests yelling and screaming gleefully as they get into the spirit of the ride.

The biggest screams of all, as usual, are for the final moments when the shuttle rolls through twenty degrees (the viewscreens make it seem steeper) as it shoots past a cruel mountain peak, uncoiling rock snakes spitting great washes of fire that clear to show the white dome of Marsport like a ripe boil on the cratered red plain. A minute later the shuttle shivers and settles. The seat belt lights go out and there's a scattering of applause which quickly dies down as everyone starts to get up. Buzz Brown is on his feet a scant moment before the guests, a tall, tanned, twenty-five-year-old in a purple jumpsuit trimmed with gold, his crisp crew cut bleached almost white by Florida sun. With the mike cable whipped once around his forearm, he delivers the last line in his script, "All you folks be sure to remember to take your stuff along with you, and have yourselves a fine time in Marsport," not much caring that the guests are too busy getting ready to leave to pay any attention to him. He and Cristal work the clunky, old-fashioned air lock doors and say good-bye to the disembarking guests, police the seats, finding nothing but candy wrappers and waxed paper cups half-full of melting ice, a well-chewed soft toy and a pair of cheap sunglasses not worth keeping, and exit through the curtained door that ostensibly leads to the cockpit.

The two stewards taking the next shift are already climbing the steep metal ramp between the big hydraulic rams at the front of the shuttle's cradle. One of them stops to ask Buzz if he's holding, and Buzz tells him what he's been telling everyone else these past few days, that he's out but he's going to connect soon, and escapes down the ramp.

Cristal dumps the bag of trash in the pneumatic tube which sucks it straight to the central incinerator, lifts off her blonde wig and shakes out her shag-cut black hair and says, "How about me, sweetie? I need some of your candy, too, and you've been telling me you're out for three days now. What's going on?"

"Nothing's going on," Buzz tells her, although he himself does not believe it. "I'm seeing Homer in a couple of hours, he got in contact with me just this morning. Everything's going to be fine."

Homer is Buzz's source, his one-time roommate at Florida State. It was Homer's idea to drop out of college and come and work here ("What else are you going to do with your media studies degree, except ask people if they want fries with their burgers five hundred times a day?"), and Homer's idea to supplement their meager wages by selling speed he cooks up in his apartment's kitchenette. Half the park's workers get by on speed or coke; because of their just-above-minimum wages, most casual temps need a lot of overtime, and need to keep the bounce in their steps and the smiles on their faces. Dealing home-cooked crank isn't how Buzz planned his life to turn out, but he thinks of it as a public service, part of the lubrication that keeps the park moving; a semi-official position even, since the management turns a blind eye to it—there's no blood or urine testing, and most leads and line managers aren't averse to the odd pill or snort. You can get fired for half a hundred infractions, for not smiling enough, for being too friendly to a guest, for not black-bagging a costume properly when carrying it to and from work, so a tentacle tip or an antenna sticks out in full view, but no one has ever been sacked for getting high.

Homer's speed is prime stuff, and he and Buzz have a nice little business going, but just lately Homer has been increasingly evasive whenever Buzz has asked him when he's going to cook up a fresh batch. Buzz feels pushed into a corner by Homer's intransigence and the demands of his customers, feels the same claustrophobic oppression, a sick clutching pressure on his heart he gets when he's stuck on a level of a virtual game with energy levels draining fast and no obvious way out. Last evening, when Homer didn't answer his phone, Buzz finally nerved himself up to drive over to his apartment building. Homer didn't answer the bell, and his window, which Buzz could see through the closed gate, beyond the little courtyard swimming pool, remained stubbornly dark. But just this morning a tech stopped Buzz as he was coming through the employees' entrance and pressed a note into his hand: a brief message, in Homer's childish, backward slanting scrawl, telling Buzz to meet him in the Bradbury section canteen at six P.M.

Cristal says, as she and Buzz enter the service tunnel, "I need a little pick-me-up right now. I'm double-shifting, another eight hours waitressing on the strip, and then tomorrow morning I'm doing auditions."

"You go for it," Buzz says absent-mindedly, still thinking about the note. Maybe it's nothing more than the delivery of a fresh batch of speed, but Buzz can't shake the feeling that Homer is up to something, that he's about to try and persuade Buzz to take another wrong turning in his life.

"I will. This ride isn't where this girl is going to spend the rest of her life. I'm a comedic actress. I should at least be out on the strip in Marsport doing one-on-one routines with the guests, but the spot I'm going for?" Cristal lifts her slim arms above her head, does a shimmy step. "It's the coolest: one of the Princesses in the Barsoom section."

Buzz has to smile at her burlesque. "You're a natural," he tells her.

"Eight years of dance classes, I don't intend to waste them. And there's no way I'm casual temping forever. I was laid off seven weeks before my last rehire. If I get the Barsoom gig,

I'm going to make it my own, and then I'm on the road to a full-time job and all those yummy benefits. So I just need a little lift, sweetie, a little something to put a spring in my step."

"Like I said, I'm out until maybe later this evening."

Cristal looks at him. She's a tall, willowy girl, with a long, mobile upper lip that lifts now in amusement. "You're too nice a guy to be a dealer, Buzz. You can't lie to save your life. I know you took a little lift from your own personal supply before the shift, I know you're holding out on me. How about I take you to this thing I know about? It's this bunch of musicians, and you know they know how to party. Someone's birthday or divorce, I forget which, tomorrow night." Cristal puts a little bump and grind into her walk. "It could be fun."

She's just twenty, pretty under the pancake and thick blue eyeshadow in a corn-fed teeth'n'tits Kansas kind of way, but Buzz has a rule not to mess around with the people he deals to, and he says, "I don't think so."

Cristal's face hardens. "Well, maybe I don't need your stuff. I hear there's something new coming in."

Buzz has heard the rumors too. It's another reason why he's been trying so hard to get hold of Homer. On impulse, he says, "You can have what I've got, but it isn't much."

"Don't do me any favors."

"This *is* a favor," Buzz protests. "I'm down to dust. But step into my office, and I'll see what I can do."

Between two green-painted dumpsters, out of sight of the tunnel security cameras, Buzz takes from the pouch hung inside the pants of his purple jumpsuit the very last glassine envelope. Cristal digs into it with a long pinkie nail, lifts the nail to her nose, sniffs up the crest of white powder, shudders with delicate pleasure.

"Buy a full bag tomorrow," Buzz tells her, "and we'll call it even."

"You're a doll," Cristal says, and treats him to the nailful. As he bends to sniff, she adds, "I'll be thinking of you when I get that gig."

"Knock 'em dead," Buzz tells her. He means it, but he feels a prick of jealousy too. She's moving on, and it seems he'll be here for the rest of his life.

In the men's locker room, he strips off his skanky costume

and throws it into a hamper, and feels the speed coming on as he showers. A sudden dryness in the throat, a tightening of the skin over his face, a sharpening of the lights and the hiss and needlepoint kiss of the shower. The crushing accumulation of his anxiety recedes a little. Maybe things will work out, he thinks, as he dresses in a clean white T-shirt and red jeans and straps on his watch, a good Timex some guest left behind a few months ago. He looks at the message on the scrap of paper for about the fiftieth time, and decides to catch Homer, who plays the child-emperor of Mars, at the end of the Bradbury section's five o'clock parade. If Homer is playing one of his silly mind games, Buzz is going to put his own spin on it.

The park is divided into twelve sections, like a neatly sliced pie, the hotels spaced around the perimeter, a fifty-meter-high scale replica of Olympus Mons at the center. Each section is its own little kingdom, with its own tunnel complex, its own set of locker rooms and break areas, its own cafeteria. Section crews don't mix. Company policy encourages fierce loyalty to your own crew, a divide and rule strategy that's created a dozen little rival factions. Sometimes there are even *West Side Story* style rumbles and spats between crews; last year, one of the Barsoom crew was knifed by a jealous boyfriend when he hassled a Marsport bar girl. Buzz has been ripped off a couple of times when he's dealt with people for other crews, and feels a flutter of apprehension under the speed's steely rush as he rides a service lift topside. In this part of the Florida panhandle, the limestone is saturated with water only a couple of feet below the surface, so the park is raised up like an ant mound, and its underground tunnels and service areas are actually the ground floor. Buzz comes up at the far edge of Marsport's geodesic dome, the first sunlight he's seen for more than nine hours blazing through its translucent panes, and makes his way through a crowded fast food area to the mock air lock which links Marsport's dome with the Face of Mars section.

Buzz puts on his shades, strides quickly along the empty walkway. The air is hot and sultry; the sunlight brassy. The red rocks and the red sands, the three rough, red pyramids and the Face itself, tilted at a viewable angle, glow like heated iron. From this aspect, the mock Olympus Mons has the profile of a cowled nun.

In five minutes, Buzz is on the other side, amongst the limpid canals and crystal towers of the Bradbury section, making his way through increasingly dense crowds to the central canal. Men and women and children in shorts and T-shirts, slacks and sports shirts, pack the bleachers. Baseball caps, sunglasses, sneakers. Children ride their fathers' shoulders or clutch their mothers' legs. Almost every adult is watching through the viewfinder of a video or still camera the dancers and musicians in skintight silvery costumes and weird masks who swirl along either side of the wide canal, where decorated barges linked nose to tail smoothly plough the limpid water.

Buzz discovers that he is grinding his teeth. He pops a stick of gum in his mouth and drops the wrapper; it's barely touched the tiles when a little maintenance robot, a slipper-sized silver teardrop, scoots over and snatches the slip of paper in its jaws and scoots away.

The child-emperor of Mars, a small skinny silvery figure with a flowing purple robe and a huge fantasticated mask and head, stands at the center of a giant crystalline flower on the last barge. As the barge glides past, Buzz sees with a stir of alarm that something's wrong. The child-emperor is sort of slumped in his cloak, and he isn't waving at the guests. Buzz keeps pace with the barge, threading through the crowds, following the last of the dancers around the barrier which shields the working part of the canal from the view of the guests, which separates the magic from the mundane.

In the backstage zoo, dancers are shucking their masks, hanging towels around their shoulders, lighting cigarettes; assistants are leaping onto the barges, helping actors disengage their headpieces. A locker room smell of sweat and talcum powder mingles with the hot oil and ozone of working machinery.

When the child-emperor's barge comes gliding under the arch of the false bridge, Buzz jumps aboard, shakes the slight, silver-clad figure's shoulders but gets no response. Homer must have fainted inside his costume, something that happens all the time; it can get as hot as a hundred thirty degrees inside the heavy costume heads, under the brutal Florida sun. Buzz finds the latches which hold the mask and head to the costume's metal shoulder rack. A steel pole runs up the back of the costume to the top of the head, and when the latches snap open the emperor slides down the pole into Buzz's arms. It isn't Homer.

A moment later, a tech jostles Buzz aside. "You go on down to the cafeteria," the man says.

"What's going on?"

The tech bends over the impostor emperor, anoints the paper-white face with water from a spray bottle. "Go on down," he says. "People are waiting for you."

The Bradbury section cafeteria, like all the other staff cafeterias in the park, is a charmless bunker carpeted in astroturf, with arctic air-conditioning and tired fluorescent lighting. Tables and chairs scattered amidst stands of fake tropical plants; a long row of vending machines that sell everything from cola to enchiladas; a gaming area at the back, with pool tables, virtual reality machines, and a dartboard. Buzz is scanning the groups of actors in half costume, techs in taupe coveralls, teenage sales persons, receptionists and restaurant staff in red jeans and white T-shirts, when someone calls his name.

It's Wolfie Look, the kingpin of the Bradbury section, a beefy, fortysomething redneck with a shaved scalp and bad skin, a wet black cheroot plugged into his grin. He runs the section's garage, and runs the numbers and drug rackets, too. He's lounging at a table with half a dozen of his cronies, all of them, like Wolfie Look, maintenance gangers. Homer sits in the middle of them.

Buzz ignores Wolfie Look and says, "What's up, Homer?"

"He's been a bad boy," Wolfie Look says.

Buzz ignores him, and tells Homer, "You weren't answering your phone for about a week, and then you ask me to come all the way over here. What's up?"

"Be cool," Homer says. He's small and squat, with a pockmarked face and coke-bottle-end glasses, the only person Buzz knows who came to work in the park because this is the next best thing to going to Mars. His half of the college room he shared with Buzz was covered with photographs of red, rocky panoramas taken by robot surveyors; he even persuaded Buzz to join the Mars Society, a group of fanatics who make endless, deeply detailed plans for terraforming Mars. Homer is a very scientific boy, but he's also deeply lazy, and he hides his laziness with an affected contempt for the straight world.

"There aren't any secrets between me and Homer," Wolfie Look says. "Not anymore. Isn't that right, boys?" There's a murmur of agreement, and Wolfie Look tells Buzz, "I knew you'd be along, speedo, chasing after that home-brewed crank your pal puts out, and here you are."

"Talk to me, Homer," Buzz says. "What have you got yourself into? Who was that guy who took your place? And why did he take your place? What's going on?"

"You'll see why I had to take time out," Homer says, "if you'll just sit down and listen."

"The guy fainted, Homer," Buzz says. "If the parade lead finds out what's going on, he'll can the substitute and he'll can you, too."

"Don't you worry about that," Wolfie Look says, with a smile that shows half a dozen gold teeth. He shifts his cheroot from one corner of his mouth to the other, pushes out a chair with his foot, and tells Buzz, "Take a load off."

Buzz knows that Wolfie Look's good ol' boy act masks a devious and dangerous mind, and says warily, "I just want a quick word with Homer, then I'll be gone."

"Oh, I don't think so, speedo. For one thing, this isn't your turf, and for another, Homer's business is my business now." Wolfie Look raps the table. There are gold rings on every one of his fat, dirty fingers. "You sit down. I'll tell you what's going down."

Buzz sits.

"What it is," Wolfie Look says, "is that Homer here is in the hole with me for about five thousand dollars."

"Five thousand three hundred and forty," one of his cronies says.

"There you go," Wolfie Look says. "So the deal is that either Homer does some business for me, or I break his arms and legs."

"He isn't interested in selling crank," Homer says. "Frankly, nor am I, not anymore."

Buzz says, "Then I don't know why I'm here," and pushes back his chair. The speed has made him bold.

"You came because I asked you to," Homer says. "This is a great opportunity. We're getting into the big time."

"Your pal's right," Wolfie Look says, his smile stretching as wide as a frog's. "I can supply you with something far superior to home-brewed crank. Focus. You might even have heard of it."

"Focus?"

"Trust me," Homer says. "We'll clean up on this stuff."

"First of all you have to do a little job for me," Wolfie Look says. "Think of it as an initiative test."

"I knew you'd come in with me," Homer says happily. "You won't regret it."

"You'd better tell just how you got so deep in the hole," Buzz says. "Five thousand dollars? I know you're not a betting man, Homer."

"It was this stuff," Homer says. He twirls the plastic bag, printed with the park's logo, that's weighted with the package Wolfie Look gave them.

"Focus?"

"Yeah. Focus. The stuff we're muling."

Buzz steps around a guest, four hundred pounds of Midwest beef crammed into Bermuda shorts and a *War of the Worlds* T-shirt who's standing in the middle of the path and panning his video camera up the side of one of the crystal towers. He tells Homer, "I wish you wouldn't call it that. It makes us sound like criminals."

"That's what we are, Buzz," Homer says. "Let's face it, that's what we've been since we started up our little business. And now we're in with the big boys," he says, and gives the plastic bag an extra-wide twirl.

"Jesus, Homer. Aren't you being, I don't know, a little insouciant about this?"

"You think someone will guess that I'm carrying a half kilo of an illegal drug in this plastic bag? No way."

A couple of guests glance at them.

"Keep your voice down," Buzz says, feeling sweat prickle his whole skin. "Be cool."

"I am cool!" Homer shouts. "I'm the king of the world! I'm the emperor of Mars!"

"Okay, okay. Jesus. Maybe you'd better tell me what this Focus shit does."

"It concentrates the mind wonderfully," Homer says.

"Like an impending execution?" Buzz's jaws ache; he's been maniacally chewing the same stick of gum for twenty minutes now. He spits the flavorless wad into his hand, drops it into one of the flower-shaped crystal waste bins, which in a tiny, tinny tinkle says *thank you.* Buzz unwraps a fresh stick and tells Homer, "You spent five thousand dollars on this stuff? No wonder you weren't answering your phone. Not to mention getting around to making up your orders."

"I was on Mars."

"You're on Mars now."

"No, seriously. That's what Focus does."

"It takes you to Mars. Right."

"It puts you wherever you want to be."

"This is a VR thing, isn't it?"

"Not exclusively," Homer says. "That's why Wolfie Look is going to clean our clocks."

"And it does what? Makes you dumb enough to believe VR is real?"

They walk through a crystal gateway into the next slice of the park's pie. Red rocks and red sand dunes saddle away into the *trompe l'oeil* distance of a painted backscene. Signs point toward the Viking landing site, the secret flying saucer factory, the Mars landing simulation, the life on Mars display.

"It works in here," Homer says, tapping his head. "Focus makes the impossible real. It suspends disbelief. It makes fake reality as real as you and me. I was plugged into one of the NASA rovers, Buzz, traveling through Nirgal Vallis. I was on Mars."

"You're on Mars right now," Buzz says, turning in a circle with his arms out, taking in the red sands (dyed Florida beach sand fixed into shape with resin), the pockmarked red rocks (each hand-carved from Arizona sandstone), the red crags (ditto).

"I never did try it in the park," Homer says, "but I'm told it works just as well here as with VR."

"You're serious about this stuff, aren't you?"

"It's the real deal. When we're done with this little job, we'll try it out. You and me, what do you say?"

"I'd say you've done so much of this stuff you don't know what's real or not anymore. Hey! Quit it!"

Because Homer has grabbed Buzz's arm, is steering him off the main path.

"I want to show you something," Homer says.

Buzz pulls free. "Man, what's wrong with you?"

"It won't take but ten minutes," Homer says stubbornly.

Buzz knows better than to argue. It's always been this way: Homer making up his mind, and Buzz going along with it. Homer is the go-getter, the man with the plan; Buzz is the sidekick.

The path winds between bigger and bigger rocks, dives down into an artfully simulated crevice in a simulated arc of a crater's rampart wall. The room beyond is low ceilinged, red lit, and, apart from a bored docent lounging in the far corner, completely deserted. Tall glass cylinders are scattered across the black rubber floor, and Homer walks straight across the room to the largest, in which a red lump of rock half a meter high sits on a black display stand.

"There," Homer says. "That there is real."

"Come on, Homer. It's just plastic. A model."

"I know that. I'm not fried. But it exists. It's sitting on Mars right this moment, in one of the canyons in Deuteronilus Mensea. A robot took twenty-eight days to scan that rock right there on Mars, and a laser stereolithograph used the information to build it up out of polymer. Look at it, Buzz. It's a fossilized stromatolite, just like the ones found in three-billion-year-old sedimentary rocks on Earth, which in turn are just like living stromatolites found in certain shallow bays of the Australian coast. See the striations, like pages in a book? Each one is a layer of sediment trapped and stabilized by a year's worth of growth of mat-forming microorganisms. There was life on Mars, once upon a time. This is the hard evidence."

"Look around you, Homer," Buzz says, exasperated. "We're the only people here. No one cares about the real Mars because no one but a bunch of robots is ever going there."

"I've been. That's the point. That's what Focus does."

"You'd rather be a robot than the emperor of Mars."

"It was like I grew into it. Like the way you grow into the corners of your car when you drive, only more intense. It was as if I was right there."

"You always were a scientific boy, Homer, but don't you think you're taking this a little too far?"

"When did you get so cynical, Buzz? You used to love this place as much as me."

"I guess when I realized I'm just another temp loser pissing away his life smiling and greeting in a second-rate amusement park. Are you done with your little lesson here? We've a job to do."

"I just want you to know that I know what I'm doing. You've got to think of it as a career opportunity."

"It's working for a redneck drug dealer, is what it is."

"Wolfie is smart, in his own way," Homer says, rooting in the plastic bag. "He wants the whole park, and with this stuff he's going to get it, too. This is the real deal, Buzz."

"He certainly has you by the balls. You'll be paying off your debt forever."

"I'll play Wolfie Look's game for now, but I have a plan, Buzz, don't you worry. I'm going to analyze the hell out of this shit. I'm going to figure out how to synthesize it and then I'm going to undercut that shit-kicker until he squeals for mercy. You and me, Buzz, what do you think?"

"I think you're crazy. What are you doing?"

Homer has pulled out the package. A dozen medium baggies, each stuffed rigid with white powder and bound together by duct tape and saran wrap.

"Christ," Buzz says. "It might as well have *Dangerous Drugs* written all over it in big red letters."

"You just need the tiniest snort," Homer says, pulling at an edge of duct tape like a child impatient with the wrapping of a present, "and it all becomes real."

Buzz grabs at the package. "If Wolfie Look's guy finds he's short, Wolfie really will break your arms and legs."

"Just one tiny snort," Homer pleads. "I want to see how real hyperreality can get."

There's a glint of wildness in Homer's eyes that alarms Buzz. He manages to snatch the package away, leaving Homer with a long curl of silvery tape in his hand. Behind them, someone says, "Can I help you guys?"

It's the docent, a tanned teenage boy in red jeans and a white T-shirt. Homer grabs the package from Buzz, drops it in the plastic bag, and says, "We were just going."

"I thought maybe you might give me a taste," the boy says. His crew cut hair is dyed yellow, as bright as a sunflower.

"There is something I can give you," Buzz says, and spits the wad of gum in the boy's hand and closed his fingers around it. "Take care of that, will you? I don't want to mess up your nice display."

Buzz and Homer pass through the *War of the Worlds* section, where amniotronic walrus-like Martians with wise, friendly faces disgorge scientific nuggets amidst fantasticated steampunk machineries, their earnest discourses mostly ignored by guests, who prefer the Battle of Dorking arena. They pass through the Malacandrian section, its bosky dells amidst giant celery trees populated by hundreds of cute amniotronic animals, a queue of parents and children for the *It's All One World* ride snaking around a dozen turns, neatly corralled by railings. And then, through a crumbling stone archway hung with green and red and gold banners, they enter the Burroughs section.

Wolfie Look told them to drop off the stuff in one of the taverns. They try to look as inconspicuous as possible while drinking root beer from paper cups at a wooden table in a corner of a big open space bounded by half-ruined arches and crowded with guests, while a trio of huge, green-skinned fourarmed amniotronic musicians play a selection of Beatle tunes. Homer, the plastic bag planted firmly between his feet, keeps glancing at his watch; they're waiting for the tavern to empty when the show begins, when Burroughs' Earth hero and his band of Martians fight the yellow Martians and rescue the Princess and her handmaidens. The Burroughs section is packed with guests waiting to see the spectacle, as Buzz can't resist pointing out.

"Disney has Tarzan, we have the nearly nude Princesses of Mars."

Homer shrugs. "The dads love them, the daughters want to be them."

"Did you ever think it would come to this, Homer? Two grown men play-acting a Mars shuttle flight attendant and the child-emperor of Mars."

"I wanted to be an astronaut," Homer says. "That's all I ever wanted to be when I was a kid. I went to space camp every year. I majored in physics and math. I even thought that being not so tall would be a help. Most astronauts aren't exactly endowed in the vertical direction."

"Except no one goes into space any more."

"The first time I took this stuff, Buzz, it really did put me there. It was like finding the place you've belonged to all your life. It was like going home. It's the new thing. It beats speed hollow."

"We're still young. We've still got our looks. We could do anything out in the world."

But Homer isn't listening. Buzz turns and sees what he's staring at: two rent-a-cops are threading through the crowded tables at the far side of the tavern, followed by a yellow-haired boy.

Homer and Buzz make it out into the crowded street by keeping a family group, from grandmother to two-year-old riding her father's shoulders, between themselves and the rent-a-cops.

"This isn't good," Homer says. He's clutching the plastic bag close to his chest.

"Where are we going?"

"We'll find a phone and make a new rendezvous," Homer says, and plunges purposefully into the crowds.

Technicians are roping off the wide avenue where the show will take place. People are camped along its edge, on the curb, under clustered palm trees and banana plants. Homer and Buzz badge themselves into the staging area behind a false stone wall. It's a chaos of buffed bodybuilders in metal-leaf kilts and red skin-paint, handmaidens in long black wigs and spray-on flesh-colored bodysuits decorated with scales at appropriate places, lizardmen and apemen, their big false heads in one hand and, cigarettes or paper cups of ice water in the other, leads with clipboards and stopwatches trying to get everyone into line, technicians talking into headsets. The actor who plays John Carter is standing in a corner, wearing a red kilt and a big brass belt and staring manfully into the far distance as his muscular torso is sprayed with glycerin by a pert teenage girl. A tech is checking the systems of the amniotronic model of a giant, shag-furred, fanged dog, typing instructions into the laptop which is plugged into the thing's back, making each of its five pairs of legs flex in turn.

Buzz follows Homer through this melee toward the office area at the back, but they're only halfway there when one of the leads challenges them. As Homer shoves the man out of the way, a rent-a-cop comes running, pushing through startled actors. Buzz and Homer dodge around a train of prop carts and a hurry down the stairs to the service tunnels. Turning left and right at random, they run past a row of steel trash cans, past someone trundling a rack of costumes, past locker rooms and a canteen, and run up a ramp and come out into the staging area, deserted now apart from techs standing in the bright sunlight at the far end. The cheers and laughter of the crowd is a dull roar through the fake stone wall. They have run in a circle.

Homer bends over and breathes hard, hands on knees.

Buzz says, "All we have to do is get out of the section."

"We have to get out of the park. And how are we going to do that? Listen."

Shouts sound faintly in the tunnel at the bottom of the ramp.

"They must have tracked us on the security cameras," Homer says.

"We're not finished yet," Buzz says. "Give me the bag."

"Don't be dumb."

"Give it to me. They don't know what's in it. If they don't have any hard evidence, all they can do is fire us."

The shouts are closer now. Suddenly, half a dozen rent-a-cops turn the corner, start running up the ramp toward them. Homer throws the plastic bag to Buzz, and Buzz takes it and runs, charging across the staging area, dodging startled techs and running out into sunlight and loud cheers, and people dancing all around him.

He's come out through an archway into the middle of the staged fight. The actor playing John Carter is dueling with a warrior with lemon-yellow skin. The nearly nude princesses of Mars are in a pen on a rough wooden wagon in the center of the wide, white avenue, stagily menaced by lizardmen. Two

white apes are chasing each other in circles. Red-skinned
swordsmen are trading sword blows with their yellow-skinned
counterparts. And a couple of rent-a-cops are pushing through
the guests pressing up against the red rope stretched on the
other side of the avenue.

Buzz picks up a sword which lies beside a "dead" yellow-
skinned warrior, who opens an eye and whispers fiercely,
"What the fuck are you doing?" The sword is made of a light,
pliable alloy, but it makes a satisfactory swish as Buzz runs
forward, hacking the air. Guests cheer, thinking this is part of
the show, a Keystone Cops comedy routine. The air prickles
with camera flashes as Buzz drives the rent-a-cops back
against the rope, then dodges a trio of bare-chested red Martians who try and bring him down. He tries to climb over the
rope, but a guest built like a linebacker enters into the spirit of
things and pushes him back.

John Carter has, on schedule, finished off his opponent and
sent the lizardmen running, and is now hacking at the big rope
around the nearly nude princesses' cage. The rope, held only
by a twist of nylon wire, parts as it is supposed to. The
princesses rush into John Carter's arms, all long limbs and
spangles and toothy squeals of delight.

Overhead, a crane lowers the flier that will carry them off,
a wooden platform on a raft of inflated bladders, its gossamer
propeller spinning in a rainbow blur.

The rent-a-cops regroup and rush at Buzz. He turns and
runs at the flier, swinging the plastic bag around his head like
David confronting Goliath. And lets it go. A rent-a-cop jumps
for it, misses. It soars through the air, hits the whirling propeller. There's an explosion of white, thinning immediately as
it's blown over Buzz and the actors and the rent-a-cops and the
guests.

The air seems to brighten. Everything swims into focus and
is intensified, from the grains of dust hung in the sunlit air to
the pull of Buzz's sheathed muscles, and every moment is as
separate and intense as the sunstruck dust grains. One half of
Buzz's brain is trying to tell the other half that it's just the
drug, but the urgent reality of the world shuts out this sensible
advice. He's on Mars.

The red and yellow warriors redouble their fight. Dejah

Thoris and John Carter, the Red Princess and the Swordsman of Mars, kiss and rekiss. Guests lower their cameras, look around themselves as if for the first time. Everyone is on Mars, in a terrible and strange city on the floor of a lost, dry sea.

Buzz runs down the ancient avenue. Crowds of Martians part before him. He runs through the ancient gate and runs on across the red sands of Mars. He's free, and so full of sudden joy that gravity seems to lessen with every step he takes.

THE WAR OF THE WORLDVIEWS

by James Morrow

AUGUST 7

One thing I've learned from this catastrophe is to start taking the science of astronomy more seriously. For six days running, the world's professional stargazers warned us of puzzling biological and cybernetic activity on the surfaces of both Martian satellites. We, the public, weren't interested. Next the astronomers announced that Phobos and Deimos had each sent a fleet of disk-shaped spaceships, heavily armed, hurtling toward planet Earth. We laughed in their faces. Then the astronomers reported that each saucer measured only one meter across, so that the invading armadas evoked "a vast recall of defective automobile tires." The talk-show comedians had a field day.

The first operation the Martians undertook upon landing in Central Park was to suck away all the city's electricity and seal it in a small spherical container suggesting an aluminum racquetball. I believe they wanted to make sure we wouldn't bother them as they went about their incomprehensible agenda, but Valerie says they were just being quixotic. In either case, the Martians obviously don't need all that power. They brought plenty with them.

I am writing by candlelight in our Delancey Street apartment, scribbling on a legal pad with a ballpoint pen. New York City is without functional lamps, subways, elevators, traffic signals, household appliances, or personal computers. Here and there, I suppose, life goes on as usual, thanks to storage batteries, solar cells, and diesel-fueled generators. The rest of us are living in the eighteenth century, and we don't much like it.

I was taking Valerie's kid to the Central Park Zoo when the Phobosians and the Deimosians started uprooting the city's power cables. Bobby and I witnessed the whole thing. The Martians were obviously having a good time. Each alien is only six inches high, but I could still see the jollity coursing through their little frames. Capricious chipmunks. I hate them all. Bobby became terrified when the Martians started wrecking things. He cried and moaned. I did my best to comfort him. Bobby's a good kid. Last week he called me Second Dad.

The city went black, neighborhood by neighborhood, and then the hostilities began. The Phobosian and the Deimosian infantries went at each other with weapons so advanced as to make Earth's rifles and howitzers seem like peashooters. Heat rays, disintegrator beams, quark bombs, sonic grenades, laser cannons. The Deimosians look rather like the animated mushrooms from *Fantasia*. The Phobosians resemble pencil sharpeners fashioned from Naugahyde. All during the fight, both races communicated among themselves via chirping sounds reminiscent of dolphins enjoying sexual climax. Their ferocity knew no limits. In one hour I saw enough war crimes to fill an encyclopedia, though on the scale of an 0-gauge model railroad.

As far as I could tell, the Battle of Central Park ended in a stalemate. The real loser was New York, victim of a hundred ill-aimed volleys. At least half the buildings on Fifth Avenue are gone, including the Mount Sinai Medical Center. Fires rage everywhere, eastward as far as Third Avenue, westward to Columbus. Bobby and I were lucky to get back home alive.

Such an inferno is clearly beyond the capacity of our local fire departments. Normally we would seek help from Jersey and Connecticut, but the Martians have fashioned some sort of force-field dome, lowering it over the entire island as blithely as a chef placing a lid on a casserole dish. Nothing can get in, and nothing can get out. We are at the invaders' mercy. If the Phobosians and the Deimosians continue trying to settle their differences through violence, the city will burn to the ground.

August 8
The Second Battle of Central Park was even worse than the first. We lost the National Academy of Design, the Guggen-

heim Museum, and the Carlyle Hotel. It ended with the Phobosians driving the Deimosians all the way down to Rockefeller Center. The Deimosians then rallied, stood their ground, and forced a Phobosian retreat to West 71st Street.

Valerie and I learned about this latest conflict only because a handful of resourceful radio announcers have improvised three ad hoc Citizens Band stations along what's left of Lexington Avenue. We have a decent CB receiver, so we'll be getting up-to-the-minute bulletins until our batteries die. Each time the newscaster named Clarence Morant attempts to describe the collateral damage from this morning's hostilities, he breaks down and weeps.

Even when you allow for the shrimplike Martian physique, the two armies are not very far apart. By our scale, they are separated by three blocks—by theirs, perhaps ten kilometers. Clarence Morant predicts there'll be another big battle tomorrow. Valerie chides me for not believing her when she had those premonitions last year of our apartment building on fire. I tell her she's being a Monday morning Nostradamus. How many private journals concerning the Martian invasion exist at the moment? As I put pen to paper, I suspect that hundreds, perhaps even thousands, of my fellow survivors are recording their impressions of the cataclysm. But I am not like these other diary keepers. I am unique. I alone have the power to stop the Martians before they demolish Manhattan—or so I imagine.

August 9

All quiet on the West Side front—though nobody believes the cease-fire will last much longer. Clarence Morant says the city is living on borrowed time.

Phobos and Deimos. When the astronomers first started warning us of nefarious phenomena on the Martian satellites, I experienced a vague feeling of personal connection to those particular moons. Last night it all flooded back. Phobos and Deimos are indeed a part of my past: a past I've been trying to forget—those bad old days when I was the worst psychiatric intern ever to serve an apprenticeship at Bellevue. I'm much happier in my present position as a bohemian hippie bum, looking after Bobby and living off the respectable income Valerie makes running two SoHo art galleries.

His name was Rupert Klieg, and he was among the dozen or so patients who made me realize I'd never be good with insane people. I found Rupert's rants alternately unnerving and boring. They sounded like something you'd read in some cheesy special-interest zine for psychotics. *Paranoid Confessions. True Hallucinations.* Rupert was especially obsessed with an organization called the Asaph Hall Society, named for the self-taught scientist who discovered Phobos and Deimos. All three members of the Asaph Hall Society were amateur astronomers and certifiable lunatics who'd dedicated themselves to monitoring the imminent invasion of planet Earth by the bellicose denizens of the Martian moons. Before Rupert told me his absurd fantasy, I didn't even realize that Mars *had* moons, nor did I care. But now I do, God knows.

The last I heard, they'd put Rupert Klieg away in the Lionel Frye Psychiatric Institute, Ninth Avenue near 58th. Valerie says I'm wasting my time, but I believe in my bones that the fate of Manhattan lies with that particular schizophrenic.

August 10
This morning a massive infantry assault by the Phobosians drove the Deimosians south to Times Square. When I heard that the Frye Institute was caught in the cross fire, I naturally feared the worst for Rupert. When I actually made the trek to Ninth and 58th, however, I discovered that the disintegrator beams, devastating in most regards, had missed the lower third of the building. I didn't see any Martians, but the whole neighborhood resounded with their tweets and twitters.

The morning's upheavals had left the Institute's staff in a state of extreme distraction. I had no difficulty sneaking into the lobby, stealing a dry-cell lantern, and conducting a room-by-room hunt.

Rupert was in the basement ward, Room 16. The door stood ajar. I entered. He lay abed, grasping a toy plastic telescope about ten centimeters long. I couldn't decide whether his keepers had been kind or cruel to allow him this trinket. It was nice that the poor demented astronomer had a telescope, but what good did it do him in a room with no windows?

His face had become thinner, his body more gaunt, but otherwise he was the fundamentally beatific madman I remembered. "Thank you for the lantern, Dr. Onslo," he said as I approached. He swatted at a naked light bulb hanging from the ceiling like a miniature punching bag. "It's been pretty gloomy around here."

"Call me Steve. I never finished my internship."

"I'm not surprised, Dr. Onslo. You were a lousy therapist."

"Let me tell you why I've come."

"I know why you've come, and as Chairperson of the Data Bank Committee of the Asaph Hall Society, I can tell you everything you want to know about Phobos and Deimos."

"I'm especially interested in learning how your organization knew an invasion was imminent."

The corners of Rupert's mouth lifted in a grotesque smile. He opened the drawer in his nightstand, removed a crinkled sheet of paper, and deposited it in my hands. "Mass: 1.08e16 kilograms," he said as I studied the fact sheet, which had a cherry cough drop stuck to one corner. "Diameter: 22.2 kilometers. Mean density: 2.0 grams per cubic centimeter. Mean distance from Mars: 9,380 kilometers. Rotational period: 0.31910 days. Mean orbital velocity: 2.14 kilometers per second. Orbital eccentricity: 0.01. Orbital inclination: 1.0 degrees. Escape velocity: 0.0103 kilometers per second. Visual geometric albedo: 0.06. In short, ladies and gentlemen, I give you Phobos-"

"Fascinating," I said evenly.

"As opposed to Deimos. Mass: 1.8e15 kilograms. Diameter: 12.6 kilometers. Mean density: 1.7 grams per cubic centimeter. Mean distance from Mars: 23,460 kilometers. Rotational period: 1.26244 days. Mean orbital velocity: 1.36 kilometers per second. Orbital eccentricity: 0.00. Orbital inclination: 0.9 to 2.7 degrees. Escape velocity: 0.0057 kilometers per second. Visual geometric albedo: 0.07. Both moons look like baked potatoes."

"By some astonishing intuition, you knew that these two satellites intended to invade the Earth."

"Intuition, my Aunt Fanny. We deduced it through empirical observation." Rupert brought the telescope to his eye and focused on the dormant lightbulb. "Consider this. A scant eighty million years ago, there were no Phobes or Deems. I'm not kidding. They were all one species, living beneath the desiccated surface of Mars. Over the centuries, a deep rift in philosophic sensibility opened up within their civilization. Eventually they decided to abandon the native planet, never an especially congenial place, and emigrate to the local moons. Those favoring Sensibility A moved to Phobos. Those favoring Sensibility B settled on Deimos."

"Why would the Martians find Phobos and Deimos more congenial?" I jammed the fact sheet in my pocket. "I mean, aren't they just . . . big rocks?"

"Don't bring your petty little human perspective to the matter, Dr. Onslo. To a vulture, carrion tastes like chocolate cake. Once they were on their respective worlds, the Phobes and the Deems followed separate evolutionary paths . . . hence, the anatomical dimorphism we observe today."

"What was the nature of the sensibility rift?"

Rupert used his telescope to study a section of the wall where the plaster had crumbled away, exposing the latticework beneath. "I have no idea."

"None whatsoever?"

"The Asaph Hall Society dissolved before we could address that issue. All I know is that the Phobes and the Deems decided to settle the question once and for all through armed combat on neutral ground."

"So they came here?"

"Mars would've seemed like a step backward. Venus has rotten weather."

"Are you saying that whichever side wins the war will claim victory in what is essentially a philosophical controversy?"

"Correct."

"They believe that truth claims can be corroborated through violence?"

"More or less."

"That doesn't make any sense to me."

"If you were a fly, horse manure would smell like candy. We'd better go see Melvin."

"Who?"

"Melvin Haskin, Chairperson of our Epistemology Com-

mittee. If anybody's figured out the Phobos-Deimos rift, it's
Melvin. The last I heard, they'd put him in a rubber room at
Werner Krauss Memorial. What's today?"

"Tuesday."

"Too bad."

"Oh?"

"On Tuesday Melvin always wills himself into a catatonic
stupor. He'll be incommunicado until tomorrow morning."

I had no troubling sneaking Rupert out of the Frye Institute.
Everybody on the staff was preoccupied with gossip and
triage. The lunatic brought along his telescope and a bottle of
green pills that he called "the thin verdant line that separates
me from my madness."

Although still skeptical of my belief that Rupert held the
key to Manhattan's salvation, Valerie welcomed him warmly
into our apartment—she's a better therapist than I ever was—
and offered him the full measure of her hospitality. Because
we have a gas oven, we were able to prepare a splendid meal
of spinach lasagne and toasted garlic bread. Rupert ate all the
leftovers. Bobby asked him what it was like to be insane.
"There is nothing that being insane is like," Rupert replied.

After dinner, at Rupert's request, we all played Scrabble by
candlelight, followed by a round of Clue. Rupert won both
games. At ten o'clock he took a green pill and stretched his
spindly body along the length of our couch, which he said was
much more comfortable than his bed at the Frye Institute. Five
minutes later he was asleep.

As I write this entry, Clarence Morant is offering his latest
dispatches from the war zone. Evidently the Deimosians are
still dug in throughout Times Square. Tomorrow the Phobosians will attempt to dislodge them. Valerie and I both hear
a catch in Morant's voice as he tells how his aunt took him to
see *Cats* when he was nine years old. He inhales deeply and
says, "The Winter Garden Theater is surely doomed."

August 11

Before we left the apartment this morning, Rupert remembered
that Melvin Haskin is inordinately fond of bananas. Luckily,
Valerie had purchased two bunches at the corner bodega right
before the Martians landed. I tossed them into my rucksack,

along with some cheese sandwiches and Rupert's telescope, and then we headed uptown.

Reaching 40th Street, we saw that the Werner Krauss Memorial Clinic had become a seething mass of orange flames and billowing gray smoke, doubtless an ancillary catastrophe accruing to the Battle of Times Square. Ashes and sparks speckled the air. Our eyes teared up from the carbon. The sidewalks teemed with a despairing throng of doctors, administrators, guards, and inmates. Presumably the Broadway theaters and hotels were also on fire, but I didn't want to think about it.

Rupert instantly alighted on Melvin Haskin, though I probably could've identified him unassisted. Even in a milling mass of psychotics, Melvin stood out. He'd strapped a dish-shaped antenna onto his head, the concavity pointed skyward—an inverted yarmulke. A pair of headphones covered his ears, jacked into an antique vacuum-tube amplifier that he cradled in his arms like a baby. Two coiled wires, one red, one black, connected the antenna to the amplifier, its functionless power cord bumping against Melvin's left leg, the naked prongs glinting in the August sunlight. He wore a yellow terry cloth bathrobe and matching Big Bird slippers. His frame was massive, his skin pale, his stomach protuberant, his mouth bereft of teeth.

Rupert made the introductions. Once again he insisted on calling me Dr. Onslo. I pointed to Melvin's antenna and asked him whether he was receiving transmissions from the Martians.

"What?" He pulled off the headphones and allowed them to settle around his neck like a yoke.

"Your antenna, the headphones—looks like you're communicating with the Martians."

"Are you crazy?" Scowling darkly, Melvin turned toward Rupert and jerked an accusing thumb in my direction. "Dr. Onslo thinks my amplifier still works even though half the tubes are burned out."

"He's a psychiatrist," Rupert explained. "He knows nothing about engineering. How was your catatonic stupor?"

"Restful. You'll have to come along some time."

"I haven't got the courage," said Rupert.

Melvin was enchanted by the gift of the bananas, and even

more enchanted to be reunited with his fellow paranoid. As the two middle-aged madmen headed east, swapping jokes and stories like old school chums, I could barely keep up with their frenetic pace. After passing Sixth Avenue they turned abruptly into Bryant Park, where they found an abandoned soccer ball on the grass. For twenty minutes they kicked it back and forth, then grew weary of the sport. They sat down on a bench. I joined them. Survivors streamed by holding handkerchiefs over their faces.

"The city's dying," I told Melvin. "We need your help."

"Rupert, have you still got the touch?" Melvin asked his friend.

"I believe I do," said Rupert.

"Rupert can fix burned-out vacuum tubes merely by laying his hands on them," Melvin informed me. "I call him the Cathode Christ."

Even before Melvin finished his sentence, Rupert had begun fondling the amplifier. He rubbed each tube as if the warmth of his hand might bring it to life.

"You've done it again!" cried Melvin, putting on his headphones. "I'm pulling in a signal from Ceres! I think it might be just the place for us to retire, Rupert! No capital gains tax!" He removed the phones and looked me in the eye. "Do you solicit me as head of the Epistemology Committee or in my capacity as a paranoid schizophrenic?"

"The former," I said. "I'm hoping you've managed to define the Phobos-Deimos rift."

"You came to the right place." Melvin ate a banana, depositing the peel in the dish antenna atop his head. "It's the most basic of *Weltanschauung* dichotomies. Here on Earth many philosophers would trace the problem back to all that bad blood between the Platonists and the Aristotelians—you know, idealism versus realism—but it's actually the sort of controversy you can have only after a full-blown curiosity about nature has come on the scene."

"Do you speak of the classic schism between scientific materialists and those who champion presumed numinous realities?" I asked.

"Exactly," said Melvin.

"There—what did I tell you?" said Rupert merrily. "I *knew* old Melvin would set us straight."

"On the one hand, Deimos, moon of the logical positivists," said Melvin. "On the other hand, Phobos, bastion of revealed religion."

"Melvin, you're a genius," said Rupert, retrieving his telescope from my rucksack.

"Should we infer that the Phobosians are loath to evoke Darwinian mechanisms in explaining why they look so different from the Deimosians?" I asked.

"Quite so." Melvin unstrapped the dish antenna, scratched his head, and nodded. "The Phobes believe that God created them in his own image."

"They think God looks like a pencil sharpener?"

"That is one consequence of their religion, yes." Melvin donned his antenna and retrieved a bottle of red capsules from his bathrobe pocket. He fished one out and ate it. "Want to hear the really nutty part? The Phobes and the Deems are genetically wired to abandon any given philosophical position the moment it encounters an honest and coherent refutation. The Martians won't accept no for an answer, and they won't accept yes for an answer either—instead they want rational arguments."

"Rational arguments?" I said. "Then why the hell are they killing each other and bringing down New York with them?"

"If you were a dog, a dead possum would look like the Mona Lisa," said Rupert.

Melvin explained, "No one has ever presented them with a persuasive discourse favoring either the Phobosian or the Deimosian worldview."

"You mean we could end this nightmare by supplying the Martians with some crackerjack reasons why theistic revelation is the case?" I said.

"Either that, or some crackerjack reasons why scientific materialism is the case," said Melvin. "I realize it's fashionable these days to speak of an emergent compatibility between the two idioms, but you don't have to be a rocket scientist to realize that the concept of materialistic supernaturalism is oxymoronic if not plainly moronic, and nobody knows this better than the Martians." He pulled the headphones over his ears.

"Ha! Just as I suspected. The civilization on Ceres divides neatly into those who have exact change and those who don't."

"The problem, as I see it, is twofold," said Rupert, pointing his telescope south toward the Empire State Building. "We must construct the rational arguments in question, and we must communicate them to the Martians."

"They don't speak English, do they?" I said.

"Of course they don't speak English," said Rupert, exasperated. "They're Martians. They don't even have language as we commonly understand the term." He poked Melvin on the shoulder. "This is clearly a job for Annie."

"What?" said Melvin, removing the headphones.

"It's a job for Annie," said Rupert.

"Agreed," said Melvin.

"Who?" I said.

"Annie Porlock," said Rupert. "She built her own harpsichord."

"Soul of an artist," said Melvin.

"Heart of an angel," said Rupert.

"Crazy as a bedbug," added Melvin.

"For our immediate purpose, the most relevant fact about Annie is that she chairs our Interplanetary Communications Committee, in which capacity she cracked the Martian tweets and twitters, or so she claimed right before the medics took her away."

"How do we find her?" I asked.

"For many years she was locked up in some wretched Long Island laughing academy, but then the family lawyer got into the act," said Melvin. "I'm pretty sure they transferred her to a more humane facility here in New York."

"What facility?" I said. "Where?"

"I can't remember," said Melvin.

"You've *got* to remember."

"Sorry."

"*Try.*"

Melvin picked up the soccer ball and set it in his lap. "Fresh from the guillotine, the head of Maximilien-Françoise-Marie-Isidore de Robespierre," he said, as if perhaps I'd forgotten he was a paranoid schizophrenic. "Oh, Robespierre, Robespierre, was the triumph of inadvertence over intention ever so total?"

I brought both lunatics home with me. Valerie greeted us with the sad news that the Winter Garden, the Walter Kerr, the Eugene O'Neill, and half a dozen other White Way theaters had been lost in the Battle of Times Square. I told her there was hope for the Big Apple yet.

"It all depends on our ability to devise a set of robust arguments favoring either scientific materialism or theistic revelation and then communicating the salient points to the Martians in their nonlinguistic language, which was apparently deciphered several years ago by a paranoid schizophrenic named Annie Porlock," I told Valerie.

"That's not a sentence you hear every day," she replied.

It turns out that Melvin is even more devoted to board games than Rupert, so the evening went well. We played Scrabble, Clue, and Monopoly, after which Melvin introduced us to an amusement of his own invention, a variation on Trivial Pursuit called Teleological Ambition. Whereas the average Trivial Pursuit conundrum is frivolous, the challenges underlying Teleological Ambition are profound. Melvin remembered at least half of the original questions, writing them out on three-by-five cards. If God is infinite and self-sufficient, why would he care whether his creatures worshiped him or not? Which thought is the more overwhelming: the possibility that the Milky Way is teeming with sentient life, or the possibility that Earthlings and Martians occupy an otherwise empty galaxy? That sort of thing. Bobby hated every minute, and I can't say I blame him.

August 12
Shortly after breakfast this morning, while he was consuming what may have been the last fresh egg in SoHo, Melvin announced that he knew how to track down Annie Porlock.

"I was thinking of how she's a walking Rosetta Stone, our key to deciphering the Martian tongue," he explained, strapping on his dish antenna. "Rosetta made me think of Roosevelt, and then I remembered that she's living in a houseboat moored by Roosevelt Island in the middle of the East River."

I went to the pantry and filled my rucksack with a loaf of stale bread, a jar of instant coffee, a Kellogg's Variety Pack, and six cans of Campbell's soup. The can opener was nowhere to be found, so I tossed in my Swiss army knife. I guided my lunatics out the door.

There were probably only a handful of taxis still functioning in New York—most of them had run out of gas, and their owners couldn't refuel because the pumps worked on electricity—but somehow we managed to nab one at the corner of Houston and Forsyth. The driver, a Russian immigrant, named Vladimir, was not surprised to learn we had no cash, all the ATMs being dormant, and he agreed to claim his fare in groceries. He piloted us north along First Avenue, running straight through fifty-seven defunct traffic signals, and left us off at the Queensboro Bridge. I gave him two cans of chicken noodle soup and a single-serving box of Frosted Flakes.

The Martian force-field dome had divided Roosevelt Island right down the middle, but luckily Annie Porlock had moored her houseboat on the Manhattan side. "Houseboat" isn't the right word, for the thing was neither a house nor a boat but a decrepit two-room shack sitting atop a half-submerged barge called the *Folly to Be Wise*. Evidently the hull was leaking. If Annie's residence sank any lower, I thought as we entered the shack, the East River would soon be lapping at her ankles.

A ruddy, zaftig, silver-haired woman in her mid-fifties lay dozing in a wicker chair, her lap occupied by a book about Buddhism and a large calico cat. Her harpsichord rose against the far wall, beside a lamp table holding a large bottle of orange capsules the size of jelly beans. Our footfalls woke her. Recognizing Rupert, Annie let loose a whoop of delight. The cat bailed out. She stood up.

"Melvin Haskin?" said Annie, sashaying across the room. "Is that really you? They let you out?"

Annie extended her right hand. Melvin kissed it.

"Taa-daa!" shouted Rupert, stepping out from behind Melvin's bulky frame. His pressed his mouth against Annie's cheek.

"Rupert Klieg—they sprang you, too!" said Annie. "If I knew you were coming, I'd have baked a fruitcake."

"The First Annual Reunion of the Asaph Hall Society will now come to order," said Melvin, chuckling.

"Have you heard about the Martians?" said Rupert.

Annie's eyes widened grotesquely, offering a brief intimation of the derangement that lay behind. "They've landed? Really? You can't be serious!"

"Cross my heart," said Rupert. "Even as we speak, the Phobes and the Deems are thrashing out their differences in Times Square."

"Just as we predicted," said Annie. Turning from Rupert, she fixed her frowning gaze on me. "I guess that'll show you doubting Thomases . . ."

Rupert introduced me as "Dr. Onslo, the first in a long line of distinguished psychiatrists who tried to help me before hyperlithium came on the market," and I didn't bother to contradict him. Instead I explained the situation to Annie, emphasizing Melvin's recent deductions concerning Martian dialectics. She was astonished to learn that the Deimosians and the Phobosians were occupying Manhattan in direct consequence of the old materialism-supernaturalism dispute, and equally astonished to learn that, in contrast to most human minds, the Martian psyche was hardwired to favor rational discourse over pleasurable opinion.

"That must be the strangest evolutionary adaptation ever," said Annie.

"Certainly the strangest we know about," said Melvin.

"Can you help us?" I asked.

Approaching her harpsichord, Annie sat on her swiveling stool and rested her hands on the keyboard. "This looks like a harpsichord, but it's really an interplanetary communication device. I've spent the last three years recalibrating the jacks, upgrading the plectrums, and adjusting the strings."

Her fingers glided across the keys. A jumble of notes leaped forth, so weird and discordant they made Schoenberg sound melodic.

"There," said Annie proudly, pivoting toward her audience. "In the Martian language I just said, 'Before enlightenment, chop wood, carry water. After enlightenment, chop wood, carry water.' "

"Wow," said Klieg.

"Terrific," said Melvin.

Annie turned back to the keyboard and called forth another unruly refrain.

"That meant, 'There are two kinds of naïveté: the naïveté of optimism and the naïveté of pessimism,'" she explained.

"Who would've guessed there could be so much meaning in cacophony?" I said.

"To a polar bear, the Arctic Ocean feels like a Jacuzzi," said Rupert.

Annie called forth a third strain—another grotesque non-melody.

"And the translation?" asked Rupert.

"It's an idiomatic expression," she replied.

"Can you give us a rough paraphrase?"

"'Hi there, baby. You have great tits. Would you like to fuck?'"

Melvin said, "The problem, of course, is that the Martians are likely to kill each other—along with the remaining population of New York—before we can decide conclusively which worldview enjoys the imprimatur of rationality."

"All is not lost," said Rupert.

"What do you mean?" I asked.

"We might, just might, have enough time to formulate strong arguments supporting a side of the controversy chosen . . . arbitrarily," said Rupert.

"Arbitrarily?" echoed Annie, voice cracking.

"Arbitrarily," repeated Rupert. "It's the only way."

The four of us traded glances of reluctant consensus. I removed a quarter from my pants pocket.

"Heads: revelation, God, the Phobes," said Melvin.

"Tails: materialism, science, the Deems," said Rupert.

I flipped the quarter. It landed under Annie's piano stool, frightening the cat.

Tails.

And so we went at it, a melee of discourse and disputation that lasted through the long, hot afternoon and well into evening. We napped on the floor. We pissed in the river. We ate cold soup and dry raisin bran.

By eight o'clock we'd put the Deimosian worldview on solid ground—or so we believed. The gist of our argument was that sentient species emerged in consequence of certain discoverable properties embedded in nature. Whether Earthling or Martian, aquatic or terrestrial, feathered or furred, scaled or smooth, all life-forms were inextricably woven into a material biosphere, and it was this astonishing and demonstrable connection, not the agenda of some hypothetical supernatural agency, that made us one with the cosmos and the bearers of its meaning.

"And now, dear Annie, you must set it all to music," I told the Communications Chairperson, giving her a hug.

Rupert and Melvin decided to spend the night aboard the *Folly to Be Wise,* providing Annie with moral support and instant coffee while she labored over her translation. I knew that Valerie and Bobby would be worried about me, so I said my farewells and headed for home. So great was my exhilaration that I ran the whole three miles to Delancey Street without stopping—not bad for a weekend jogger.

I'm writing this entry in our bedroom. Bobby's asleep. Valerie wants to hear about my day, so I'd better sign off. The news from Clarence Morant is distressing. Defeated in the Battle of Times Square, the Deimosians have retreated to the New York Public Library and taken up positions on the steps between the stone lions. The Phobosians are encamped outside Grand Central Station, barely a block away.

There are over two million volumes in the New York Public Library, Morant tells us, including hundreds of irreplaceable first editions. When the fighting starts, the Martians will be firing their heat rays amidst a paper cache of incalculable value.

August 13

Phobos and Deimos. When Asaph Hall went to name his discoveries, he logically evoked the two sons and companions of Ares, the Greek god of war. Phobos, avatar of fear. Deimos, purveyor of panic.

Fear and panic. Is there a difference? I believe so. Beyond the obvious semantic distinction—fear the chronic condition, panic the acute—it seems to me that the Phobosians and the Deimosians, whether through meaningless coincidence or Jungian synchronicity, picked the right moons. Phobos, fear. Is fear not a principal engine behind the supernaturalist worldview? (The universe is manifestly full of terrifying forces controlled by powerful gods. If we worship them, maybe they won't destroy us.) Deimos, panic. At first blush, the scientific worldview has nothing to do with panic. But consider the etymology here. *Panic* from Pan, Greek god of forests, pastures, flocks, and shepherds. Pan affirms the physical world. Pan says yes to material reality. Pan might panic on occasion, but he does not live in fear.

When I returned to the *Folly to Be Wise* this morning, the lunatics were asleep, Rupert lying in the far corner, Annie curled up in her tiny bedroom, Melvin snoring beside her. He still wore his dish antenna. The pro-Deimosian argument lay on the harpsichord, twelve pages of sheet music. Annie had titled it "Materialist Prelude and Fugue in C-Sharp Minor."

I awoke my friends and told them about the imminent clash of arms at the New York Public Library. We agreed there was no time to hear the fugue right now—the world premiere would have to occur on the battlefield—but Annie could not resist pointing out some of its more compelling passages. "Look here," she said, indicating a staff in the middle of page three. "A celebration of the self-correcting ethos at the heart of the scientific enterprise." She turned to page seven and ran her finger over the topmost measures. "A brief history of postmodern academia's failure to relativize scientific knowledge." She drew my attention to a coda on page eleven. "Depending on the definitions you employ, the materialist worldview precludes neither a creator-god nor the possibility of transcendence through art, religion, or love."

I put the score in my rucksack, and then we took hold of the harpsichord, each of us lifting a corner. We proceeded with excruciating care, as if the instrument were made of glass, lest we misalign any of Annie's clever tinkerings and canny modifications. Slowly we carried the harpsichord across the deck, off the island, and over the bridge. At the intersection of Second Avenue and 57th Street, we paused to catch our breath.

"Fifteen blocks," said Rupert.

"Can we do it in fifteen minutes?" I asked.

"We're the Asaph Hall Society," said Annie. "We've never failed to thwart an extraterrestrial invasion."

And so our great mission began. 56th Street. 55th Street. 54th Street. 53rd Street. Traffic being minimal, we forsook the sidewalks with their frequent impediments—scaffolding, trash barrels, police barriers—and moved directly along the asphalt. Doubts tormented me. What if we'd picked the wrong side of the controversy? What if we'd picked the right side but our arguments sounded feeble to the Phobosians? What if panic seized Annie, raw Deimosian panic, and she choked up at the keyboard?

By the time we were in the Forties, we could hear the Martians' glissando chirpings. Our collective pace quickened. At last we reached 42nd Street. We turned right and bore the peace machine past the Chrysler Building and the Grand Hyatt Hotel. Arriving at Grand Central Station, we paused to behold the Phobosian infantry maneuvering for a frontal assault on the Deimosian army, still presumably holding the library steps. The air vibrated with extraterrestrial tweets and twitters, as if midtown Manhattan had become a vast pet store filled with demented parakeets.

We transported the harpsichord another block and set it down at the Madison Avenue intersection, from which vantage we could see both Grand Central Station and the library. The Phobosian army had indeed spent the night bivouacked between the stone lions. Inevitably I thought of Gettysburg— James Longstreet's suicidal sweep across the Pennsylvania farmlands, hurtling his divisions against George Meade's Army of the Potomac, which had numerical superiority, a nobler cause, and the high ground.

Rupert took the score from my sack, laid the twelve pages against the rack, and made ready to turn them. Melvin removed his dish antenna and got down on all fours before the instrument. Annie seated herself on his massive back. She laid her hands on the keyboard. A stiff breeze arose. If the score blew away, all would be lost.

Annie depressed a constellation of keys. Martian language came forth, filling the canyon between the skyscrapers.

A high bugling wail emerged from deep within the throats of the Deimosian officers, and the soldiers began their march. Annie played furiously. "Materialist Prelude and Fugue," page one . . . page two . . . page three . . . page four. The soldiers kept on coming. Page five . . . page six . . . page seven . . . page eight. The Deimosians continued their advance, parting around the harpsichord like an ocean current yielding to the prow of a ship. Page nine . . . page ten . . . page eleven . . . page twelve. Among the irreplaceable volumes in the New York Public Library, I recalled, were first editions of Nicolaus Copernicus' *De Revolutionibus,* William Gilbert's *De Magnete,* and Isaac Newton's *Principia Mathematica.*

Once again the Deimosian officers let loose a high bugling wail.

The soldiers abruptly halted their advance.

They threw down their weapons and broke into a run.

"Good God, is it working?" asked Rupert.

"I think so," I replied.

"It worked!" insisted Annie.

"Really?" said Melvin, whose perspective on the scene was compromised by his function as a piano stool.

"We've done it!" I cried. "We've really done it!"

Within a matter of seconds the Deimosians accomplished a reciprocal disarmament. They rushed toward their former enemies. The two forces met on Fifth Avenue, Phobosians and Deimosians embracing passionately, so that the intersection seemed suddenly transformed into an immense railroad platform on which countless wayward lovers were meeting sweethearts from whom they'd been involuntarily separated for years.

Now the ovation came, two hundred thousand extraterrestrials cheering and applauding Annie as she climbed off Melvin's back and stood up straight. She took a bow, and then another.

A singularly appreciative chirp emerged from a Phobosian general, whereupon a dozen of his fellows produced the identical sound.

Annie got the message. She seated herself on Melvin's back, turned to page one, and played "Materialist Prelude and Fugue in C-Sharp Minor" all over again.

August 18
The Martians have been gone for only five days, but already Manhattan is healing. The lights are back on. Relief arrives from every state in the Union, plus Canada.

Valerie, Bobby, and I are now honorary members of the Asaph Hall Society. We all gathered this afternoon at Gracie

Mansion in Carl Schurz Park, not far from Annie's houseboat. Mayor Margolis will let us use his parlor whenever we want. In fact, there's probably no favor he won't grant us. After all, we saved his city.

Annie called the meeting to order. Everything went smoothly. We discussed old business (our ongoing efforts to contact the Galilean satellites), new business (improving patient services at the Frye Institute and the Krauss Clinic), and criteria for admitting new participants. As long as they remember to take their medicine, my lunatics remain the soul of reason. Melvin and Annie plan to marry in October.

"I'll bet we're all having the same thought right now," said Rupert before we went out to dinner.

"What if Dr. Onslo's quarter had come up heads?" said Melvin, nodding. "What if we'd devised arguments favoring the Phobosians instead? What then?"

"That branch of the reality tree will remain forever hidden from us," said Annie.

"I think it's entirely possible the Deimosians would've thrown down their arms," said Valerie.

"So do I," said Melvin. "Assuming our arguments were plausible."

"Know what I think?" said Rupert. "I think we all just got very lucky."

Did we merely get lucky? Hard to say. But I do know one thing. In two weeks the New York Philharmonic will perform a fully orchestrated version of "Materialist Prelude and Fugue in C-Sharp Minor" at Lincoln Center, which miraculously survived the war, and I wouldn't miss it for the world.

Editor's Note: The author wishes to mention that he composed this story nearly a year before the tragic events of September 11, 2001.

NEAR EARTH OBJECT

by Brian Aldiss

O'DEERE thought he saw something moving. He looked again, and it was gone.

It could have been nothing. The crapout stretched away into the distance, growing dim as the sun sank. Shadows lay across the view as if painted there. The surface of the knee-high atmosphere shone like a dull bronze shield in the oblique light.

Oh, yes, it held beauty. Only the silence was threatening. Being inside the dome, he could hear nothing outside. Inside, the conversation between his partner, Frere, and Imo Loko was all too audible. They were discussing how hair should be cut and why cutting was not a painful process. They were tittering.

Set against their triviality was the weighty seriousness of the outside world. Its silence had a material quality, a texture quite different from terrestrial silences. Perhaps his lapsed Catholicism led him to seek a religious significance in the wastes outside, and in the coming of night.

Searching again for that furtive movement, O'Deere recalled the noise of the city into which he had been born. It never knew silence. There was always noise, the enemy of thought: the banshee scream of police cars, the shriek of ambulances and fire trucks, the constant rumble of traffic, the clatter of helicopters overhead. And inside the building where his boyhood was spent, the babble of television sets burning night and day, screams, shouts, the yatter of children.

He had once known a girl in those days. He had forgotten her name by now. She had sung to him, and that sound was sweeter than silence. The song she sang, so she told him, was a folk song. "Up, up and away-ay, in my beautiful balloon . . ."

The words drifted through the lonely regions of his mind.

As he turned from the observation window, he glimpsed it again. It was out there, a veritable ghost! He called Frere to come over and look.

So Digby O'Deere and Martin Frere started arguing, that evening the strangers flew in uninvited from Asteroid A4949.

The two men had always argued, sometimes in friendship, often in hate. Both men loathed their duties, but for different reasons. Now it was a specter they were quarreling over. Sometimes they quarreled over abstract issues. Frere, O'Deere maintained, never thought in abstracts. O'Deere sought to feel something profound in being on Mars; he looked for the deeper mysteries of how humanity's extended consciousness had come into being, and for riddles of the universe. And all he found was the stifling career of a soldier, stationed on an outpost in a remote desert, frozen into silence seventy degrees below zero. Secretly, he hated Frere. Frere reinforced his feeling that he was imprisoned in hell.

From their outpost on Hellas Planitia, during the mid-watch, both men saw their first Martian ghost. Frere came to the observation window with their shared woman, Banzi Imo Loko. The specter seemed to be making for a rock outcrop nearby, vanishing before it reached it.

"What in all get-out . . ." said Imo Loko, leaving her jaw hanging. She was a wonderful simulation of a human being.

O'Deere found it hard to determine whether the specter made the outlook more lonely or less. From the observation window, he could see north and south over the Noachian plain, a flat, desolate waste, troubled by winds which raised small flat-topped dust storms. The machinery for which they were responsible turned its trellised head a few degrees this way, a few degrees that way, like a crazed thing, forever searching a quadrant of space for oncoming near-Earth objects. This watchdog was one of the Martian stations for which the military had built and manned the Hellas outpost.

Any object hurtling in from the Kuiper Belt or elsewhere toward Earth and—*kerpow!*—the military blew it into fragments. Between the installation and the dome in which the men and their woman were stationed lay a number of untidy waste items, some bagged up, awaiting the monthly trash clipper's call, some mere skeletons of machines, obsolete and abandoned to rust.

The landscape was not encouraging. The fact that dusk was coming on added to its gloom at this time.

The curious thing was that the soldiers seemed to have seen different specters. O'Deere said his looked like the ghost of a large robot, colorless, headless, with a mechanical walk. Frere claimed he saw a vehicle of some kind. Imo Loko just did not know. They argued about what they had seen, and what it might mean, in a desultory way.

They ceased shouting at each other when a sharply defined rectangular cloud much resembling a block of ice filled the operations room. It moved slowly away, through the outer walls, and was lost.

A message coming over the ambient distracted them, drawing them away from their shock.

"This is Pilot Mark Bigsby calling. I have a complexitor. I'm coming in to your landing strip in thirty minutes. With me is a sick person. Prepare to receive her."

Frere answered. "Hold it! This is a military outpost. You need clearance to land here. No unauthorized landings permitted."

He looked askance at O'Deere, who gave a nod, although he had never heard of such a regulation. *"Complexitor?"* he asked himself in a low voice.

"Clearance nothing!" said the voice over the ambient. "This is an emergency, my fellow! I am arriving from the asteroid belt. Due to land in twenty-eight minutes. It's an emergastrophe. I have a delusional victim aboard who had to quit A4949 immediately."

"Emergastrophe?" echoed O'Deere, half-amused.

Frere again. "There are only two of us on duty here. We have no facilities. Deflect to Marsopolis center."

"No compliance. I'm low on fuel and am already beamed on your beacon. Make preparassments to receive me, will you?"

Frere asked for Bigsby's code.

"I'm in a Jupiter Javelin, Code CC335. Out."

Frere and O'Deere looked at each other. "What in hell's name is a Jupiter Javelin?" they asked each other in unison.

O'Deere looked up CC335 in the Operators' Handbook. No sign of CC335.

They called Bigsby to check if he was military. Only military were allowed in this sector of space, since civilian craft would have interfered with the search for the current obsession, Near Earth Objects. Bigsby gave no answer to their signal.

"Useless just standing here," said O'Deere. "Better go and meet with him."

So they climbed into the atmobile, defrosted it, drove it out of its garage, and headed for the landing strip, leaving Imo Loko in charge.

They could feel the silence and cold through the insulated walls of their vehicle. Low over Huygens, the sun spread its feeble shrunken glow.

"This guy Bigsby sounds like something's deeply wrong," O'Deere said. "Complexitor? Emergastrophe?"

Frere merely nodded. Maybe there was trouble ahead. Anything was better than the isolation of the three-month stint on Hellas Planitia Station. And being stuck with this superior-minded idiot O'Deere. He had served two of the three months. A month to go before his relief. That month stretched before him as barren as the Martian desert itself. O'Deere took philosophy and cosmogony courses; Frere could not be bothered.

Turning to O'Deere, he said, "It's not just that you are so frigging ugly, it's just that I am mega-tired of your conversation, such as it is."

O'Deere folded his hands together and tucked them between his thighs. Looking ahead into the crapout, he replied, "But, Augustus, what conversation can I have with you? You think only of this petty life. The cosmos has never got to you. You're a Tiny Details Man. Remember yesterday, you wanted to discuss the schedule of flights by Olga Lines out of Detroit?"

"If you call me Augustus again, I'll sock you, okay? I knew a man who worked for Olga Lines, is all. He was in charge of freight movements," explained Frere, in a hangdog way. "I'm just as fond of the cosmos as you are. I just don't want to live there." There were no more exchanges between them until they reached the strip.

Suddenly a belt of fire blazed up ahead, tall as a tree, dazzling in its brilliance. Then it was gone, even before they had time to kick the truck to a halt.

"Seeing things . . ." muttered Frere.

"Le cafard," muttered O'Deere.

They were nervous after that, after saying that it did not happen.

Frere flicked on the astrochart, punching up Asteroid A4949. There it was, a broken egg shape, 65 kilometers at its greatest radius, rotation 8.2 hours, orbital period of 5.33 years, mean distance from Sun 2.96 AU, name Robina. Currently being mined by the Azure Nuts Co plc, under a twenty-year lease.

O'Deere punched his wrisputer with the tip of his ballpoint pen. "So, at present 4949 is only three two five thousand kilometers from Mars."

"This guy Bigsby—he has no business coming here. It only means trouble for us. No promotion if things go pear-shaped."

"At least it's a diversion," O'Deere said. "Someone to talk to. Perhaps he will be intelligent."

A deadening silence fell between the two soldiers. O'Deere zapped in the landing guide lights. The lighting on the strip emphasized the surrounding darkness.

"God, how I hate Mars," Frere said. "It is so frigging ugly. Nothing but frozen desert. Rocks. Wind. Dust."

"It's beautiful. You just have to see it properly."

"See it properly! You want your head examined!"

"No, it's beautiful, Martin, you dimwit. Can't you see that? Nothing but rocks, wind, dust. No footprints. Unspoiled. Beautiful."

A signal came through on the right-hand screen, a blip trailing numbers. Bigsby and his Javelin, coming in fast. Instinctively, both men peered out at the sky, dark, pink-rimmed like an inflamed eye. Frere turned to his partner to make a comment and saw in his place a grand well-coiffeured woman with an unostentatious tiara snug in her blonde hair, wearing a lace blouse and ankle-length skirt. Her tight lace collar was girded by a pearl necklace wound tightly about her throat. Her face was the face of an Egyptian mummy.

"Save me!" he exclaimed, but the vision was gone.

O'Deere was his normal self, slouched in his drab overalls, with the shoulder flash saying NEOC.

"Better get the chicken ready," said O'Deere; then, "I mean to say, the rear doors." They slicked on their atmomasks and climbed down from the cab. The cold bit their bones. A gigantic shadow passed slowly over the vehicle. It seemed, as far as they could tell, to be plane-shaped. Or bird-shaped. But it was a monstrous bird. Frere fell flat on the ground.

"What in all hell's name . . ."

Both men crawled under their atmobile and lay flat. Only an urgent beeping from the cab drew them forth again. They ran in, with hasty glances upward. The sky rained stars. Darkness had fallen. The sun had gone off duty for the day.

"What was that?" O'Deere asked.

"Search me."

On their screens, an orange dot moved among a crisscross of lines. Shortly, they had visual contact. The Javelin came down on an integrated column of mesons. O'Deere started their vehicle rolling toward it. He had never seen a spacer like the Javelin before, so bulky, with great clawed metal feet.

A hatch on the side of the Javelin slowly swung open. Out of it climbed a suited figure, activating an injury pod. Once on the regolith, retractable wheels protruded and the pod began rolling. O'Deere and Frere met it and conducted it and the astronaut to their vehicle.

Once they were in the dome again, the astronaut unsuited. He climbed onto a couch and lay back, demanding a hot drink.

He was a tall stringy man, aged about fifty—so Imo Loko estimated as she brought him a coffdrink. His hair had been dyed a bright yellow. He wore a suit of unusual texture which fitted his spare figure cozily. He pulled a face at the drink, but sipped it without complaint.

"So, how's about telling us who in the living hell you are, buddy?" said Frere. "You're Bigsby? We could have you locked in the cells."

"What year is this, talking of living hell?" the man asked, with a casual inflection.

"Come on, you can't be that out of touch," said O'Deere, irritated by the stranger's manner. "It's 2050 and we're halfway through March, Earth-time."

"It's worse than I thought," said Bigsby, as if to himself. "2050, eh? Well, I estimess it *could* be worse. It could have been 2005, for instance, before the first manned expedition reached Mars. Then I'd be really schtuckkered . . ." He turned his gaze on O'Deere. "You look the least cretinous of the three of you, so tell me. Year 2050—this means Mars is still a planet entirely occupied by the U.S.A. military, if I recall? Is that uncounteractable?"

"There's a Chinese outpost in the South Polar region. What is it with all these questions? Are you a spy or something?"

"A typical question to issue forth from a military mund," remarked Bigsby.

"What's a mund?" asked Frere.

"You don't know? It's a dim form of mind. Of course I'm not a spy, you fools! Spies operate secraticly. They don't come mesonneting in in a Javelin. Nor, I imagine, could a spy find much to outterest himself in your dingy little station."

"We are serving our term of duty. We can't help it if it's dingy. So if you're not a spy, what are you? A time traveler?" Frere laughed at the absurdity of the idea.

"In a sense, yes. Purely involuntary, I assure you. Perhaps I ought to explarify—before we open up the injury pod and talk with Jessica Jeans Two. That is, if she is still capable of talking. She's had something of a shoirick."

"A shoirick?"

"Yes, an extreme shock. You are not familiar with the term?"

It was hard to listen sensibly to him, O'Deere thought, when his body kept turning transparent and delicate slices of a silvery metal were passing through it. And through the entire station. The slices formed themselves into spirals in the corners of the chamber and then dissolved.

Bigsby explained that he was a civilian pilot. He was licensed by his company to travel among the bodies of the asteroid belt, visiting any that beaconed him, bringing in supplies or taking astoridians (as he called them) to another asteroid or to hospidalle. There was, in his day, he assured them, a brilliant hospidalle for xenosicknesses on Ceres, in Ceropolis—a nonmilitary hospidalle, he stressed. He had been beaconed for assistacity from Asteroid Robina.

"Oh, that's under lease to the Azure Nuts Company!" said Frere brightly, remembering the data on the astrochart.

"Never heard of them," said Bigsby severely. "In my day, all asteroids are depredised."

He went on to say that he lived and operated in the year 2081; still the illusory shafts curled through him. His manner was one of effortless superiority. As the Javelin was approaching Robina, he said, he found himself bombarded by fleeting ghostly images. These were characterized by extreme extrangeners. Frere and O'Deere looked at each other.

He had anchored his craft in orbit ten kilometers above Robina and had descended in the skelevator. He did not clarify this term. Robina, he said, was pormango-shaped and no more than sixty-five kilometers at its biggest radius. Living accommodation was consequently modest, although it boasted a cypermart, an opera house, and a nondenominational chusque.

"The place was in a yuproar. Only ten real humans habinited Robina, together with a number of andumans, who kept things running."

"Andumans?" asked Imo Loka, in puzzlement.

"Half-androids," said Bigsby impatiently. "Androids with psyches. I was forgetting that in your day . . . 2050, you said? Well . . ."

The andumans had broken down, while the ten humans were all distraught. Not least distraught was Jessica Jeans Two. She and the other inhabitants were being boombarked by incomprensible images.

"I'm ninety-seven and have never experienced anything like it."

Having said this, Bigsby eased himself gingerly off the couch and approached the injury pod, saying that it was time to have a look at the lady.

"I saved her. She was overcome by the visitoxations. I necessarily had to remove her from their proximity. Unfortunately, I reckoned without the temporal dislocations. How I will manage to return to 2081 and gnostization I do not know."

Shaking his head gloomily, Bigsby unlocked the clamps on the injury pod and folded back its plastoid door. By so doing, he revealed the face and body of a haggard young woman. Her

eyes were closed, her brown hair straggled across her forehead.

"Jessica!"

Her eyes opened. She struggled to sit up, an expression of
fear on her face. Steam poured from her confining pads.

"Where am I?"

Bigsby said, "The force of the tomb you opened was overwhelming you. It was necessary to take you away. I am sorry
to tell you we were projected back in time by its effluent, into
the Post-Human Age. Here we are, relatively safe and sound,
in year 2050. I must apologize for the inconventance. Here
stand a couple of denizens—soldiery, of course, but harmless
enough, it seems."

"I was insane," she said, as if to herself. "Maybe I still am.
I can't believe what occappered . . . 2050 . . . how awful-
gent . . ."

Her gaze traveled over the two soldiers and Imo Loka. They
felt it like a cool breeze. She climbed briskly from the pod.

"They don't look too fierce, Mark," she told Bigsby.
"Hello, guyllows, I'm placked to see you, if not placked to be
here."

"You're foreign?" Frere asked. "You shouldn't be here: this
is U.S. Space Force territory. We should lock you up."

"All the same, we're pleased—um, *placked* to see you,"
added O'Deere hastily. "It seems you've had a bad time."

Jeans Two looked questioningly at Bigsby.

"He means unstimtempo. He's doing his best."

"I'll get you a coffdrink," said Imo Loko. "If you're really
from 2081, you must be thirsty."

As she left, Jeans Two asked Bigsby why he had come to
this fathforsaken place. To which he replied that he was low on
mesonnetry and Mars happened to be the proximerest body. It
was the event on Robina which had proulsed their craft backward in time.

Frere felt it was time he exerted a little authority.

"By rights we should lock you two in the cooler and call
Mars City to get you moved there for trial, regarding the offense of trespass on military territory. You pair of weird people better explain how and why you are here."

Bigsby and Jeans Two stood together, whispering to each

other. The soldiers caught the question, "Are they mentally equipped to comprestand the situvent?" It was the first time they had seen Bigsby looking undecided.

Bigsby said that it was beyond any of them to comprestand the unique event which had occurred. Deep thought was required.

"Fine, then we'll lock you up," said Frere. "Get moving!"

"A typical mentalanity of the age," said Bigsby to Jeans Two, smiling resignedly. He walked with her, giving no resistance, into the unit's cell, where Frere applied the electronic locks.

O'Deere sat with his head in his hands, trying to think. When Frere asked him something, he waved him away.

Considering the situation, he concluded that a) Bigsby and Jeans Two might be some kind of impostors, out for some kind of gain which he could not fathom, for it was difficult to believe that they had actually come from a future thirty years ahead; he did not believe anyone lived in the future. Then b) they really had come from the future, not by accident, as they claimed, but by design, because they were criminals escaping the law of their own time. Or c) the situation was as they represented it, and some unimaginable event had taken place on A4949, the nature of which they had yet to discover.

All these possibilities neglected the array of strange phenomena which had broken out, and with which Bigsby's space vehicle, the Javelin, was evidently connected but not responsible. This led O'Deere to d) the unwilling conclusion that the solitudes of the Hellas Planitia had turned him and Frere mad, and they were suffering from delusions.

He opened up the ambient and called the padre, Major Blake, in Areopolis Military H.Q., for help and advice.

A little fat man dressed as a chicken appeared on the screen.

"Sorry," he said, amiably, "I've been visiting a difficult convert. How may I help?" He divested himself of beak and comb as he spoke.

Explaining what had happened, O'Deere felt himself to be inarticulate, although the padre nodded encouragingly, as if he understood everything.

Finally, the holy man spoke. "As you know, my dear O'Deere, we religious people regard the afterlife as divided between heaven and hell—the hot and the cold, as it were. Stationed on Mars, which may be regarded as the cold, it is not unnatural to become obsessed with visions of warmth—of hell, in fact. You have imagined yourself into an unanswerable predicament. That is hell. You must pray and unimagine the situation."

"You mean to say our two visitors from A 4949 are imaginary, padre?" asked O'Deere in astonishment.

"The mere visit by unexpected visitors has tipped the balance of your mind, my son. Temporarily at least, you are insane. It has happened to me, so I understand. You are not really in hell. That comes after death."

"This has nothing to do with hell or death, father. It's a real life predicament I'm consulting you about."

The padre bit his lower lip. "My son, has it occurred to you that you may actually be dead? I have often had to converse with the dead before this."

As O'Deere switched off, the padre was reassuming his chicken apparel. "Shit," said O'Deere. Turning, he found that Frere and Imo Loko were standing silently behind him.

"We have to deal with this situation ourselves, Martin. Let's get those two strangers out of the cooler and force an explanation from them. It seems as if something peculiar happened on 4949, and we should know about it."

"Pee-culiar!" exclaimed Frere. "Jeez, what a master of language you are, Dig!"

"What if it is beyond our limited brain power to understand what they tell us?" said Imo Loko.

"Let's try it."

"Okay. Then I'll get them some coffdrink."

Bigsby and Jeans Two were released with something approaching an apology. Jeans Two smoothed hair away from her forehead and looked contemptuous.

"It is the mentalanity of your age to lock people up," said Bigsby. "Don't apolophrase. Your perceptions are not as free as ours."

He sauntered over to the observation window to peer out at the night. An electric storm was in progress. The newly imposed atmosphere of Mars was now about knee-high as oxygen held in the rocks began to thaw out. This proto-atmosphere still contained poisonous CFC gases. Fragmentary sheet lightning played low over the ground, as if spun by demented spiders. Thunder gave an occasional low-pitched squeak.

"This terraforming will not work," Bigsby said, turning to address the soldiers. "It is an iridictmentation of *mankinder* trying to grasp more things beyond his reach. I assure you that within a decade this planet will be depredised."

"If *mankinder,* as you call us, don't reach out, they achieve nothing," retorted Frere. "What makes you so high and mighty?"

"Because I am a product of a gnostization that has espoused knowledge and wisdom, rather than power."

"Oh? How did that change come about?" asked O'Deere.

"Primpted by the total evacuation of Mars in—mm, I believe if my history serves that it was in year 2051."

"But that's next year!"

"To you I suppose it is."

A painful memory returned to O'Deere's mind—or was it *mund*? Back in his childhood, his family had been situated in the slum quarter of one of the world's giant cities. To escape his father's rages, young Digby would climb to the top of their high-rise, to the flat roof. He would wrap a floor rug about his shoulders to protect himself from the cold of night. There he would stand among the grimy ventilation and elevator machinery, staring up at the sky and stars—when they could be seen free of clouds.

There he had imagined better worlds than Earth, where society was more just, more clement.

He longed to escape from this slum, from this city, even from this planet. Up, up and away. . . . At the age of sixteen, he had left his home and joined what the military liked to call the Interplanetary Corps of the Army.

He had reached Mars. But had found in the military life there was no justice and little clemency, only oppression and a baffling series of regulations.

How wonderful if life were to improve. . . .

Half-fearful, almost parenthetically, he asked Bigsby what life was like, thirty years in the future.

Bigsby said that they had cleared away a lot of "emotional

mess." The number of children being born was better super-
vised, and those children were loved and taken care of. They
were shown, both pre- and postnatally, the pleasures of learning and wisdom; they were taught social skills. Almost immediate moderation, as he termed it, was evident in society.
Not only did crime figures go down, but the armed forces
began to disintegrate together with nationalism, while Peace
Promotion flourished. By 2080, a renaissance of ideas was
blossoming, coupled with universal expressions of greater
happiness.

O'Deere tried to grasp what he had been told. "You mean
to say that in just one contented generation . . ."

"Let's not say 'contented.' Better is 'fulfilled.' "

"Fulfilled!"

Bigsby perceived something of O'Deere's confusion. Perhaps he felt he had said enough, or too much. Or perhaps he
was deciding whether to say more; but at this juncture, Frere
grasped O'Deere's arm and pointed out into the night.

"We're locked out from that future he was describing," said
O'Deere, bitterly.

"Forget that shit! We're in trouble!"

They stared out, horrified. For as far as they could see, a
fiery cloud was advancing on the outpost. Within it floated
shadowy men, five abreast. But not men. Not human. Not even
mankinder. Bulky black objects, possibly three-legged, with
stiff—was it hair or spines?—protruding from their backs. All
difficult to discern from amid the fierce glow and the attendant
streaks of smoke which accompanied their march.

"Man the guns!" shouted Frere. But as he spoke, the approaching column faded and disappeared, leaving only the
webbed lightning to haunt the crapout.

Pale of face, the two soldiers stared at each other questioningly.

"Another chimera from Robina 4949," said Bigsby, dismissively.

"I'll get us some coffdrink," said Imo Loko.

When Frere asked what the floating things were, Jeans Two
laughed and said that they needed explanation. It might be difficult to make Frere and O'Deere comprestand.

"Sit down and try and make us comprestand," said O'Deere grimly.

They sat on the benches fixed to the mess table, the two men and Imo Loko on one side, Bigsby and Jeans Two on the other, with mugs of coffdrink steaming at their elbows.

"You had better do the explanations," said Bigsby to Jeans Two. "Keep it simple."

"But it is not simple. It is complex and scarifying, and I cannot fully comprestand the situation myself." With this preamble, Jeans Two clasped her hands together, placed them on the table in front of her, and began.

She said she was an astropaleontologist, specializing in cataloging the age and variety of the minor planets in the asteroid belt between Mars and Jupiter. She went into some detail about the attractions and hazards of her profession. On some asteroids, notably Ceres and Nausicaa, remains had been discovered which seemed to indicate the existence of a past life-form, mainly in evidence of unexpected traces of radioactivity.

She had visited 4949 at the request of the mayor of Robina City, to whom traces of local radioactivity had been reported. After getting permission to dig, she had gone with two andumans to the site. It lay in an indent or small valley. She enjoyed the sheer vacancy of the site, with the horizon a matter of meters away and stars and the distorted disks of nearby asteroids overhead. It was for this kind of environment that she had adopted her chosen profession. They pitched their atmotent and began to drill.

All this was clear enough to the soldiers and to Imo Loko, despite Jeans Two's use of her own variety of 2081's English. She went on to say that the rock was pummicelike, brittle, but easy to quarry. Within two eight-hour shifts, they came upon the outer casing of an alien object. It had struck the asteroid when the minor planets were still in semiliquid state. Its casing was of an ultra-hard and much-pockmarked metal; no torch would cut it. Eventually, the team excavated round the object, brought in a crane, and lifted it from the hole. It was the size of a small room, of a dull bluish material—clearly an artifact, but with no discernible door or other opening in its sides.

Jeans Two had worked round it, pressing it with gloved hands, seeking for cracks. She had triggered a signal. It took the form of a thick rod, suddenly protruding from the casing. The rod had what seemed to be an inscription on it. It was removed for decipherment. After a terrestrial year, about a fifth of Robina's year, no progress had been made in decipherment; indeed, the so-called inscription was dismissed in some quarters as simple random scratch marks. Then, one of the andumans had the idea of super-heating the rod. Immediately, they obtained results—results of a dramatic nature.

"The alien object was a tomb," said Bigsby, breaking into Jeans Two's account. "It cracked open. It was the tomb of a whole species! A species which had once roamed the entire universe. Never before had anything remotely like it been found."

As the tomb opened, Jeans Two experienced a hot blast of a thick element—"almost like honey," in her words. With it were released all the phantasms which had so afflicted her, and which had now percolated—though more faintly—as far as the Mars outpost. No doubt they would soon reach Earth, in an etiolated form.

"So what was this stuff, this thick element like honey? What's it all mean?" Frere asked, with some show of impatience.

"We are coming to that . . ."

"I can't make sense of this tale you're telling us."

"It has taken us a while to make sense of it," said Jeans Two. She went on to explain that inside the tomb they had seen the bodies of what had once been sentient creatures—"sentient if not actually living," was her phrase.

These creatures, or *beings,* she said, was a better term, had three paddles, with bodies like cauldrons from which protruded many sensory organs, some rigid, some flexible. No heads as such. With age, they had become as brittle as dried seaweed. Beside them were various artifacts, still being examined.

Dating systems revealed that the beings were in the region of nine billion years old.

O'Deere whistled. "That's impossible! The universe is only—what? Thirteen billion years old. You're saying these things existed when the universe—"

"—was practically in a compressed nuclear state," said Jeans Two, completing the sentence for him. "It then had a density a billion times that of water. There were certainly no planets extant at that time. No oxygen—primordial hydrogen and helium were then the only elements extant. These beings were certainly not carbon-based. They did not breathe. They may have been born when the universe was born—as a species, that is, if species is a word you can use.

"One theory is that they, whatever they were, were complex clusters of defective protons, turning into fairly normal solid beings only in their extinction. Their medium must have been movement, forever scudding through that dense super-hot ylem . . .

"When we found them, they had withered into things of quasi-metal, wizened like mummies. There's no telling what they looked like exactly when—when active."

"But they had technology?" Imo Loko asked.

"Of a kind, yes. It is impossible to guess at their living conditions."

Nevertheless, O'Deere was trying to imagine just that, imagining these beings, "sentient if not actually living," riding the storms of the early universe, in fluid environments too hot for flame. Forging for themselves some kind of terminal habitation. They themselves always burning, burning.

He thought, startled, " Why, they were creatures of hell . . ."

Jeans Two was saying, "I needed rescue. The phantasms these dead beings released were overpowering my brain. Those phantasms, so ancient, repressed for so long . . ."

"It doesn't make sense to me," Frere said. "If they could survive those high temperatures—we're talking billions of degrees, aren't we—why did they die out?"

Bigsby said that so far they had pieced together only part of the story. But the answer to that question was clear. Gradually, the universe had become too cool for the creatures to survive in. The emergence of heavier elements had spelled their doom. For them, an Ice Age had set in, a universal ice age still continuing. Maybe there were tombs similar to the one on 4949 to be found elsewhere throughout the galaxy.

Speaking almost to herself, Jeans Two said it was impossible even to guess for how many millions of years these creatures had—no, not *lived,* as she understood life, but . . . had their being. . . .

"I've got to get out of here," O'Deere said. The small room had become too oppressive, the speculations too immense. He shruggled himself into a full space suit and headed for the air lock. As he left them, he heard Frere asking, "Okay, but—what was this honeylike stuff that came blasting out at you when you opened the tomb?"

O'Deere did not wait to hear the answer. He thought he knew it. He staggered through the lock, out into the chill Martian night. The ground lightning had died, leaving only leaden dark behind. The expanse of uninhabited nothingness confronted him like a presence, with its material quality. He felt like vomiting, but knew the unpleasantness of vomiting inside a space suit. He leaned against the chill wall of the dome, breathing deeply. To calm himself, he repeated over and over, like a mantra, "*Up, up and away . . .*"

Fulfilled? He could not recall whether he had dared even to kiss that darling girl who sang to him. Probably not. His Catholic upbringing had got in his way. But supposing he *had* kissed her, that there had been courage enough, or time . . . Then he would be a major, a colonel, by now, living far from this astronomical backwater. The whole world would have been changed by that one kiss . . .

He could guess the nature of the ichor pouring from that newly opened tomb on 4949. It had been preserved from the early universe, when space-time was a flux. It had been Time itself which poured forth—Time when it was a different material, Time undiluted, Time as nutrient syrup, a material of the womb.

And those marvelous beings of fire. They had no need for kisses, his sad, unfulfilled need. They could—what?—skate?—*speed* through the entire universe, free, free of gravity. He supposed that in their long epochs, gravity had been as nonexistent as oxygen. And somehow those dreadful, enviable beings had left a legend behind them: the legend of hell as a perpetual torment. Hell had existed long before the cold rule-giving God in heaven was born. Hell was the only faint folk memory mankind—the *humankinder* had of their primal universe. The memory had somehow been passed on, when the universe grew chill. When sentient beings were confined to the laws of planets instead of riding forever on the storms of furnace fire . . .

THE ME AFTER THE ROCK

by Patrick O'Leary

CAN you please, please, please stop talking?"

"I can't. I can't anymore. I've been quiet for days. I'm through with quiet."

"Just watch your mouth."

"Okay. I'm watching it. So what do we tell them, Captain? What do we say?"

"We say: There is no life on Mars. That's what we say. That's it. End of story."

"They won't believe us. Not after our transmissions. They're on record. Recorded history. I bet they're listening to every word we say. I bet this whole conversation is being recorded."

00:10 SILENCE

"Don't be paranoid."

"I don't care what they hear. We have an obligation. People need to know the truth. Mars is not a rock. It is a sentient planet that loves."

"Awww shuttup."

"I love you."

"Stop it."

"I do, you know."

"Shuttup, already! It's not enough I had to put up with . . ."

"With what?"

"You. All the way back. Looking at me."

"I couldn't help myself."

"Well, try."

"I am. I can't."

"Try harder."

"Harder?"

"It's not a joke to me, you know!"

"No need to raise your voice. They can hear everything."

"I mean you weren't this way when we signed on."

"No."

"You were screened for it."

"Right."

"So what happened? And don't give me that rock shit."

"People change."

"Not that much, for Christ's sake."

"It was Mars."

"Mars is a rock. A cold red rock."

"We both saw it."

"Shuttup. I never touched it."

"But you saw it."

"It could have been . . ."

"What?"

"It could have been anything. Light. Shadow. Our tank mixture. Stop laughing."

"I'm laughing at myself. It's hopeless. I'm hopeless. Denial makes you so beautiful."

"Stop it."

"You think I'm making this up?"

"I think you're crazy."

"You never met any gay guys before?"

"Not like you."

"Well, there's no one like me, that's for sure."

"You could have warned me."

"You don't get it. I was never gay, Brian. Never. I never felt those feelings about men. I did not just come out of the closet. I was changed."

"By a rock."

"Yes."

"A sentient rock."

"Yes."

"You didn't even touch it. You had gloves on."

"They went through the gloves."

"They?"

"They. It. Whatever. Mars."

"That's impossible."

"There's no other explanation."

"Intelligent rocks that turn people gay. They're going to put you away."

"We already are. What do you call this?"

"This is the transitional—stop laughing. Containment is procedure."

"Three days is procedure. One week is prison."

"Precaution. Quarantine. Whatever you call it, you want to get out of this white room, Bob, you better shut the fuck up about all this smart rock shit. It didn't happen to me."

"You sound jealous."

"Look. Stop it. You're gonna drive me— Okay. I believe you. Are you happy? Will you shuttup now?"

"I can't."

"Then they'll never let us out of here."

"Now who's paranoid?"

"Can we just stop talking? I have a headache."

01:36 SILENCE

"You haven't considered another option."

"Jesus."

"Maybe they didn't change me. Maybe they changed you."

"What are you talking about?"

"Maybe they changed you into something I could love. Don't you remember? I hated you."

"We barely knew each other."

"Six months of training. One month of isolation. I'd say we knew—"

"I don't care what you say. I'm the same. I'm no different. I'm the same man I was when we launched!"

"You don't have to talk to the ceiling. They can hear you. Okay, I vouch for you. He's the same guy he was. The single most irritating, human I'd ever met. Pilot Brian. Captain Regulation. Everything by the book. God, how I hated you. But now—"

"I don't want to hear it, Bob."

"I love the way you say my name."

"Shut the fuck up."

"Maybe that's it. Maybe they talked, but you didn't listen. So the rocks didn't talk to you?"

"Jesus, you never said they talked."

"I'm joking, Brian."

"Goddammit, stop it!"

02:16 SILENCE

"What's so funny?"

"This is why I hate public transportation."

"Not . . . really . . . following you here, Brian."

"You know what this is like? This is like that movie. The one with Robert De Niro and what's his face? The one where the fugitive and the bounty hunter are stuck together."

"Shackled?"

"No, not shackled. Stuck. He was a mob accountant and he's flown on his bail and De Niro's gotta get him across country to LA to pick up the reward and they're riding a train and he won't stop pestering De Niro—the bounty hunter. And he's on him about everything. His smoking. His watch that won't work. And the guy can't stop talking."

" 'That's a nice looking chicken.' "

"What?"

"I remember now. Charles Grodin."

"Who?"

"The other guy. The fugitive. Charles Grodin."

"I thought it was Steve Martin."

"No. They never did a movie together."

"Anyway he was a pest."

" 'That's a nice looking chicken.' "

"You keep saying that."

"It was the line on the train. When they're riding the train and they've been on the run and they're starting to warm up to each other."

"*Midnight Run.* That's the title."

"Right. Anyway they're stuck and they're probably horny."

"Watch it."

"I'm not even talking about that. And they walk through some chickens. And Grodin says, 'Those were some pretty nice looking chickens back there.' "

"I remember now."

"And De Niro agrees. That's when the ice melts."

"The ice?"

"Like the polar caps. That's when it started."

"What started?"

"You know, there was a thaw in the air."

"A thaw?"

"I mean that's when they fall in love."

"Nobody falls in love. It's got nothing to do with, it's a buddy movie, for chrissake!"

"No, I think there's a definitive thaw there."

"There's no thaw whatsoever. They . . . reconcile."

"No, I think they fall in love. At the end."

"Bullshit."

"Well, Grodin gives him his belt."

"It's a money belt! It's about the money."

"I think it's about love."

"You're warped. Simple fact. Warped."

"Like I had any choice in the matter. I never asked for this, Brian. Falling in love with you was not on my agenda."

"You know how annoying this is? Can we keep love off the table here?"

"Are you one of those bigots, those Bible thumpers who think it's a goddamn choice? A moral choice?"

"No, I'm not. I just never, it was never . . . personal before."

"Nobody ever had a crush on you?"

"No."

"Not even in Boy Scouts?"

"You know, you keep making jokes. There's nothing funny about this. You keep making jokes and they're gonna keep you in here forever. Stuck."

"Like De Niro and Grodin."

"There is no life on Mars, Bob. That's my story, and I'm sticking to it."

00:32 SILENCE

"Anyway. What makes us think we got the right definition of life?"

"Christ almighty."

"Carbon-based. Bipedal. Mammalian. Territorial. When the simplest thing could change it all. Gravity. Proximity to the sun. Atmosphere."

"CAN WE GET SOME MORE LIGHT IN HERE?"

"Jesus, chill, Brian. You think they can't hear every word we say?"

"I would like a little more light, please."

"There, see? They heard you."

"Thanks. Thank you."

"Siddown. Stop groveling, Captain."

"I'm ready for my debriefing now. I'm ready to talk to someone. I need to be debriefed."

"I'll debrief you."

"Shut the fuck up!"

"They're not going to answer. Haven't you learned that yet? They'll fume us any moment now. And leave us the food."

"I would like to talk to someone!"

"You're talking to me."

"I would like to talk to someone else!"

"Why do you even bother?"

"Please!"

"Relax, Brian. Deep breaths. In through that lovely mouth. Out through that lovely nose."

"Shut the fuck up."

03:12 SILENCE

"Funny, how we know they're there even though we can't see them. Like we had to figure out about the fumes here. I'm surprised they didn't tell you about the fumes. I mean, I can understand them not telling me. I'm just the rock man. But you're the mission commander. You'd think they might have mentioned Quarantine. Courtesy, you know. They might have prepped us."

"They did."

00:10 SILENCE

"They mentioned the possibility of contamination. And a new facility they were working on. In Dallas."

"You knew this and you didn't tell me?"

"What difference does it make?"

"Well, for one thing it would have been nice to know we were in Texas. I mean to have a name for this white room. That would have helped."

"I'm sorry, I should have told you."

"You were playing dumb. You knew all about the fumes, didn't you?"

"I'm sorry."

"If I didn't love you, I would really be pissed right now."

"Get pissed, I don't care."

"It won't work, Brian. I'm not that easily discouraged. My love is steadfast."

"Fuck you."

"See, that won't work either. I see the real you. I know you did what you did for the highest motives. You were following the chain of command. It was a need-to-know thing, right?"

"Right."

"So Okay. I forgive you. I admire you. I love you."

"Shut the fuck up."

"I just would have liked to have known we were in Texas. I've got relatives here."

00:42 SILENCE

"What if they're microscopic?"

"Who?"

"You know who."

"There is no life on Mars, Bob. Get it through your thick skull. We have no evidence."

"But what if they're too small for anyone to see with the naked eye? Or subatomic."

"What if they were Fairy Dust? Christ, start acting like a scientist!"

" 'Fairy dust.' That's funny. That's maybe the first joke I've ever heard you make. My point is, my logical scientific thesis is: Where's it say that life has to be recognizable to us? On our terms. I mean you were there; you remember. We both knew we were not alone."

"Speak for yourself."

"We both felt someone, something watching us. But why me? Why me?"

00:51 SILENCE

"I'm a geologist. Maybe that's why it happened. I love rocks. I know their names. But that one. You know the one I'm talking about."

"I never touched it."

"No, but neither of us could take our eyes off it. The color. It wasn't a color."

"It had to be some color. What's so funny?"

"We're scientists and we cannot even describe the color of a rock!"

"It was bluish, blackish."

"Blackish, greenish, I would say."

"It doesn't matter."

"It scared you. It still does. Admit it, Brian."

"I'm not afraid of rocks."

"You were. You practically begged me to come back to the lander."

"For the record: I was concerned about our oxygen."

"You were afraid you were hallucinating."

"I was the pilot. I was responsible for the safety of the mission."

"You were pissing in your suit. And you said you saw it move."

"I did not!"

"You did. I recall your exact words: 'Did you see it move? Did it move?' "

00:12 SILENCE

"It was just a pretty rock until I touched it. Held it in my hand. There was the me before the rock and the me after the rock. Two totally different people. I held it in my hand and looked at you in your suit, and even though I couldn't see your eyes through the visor you were the most beautiful creature I'd ever encountered."

"You gotta stop this, Bob. You're scaring me."

"You have no reason to fear me. I would leap in front of lions for you. I would lie and cheat and steal and kill for you."

"I would like another room, now!"

"You don't even have to touch me, Brian. I just want to be around you, wherever you go."

"Stay on your side."

"I didn't know how lonely I was until that moment."

"I'm warning you."

"It was like I'd spent my entire existence with no one to talk to. Just an endless cycle of cold and colder. Day and night. Rocks and more rocks. And then, it changed. There was somebody to talk to. Somebody to listen. And it was like I'd spent a lifetime waiting for something and I didn't even know it until it was there. Finally there."

02:12 SILENCE

"Brian? Can I ask you a question? Do you think it's possible for a planet to be lonely? I know you don't want to talk about rocks. I know: There is no life on Mars. 'Shut the fuck up.' Let's talk about paradigm shifts. Like twenty years the Mets are losers and suddenly one day they're in the series."

"I didn't know you were a Mets fan."

"There, see? We've got something in common. Relax. You ever have a paradigm shift?"

"Not recently."

"My Uncle George did. In China. He took me out to dinner when I got my degree and we're eating fried rice in this Chinese place on 20th."

"Fu's?"

"No."

"Wu's?"

"I forget the name. Anyway, Uncle George told me he was stationed in China during The Big One."

"World War Two?"

"Right. A cushy job, he said: all the action was elsewhere. But on weekends he got to see some strange stuff, like this huge green cave scooped out of a mountain. And inside there was this temple and a thousand candles and this giant golden Buddha about the size of three fridges. You know how they sit. Kinda contorted but kinda sleepy, too. He's gotta get a picture of this, but the Buddha's too big and he has to step way back to fit it into frame. He worries about the light 'cause the gold's tarnished and the cave is full of shadows. He takes the picture. He doesn't expect much. When he gets the picture, he sees what he didn't see: this giant Buddha is not a giant but a golden baby in the lap of its papa: a gargantuan Buddha carved out of the green mossy rock of the cave wall. Three stories high. I remember he laughed and some rice dribbled out of his mouth onto the china."

00:10 SILENCE

"Or like the time I went back to the town where I was born and everything was smaller. The houses. The ditches. The dirt roads."

"Why was it smaller?"

"I was a kid then. I'm bigger now. Grown."

"Oh, I see."

"Actually, I was always the smallest kid in class. I mean the girls were giants. And everybody used to rub my head for good luck. Like I was a mascot or something. But now. Now. Christ, I feel like I'm the biggest person in the world. What did Whitman say?"

"The guy in Mission Control?"

"The poet. 'I am Big. I contain multitudes.'"

"What are you talking about?"

"It's like I'm bigger somehow. Enlarged. Like I'm looking down on everybody. Like I'm so big nobody can fit their arms around me."

"Aww, Christ."

"I'm sorry."

"Don't. Don't!"

"I CAN'T HELP IT!"

"You don't have to cry."

"I didn't ask for this. I was a perfectly happy geologist. I DIDN'T WANT TO TOUCH A PLANET AND FALL IN LOVE WITH YOU!"

"Hello? Is anybody listening? My buddy needs some help here. And, frankly, I'd like my own room."

"Don't leave me!"

"Aww, Christ."

"I'll go crazy without you here."

"Somebody! Anybody! There's a situation here! A situation! Just stay away from me!"

"I'm not gonna hurt you! I would never hurt you."

"Just siddown and cool it. Don't!"

"You don't understand. I got a whole planet in me, and it's lonely and it's sad and it can't bear it any longer."

"SOMEBODY!"

"I'm not gonna hurt you."

"Don't!"

"I promise I won't."

"No touching."

"I won't touch you if you hold me."

"I'm not gonna— Just siddown, would ya?"

"Please."

"SOMEBODY!"

"Please!"

"ANYBODY!"

02:24 SILENCE

"See? I didn't hurt you, did I?"

"Just shuttup."

"I promised."

"All right. Just shuttup."

"Thanks. I'm getting your shirt wet."

"Don't worry about it."

"Have you ever held a man before?"

"My son. It was at my dad's funeral."

"I feel better now. You can let go. Thanks."

"Damn."

"What?"

"I'm soaking."

"I'm sorry."

"I didn't know you could cry that much."

"A world of tears."

"Don't start."

"That's what it is: A world of tears. I'm sorry about your dad."

"It's okay. He was an asshole anyway."

"Did you love him?"

"Sure."

"Even though he was an asshole?"

"He was my dad. I didn't have much choice in the matter."

"My mother died. She was a star. The biggest, brightest . . . I mean she could light up a room. But she died ages ago. I don't even remember when."

"Was she anybody I might have heard of? Like on TV? What are you smiling for?"

"We come from the same stuff, you know. Stardust. That's why I love you. You're the closest thing I got to a brother. The same stuff."

"You're going crazy on me again."

"Sorry. I'm okay. That was nice of you to hold me."

"Don't mention it."

"No. Really. It meant a lot."

"I said don't mention it."

" 'Shut the fuck up.' "

"What?"

"That's what De Niro keeps saying to Grodin. 'Shut the fuck up.'"

"We're back to that movie."

"The love story."

"It was a buddy movie. There was no sex involved."

"I didn't say sex. Male love. Friendship."

"Right."

"Guy love. Between guys."

"It's the norm."

"Okay. It's the norm. I'll grant you that."

00:16 SILENCE

"Like warriors. Soldiers. The bond of battle. You ever felt that?"

"Some."

"When?"

"I don't want to talk about it."

"Desert Storm. It was in your bio. You flew that?"

"Yes."

"You bombed Iraq?"

"We all did."

"You lost . . . ?"

"Read the papers. We won."

"I mean: casualties. I mean . . . buddies."

"Yeah."

"I'm sorry."

"It's war. You get close in a way . . . I can't explain."

"A bond. The mission. Maybe that's what happened to us. The war bond. Between men."

"What the fuck are you talking about?"

"Mars. The angry red planet. The god of war."

"I need a beer."

"It's mythology. Didn't they teach you that at flight school? War? Mars? Rome?"

"No. I can't say that was a critical part of the curriculum."

"See, maybe they got the myth wrong. Maybe it's about the bond of men at war. Brothers in Arms. The only time they can let themselves love each other."

"Are we back to that again?"

"Red. Maybe it's passion, lust, desire."

"That's Venus. I do know that."

"But there's no life on Venus, Brian."

"Fuck off."

"I still love you."

"Fuck you!"

"You can accept that?"

"Do I have a choice?"

"No. You're stuck with it. We're brothers now."

"We're not even related."

"We're brothers. You can shut me down. Or keep me locked up here forever. But that's the truth. We're brothers."

"Somebody?"

"Don't bother. They won't come. They're not gonna answer. We're alone."

"I should have never hugged you."

"Jesus. Relax. I'm not touching you again."

"Don't."

"I won't. I promise."

"Good. Once was enough."

"I said I wouldn't. Relax."

00:11 SILENCE

"Besides. Now you got it."

"What?"

"It. Me. That's what it wants. It wants me to touch everybody. So I started with you."

"SOMEBODY!"

"You can yell and scream, but they won't let you out. You've touched me now. My tears are all over you."

"PLEASE! SOMEBODY!"

"They know, you see. They must. That's why we're here. And soon you'll feel the same way I do and I won't have to fight you anymore. We'll want the same things. We won't be different. We'll want each other. And we'll never want to leave each other."

01:02 SILENCE

"Don't cry. Please don't cry, Brian. Don't cry, my love. I'll take care of you. I take good care of anyone who lets me touch them. I promise."

LOST SORCERESS
OF THE SILENT CITADEL

by Michael Moorcock

(Homage to Leigh Brackett)

*T*HEY *came upon the Earthling naked, somewhere in the
Shifting Desert when Mars' harsh sunlight beat through
thinning atmosphere and the sand was raw glass cutting into
bare feet. His skin hung like filthy rags from his bloody flesh.
He was starved, unshaven, making noises like an animal. He
was raving—empty of identity and will. What had the ghosts of
those ancient Martians done to him? Had they traveled
through time and space to take a foul and unlikely vengeance?
A novella of alien mysteries—of a goddess who craved life—
who lusted for the only man who had ever dared disobey her.
A tale of Captain John MacShard, the Half-Martian, of old
blood and older memories, of a restless quest for the prize of
forgotten centuries. . . .*

CHAPTER ONE

Whispers of an Ancient Memory

"That's Captain John MacShard, the tomb-thief." Schomberg
leaned his capacious belly on the bar, wiping around it with a
filthy rag. "They say his mother was a Martian princess turned
whore, and his father—"

Low City's best-known antiquities fence, proprietor of the
seedy Twenty Capstans, Schomberg murmured wetly through
lips like fresh liver. "Well, Mercury was the only world would
take them. Them and their filthy egg." He flicked a look toward the door and became suddenly grave.

Outlined against the glare of the Martian noon a man appeared to hesitate and go on down the street. Then he turned and pushed through the entrance's weak energy gate. Then he paused again.

He was a big, hard-muscled man, dressed in spare ocher and brown, with a queer, ancient weapon, all baroque unstable plastics and metals, prominent on his hip.

The Banning gun was immediately recognized and its owner identified by the hardened spacers and *krik* traders who used the place.

They said only four men in the solar system could ever handle that weapon. One was the legendary Northwest Smith; the second was Eric John Stark, now far off-system. The third was Dumarest of Terra, and the fourth was Captain John Mac-Shard. Anyone else trying to fire a Banning died unpleasantly. Sometimes they just disappeared, as if every part of them had been sucked into the gun's impossible energy cells. They said Smith had given his soul for a Banning. But MacShard's soul was still apparent, behind that steady gray gaze, hungering for something like oblivion.

From long habit Captain John MacShard remained in the doorway until his sight had fully adjusted to the sputtering naphtha. His eyes glowed with a permanent feral fire. He was a lean-faced, slim-hipped wolf's head whom no man could ever tame. Through all the alien and mysterious spheres of interplanetary space, many had tried to take the wild beast out of Captain John MacShard. He remained as fierce and free as in the days when, as a boy, he had scrabbled for survival over the unforgiving waste of rocky crags and slag slopes that was Mercury and from the disparate blood of two planets had built a body which could withstand the cruel climate of a third.

Captain John MacShard was in Schomberg's for a reason. He never did anything without a reason. He couldn't go to sleep until he had first considered the action. It was what he had learned on Mercury, orphaned, surviving in those terrible caverns, fighting fiercely for subsistence where nothing would grow and where you and the half-human tribe which had adopted you were the tastiest prey on the planet.

More than any Earthman, he had learned the old ways, the sweet, dangerous, old ways of the ancient Martians. Their descendants still haunted the worn and whispering hills which were the remains of Mars' great mountain ranges in the ages of her might, when the Sea Kings ruled a planet as blue as turquoise, as glittering red as rubies, and as green as that Emerald Isle which had produced Captain John MacShard's own Earth ancestors, as tough, as mystical and as filled with wanderlust as this stepson of the shrieking Mercurian wastelands, with the blood of Brian Borhu, Henry Tudor, and Charles Edward Stuart in his veins. Too, the blood of Martian Sea Kings called to him across the centuries and informed him with the deep wisdom of his Martian forebears. That long-dead kin had fought against the Danes and the Anglo-Saxons, been cavaliers in the Stuart cause and marshals in Napoleon's army. They had fought for and against the standard of Rhiannon, in both male and female guise, survived blasting sorcery and led the starving armies of Barrakesh into the final battle of the Martian pole. Their stories, their courage and their mad fearlessness in the face of inevitable death were legendary.

Captain John MacShard had known nothing of this ancestry of course and there were still many unsolved mysteries in his past, but he had little interest in them. He had the instincts of any intelligent wild animal, and left the past in the past. A catlike curiosity was what drove him and it made him the best archaeological hunter on five planets—some, like Schomberg, called him a grave-looter, though never to his face. There was scarcely a museum in the inhabited universe which didn't proudly display a find of Captain John Mac-Shard's. They said some of the races which had made those artifacts had not been entirely extinct until the captain found them. There wasn't a living enemy didn't fear him. And there wasn't a woman in the system who had known him that didn't remember him.

To call Captain John MacShard a loner was something of a tautology. Captain John MacShard was loneliness personified. He was like a spur of rock in the deep desert, resisting everything man and nature could send against it. He was endurance. He was integrity, and he was grit through and through. Only one who had tested himself against the entire fury of alien Mercury and survived could know what it meant to be Mac-Shard, trusting only MacShard.

Captain John MacShard was very sparing in his affections but gave less to himself than he gave to an alley-*brint*, a wounded ray-rat, or the scrawny street kid begging in the hard sour Martian sun to whom he finally tossed a piece of old silver before striding into the bar and taking his usual, which Schomberg had ready for him.

The Dutchman began to babble something, but Captain John MacShard placed his lips to the shot glass of Vortex Water, turned his back on him, and surveyed his company.

His company was pretending they hadn't seen him come in.

From a top pocket MacShard fished a twisted pencil of Venusian talk-talk wood and stuck it between his teeth, chewing on it thoughtfully. Eventually his steady gaze fell on a fat merchant in a fancy fake *skow*-skin jerkin and vivid blue tights who pretended an interest in his fancifully carved flagon.

"Your name Morricone?" Captain John MacShard's voice was a whisper, cutting through the rhythmic sound of men who couldn't help taking in sudden air and running tongues round drying mouths.

His thin lips opened wide enough for the others to see a glint of bright, pointed teeth before they shut tight again.

Morricone nodded. He made a halfhearted attempt to smile. He put his hands on either side of his cards and made funny shrugging movements.

From somewhere, softly, a *shtrang* string sounded.

"You wanted to see me," said Captain John MacShard. And he jerked his head toward a corner where a filthy table was suddenly unoccupied.

The man called Morricone scuttled obediently toward the table and sat down, watching Captain John MacShard as he picked up his bottle and glass and walked slowly, his antique *ghat*-scale leggings chinking faintly.

Again the *shtrang* string began to sound, its deep note making peculiar harmonies in the thin Martian air. There was a cry like a human voice which echoed into nowhere, and when it was gone the silence was even more profound.

"You wanted to see me?" Captain John MacShard moved the unlit stogie from one side of his mouth to the other. His gray, jade-flecked eyes bore into Morricone's shifting black pupils. The fat merchant was obviously hyped on some kind of Low City "head chowder."

There wasn't a drug you couldn't buy at Schomberg's where everything was for sale, including Schomberg.

The hophead began to giggle in a way that at once identified him as a *cruffer,* addicted to the fine, white powdered bark of the Venusian high tree cultures, who used the stuff to train their giant birds but had the sense not to use it themselves.

Captain John MacShard turned away. He wasn't going to waste his time on a druggy, no matter how expensive his tastes.

Morricone lost his terror of Captain John MacShard then. He needed help more than he needed dope. Captain John MacShard was faintly impressed. He knew the kind of hold *cruff* had on its victims.

But he kept on walking.

Until Morricone scuttled in front of him and almost fell to his knees, his hands reaching out toward Captain John MacShard, too afraid to touch him.

His voice was small, desperate, and it held some kind of pain Captain John MacShard recognized. "Please . . ."

Captain John MacShard made to move past, back into the glaring street.

"Please, Captain MacShard. Please help me . . ." His shoulders slumped, and he said dully: "They've taken my daughter. The Thennet have taken my daughter."

Captain John MacShard hesitated, still looking into the street. From the corner of his mouth he gave the name of one of the cheapest hotels in the quarter. Nobody in their right mind would stay there if they valued life or limb. Only the crazy or desperate would even enter the street it was in.

"I'm there in an hour." Captain John MacShard went out of the bar. The boy he'd given the silver coin to was still standing in the swirling Martian dust, the ever-moving red tide which ran like a bizarre river down the time-destroyed street. The boy grinned up at him. Old eyes, young skin. A slender snizzer lizard crawled on his shoulder and curled its strange, prehensile tail around his left ear. The boy touched the creature tenderly, automatically.

"You good man, Mister Captain John MacShard."

For the first time in months, Captain John MacShard allowed himself a thin, self-mocking grin.

CHAPTER TWO

Taken by the Thennet!

Captain John MacShard left the main drag almost at once. He needed some advice and knew where he was most likely to find it. There was an old man he had to visit. Though not of their race, Fra Energen had authority over the last of the Memiget Priests whose Order had discovered how rich the planet was in man-made treasure. They had also been experts on the Thennet as well as the ancient Martian pantheon.

His business over with, Captain John MacShard walked back to his hotel. His route took him through the filthiest, most wretched slums ever seen across all the ports of the spaceways. He displayed neither weakness nor desire. His pace was the steady, relentless lope of the wolf. His eyes seemed unmoving, yet took in everything.

All around him the high tottering tenement towers of the Low City swayed gently in the glittering light, their rusted metal and red terra cotta merging into the landscape as if they were natural. As if they had always been there.

Not quite as old as Time, some of the buildings were older than the human race. They had been added to and stripped and added to again, but once those towers had sheltered and proclaimed the power of Mars' mightiest sea lords.

Now they were slums, a rat warren for the scum of the spaceways, for half-Martians like Captain John MacShard, for stranger genetic mixes than even Brueghel imagined.

In that thin atmosphere you could smell the Low City for miles and beyond that, in the series of small craters known as Diana's Field, was Old Mars Station, the first spaceport the Earthlings had ever built, long before they had begun to discover the strange, retiring races which had remained near their cities, haunting them like barely living ghosts, more creatures of their own mental powers than of any natural creation—ancient memories made physical by act of will alone.

Millennia before, the sea lords and their ladies and children died in those towers, sensing the end of their race as the last of the waters evaporated and red winds scoured the streets of all ornament and grace. Some chose to kill themselves as their fine ships became so many useless monuments. Some had marshaled their families and set off across the new-formed deserts in search of a mythical ocean which welled up from the planet's core.

It had taken less than a generation, Captain John MacShard knew, for a small but navigable ocean to evaporate rapidly until it was no more than a haze in the morning sunlight. Where it had been were slowly collapsing hulls, the remains of wharfs and jetties, endless dunes and rippling deserts, abandoned cities of poignant dignity and unbelievable beauty. The great dust tides rose and fell across the dead sea bottoms of a planet which had run out of resources. Even its water had come from Venus, until the Venusians had raised the price so only Earth could afford it.

Earth was scarcely any better now, with water wars turning the Blue Planet into a background of endless skirmishes between nations and tribes for the precious streams, rivers, and lakes they had used so dissolutely and let dissipate into space, turning God's paradise into Satan's wasteland.

And now Earth couldn't afford Venusian water either. So Venus fought a bloody civil war for control of what was left of her trade. For a while MacShard had run bootleg water out of New Malvern. The kind of money the rich were prepared to pay for a tiny bottle was phenomenal. But he'd become sickened with it when he'd walked through London's notorious Westminster district and seen degenerates spending an artisan's wages on jars of gray reconstitute while mothers held the corpses of dehydrated babies in their arms and begged for the money to bury them.

"Mr. Captain John MacShard."

Captain John MacShard knew the boy had followed him all

the way to the hotel. Without turning, he said: "You'd better introduce yourself, sonny."

The boy seemed ashamed, as if he had never been detected before. He hung his head. "My dad called me Milton," he said.

Captain John MacShard smiled then. Once. He stopped when he saw the boy's face. The child had been laughed at too often and to him it meant danger, distrust, pain. "So your dad was Mr. Eliot, right?"

The boy forgot any imagined insult. "You knew him?"

"How long did your mother know him?"

"Well, he was on one of those long-haul ion sailors. He was a great guitarist. Singer. Wrote all his own material. He was going to see a producer when he came back from Earth with enough money to marry. Well, you know that story." The boy lowered his eyes. "Never came back."

"I'm not your pa," said Captain John MacShard and went inside. He closed his door. He marveled at the tricks the street kids used these days. But that stuff couldn't work on him. He'd seen six-year-old masters pulling the last Uranian *bakh* from a tight-fisted New Nantucket blubber-chaser who had just finished a speech about a need for more workhouses.

A few moments later, Morricone arrived. Captain John MacShard knew it was him by the quick, almost hesitant rap.

"It's open," he said. There was never any point in locking doors in this place. It advertised you had something worth stealing. Maybe just your body.

Morricone was terrified. He was terrified of the neighborhood and he was terrified of Captain John MacShard. But he was even more terrified of something else. Of whatever the Thennet might have done to his daughter.

Captain John MacShard had no love for the Thennet, and he didn't need a big excuse to put a few more of their number in hell.

The gaudily dressed old man shuffled into the room, and his terror didn't go away. Captain John MacShard closed the door behind him. "Don't tell me about the Thennet," he said. "I know about them and what they do. Tell me when they took your daughter and whatever else you know about where they took her."

"Out past the old tombs. A good fifty or sixty versts from

here. Beyond the Yellow Canal. I paid a breed to follow them. That's as far as he got. He said the trail went on, but he wasn't going any farther. I got the same from all of them. They won't follow the Thennet into the Aghroniagh Hills. Then I heard you had just come down from Earth." He made some effort at ordinary social conversation. His eyes remained crazed. "What's it like back there now?"

"This is better," said Captain John MacShard. "So they went into the Aghroniagh Hills? When?"

"Some two days ago . . ."

Captain John MacShard turned away with a shrug.

"I know," said the merchant. "But this was different. They weren't going to eat her or—or—play with her . . ." His skin crawled visibly. "They were careful not to mark her. It was as if she was for someone else. Maybe a big slaver? They wouldn't let any of their saliva drip on her. They got me, though." He extended the twisted branch of burned flesh that had been his forearm.

Captain John MacShard drew a deep breath and began to take off his boots. "How much?"

"Everything. Anything."

"You'll owe me a million hard *deens* if I bring her back alive. I won't guarantee her sanity."

"You'll have the money. I promise. Her name's Mercedes. She's sweet and decent—the only good thing I ever helped create. She was staying with me . . . the vacation . . . her mother and I . . ."

Captain John MacShard moved toward his board bed. "Half in the morning. Give me a little time to put the money in a safe place. Then I'll leave. But not before."

After Morricone had shuffled away, his footsteps growing softer and softer until they faded into the general music of the rowdy street outside, Captain John MacShard began to laugh.

It wasn't a laugh you ever wanted to hear again.

CHAPTER THREE

The Unpromised Land

The Aghroniagh Hills had been formed by a huge asteroid
crashing into the area a few million years earlier, but the wide
sweep of meadowland and streams surrounding them had never
been successfully settled by Captain John MacShard's people.
They were far from what they seemed.

Many settlers had come in the early days, attracted by the
water and the grass. Few lasted a month, let alone a season.
That water and grass existed on Mars because of Blake, the
terraplaner. He had made it his life's work, crossing and re-
crossing one set of disparate genes with another until he had
something which was like grass and like water and which
could survive, maybe even thrive and proliferate, in Mars' barren climate. A sort of liquid algae and a kind of lichen, at root,
but with so many genetic modifications that its mathematical
pedigree filled a book.

Blake's great atmosphere pumping stations had transformed the Martian air and made it rich enough for Earthlings
to breathe. He had meant to turn the whole of Mars into the
same lush farmland he had seen turn to dust on Earth. Some
believed he had grown too ambitious, that instead of doing
God's work, he was beginning to believe he, himself, was
God. He had planned a city called New Jerusalem and had designed its buildings, its parks, streams, and ornamental lakes.
He had planted his experimental fields and brought his first
pioneer volunteers and given them seed he had made and fer-
tilizer he had designed, and something had happened under the
unshielded Martian sunlight which had not happened in his
laboratories.

Blake's Eden became worse than Purgatory.

His green shoots and laughing fountains developed a kind
of intelligence, a taste for specific nutrients, a means of finding them and processing them to make them edible. Those nutrients were most commonly found in Earthlings. The food
could be enticed the way an anemone entices an insect. The
prey saw sweet water, green grass and it was only too glad to

fling itself deep into the greedy shoots, the thirsty liquid, which was only too glad to digest it.

And so fathers had watched their children die before their eyes, killed and absorbed in moments. Women had seen hard-working husbands die before becoming food themselves.

Blake's seven pioneer families lasted a year and there had been others since who brought certain means of defeating the so-called Paradise virus, who challenged the hungry grass and liquid, who planned to tame it. One by one, they went to feed what had been intended to feed them.

There were ways of surviving the Paradise. Captain John MacShard had tried them and tested them. For a while he had specialized in finding artifacts which the settlers had left behind, letters, deeds, cherished jewelry.

He had learned how to live, for short periods at least, in the Paradise. He had kept raising his price until it got too high for anybody.

Then he quit. It was the way he put an end to his own boredom. What he did with all his money nobody knew, but he didn't spend it on himself.

The only money Captain John MacShard was known to exchange in large quantities was for modifications and repairs to that ship of his, as alien as his sidearm, which he'd picked up in the Rings and claimed by right of salvage. Even the scrap merchants hadn't wanted the ship. The metal it was made of could become poisonous to the touch. Like the weapon, the ship didn't allow everyone to handle her.

Captain John MacShard paid a halfling *phunt*-renter to drive him to the edge of the Paradise, and he promised the sweating driver the price of his *phunt* if he'd wait for news of his reappearance and come take him back to the city. "And any other passenger I might have with me," he had added.

The *phunter* was almost beside himself with anxiety. He knew exactly what that green sentient weed could do, and he had heard tales of how the streams had chased a man halfway back to the Low City and consumed him on the spot. *Drank him, they said.* No sane creature, Earthling or Martian, would risk the dangers of the Paradise.

Not only was the very landscape dangerous, there were also the Thennet.

The Thennet, whose life-stuff was unpalatable to the Paradise, came and went comfortably all year round, emerging only occasionally to make raids on the human settlements, certain that no posse would ever dare follow them back to their city of tunnels, Kong Gresh, deep at the center of the Aghroniagh Crater, which lay at the center of the Aghroniagh Hills, where the weed did not grow and the streams did not flow.

They raided for pleasure, the Thennet. Mostly, when they craved a delicacy. Human flesh was almost an addiction to them, they desired it so much. They were a cruel people and took pleasure in their captives, keeping them alive for many weeks sometimes, especially if they were young women. But they savored this killing. Schomberg had put it graphically enough once: *The longer the torment, the sweeter the meat.* His customers wondered how he understood such minds.

Captain John MacShard knew Mercedes Morricone had a chance at life. He hoped, when he found her, that she would still want that chance.

What had Morricone said about the Thennet not wishing to mark her? That they were capturing her for someone else?

Who?

Captain John MacShard wanted to find out for himself. No one had needed to pay the Thennet for young girls in years. The wars among the planets had given the streets plenty of good-looking women to choose from. Nobody ever noticed a few missing from time to time.

If the Thennet were planning to sell her for the food they would need for the coming Long Winter, they would be careful to keep their goods in top quality, and Mercedes could well be a specific target. The odds were she was still alive and safe. That was why Captain John MacShard did not think he was wasting his time.

And it was the only reason he would go this far into the Aghroniaghs, where the Thennet weren't the greatest danger.

CHAPTER FOUR

Hell Under The Hill

It was hard to believe the Thennet had ever been human, but there was no doubt they spoke a crude form of English. They were said to be degenerated descendants of a crashed Earth ship which had left Houston a couple of centuries before, carrying a political investigative committee looking into reports that Earth mining interests were using local labor as slaves. The reports had been right. The mining interests had made sure the distinguished senators never got to see the evidence.

Captain John MacShard was wearing his own power armor. It buzzed on his body from soles to crown. The silky energy, soft as a child's hand, rippled around him like an atmosphere. He flickered and buzzed with complex circuitry outlining his veins and arteries, following the course of his blood. This medley of soft sounds was given a crazy rhythm by the ticking of his antigrav's notoriously dangerous regulators as he flew an inch above the hungry, whispering grass, the lush and luring streams of Paradise.

Only once did he come down, in the ruins of what was to have been the city of New Jerusalem and where the grass did not grow.

Here he ran at a loping pace which moved him faster over the landscape and at the same time recharged the antigrav's short-lived power units.

He was totally enclosed in the battlesuit of his own design, his visible skin a strange arsenical green behind the overlapping energy shields, his artificial gills processing the atmosphere to purify maximum oxygen. Around him as he moved was an unstable aura buzzing with gold and misty greens, skipping and sizzling as elements in his armor mixed and reacted with particles of semi-artificial Martian air, fusing them into toxic fumes which would kill a man if taken straight. Which is why Captain John MacShard wore his helmet. It most closely resembled the head of an ornamental dolphin, all sweeping flukes and baroque symmetry, the complicated, delicate wiring visible through the thin plasdex skin, while the macro-engineered plant curving from be-

tween his shoulder blades looked almost like wings. He
could have been one of the forgotten beasts of the Eldren
which they had ridden against Bast-Na-Gir when the first
mythologies of Mars were being made. The transparent steel
visor plate added to this alien appearance, enlarging and giving exaggerated curve to his eyes. He had become an unlikely creature whose outline would momentarily baffle
any casual observer. There were things out here which fed
off Thennet and human alike. Captain John MacShard
only needed a second's edge to survive. But that second was
crucial.

He was in the air again, his batteries at maximum charge.
He was now a shimmering copper angel speeding over the
thirsty grass and the hungry rivers of Paradise until he was at
last standing on the shale slopes of the Aghroniagh Mountains.

The range was essentially the rim of a huge steep-sided
crater. At the crater's center were peculiar pockets of gases
which were the by-product of certain rock dust interacting
with sunlight. These gases formed a breeding and sleeping environment for the Thennet, who could only survive so long
away from what the first Earth explorers had called their
"clouds." Most of the gas, which had a narcotic effect on humans, was drawn down into their burrows by an ingenious system of vents and manually operated fans. It was the only
machinery they used. Otherwise they were primitive enough,
though inventive murderers who delighted in the slow, per-
verse death of anything that lived, including their own sick and
wounded. Suicide was the commonest cause of death.

As Captain John MacShard raced through the crags and
eventually came to the crater walls, he knew he might have a
few hours left in which to save the girl. The Thennet had a way
of letting the gases work on their human victims so that they
became light-headed and cheerful. The Thennet knew how to
amuse humans.

Sometimes they would let the human feel this way for days,
until they began to get too sluggish.

Then they would do something which produced a sudden
rush of adrenaline in their victim. And thereafter it was
unimaginable nightmare. Unimaginable because no human

mind could conceive of such tortures and hold the memory or its sanity. No mind, that is, except Captain John MacShard's. And it was questionable now that Captain John MacShard's mind was still in most senses human.

Here's where I was too late. There's her bone and necklace again. That's the burrow into middle chamber. Gas goes low there. All these thoughts passed through his head as he retraced steps over razor rocks and unstable shale. He had been paid four times to venture into Thennet territory. Twice he had successfully brought out living victims, both still relatively sane. Once he had brought out a corpse. Once he had left a corpse where he found it. Seven times before that, curiosity had taken him there. The time they captured him, his chances of escape had been minimal. He was determined not to be captured again.

Now, however, there was something different about the sinister, smoking landscape of craters and spikes. There was a kind of silence Captain John MacShard couldn't explain. A sense of waiting. A sense of watching.

Unable to do anything but ignore the instinct, he dropped down into the fissures and began to feel his way into the first flinty corridors. He had killed five Thennet guards almost without thought by the time he had begun to descend the great main passage into the Thennet underworld. He always killed Thennet at a distance, if he could. Their venom could sear into delicate circuitry and destroy his armor and his lifelines.

Three more Thennet fell without knowing they were dead. Captain John MacShard felt no hesitation about killing them wherever he came across one. He killed them on principle, the way they killed by habit. The less of the Thennet there were, the better for everyone. And each corpse offered something useful to him as he crept on downward into the subsidiary tunnels, following still familiar routes.

The walls of the caverns were thick with flaking blood and ordure, which the Thennet used for building materials. Mostly it had hardened, but every so often it became soft and slippery. Captain John MacShard had to adjust his step, glad of his gills as well as his armor, which meant he did not have to smell or touch any of the glistening stuff, though every so often his air system overloaded and he got just a hint of the disgusting stench.

But something was wrong. His armor began to pop and tremble. It was a warning. Captain John MacShard paused in the slippery passage and considered withdrawing. There would normally be more Thennet, males and females, shuffling through the passages, going about their business, tending their eggs, tormenting their food.

He had a depressing feeling that he couldn't easily get back, that he was already in a trap. Was it a trap which had been set for him specifically? Or could anyone be the prey? This wasn't the Thennet. Could it be the Thennet had new leadership and wider goals? Captain John MacShard could smell intelligence. This was intelligence. And it wasn't a kind he'd smelled before. Not in Thennet territory. Mostly what you smelled was terror and ghastly glee.

There was something else down here. Something which had a personality. Something which had ambitions. Something which was even now gathering power.

Captain John MacShard had learned to trust his instincts, and his instincts told him he would have to fight to return to the surface. What was more, he had an unpleasant feeling about what he might have to fight. . . .

His best chance was to pretend he had noticed nothing, but keep his attention on that intelligence, even as he sought out the merchant's daughter. What was her name? Mercedes?

The narrow, fetid tunnels of the Thennet city were familiar, but now they were opening up, growing wider and taller, as if the Thennet had been working on them. But why?

And then, suddenly, a wave of thought struck against his own mind—a wave which boomed with the force of a tidal wave. It almost stopped him moving forward. It was a moment before the sense of the thoughts began to filter in to him.

No longer. No longer. I am the one. And I am more than one. I am Shienna Sha Shanakana of the Yellow Price, and I shall again become the goddess I once was when Mars was young. I have paid the Yellow Price. I claim this star system as my own. And then I shall claim the universe. . . .

The girl? Captain John MacShard could not stop the question.

All he received was a wave of mockery which again struck with an almost physical weight.

CHAPTER FIVE

Ancient and Modern

A voice began to whisper through the serpentine tunnels. It was cold as space, hard and sharp as Mercurian steel.

The female Mercedes is gone. She is gone, Earther. There is nothing of her, save this flesh, and I am already changing the flesh so that it is more to my taste. She'll produce the egg. First the body, then the entire planet. Then the system. Then the stars. We shall thrive again. We shall feast at will among the Galaxies.

So that was it! Yet another of Mars' ancient ghosts trying to regain its former power. These creatures had been killed, banished, imprisoned long ago, during the last of Mars' terrible wars.

They had reached an enormous level of intellectual power, ruling the planet and influencing the whole system as they became capable of flinging their mental energy through interplanetary space, to control distant intelligences and rule through them.

They considered themselves to be gods, though they were mortal enough in many respects. It had been their arrogance which had brought them low.

So abstract and strange had become their ambitions that they had forgotten the ordinary humans, those who had chosen not to follow their bizarre path, whose lives became wretched as the Eldren used all the planet's resources to increase their powers. They had grown obsessed with immortality, recording themselves onto extraordinary pieces of jewelry containing everything needed to reconstitute the entire individual. Everything but ordinary humans to place the jewels in their special settings and begin the process, which required considerable human resources, ultimately taking the lives of all involved. For most of the ordinary humans had died of starvation and dehydration as those powers plundered their planet of all re-

sources, melting the poles so that first there was an abundance
of water, the time of the beginnings of the Sea Kings' power,
but then, as quickly, the evaporation had begun, dissipating
into empty space, no longer contained by the protective layers
of ozone and oxygen. The water could not come back. It was
a momentary shimmer in the vastness of space as it was drawn
inevitably toward the sun.

Captain John MacShard knew all this because his mother
had known all this. He had not known his mother, had not
known he had emerged, a brawling, bawling independent
creature from the egg she had saved, even as she and her husband died, victims of the planet's unforgiving climate. He had
not known how he had come to live among the aboriginal ape
people. The fiercely tribal Mercurians had been fascinated by
his tanned, pale hide, so unlike their own dark green skins.
They had never thought him anything but one of themselves.
They had come to value him. He had been elected a kind of
leader. He had taken them to food and guarded them against
the giant rock snakes. He had taught them to kill the snakes,
to preserve their meat. They named him Tan-Arz or Brown-
Skin.

Tan-Arz was his name until the Earthlings found him at
last. His father's brother had paid for the search, paid to bring
him back to Earth during that brief Golden Age before the
planet again descended into civil war. Back to the Old Country. Back to Ireland. Back to Dublin and Trinity College. Then
to South London University.

Dublin and London had not civilized Captain John Mac-
Shard, but they had taught him the manners and ways of a gen-
tleman. They had not educated Captain John MacShard, but
they had informed his experience. Now he understood his enemies as well as his friends. And he understood that the law of
the giant corporations was identical to the law he had learned
on Mercury.

Kill or be killed. Trust nothing and no one. Power is survival. He smelled them. He was contemptuous of most of
them, though they commanded millions. They were his kind.
They were his kind gone soft, obscenely greedy, decadent to
the marrow.

His instinct was to wipe them out, but they had trained him

to serve them. And he had served them. At first, when the wars had begun, he had volunteered. He had served well and honorably, but as the wars got dirtier and the issues less clear, he found himself withdrawing.

He realized that he had more sympathy, most of the time, with the desperate men he was fighting than with the great patricians of Republican Earth.

His refusal to take part in a particularly bloody operation had caused him to be branded a traitor.

It was as an outlaw he had arrived on Mars. They had hunted him into the red wastelands and known he could not have lived.

But Mars was a rest cure compared to Mercury. Captain John MacShard had survived. And Captain John MacShard had prospered.

Now he captained his own ship, the gloriously alien *Duchess of Malfi*, murmuring and baroque in her perpetually shifting darkness. Now he could pick and choose whom he killed and whom he didn't kill.

He had no financial need to continue this dangerous life, no particular security to be derived, even the security of familiarity. Nothing to escape from. Nothing within him he could not confront. He did it because he was who he was.

He was Captain John MacShard and Captain John MacShard was a creature of action, a creature which only came fully alive when its own life was in the balance. A wild creature that longed for the harsh, savage places of the universe, their beauties and their dangers.

But Captain John MacShard had no wish to die here in the slimey burrows of the unhuman Thennet. He had no desire to serve the insane ends of the old Martian godlings who saw their immortality slowly fading and longed for all their power again.

You, Captain John MacShard, will help me. And I will reward you. Before you die, I will make you the sire of the supernatural. Already the blood of my Martians mingles with your own. It is why you are so perfect for my plans.

John MacShard: You are no longer the Earthboy who grew up wild with the submen of Mercury. You are of our own blood, for your mother drew her descent directly from the greatest of

*the Sea Kings and the Sea Kings were our own children—so
much of our blood has mingled with yours that you are now almost one of us.*

Let your blood bring you home, John MacShard.

"My blood is my own! It belongs to nobody but me! Every
atom has been fought for and won."

*It is the blood of gods and goddesses, John MacShard. Of
kings and queens.*

"Then it's still mine. By right of inheritance!" John Mac-
Shard was all aggression now, though the voices speaking to
him were patient, reasonable. He had heard similar voices before. As he lay writhing in his own filthy juices on one of the
Old Ones' examining slabs.

*It is your Earth blood, however, which will give us our
glory back. That vital, sturdy, undiluted stuff will bring us back
our power and make Mars know her old fear of the unhumans
who ruled her before the Sea Kings ruled.*

*Welcome home, Captain John MacShard, last of the Sea
Kings. Welcome home to the Palace of Queen Shienna Sha
Shanakana, Seventh of the Seven Sisters who guard the Shrine
of the Star Pool, Seventh of the Seven Snakes, Sorceress of the
Citadel of Silence where she has slept for too many centuries.*

*The little mortal did its job well, though unconsciously. I
needed its daughter's womb and I needed you, John Mac-
Shard. And now I have both. I will reemerge from the great egg
fully restored to my power and position.*

*Behold, Captain John MacShard! The Secrets of the Silent
Citadel!*

CHAPTER SIX

Queen of the Crystal Citadel

All at once the half-Martian was surrounded by crystal. Crystal
colored like rainbows, flashing and murmuring in a cold wind
that blew from all directions toward the center where a golden
woman sat, smiling at him, beckoning to him, and driving all
thought momentarily from his mind as he began to stumble for-

ward. He wanted nothing else in the world but to mate with her. He would die, if necessary, to perform that function.

It took Captain John MacShard a few long seconds to bring himself back under control. Faces formed within the crystal towers. Familiar faces. The faces of friends and enemies who welcomed Captain John MacShard and bid him join them, in their good company, for eternity. These were the siren voices which had tempted Ulysses and his men across the void of space. Powerful intelligences trapped within indestructible crystal. Intelligences which, legend had it, could be freed by the stroke of a sacred sword held in the hand of one man.

Captain John MacShard shuddered. He had no such sword. Only his jittering Banning cannon in its heavy webbing. He laid his hand on the gun and seemed to draw reassurance from it.

His white wolf's teeth were clenched in his lean jaw. "No. I'm not your dupe and I'm not Earth's dupe. I'm my own man. I'm Captain John MacShard. There is no living individual more free than me in the universe and no one more ready to fight to keep that freedom."

Yes, murmured the voice in his head. It was a seductive voice. *Think of the power and therefore the freedom you have when we are combined . . . Power to do whatever you desire, to possess whatever you desire, to achieve whatever you desire. You will be reborn as Master of the Universe. The whole of existence will be yours, to satisfy your rarest appetites. . . .*

The voice was full of everything feminine. He could almost smell it. He could see the figure outlined at the center of the crystal palace. The lithe young body with its waves of golden hair, clad in gold, with golden threads cascading down her perfect thighs, with golden cups supporting her perfect breasts and golden sandals on her perfect feet. He could see her quite clearly, yet she seemed the length of a football field away. She was beckoning to him.

"All I want is the power to be free," said Captain John Mac-Shard. "And I already have that. I got it long ago. Nobody gave it to me. I took it. I took it on Mercury. I took it on Earth. I took it on Mars, and I took it on Venus. Not a year goes by when I do not take that freedom again, because that is the only way you preserve the kind of freedom I value. My very marrow is freedom. Everything in me fights to maintain that freedom. It is unconscious and as enduring as the universe itself. I am not the only one to possess it or to know how to fight to keep it. It is the power of all the human heroes who overcame impossible odds that I carry in my blood. You cannot defeat that. Whatever you do, Shienna Sha Shanakana, you cannot defeat that."

She was laughing somewhere in his mind. That laughter coursed along his spine, over his buttocks, down his legs. It was directed. She was displaying the powers of her own incredible mentality.

Captain John MacShard examined the body of the girl he had come to rescue. Of course the Martian sorceress possessed her, probably totally. But was there anything of the girl left? It was crucial that he know.

He forced himself to push forward and thought he saw something like astonishment in the girl's eyes. Then another intelligence took control of her face and the eyes blazed with eager fury, as if the goddess had found a worthy match. There was an ancient knowledge in those eyes which, when they met Captain John MacShard's, saw its equal in experience.

But all Captain John MacShard cared about was that he had glimpsed human eyes, a human face. Somewhere, Mercedes Morricone still existed. That body which pulsed with strange, stolen life and glaring intelligence, still contained the girl's soul. That was what he had needed to know.

"Give the human its body back," said Captain John MacShard, switching to servos so that his arm whined up, automatically bringing the Banning cannon to bear on the golden goddess who now smiled at him with impossible promises. "Or I will destroy it and in so doing destroy you. I am Captain John MacShard, and you must know I have never made a threat I was not prepared to follow through."

You cannot destroy me with that, with a mere weapon. I draw my strength from all this—all these—from all my companions still imprisoned in the crystal. Ultimately, of course, I may release them. As they come to acknowledge that I am Mistress of the Silver Machine.

And now Captain John MacShard looked up. It was as if

someone had tilted him by the chin. And above him stretched the vibrating wires and twisting ribbons of silver that told him the terrible truth. Inadvertently he had stepped into the core of one of the ancient Martian machines.

The sorceress had set a trap. And it had been a subtle trap, a trap which showed the mettle of his enemy.

The trap had used his own stupid pride against him.

He cursed himself for an idiot, but already he was inspecting the peculiar twists and loops of the machine, which seemed to come from nowhere and disappear into nothing. A funnel of silver energy was at the apex, high above.

Yet, perhaps most impressively, this silver citadel of science was absolutely silent.

Silent, save for the faintest whisper, like the hiss of a human voice, far away, the sweet, persuasive suggestions of this seductive sorceress slipping into his synapses, soothing his ever-wary soul, preparing him for the big sleep, the long good-bye. . . .

Everything that was savage. Everything that had made him fight to survive in the wastelands of Mercury. Everything that he had learned in the cold depths of space and the steamy seas of Venus. Everything he had been taught in the seminaries of Dublin and the academies of London. Everything came to Captain John MacShard's aid then. And there was a possibility that everything would not be enough.

The silent crystals around him began to vibrate, almost in triumph. And there, below the pulsing silver fire, the goddess danced.

He knew why Shienna Sha Shanakana danced and he tried desperately to take his eyes off her. He had never seen anything quite so beautiful. He had never desired a woman more. He felt something close to love.

With a strangled curse which peeled his lips back from his teeth, he took the Banning in both hands, his fingers playing across the weird lines and configurations of the casing as if he drew music from an instrument.

The goddess smiled but did not stop dancing. Neither did the crystals of her citadel stop dancing. Everything moved in delicate, subtle silence. Everything seduced him. If there had been music, he might have resisted more easily. But the music was somewhere in his head. There was a tune. It was taking charge of his arms and legs. Taking over his mind. Was he also dancing? Dancing with her in those strange, sinuous movements so reminiscent of the snakes which had pursued them on Mercury until he had become the hunter and turned them into food for himself and his tribe?

Oh, you are strong and resourceful and mighty and everything a hero should be. A true demigod to mate with a demigoddess and create a mighty god, a god who in turn will create entire new universes, an infinity of power. Look how beautiful you are, Captain John MacShard, what a perfect specimen of your kind.

A silver mirror appeared before him and he saw not what she described but the wild beast which had survived the deadly wastes of Mercury, the demonic creature who had slain the Green Emperor of Venus and wrested a planet from the grip of Grodon Worbn, the pious and vicious Robot Chancellor of Ganymede.

But the sweetness of her perfume, the sound of those golden, silky threads brushing against her skin, the rise and fall of her breasts, the promise in her eyes . . .

All this Captain John MacShard shook off, and he thought he saw a look of some astonishment, almost of admiration, in those alien orbs. His fingers would scarcely obey him, but they moved without thought, from pure habit, flicking across the Banning, touching it here, adjusting something there. An instrument made for aliens.

No human hand had ever been meant to operate the Banning, which was named not for its maker but for the first man who had died trying to find out how it worked. General Banning had prided himself on his expertise with alien artifacts. He had not died immediately, but from the poisons which had eaten into his skin and slowly digested his flesh. Captain John MacShard had never bothered to find out how the Banning worked. He simply knew how to work it. The way so many Spanish boys simply know how to coax the most beautiful music from the guitar.

The same intelligences, who Captain John MacShard believed to have perished out beyond Pluto, had also made his ship. There was a philosophy inherent to his ship, which rejected most who tried to board her vast, echoing interior, whose very emptiness was essential to her function, to her existence, and the weapon, and somehow Captain John Mac-Shard understood the philosophy and loved the purity of the minds which had created it.

His respect was what had almost certainly saved his life more than once as he learned the properties and sublime beauty of the Banning and the ship.

He was panting. What had he been doing? Dancing? Before a mirror? The mirror was gone now. The goddess had stopped dancing. Indeed, she was leaning forward, fixing Captain John MacShard with strange eyes in which flecks of rainbow colors flashed and flared. The red lips parted to show white, even teeth. The young flesh glowed with inner desires, impossible promises . . .

Come, John MacShard. Come to me and fulfill your noble destiny.

Then Captain John MacShard was sweeping the Banning around him in an arc. He aimed at the crystals while the gun's impossible circuits and surfaces plated and replated in a blur of changes, from gold to copper to jade to silver to gold as the great gun seemed to expand under Captain John MacShard's urgent caresses. Yet nothing dramatic happened to the crystals. They darkened, but they did not break. The light went from glaring day to misty night.

A terrifying silence fell.

He swept the gun again. Still the crystal held. And whatever was within the crystal held, too. It was harder to see movement, perhaps because the inhabitants were protecting themselves. But the gun had done nothing.

The silence continued.

Then the golden girl laughed. Her laughter was the sweetest music in the universe.

Did you think, Captain John MacShard, your famous gun could conquer Shienna Sha Shanakana, Priestess of the Silent Citadel, Sorceress of the Seven Dials? The stupid Knights of the Balance who came against us from far Cygnus met their match. They planned to conquer us, but we killed them all, even before they reached the inner planets. . . .

He looked up. She was so much closer now. Her wonderful

beauty loomed over him. He gasped. He refused to take a step
back.

Those human lips were filled with the stored energy of ancient Mars as they smiled down at him. *Oh, yes, Captain John
MacShard. You are not here by accident. I did not send the
Thennet to take the girl until I knew you were about to land at
Old Mars Station. And it was I who let the father know you
were the only creature alive that could find his daughter. And
you did find her, didn't you? You found me. You found Shienna
Sha Shanakana who has been dust, who has not known this desire for uncountable millennia, who has not felt such need,
such joyous lust. . . .*

Now Captain John MacShard took that backward step, the
great Banning cannon loose on its webbing, swinging as his
hands sought something in his clothing. Now his fists were
clenched at his sides.

The goddess licked her sublime lips.

*Is that sweat I see on your manly brow, Captain John Mac-
Shard?* A hand reached out and whisked lightly across his
forehead. He felt as if a flaming knife had been drawn through
his flesh. Yet he would have given his whole life to experience
that touch again.

He tasted a tongue that was not a human tongue. It licked at
his flesh. It reveled in his smell, the feel of his hard, muscular
body, the racing blood, the pounding heart, the sight of his perfect manhood. He was everything humans or Martians could
be; everything the female might desire in a male.

Her touch yielded to him, offered him a power he knew she
would never really give up. He had enjoyed the most expert
seductresses, but this creature brought the experience of centuries, the instincts of her stolen body, the cravings of a female
which had not known any kind of feeling, only a burning ambition, for longer than most of Earth's greatest civilizations
had come and gone. And those cravings were centered on Captain John MacShard.

You will sire the new Martian race, she promised, as she
moved her golden breastplates against his naked chest. *You
will die knowing that you have fulfilled your greatest possible
destiny.*

And Captain John MacShard believed her. He believed her

to the depths of his being. He wanted nothing else. Nothing but
to serve her in any way she demanded. The gun hung forgotten at his side. He reached out his arms to receive from her
whatever she desired to give, to give to her whatever she
needed to take. It was true. He was hers. Hers to use and then
to bind so that later his own son might feed upon his holy flesh
and become him. That was his destiny. The eternal life which
lay before him.

But first, she whispered, *you must entertain me.*

Then he suddenly knew the son must be sired, the remains
of the humans driven from the bodies and the blood mingled
in the painful and protracted mating rituals of those first Martians.

She moved to enfold him in that final, lethal embrace.

CHAPTER SEVEN

The Poisoned Chalice

They came upon the Earthling naked, somewhere in the Shifting Desert, almost a hundred *versts* from the Aghroniagh Hills.
He had no armor, no weapons. His skin hung like filthy rags on
his bloody, blistered flesh. Both his legs had long, deep red
lines running from thigh to heel, as if a white-hot sword blade
had been placed on the limbs. He could see, but his eyes were
turned inward. He was mumbling to himself. There was foam
on his mangled lips. He was raving, seemingly empty of identity and will, and the noises that came occasionally from deep
in his chest were the sounds a wild beast might make. At other
times, he seemed amused.

The patrol which found him had been looking for Venusian
chuff runners and couldn't believe anything lived in his condition. They were superstitious fellows. They thought at first he
was a ghost. Then they decided he had fallen among ghosts,
within the influence of those mythical Martians frozen in jewels and dreaming deep within the planet. Some of the customs
people had seen Earthling explorers who had returned from
expeditions in a state not much better than this.

But then one of the patrol recognized Captain John Mac-

Shard and they knew that whatever enemy he had met out
here, it must have been a powerful one. They identified the
long scars down his legs and on his hands as burns from Thennet venom. But how had they gotten there? The marks did not
look typical of Thennet torture.

They began to take him back to Old Mars Station where
there was a doctor, but he roused himself, gathered his senses
and pointed urgently toward the Aghroniaghs. It seemed he
had a companion.

They had gone seventy *versts* before their instruments detected a human figure lying in the shade of a rock, a small bottle nearby. Indications were that the figure was barely alive.

Captain John MacShard sank back into the craft as soon as
he saw Mercedes Morricone. He let go. He allowed oblivion at
last to overcome him.

He would never deliberately recall and would never tell
anyone what Shienna Sha Shanakana, Sorceress of the Silent
Citadel, had made him do, as she took hold of his mind. He
would never admit what he had allowed her to do in order to
ensure the success of a desperate, maybe suicidal, plan.

She knew she could not fully control him and it had whet-
ted her curiosity, made her test her powers in ways she had
never expected to test them. She fed off him. She tasted at his
brain the way a wealthy woman might take a delicate bite of a
chocolate to see if it suited her. Some of what she took from
him she discarded as so much waste. Memories. Affections.
Pride.

But then she had become puzzled. Her own power seemed
to ebb and flow. He was naked, and he had torn his own flesh
for her amusement, had capered and drooled for her amusement. John MacShard was no longer a thinking being. She had
sucked him dry of everything she herself lacked. Dry of everything human.

Or so it had seemed . . .

For Captain John MacShard had learned all he had needed
to learn from the veteran priest he had talked to in Old City before he left. He had kept some of his wits by tapping the venom
from the Thennet he had killed, keeping it in crushable vials
until the moment came when he needed that level of pain to
keep his mind from the likes of Shienna Sha Shananaka's se-

ductions. It had been her embrace that had seared them both. But he intended to reverse her spell. He had reversed the path of most of the energy she had been drawing from her compatriots in their crystal prisons. He had absorbed it in the gun.

For the gun didn't merely expel energy, it also attracted energy. It processed its own power from the planet's energy, wherever that energy was to be found. The blood and soul she had sucked from him was still under his control. He had let her draw him in, let her take his very soul, somehow keeping his own consciousness as he was absorbed into her, somehow linking with that other terrified fragment of soul-mind that was the girl to whom he was able to give strength, a chance at life.

Somewhere in that ruined, apparently lunatic skull, there was a battle still taking place, through the twists and turns of an alien space and time—a battle for control of a human creature that had perished so that a goddess might survive. It was not only Captain John MacShard's vigorous blood she had sucked, nor his diamond-hard mind, but his will. A will which, ironically, she could not control. A will strong enough to take possession of a demigoddess.

Captain John MacShard was still there. Actually inside her. Actually working to destroy her. There had never been an individual more ruggedly determined to maintain its identity against all odds. He had summoned everything he possessed as she embraced him and had broken the vials containing the venom he had gathered from the Thennet. The venom burned his body as well as hers. The girl's body became useless to her. She began to remove herself from it. And Captain John MacShard, the skin of his hands and legs bubbling as the venom ate into them, kept his will directed to his goal.

She had been astonished to discover a mind as powerful as her own—as thoroughly trained as her own in the Martian forms of mental control and counter-control which Earthers had nicknamed "brain-brawling" and which more subtle observers knew as a combination of mental fencing and mental chess whose outcome could annihilate the defeated.

But the searing venom kept his mind free enough from her dominance and ultimately allowed him to break from her embrace. She had advanced on him, a roaring, shouting thing of raw energy, the ruined human body abandoned.

Then Captain John MacShard forced himself toward his fallen Banning cannon. The gun lay in a heap of clothing and circuitry which he had stripped from his own body before beginning to strip the flesh as she had demanded.

But all the while his iron will had kept the crucial parts of himself free. Now he had the gun in his hands and the golden whirlwind that was the true form of Shienna Sha Shanakana, Sorceress of the Silent Citadel, was advancing toward him, triumphant in the knowledge that the gun had already failed to break the crystal coffins in which her kinfolk were still imprisoned.

But Captain John MacShard knew more about the people who had made the Banning than she did. Her folk had merely killed them. Captain John MacShard had examined the culture they had left behind in their great, empty ship. Captain John MacShard had a human quality which the ancient Martians, for all their powers, always lacked and which would always undo them. They had no curiosity about those they fed upon. Captain John MacShard had the curiosity of the Venusian saber-tooth whose reactions matched his own. He had learned so much from *The Duchess of Malfi.*

He had never meant to destroy the crystal tombs with his gun. That would have released even more of the greedy immortals from their already fragile captivity. Instead he had used the gun's powering devices, the cells which sucked in energy of cosmic proportions, which in turn powered the gun when it was needed. The instrument in his hands could contain the raw power of an entire universe—and expel that same power wherever it was directed.

The gun hadn't failed to break the crystals, but it had absorbed their enormous energy.

It had gathered the power of the silent crystals into the gun so that the Sorceress could no longer call upon it. Her energy, uncontained, began to dissipate. She began to return to the body of the girl. But she had reckoned without the power of the Banning cannon.

She was held in balance between her own desperate lust for flesh and the relentless draw of the Banning.

MacShard's last act had been to take the girl's apparently lifeless body and carry it through the winding, filthy tunnels of the Thennet, who had all long since fled, and somehow get her up to the surface as a goddess shrilled and boomed in the crystal chamber. The whole planet seemed to shake with her frustrated attempts to draw more strength from her imprisoned brothers and sisters.

She was outraged. Not because she knew she might actually die, but because a puny little halfling threatened to best her. She could not bear the humiliation.

He saw an intense ball of light pursue him for a few moments and then become a face. Not the face he had seen before but a face at once hideous and obscenely beautiful. She was being dragged down to him, down to where the alien gun sucked at her very soul. Then she stopped resisting it. She might have lived on, as she had lived for millennia, but she chose oblivion. She let go of her consciousness. Only her energy remained in the gun's energy cells. But Captain John MacShard would never be sure.

Nothing but natural hazards blocked his progress to the top. At last he was stretched, gasping on the thin, sour air, staring upward.

Suddenly a sad wind began to stretch a curtain of dark blue across the sky. It seemed for a moment that Mars lived again, lived when the seas washed her wealthy, mysterious beaches.

At the surface, Captain John MacShard realized he would have to leave the Banning behind if he was to get the girl to safety. He must risk it. It had enough charge to do extraordinary damage. If mishandled, it would not only destroy any living thing within a hundred yards, it would probably destroy a good-sized portion of the planet or worse. He suspected that it was as safe from the Thennet as it was from the Sorceress of the Silent Citadel. He hoped to cross the Paradise before he smelled human again.

It had not been until the following night that he had stopped. The girl was just conscious, a shoulder and leg raw from Thennet venom, though her face, by a miracle, had not been touched. He had left her what little water he had brought and had stumbled on. He had been walking toward the Old City when the customs patrol found him.

The port doctors shook their heads. They could see no hope of saving him. But then Morricone stepped in. He flew Captain John MacShard to Phobos and the famous Clinique Al Rhabia, where his daughter was already recovering. They had worked on him. A billion *deen* had been spent on him, and they had saved him.

And in saving Captain John MacShard they instilled the germ of a new kind of anger, a profound understanding of the injustice which could let crippled boys beg in the Martian dust but fly the privileged to Phobos and the finest new medicine science could create.

He wasn't ungrateful to Morricone. Morricone had kept his bargain, paid the price and better. He didn't blame Morricone for his failure to understand, for not having the imagination to see that for every hero's life he saved, there were millions of ordinary people who would never be given the chance to be heroes.

They found his gun for him. Nobody dared handle it, but they picked it out of a dune with their waldos and brought it to him in a sealed canister.

Captain John MacShard saw Mercedes Morricone a couple of times after he left the Clinique and was waiting for his ship to be recircuited according to his new instructions. Plastic surgery had rid her of most of the scars. She was more than grateful to him. She knew him in a way no woman had ever known him before. And she loved him. She couldn't help herself. She understood Captain John MacShard had nothing to offer her now that he had given her back her life.

Yet maybe there was something. A clear feeling of affection, almost a father's love for a daughter. He realized, to his own surprise, that he cared about her. He even let her come along when he took the kid aboard *The Duchess of Malfi* and showed him the wild, semistable gases and gemstones which were her controls. He wanted the boy to remember that the ship could be understood and handled. And Mercedes had fallen in love all over again, for the ship had a beauty that was unique.

Pretending to joke, she said they could be a hardy little pioneer family, the three of them, setting off for the worlds beyond the stars. How marvelous it would be to stand at his side

as he took the alien ship into the echoing corridors of the mul-
tiverse, following fault lines created in the impossibly remote
past through the infinitely layered realities of intraspatial matter. How marvelous it would be to see the sights that he would
see.

He was loading the heavy canister down into a cradle he'd
had made for it and which fitted beside his compression bed.
He had commissioned himself a new power suit. It rippled
against his body, outlining muscles and sinews as he moved
gracefully to his familiar tasks, checking screens and globes,
columns of glittering force.

The boy was content to look, wide-eyed. And maybe he understood. Maybe he just pretended.

And maybe Captain John MacShard pretended not to understand her when she spoke of that impossible future. He
didn't tell her what you had to become to steer *The Duchess*
through time and space. What you must cease to be. What you
must learn never to desire, never to think about.

He was gentle when he escorted her home from the spaceport, took her and the boy to her father's big front door, kissed
her cheek, and bade her good-bye for the last time.

She held the boy's hand tight. He was her link to her dream.
He might even become her best dream. She was going to get
him educated, she said, as best you could these days.

The girl and the boy watched Captain John MacShard
leave.

His perfect body was suddenly outlined against the huge,
scarlet sun as it settled on the Martian horizon. Ribbons of red
dust danced around his feet as he strode back up the drive of
her father's mansion, between the artificial cedars and the
holograph fountains. He walked to the gates, seemed about to
turn, changed his mind, and was gone.

The girl and the boy were standing there again in the morning at Old Mars Station as *The Duchess* blasted off en route for
the new worlds beyond Pluto where Captain John MacShard
thought he might find what he was looking for.

He had gained something more than the cosmic power
which resided in his gun. He now knew what love—ordinary,
decent, celebratory human love—was. He had felt it. He still
felt it.

The ship was cruising smoothly, her own intelligence taking over. He turned away from his instruments and poured himself a much-needed shot of Vortex Water.

Staring up at the great tapestry of stars, thinking about all the worlds and races which must inhabit them, Captain John MacShard turned away from his instruments.

Like the wild creature that he was, he shook off the dust and the horror and the memory of love.

By the time his alien ship was passing Jupiter, Captain John MacShard was his old self again. He patted the gun in its special case; his Banning was now powered by the life-stuff of the gods.

Soon he could start hunting the really big game.

The interstellar game.

AUTHORS' BIOGRAPHIES

Brian Aldiss feels that good things lie ahead for him . . . and it's not surprising. He's in Paris, Athens, and Buenos Aires this year, following translations of his books; the Spielberg film, *A.I.* (based on his story "Supertoys Last All Summer Long") is doing well—along with the paperback collection of that name—and the House of Stratus is currently reprinting forty of his backlist titles. "These are beautifully produced editions," he says, "trendy covers, high grade paper, and so on. And two new novels with Greek backgrounds are to be published in 2001-02—*The Cretan Teat* and *Jocasta*. I'm hoping *Jocasta* will transform into an opera."

Aldiss recently finished an SF novel, *Super-State*, portrait of the EU forty years on. "It's meant to be funny," he says, "but we shall see. At least the French like it.

"Traditionally," he says, when asked about the Red Planet, "Venus was peaceful and female, Mars warlike and male. Funny how we are having to make our accommodations with Mars."

Stephen Baxter is no stranger to Mars—his novel *Voyage* described how NASA might have reached the planet in the 1980s. He is the author of twenty science fiction novels and collections and over a hundred published short stories, and his work has won awards in Britain, the U.S., Japan, Germany, and elsewhere. His next books are *Origin*, the third novel in the *Manifold* series; a collection in the same series; and a novel called *Evolution*. "This story," he says, "is for Colin Pillinger and the Beagle 2 team."

M. Shayne Bell has published short fiction and poetry in *Asimov's, Fantasy and Science Fiction, Interzone, Amazing Stories, Tomorrow, Science Fiction Age, Gothic.Net, SciFiction,* and *Realms of Fantasy,* plus numerous anthologies, including each of the three Star Wars short story collections. His short story, "Mrs. Lincoln's China" (*Asimov's,* July 1994) was a 1995 Hugo Award finalist and his poem "One Hundred Years of Russian Revolution" (*Amazing Stories,* 1989) was a Science Fiction Poetry Association Rhysling Award finalist. He worked for six years as poetry editor of *Sunstone* magazine. In 1991, he received a Creative Writing Fellowship from the National Endowment for the Arts.

Bell is author of the novel, *Nicoji* and editor of the anthology *Washed by a Wave of Wind: Science Fiction from the Corridor* for which he received an AML award for editorial excellence. More recent novels continue to languish on the desks of editors in New York. His story collection *How We Play the Game in Salt Lake and Other Stories* will be released in e-book format in May.

He has backpacked through Haleakala Volcano on Maui, from the summit to the sea, retracing an expedition Jack London went on at the turn of the century. In the fall of 1996, Bell joined an eight-day expedition to the top of Kilimanjaro, the highest mountain in Africa. He lives in Salt Lake City.

"When I was twelve," he says, "my best friend's father bought his family a telescope: a beautiful Bausch and Lomb precision instrument that promised to show us wonders. My friend lived far out from town, near an extinct volcano on the Snake River plain, and the nights were clear and free of city lights. Stars filled the huge Idaho sky.

"They invited me to stay over one night to look through the telescope. I wanted to see Mars. I remember sitting as patiently as I could while my friend's father adjusted the telescope, bringing Mars into view. After a moment, he called me over: and there it was, shimmering in the sights. Seeing it through that telescope was better than seeing photographs because I was looking at the real planet in real time. I could see the northern ice cap. I could see the dark areas we hoped were forests. No canals. Everyone wanted to look, then we took turns looking again. It seemed anything could happen while we watched it.

"Of course, we had all been to Mars before. All of us—his family, my family—had read the Burroughs' John Carter books. We had explored that planet thoroughly with John Carter and Dejah Thoris and all the others, and we loved its stark, cold beauty: the adventure it promised, the love for life its characters possessed. I have never forgotten any of it—the thrill of seeing the actual planet; the romance of the literary world. I enjoyed coming back to it with another friend in this story."

Ray Bradbury received an award from The American Book Foundation for his contribution to American literature. This year will see the publication of a new Hallowe'en book—*From the Dust Returned*—a new collection of short stories (*One More for the Road*), a book of essays (*A Chapbook for Burntout Priests, Rabbis, and Ministers*) and a book of poetry, to be published in Ireland, entitled *I Live by the Invisible*.

"I was at the Mars *Viking* landing twenty years ago with Carl Sagan," he says. "We stayed up all night and the first photographs came through early in the morning. I was surrounded by incredibly happy people who were dancing around, laughing and crying, including myself.

"At 9:00 A.M., Roy Neill interviewed me on NBC TV and said, 'How does it feel, Mr. Bradbury, to have been writing about Mars all these years? You put a civilization up there, with cities and people and canals . . . and now we've landed and there's nothing there. There is no life on Mars. How does it feel?' I said, 'Stupid—there is life on Mars—and it's us!'"

Eric Brown was born in England, in 1960. He has lived in Australia, India, and Greece, and now lives in Haworth, West Yorkshire where he writes full-time. Among his published novels are *Engineman*, *Penumbra*, and *New York Nights*, forthcoming are *New York Blues* and *New York Dreams*, the second and third books of the *Virex* trilogy. His short story collections are: *The Time-Lapsed Man and Other Stories*, and *Blue Shifting*, *Parallax View*, written in collaboration with Keith Brooke, and *Deep Future*. He has published over sixty short stories in the U.K. and U.S. in magazines and anthologies including *Interzone*, *SF Age*, *New Worlds*, and *Moon Shots*. He is only mildly interested in the Red Planet, but his fascination with crustaceans dates from childhood holidays on the south Wales coast.

Peter Crowther has written and published around one hundred stories, four chapbooks, and a collaborative novel (with James Lovegrove). In addition, he has produced more reviews, columns, and interviews than he cares to think about, and has edited sixteen anthologies, three of which (including this volume) have been collaborative projects with Martin H. Greenberg—"And, without any doubt," he says, "those have gone the smoothest!"

He has recently adapted his work for British TV and for "reluctant readers" (thirteen- to sixteen-year-olds with a reading age of around eight+), and is just now settling down to work on a mainstream novel entitled *Thanksgiving* while the idea for a hard-boiled crime novel sits drumming its fingers, anxious for the starting whistle to be blown. This year sees the publication of *Infinities*—the second anthology quartet of the best in current British SF—and *Darkness, Darkness*, the first in a four- or five-book 35,000-word novella cycle entitled *Forever Twilight*, which he describes as, ". . . a kind of *Invasion of the Body Snatchers* meets *Assault on Precinct 13*."

Peter first encountered Mars in the pages of the late-lamented DC comic books, *Strange Adventures* and *Mystery In Space*. "I was amazed to think," he says, "how many different-looking races there could be living on the one planet. From there on, Patrick Moore, Edgar Rice Burroughs, and the incomparable Ray Bradbury, plus a whole host of other fine and wonderful tall-tale-tellers spinning yarns, kept—and continue to keep—me enraptured to this day." He respectfully dedicates *Mars Probes* to all of them.

Paul Di Filippo has sold over one hundred short stories since his first in 1977, and the latest batch to reach hardcover publication appeared in *Strange Trades* in the autumn of 2001. He and his mate, Deborah Newton, recently celebrated their twenty-fifth anniversary with a trip to Hong Kong.

"As a dedicated and ardent admirer of Earth's satellite," he says (he and Deborah faithfully chart the Moon's phases on an annual calendar), "I look forward someday, however improbably, to standing on a globe that affords a celestial ballet involving *two* moons!"

James Lovegrove was born on Christmas Eve, 1965, and is the author of *The Hope, Days,* and *The Foreigners,* and coauthor (with Peter Crowther) of *Escardy Gap.* He is also the author of numerous short stories, with his first collection, *Imagined Slights,* due out soon. In addition, he has published a novella, *How the Other Half Lives,* and a children's book, *Wings.* His next major novel, *Untied Kingdom,* should see the light of day shortly. Like the father in his story, he has the knack of being able to pick out Mars in a clear night sky. It is a power he has vowed to use only for good, never for evil.

Paul McAuley received the Philip K. Dick Memorial Award for his first novel, *Four Hundred Billion Stars,* and the Arthur C. Clarke Award and the John W. Campbell Award for *Fairyland,* his fifth. His short stories have been collected in two volumes—*The King of the Hill* and *The Invisible Country,* the latter containing the widely anthologized story "Gene Wars" which has been used as a teaching aid in at least two university courses . . . one biology and the other law. His latest novels are *The Secret of Life*—which is in part about life on Mars—and *Whole Wide World.*

"We live in very strange times, but surely there's nothing stranger than to see a myth displaced by hard reality," McAuley says. "But that is exactly what has happened to Mars.

"One of the first proper, grown-up SF books I read, right in the middle of the Space Age, was Ray Bradbury's *The Martian Chronicles,* that dreamy collision of mythic nostalgia and American culture, where ancient crystal cities stood by broad canals, and ex-astronauts set up hot-dog stands in the Martian deserts and scoffed at the ghosts of the culture they'd destroyed. Bradbury's parable of cultural imperialism can these days be read as a paean to the lost dreams of SF; to those canals and ancient empires dreamed of by Lowell and a whole generation of SF writers that have been vaporized by the pitiless scrutiny of robot probes. Mars is no longer a theater of mythic dreams, but a landscape, an epic of geology. But heck, even if those lovely old myths exist nowhere but in a theme park, a person can still dream, can't he?"

Ian McDonald was born in Manchester, England in 1960. His most recent publications are "Tendeleo's Story"—a novella in his *Chaga* cycle—and the novel *Ares Express* (a companion to *Desolation Road*). He currently works with an independent TV production company and has had a couple of short films commissioned by the BBC.

"Mars has always been a mirror," he says, "hanging up there in our nights, close enough for us to get a clear (if red-tinted) reflection of ourselves and our Earth. It's our fears and our hopes, our fantasies and our horrors, all pushed out there where we can deal with them. And it challenges us, as humans and as writers. Our scientific knowledge of her—I always think of Mars as female: Venus, we now know, is defiantly male—calls us constantly to reinvent the stories we have to tell about her, to fit our new cultural obsessions (far different from those of Wells' or Heinlein's day) on to her.

"I've always thought of Mars as the people's planet: her bare openness, everything on show . . . 'here it is, make what you can of me.' I've said elsewhere about Mars being beyond the Third World, even the Fourth World: it's the Fifth World. I think I believe that more steadfastly now. She's calling—'Give me your poor, your hungry, your huddled masses . . . and I'll give them a world of their own.' Hopelessly romantic, but . . . hey, it's Mars!"

Michael Moorcock is feeling somewhat triumphalist about Mars. He has always continued to insist that Mars is more or less the planet invented between them by Edgar Rice Burroughs, Leigh Bracket, and Ray Bradbury. "This is the real Mars," Moorcock says, "and I have had no difficulty setting stories there. What is very satisfying is that bit by bit and very slowly—probably even a bit reluctantly—the scientists are beginning to find increasing evidence that the three Bs described pretty much the planet as it is. I based my story entirely on their evidence. Further proof that science fiction, no matter how derided, always gets it right."

In some glorious parallel universe, Moorcock has won the Nobel Prize for Outstanding Services to Science Fantasy, the Milosevitch Peace Prize and the George Bush Award for Services to the Communications Industry. In our own dimension, however, he's been restricted to picking up merely all the major SF awards apart from the Hugo. "Maybe that's because I really don't like spaceships," he says. The award of which he's most proud is the Guardian Fiction Prize, given by a panel of the *Guardian*'s reviewers. "Most other prizes," he says ruefully, "are political as much as they are appreciative and I'm really against the whole idea, which is more to do with stimulating book sales than awarding merit." Nevertheless, Moorcock did enjoy receiving the World Fantasy Long Service Award— ". . . a bit like the Purple Heart," he says. "You get it as soon as they see you walking with a cane. God knows what you get if they see you with a zimmer frame."

Moorcock moved from London to Texas some years ago. When asked why, he said it was for the same reasons most people originally came to Texas—he was on the run. "The climate's killing me," he concludes jovially, "but at least someone managed the good old Texas trick of rigging an election and getting rid of our governor for us."

Sir Patrick Moore CBE FRS, Britain's best-known astronomer, is the author of many highly respected books in the field. He has presented the BBC TV program *The Sky at Night* for more than forty years, a world record in television. Astronomy, his childhood passion, grew into a lifetime's work that has made him a familiar figure in observatories and broadcasting studios around the world. A minor planet was named "Moore" in his honor in 1982.

Among several works of fiction for younger readers, Sir Patrick wrote, in the 1960s, a sequence of books set on Mars.

He is a Fellow and past President of the British Astronomical Association and was awarded the CBE in 1988 and knighted in 2000. Once, when health allowed, Sir Patrick was a fervent amateur cricketer, an accomplished xylophonist, and a prolific composer of marches and waltzes for military bands. But he has always been happiest observing the night skies—

and, of course, when conditions allowed it, Mars—from his own observatory at home in Selsey on the Sussex coast.

Patrick O'Leary was born in 1952 in Saginaw, Michigan. He has a BA in Journalism from Wayne State University in Detroit. His poetry has appeared in literary magazines across North America. His short fiction has appeared in *Talebones* magazine and *Infinity Plus* (online). His first novel *Door Number Three* was chosen by *Publishers Weekly* as one of the best novels of the year. His second novel, *The Gift* was a finalist for the World Fantasy Award and The Mythopoeic Award. His collection of fiction, nonfiction, and poetry, *Other Voices, Other Doors* came out in January, 2001. His third novel *The Impossible Bird* was published in January 2002. His novels have been translated into German, Japanese, Polish, French, and Braille. Currently he is an Associate Creative Director at an advertising agency and his work has won numerous industry awards. He travels extensively, but makes his home in the Detroit area with his wife and sons.

Although O'Leary has never actually been to Mars, he feels the same cannot be said for several of his relatives. He cannot help but feel a twinge of terror when recalling the original *Invaders from Mars* movie. "The mark on the back of the neck of that poor kid's dad," he says somewhat hysterically, "and the zombie way his mom talked. And that vortex of quicksand in the backyard . . . the Green Monstrosity Head In-A-Bottle . . . with *claws!*" (He actually only imagined the 'green' bit— O'Leary saw the movie on a black-and-white TV in the 1950s.) Nevertheless, this certainly was Bad Dream Stuff and it cost him many sleepless nights until he discovered the *true* aliens: girls—creatures who, in his opinion, control your thoughts from afar, suck you into a vortex of desire (from which there is no escape) and mark you for life. But it's not *all* bad. "Thankfully, they have torsos," he says, "and they aren't green and the hypnosis is occasionally mutual. And the touching . . . Well, the touching is the best part. But you already knew that. What were we talking about? Oh, yeah. Mars . . ."

Mike Resnick is the author of more than forty novels, ten collections, 125 stories, two screenplays, and the editor of more than twenty anthologies. He has won four Hugos and a Nebula, plus major and minor awards in America, Poland, Japan, France, Spain, and Croatia. His work has been translated into twenty-two languages.

His most recent novel is *The Outpost*, and his next will be *The Return of Santiago*.

"I think it's almost a dead certainty that we'll discover that life once existed on Mars," he says. "I think it's even possible that some form of life still exists. On the other hand, in neither case is it likely to be anything you'd ever want to sit down and have a beer with."

Alastair Reynolds was born in Wales on March 13, 1966, exactly 111 years after the birth of Percival Lowell, the astronomer who popularized the theory of an inhabited Mars. "As a child," he says, "I was an avid collector of the cards that appeared in boxes of Brooke Bond tea, and one of them, I recall, prophesied that we would most likely have sent someone to Mars by 1980. I remain bitterly disappointed that, even some twenty years later, we still haven't managed to do that."

Reynolds wrote two science fiction novels in his teens, and his first published short story appeared in *Interzone* in 1990. Since then he has gone on to sell stories to *Interzone*, *Asimov's*, *Spectrum SF*, *In Dreams*, as well as various reprints and *Year's Best* collections. His debut novel, *Revelation Space*, appeared in the U.K. in 2000 and in the United States in 2001. His second novel, *Chasm City*, appeared in 2001 and a third book, *Redemption Ark*, will be published in the UK in June 2002. *Revelation Space* was shortlisted for both the Arthur C. Clarke and the British Science Fiction Association awards and *Chasm City* is currently on the BSFA shortlist..

He studied astronomy in Newcastle and St. Andrews, and since 1991 has lived in the Netherlands, where he works for the European Space Agency on various projects; most recently involving the development of a new class of astronomical detector. He and his partner Josette enjoy star-watching, horseback riding and Indian restaurants . . . though, presumably, not all at the same time.

"My favorite songs about Mars include 'Bird Dream of Olympus Mons' by the Pixies and 'Red Planet Revisited' by Sheffield's late, lamented Comsat Angels (who also provided the title for the story in this anthology). My favorite color is red."

Allen Steele is the author of nine novels and three collections of short stories. His work has twice received both the Hugo and the Locus awards, as well as the Seiun Award, the Asimov's Readers' Award, and the AnLab Award, and has been nominated for the Nebula, the Sturgeon, and John W. Campbell Awards. He lives in western Massachusetts.

"Ray Bradbury got it right," Steele says. "Mars *is* heaven.

"Just as everyone has their own personal conception of what the afterlife may (or may not) be like, Mars is a canvas upon which we project both our fondest dreams and our worst nightmares. Which is why the planet remains one of the most popular settings for science fiction stories; writers can do whatever they want with the place, and no two visions are exactly alike. It's almost a shame that humankind will eventually go there, because it'll mean the end of one of our last great fantasy frontiers."

Gene Wolfe has taught Clarion East and Clarion West, plus workshops for Florida Atlantic University and, in 1996, a semester of creative writing for Columbia College. Although his work has received three World Fantasy Awards, two Nebulas, the British Fantasy Award, the British Science Fiction Award, and several others—including awards from France and Italy—he has never won the Hugo, despite being nominated eight times. "So far," he adds dryly.

Wolfe believes he was always destined to become a science fiction fan . . . and, indeed, to write about Mars. But this predestiny only became clear when he met Jack Rasnick. "A teacher demanded that I name my favorite book, giving me no time at all to consider that difficult choice," Wolfe recalls. "Utterly taken aback, I blurted out the first title that occurred to me: 'Tarzan of the Apes.' After class, another student—Jack Rasnick—cornered me in the hall. 'You like Tarzan? So do I! I've got all the Tarzan books.' And he did. In fact, he had about five feet of Edgar Rice Burroughs, including *A Princess of Mars* and its sequels . . . all of which Jack loaned me. I have worn a sword and a radium pistol ever since; you can't see them, but they are there."

C.S. Friedman

☐ **THIS ALIEN SHORE**   UE2799—\$6.99

It is the second age of human space exploration. The first age ended in disaster when it was discovered that the primitive FTL drive caused catastrophic genetic damage—leading to the rise of new mutated human races on the now-abandoned colonies. But now one of the first colonies has given rise to a mutation which allows the members of the Gueran Outspace Guild to safely conduct humans through the stars. To break the Guild's monopoly could bring almost incalculable riches, and to some, it would be worth any risk—even launching a destructive computer virus into the all-important interstellar Net. And when, in this universe full of corporate intrigue, a young woman called Jamisia narrowly escapes an attack on the corporate satellite that has been her home for her entire life, she must discover why the attackers were looking for *her*. . . .

☐ **IN CONQUEST BORN**   UE2198—\$6.99

☐ **THE MADNESS SEASON**   UE2444—\$6.99

THE COLDFIRE TRILOGY

Centuries after being stranded on the planet Erna, humans have achieved an uneasy stalemate with the *fae*, a terrifying natural force with the power to prey upon people's minds. Damien Vryce, the warrior priest, and Gerald Tarrant, the undead sorcerer must join together in an uneasy alliance confront a power that threatens the very essence of the human spirit, in a battle which could cost them not only their lives, but the soul of all mankind.

☐ **BLACK SUN RISING (Book 1)**   UE2527—\$6.99

☐ **WHEN TRUE NIGHT FALLS (Book 2)**   UE2615—\$6.99

☐ **CROWN OF SHADOWS (Book 3)**   UE2717—\$6.99

JULIE E. CZERNEDA

"One of the fastest-rising stars of the new millennium"—Robert J. Sawyer

Web Shifters

☐ BEHOLDER'S EYE (Book #1)   0-88677-818-2—$6.99

☐ CHANGING VISION (Book #2)   0-88677-815-8—$6.99

It had been over fifty years since Esen-alit-Quar had revealed herself to the human Paul Ragem. In that time they had built a new life together out on the Fringe. But a simple vacation trip will plunge them into the heart of a diplomatic nightmare— and threaten to expose both Es and Paul to the hunters who had never been convinced of their destruction.

The Trade Pact Universe

☐ A THOUSAND WORDS FOR STRANGER (Book #1)
                                                0-88677-769-0—$6.99

☐ TIES OF POWER (Book #2)   0-88677-850-6—$6.99

Kate Elliott

The Novels of the Jaran: